D0481466

Bred to Kill

ALSO BY FRANCK THILLIEZ

Syndrome E

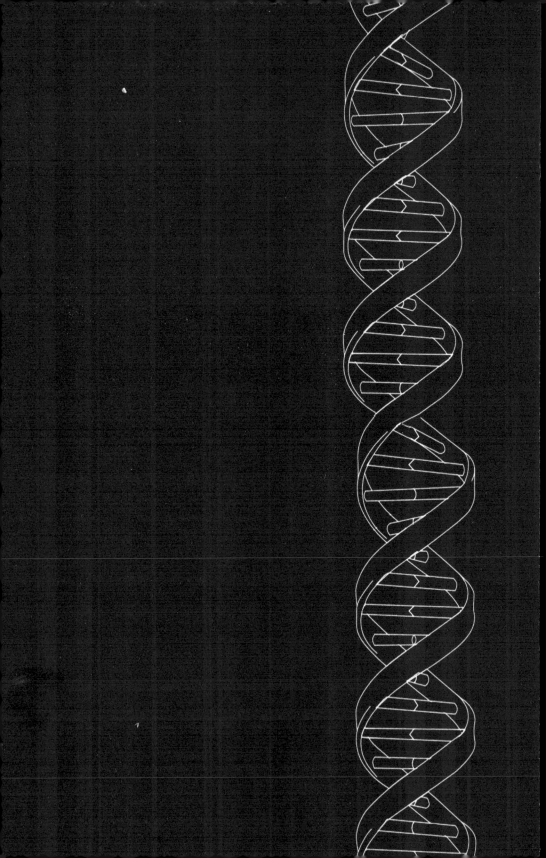

Bred to Kill

Franck Thilliez

TRANSLATED FROM THE FRENCH BY
Mark Polizzotti

VIKING

VIKING
Published by the Penguin Group
Penguin Group (USA) LLC
375 Hudson Street
New York, New York 10014

USA | Canada | UK | Ireland | Australia | New Zealand | India | South Africa | China
penguin.com
A Penguin Random House Company

First published by Viking Penguin, a member of Penguin Group (USA) LLC, 2015

Originally published in French under the title *Gataca* by Fleuve Noir,
departement d'Univers Poche

LIBRARY OF CONGRESS CATALOGING-IN-PUBLICATION DATA
Thilliez, Franck.
[Gataca. English]
Bred to kill : a thriller / Franck Thilliez ; Translated from the French by Mark Polizzotti.
pages cm
"Originally published in French under the title Gataca by Editions Fleuve Noir,
Départment d'Univers Poche, Paris."   *5543 6827*   *0/15*
ISBN 978-0-670-02597-8
I. Polizzotti, Mark, translator. II. Title.
PQ2720.H58G3813 2015
843'.92—dc23   2014038469

Printed in the United States of America
10 9 8 7 6 5 4 3 2 1

Set in Minion Pro
Designed by Francesca Belanger

Bred to Kill

Prologue

August 2009

It should not have been a sunny day.

Nowhere on earth should people have had the right to laugh, to run along the beach or exchange gifts. Something or someone should have stopped them. No, they had no right to be happy or carefree. Because somewhere else, in a refrigerated room, at the end of a dank, neon-lit hallway, a little girl was cold.

That cold would never leave her. Not ever.

Reports came through that the unrecognizable corpse of a little girl—estimated age seven to ten—had been found near a local highway between Niort and Poitiers. Lucie Henebelle didn't yet know the exact circumstances surrounding the discovery, but the minute the news had hit the Criminal Investigations Division in Lille, she'd been out of there like a shot. More than three hundred miles fueled by pure adrenaline, despite her fatigue and emotional pain, her constant fear of the worst. And always, that one sentence she kept repeating like a mantra: "Please don't let it be one of my daughters, please, God, don't let it be one of my girls." She who never prayed, who no longer remembered the scent of church candles, was begging. She let herself dare believe it was someone else's child, a little girl who'd just now gone missing and hadn't yet found her way into the system. Other parents would grieve, but not she.

Oh, no, not she.

Lucie convinced herself one more time: it was someone else's child. The relative proximity of Les Sables d'Olonne, where Clara and Juliette had been kidnapped, to where hikers had found the body could only be coincidence. Same thing for the short amount of time, five days, between the

1

little girls' disappearance and the moment Lucie stepped onto the parking lot of the Poitiers forensic building.

Someone else's child . . . So why was Lucie there, alone, so far from home? Why was bile coming up her throat, making her want to gag?

Even in late afternoon, the blacktop of the parking area was burning hot. Between the police cars and staff vehicles, the bitter odors of melting tar and hot tires stank up the air. That summer of 2009 had been hell in every way. And the worst was still to come, with that horrible word throbbing in her head: unrecognizable.

The girl stretched out in there is not one of my daughters.

Lucie looked at her cell phone yet again, called voice mail even though there was no envelope icon on the screen. Maybe there'd been a network outage while she was en route, maybe someone had left her an urgent message: they'd found Clara and Juliette; the girls were unharmed and would soon be back home, surrounded by their toys.

A van door slamming wrenched her back to reality. No messages. She put away her cell and entered the building. Lucie knew forensic institutes by heart. Always the same layout: reception straight ahead, labs on the first and second floors, morgue and autopsy rooms symbolically located underground. The dead were no longer allowed to see light.

The police lieutenant with sunken features and red-rimmed eyes got the information from the secretary. Her voice was hesitant and uncertain, vocal cords made hoarse by too many screams, sobs, and sleepless nights. According to the registrar, the subject—another awful word that squeezed her heart—had come in at 6:32 p.m. The medical examiner was probably finishing up the external exam. At that very moment, he was no doubt reading the events of the subject's final moments in the very substance of her flesh.

Another little girl. Not Clara or Juliette.

Lucie had trouble staying on her feet; her legs buckled, urging her to run out of there. She hobbled down the corridor, one hand on the wall, moving in slow motion, bathed in shadow, while somewhere outside, in the midsummer air, people were dancing and singing. The contrast was so hard to fathom: everywhere else life went on, whereas here . . .

Thirty seconds later, she was standing in front of a swinging door with an oval window. The place reeked of death. Lucie had led parents, brothers, sisters down these ink-dark tunnels to "identify the body." Most of them collapsed before the viewing. There was something terribly inhuman about entering this place. Something unnatural.

In her field of vision, on the other side of the window, a masked face directed an intent gaze toward a stainless steel table that Lucie couldn't see. She had lived through this scene so many times; and so many times, she had seen only the start of a new case, a file she hoped would prove exciting, unusual. She had been like that cursed ME, who was just examining one case among many, and who would go home that night, pour himself a drink, and turn on the TV.

But today, everything was so horribly different. She was both the cop and the victim. The hunter and the prey. And just a mother, faced with the body of a dead child.

Not one of my daughters. Some anonymous little girl. Other parents will soon be suffering instead of me.

Drawing renewed courage from those words, Lucie flattened both hands against the door, took a deep breath, and pushed.

The fifty-something-year-old man had parked in the back of the forensic institute lot, behind a van delivering medical supplies. A strategic spot that allowed him to watch people coming and going from the building without attracting attention. Eyes hidden behind patched sunglasses, several days' stubble on his cheeks, sweat beading on his forehead. The heat, this lousy, thick, oppressive heat . . . He raised his glasses and mopped his eyelids with a tissue, fretting. Should he go in and get more information about the dead child? Or should he wait for the Criminal Investigations cops to come out after witnessing the autopsy and get the intel from them?

Pressed back in his seat, Sharko massaged his temples. How many hours since he'd slept? How many nights had he spent tossing and turning in bed, huddled up like some guilty kid? The faint trickle of music from the dashboard radio and the thin drizzle of stifling air between the two open windows made his eyelids droop. His head lolled to one side; the sensation of free fall jolted him awake again. His body wanted to sleep, but his mind wouldn't let him.

Franck Sharko, chief inspector at the Violent Crimes Unit in Nanterre, poured tepid mineral water into the hollow of his hand, wiped it over his face, and got out to stretch his legs. The outside air clung to his drenched clothes. At that moment, he felt incredibly stupid. He could have gone into the building, shown his police ID, and watched the autopsy. Gathered information, mechanically and professionally. In more than twenty-five years on the job, including twenty in Homicide, how many remains had he already watched being sliced up by an ME's saw? Two hundred? Three times that?

But when it came to children, he couldn't anymore, hadn't for a long time. The scalpel was way too shiny next to those pale little hairless chests. It was like the kiss of pure evil. He had loved the way the little Henebelle girls looked at him, that day on the beach. They had played ball, jumped in puddles together, under their mother's gaze. It was the holidays, a time to be carefree, to enjoy the simple pleasures of sharing. And the twins with their beautiful blue eyes had disappeared because of him.

That was barely a week earlier.

One of the longest, most agonizing weeks he'd known since his own family had been taken from him.

What would they learn from the autopsy, the internal exams and toxicology screens? What horrors would be spit out of the lab's printer? He knew the circuit of death by heart, that implacable logic within the illogical. He knew perfectly well that a dead body in the hands of the police and medical examiners would never be granted final rest until the investigation was closed. This desecration of a human being that had once harbored so much light disgusted him. As for child-killers . . . The inspector clenched his fists until his knuckles turned white.

From the sound of a car engine, Sharko knew someone was parking nearby. Hidden by the van, he stretched for a few more seconds on that burning asphalt. His joints cracked like dry wood. Finally, he got back into his ailing vehicle, which was always on the point of giving up the ghost but which held out, then held out some more . . .

It was at that very moment that he saw her, and his insides shattered still further. In jeans and untucked gray T-shirt, her hair clumsily pulled back in a ponytail. Her sky-blue eyes no longer lit up her face. She looked like an old, ruined canvas by some past master—as no doubt did he. Seeing her that way, listing to the side like an ill-rigged sailboat, pained him to his inner core.

So Lucie Henebelle had heard the news, too. She had scanned the *computerized case logs from every unit, picked up on any investigation involving children, made the phone calls. And at the first sign of trouble she had flown down here, pedal to the metal. Good God, what had she come to this mausoleum for? To watch one of her own children be cut into pieces? Even he, Sharko, hadn't been up to seeing the postmortem of his little Eloise, so long ago. It was worse than swallowing a live grenade.*

So then how could a mother, with all of her love, find the strength to do this? Why this need to suffer, to sharpen her hatred still further? And what if it turned out to be some anonymous kid? Would Lucie be condemned to wander from morgue to morgue, searching for her two children, until it wore her down to nothing? And what if she found one and never found the other—how does one keep from going insane?

His fingers gripping the steering wheel, Sharko hesitated a long time about what to do. Should he go in after her? Sit here and wait for her to reappear? But how could he let Lucie leave the building, legs wobbling and drunk with grief, without throwing himself into her arms? How could he not crush her to his heart with all his might, whisper in her ear that someday things would surely be better?

No, there was only one solution. Run away. He loved the woman too much.

He switched on the ignition and drove off toward Paris.

When the monstrous outline of the forensic building had faded in his rearview mirror, Sharko realized that he would probably never see her again.

Never had he felt such sorrow, or such hatred.

Follow the road, without thinking about the pain in her head, the burning tears. Get as far away as possible from that death-haunted place. Lucie had not eaten or drunk anything. Only retched. Going much faster than the speed limit, she drove back along the screaming floods of highway lamps, heading north. And too bad if she smashed against the guardrails. Drive to the point of exhaustion. Rack up the asphalt miles so as not to think, never to think. But despite everything, images rained down, flooding her memory. The tiny body, so out of place on the huge autopsy table. The merry gleam of the tools under the scialytic lamp . . .

And not to know. Not even to be able to recognize one of her own children. Those fountains of life that she had carried, accompanied for eight years, day and night, through illnesses and school fairs; whose every feature she knew, every hidden detail, down to the most minute differences between their faces.

The blood of her blood.

She had to wait a bit longer. The seconds would now drip like slow poison through her veins, with only horror at the end of it: either one of her twins was dead, or she was still trembling in the hands of her torturer. The worst, or worse still . . .

What monster had taken them? Why? Clara and Juliette had gone missing while buying ice cream, on the beach at Les Sables d'Olonne. In less than a minute they had vanished into the crowd. Had someone kidnapped them just by sinister chance? Had he been targeting them? To what end? Lucie couldn't help trying out every possibility, every variation on the sordid theme, until she felt ill. The reel of horrors never ran out.

These constant waves of darkness, and all because of Franck Sharko. She hated him to the depths of her soul, and never, ever, did she wish to see him again—which was just as well, because she would gladly have leapt at him and ripped out his throat.

What would the next days be like, waiting for the lab results, the investigation, the manhunt for the killer? What kind of monster could do something like that to a child? Wherever he was on this earth, Lucie would track him down with her last iota of strength.

Not Clara or Juliette. It wasn't Clara or Juliette I saw this evening. It was . . . something else.

A timid light trembled in the window of her apartment, in the heart of Lille's student quarter. A pleasant area, usually, full of life, conversations, human warmth. Now the boulevard was empty; the traffic lights spat out their greens, reds, and yellows, monotonous like the end of the world. Lucie was afraid to go home. Those four walls, without Clara and Juliette at her sides, were worse than a sarcophagus.

Her mother, Marie Henebelle, was downing coffee after coffee and pill after pill to stay awake. It was three in the morning, and the woman with dyed blond locks, who usually had energy to burn, had aged ten years in the space of a few days. It was she who had raised the girls since they were born, because of their mother's job. It was she who had changed their diapers, heated their bottles, sat at their bedside when they were sick, or when stakeouts called Lucie away in the night.

And today, dear God, today . . .

Lucie stood immobile in the doorway, jaws clenched, facing her mother. If only she'd been able to run away, far away from here, and never come back. Walk down a long stretch of sand as it sank into the middle of the ocean. She was already thinking of the next day. The empty beds in the pink-and-green room. Those stuffed toys waiting to be hugged. Juliette's elephant that she'd won at the street fair, the hippo that Clara so loved to squeeze against her chest. All those memories, which had now become gaping wounds.

Because Lucie didn't move, her mother got up and held her, not saying a word. What could she say at a time like this? That they'd end up finding the twins safe and sound? That everything would go back to normal? A cop, and consequently the mother of a cop, knew better than anyone that, after forty-eight hours, the chances of finding a child alive were next to nothing. Reality and statistics simply worked that way.

Marie noticed the transparent, hermetically sealed bag her daughter was squeezing in her white fist. She immediately understood. The packed kit contained a mask, a tube, a pair of latex gloves, an index card, and three cotton swabs for taking DNA samples.

Lucie murmured into her mother's back.

"How am I going to do this, Mom? How am I going to get through this?"

Marie Henebelle sat on the couch, exhausted.

"I'll be here. I'll always be here."

Lucie nodded with a sniffle.

"The child, on the autopsy table . . . I cursed her, Mom; I cursed her for leaving me in doubt. It's not my child. Deep inside me, I know it's not mine. How could one of my little girls end up on one of those? How could . . . how could anyone want to harm them? It just isn't possible."

"I know it isn't."

"I'm sure that monster . . . I'm sure he stood there while . . . while the flames spread. He was watching."

"Lucie . . ."

"Maybe they'll catch him fast. Maybe he's got other little girls . . ."

Marie answered in a resigned voice: the sign, Lucie thought, of an unshakable fatalism.

"Maybe, Lucie. Maybe."

The cop no longer had the strength to talk. In the half darkness, she went to wash her hands and tore open the packet the CSI lab had given her. Each of her movements weighed a ton. Once she'd pulled on the gloves, she came back into the living room. Her gaze met her mother's, who recoiled, fingers trembling on her lips.

As an officer of the law, Lucie cautiously slid the swab into her own mouth, delicately moved it around so that its white cotton-wool tip would become saturated with saliva. She wiped her tear-streaked face on her shoulder: nothing could be allowed to contaminate her movements, not even her maternal grief. She knew what she was doing was hateful, unreal: she was seeking in her parental DNA the proof that one of her daughters might be dead.

Lucie then rubbed the tip of the swab on the spot indicated on the pink FTA card until she'd impregnated it with her DNA; she placed the card in the bag, which she carefully sealed along the wide red self-adhesive strip: "Police seal. Do not open."

The sample would go off first thing the next morning to a private laboratory, where it would be stacked up among hundreds of others. Her future—their future—depended on a common molecule that she couldn't even see. A succession of millions of letters—A, T, G, C—that constituted a unique genetic fingerprint (except in the case of monozygotic twins), which so often had guided investigators and tripped up suspects.

Despite her beliefs, her hopes, Lucie couldn't help thinking that she might, soon, have to learn to survive without her little stars. And if that were to happen, how could she possibly keep on living?

1

One year later

Manien's group, from the Paris Homicide squad, had been first on the scene. The murder had been committed in the Vincennes woods, near the zoo, not far from Daumesnil Lake and only a few miles from Homicide's own headquarters at 36 Quai des Orfèvres. Blue sky, warm water, but moderate temperatures that early September day. A muted, variable summer, often traversed by torrential rains that allowed the capital to catch its breath.

A lifeless body had been found by a jogger early that morning. The runner, cell phone in his waist pouch, had first called Emergency. In less than an hour, the information had been relayed by first responders to the Homicide switchboard, before reaching the third floor, Stairway A, and yanking the detectives from their seats.

Slumped at the wheel of his green Polo, a man of about forty had, at first glance, taken several knife wounds to the thorax. He was still wearing his seatbelt. It was the strange position of his head—chin resting heavily on his chest—that had alerted the jogger. The driver's-side window was completely lowered.

Franck Sharko, second in command in the group of four policemen, stayed as close to the front as he could. He walked with a firm step, intent on arriving first at the crime scene. Followed some ten yards back by his boss and two colleagues, he crossed the boundary set up by the two uniforms and approached the vehicle parked in an area surrounded by trees, sheltered from prying eyes.

The men from Quai des Orfèvres knew the Vincennes woods all too well, especially the areas around the boulevards, popular with prostitutes and transvestites. Still, this particular place, between the zoo and the lake, was a bit more remote and usually quiet—in other words, the ideal spot for an unwitnessed murder.

After pulling on latex gloves, Sharko, wearing jeans that were too big for him, a black T-shirt, and docksiders on the verge of disintegration, thrust his arm through the car's open window, grabbed the victim by the chin, and wrenched the face toward him. Captain Bertrand Manien, fifty years old, more than twenty-two of them on the job, rushed up and furiously grabbed Sharko by the collar of his T-shirt.

"What the *fuck* are you doing?"

Sharko gently pushed the corpse's head back inside the car. He looked at the victim's bloodstained clothes, dead eyes, and pallid face.

"I think I know this guy. Don't you recognize him?"

Manien was fuming. He jerked the inspector away, as if he were just some delinquent.

"Correct procedures mean anything to you? Are you shitting me?"

"Frédéric Hurault . . . That's it, Frédéric Hurault. He came through our place about ten years ago. I was the one who handled his case at the time, back when *you* were working for *me*. Don't you remember?"

"What I'm interested in right now is *you*."

Sharko glared at this boss with a lower rank than his. Since his voluntary reassignment to Homicide, he was no longer a chief inspector—other than in the nickname people sarcastically gave him: "How's it going, *Chief Inspector*?" No, he was now just a simple police lieutenant. It was the price he'd had to pay to return to the grime of the streets, the slums, the filth of crimes committed for money, after several years in the pristine offices of the Violent Crimes Unit in Nanterre, Behavioral Analysis section. Sharko had asked for this reassignment, even if it meant working with an asswipe like Manien. His request had shocked all his former superiors: demotions were extremely rare in the French police system. As compensation, they'd offered to let him run his own group in Homicide. He'd refused. He wanted to end up the way he'd begun: hedgehopping, a gun in his fist, facing off with the shadows.

"And do you remember why Hurault was convicted?" he said in a dry voice. "Because he killed two little girls who weren't even ten years old. His own daughters."

Manien pulled out a cigarette, which he lit between two fingers with chewed nails. He was the thin, nervous type, with a face like rolling paper: pale, rough, and taut. He worked a lot, ate little, and laughed even less. A sleazebag for some, a real son of a bitch for others. For Sharko, he was both.

Manien didn't mince words: "You've really done it now. You've been pulling my chain since Day One, and I don't need any loose cannons on my team. Something's coming open with Bellanger—Fontès is moving to the islands at the end of the week. Clear out without making a fuss. It'll be good for you and good for me."

Sharko nodded.

"Amen."

Manien puffed greedily on his coffin nail, squinting behind a cloud of smoke that quickly dissipated.

"Tell me, when's the last time you got any sleep? More than two hours a night, I mean?"

Sharko rubbed his forehead. Three deep, perfectly parallel furrows appeared under the graying locks that spilled over his ears. He who, during his entire career as a cop, had always kept his hair short, hadn't been to the barber in months.

"How should I know?"

"You know perfectly well. I didn't think it was physically possible for anyone to last this long. I always thought you could die from lack of sleep. You're falling off the deep end, *Chief Inspector*. You never should have left that desk in Nanterre. You can remember some guy you haven't seen in ten years, but you've got no clue where you misplaced your weapon. So right now, you're going home and you're going to sleep like there's no tomorrow. And wait for Bellanger's call. Go on, now, beat it."

Manien walked away with those words. Firm step of a military man. A real bastard, and proud of it. He went off to greet the CSI techs and the procedural expert, who were just arriving with their equipment, paperwork, and serious faces. Always the same, thought Sharko: a bunch of carrion-eating maggots ready to throw themselves on the corpse. Time went by, nothing changed.

With pinched lips, he stared one last time at the victim, whose pupils were already filming over. Frédéric Hurault had died with amazement deep in his eyes, probably without understanding why. Middle of the night, darkness, not even a lamppost nearby. Someone had knocked on his window and he'd rolled it down. The knife had flashed and struck him in the chest several times. A crime committed in less than twenty seconds, without noise or blood spatter. And without witnesses. Now it was time to gather clues, perform the autopsy, canvass the neighborhood: a tried-and-true routine that helped them solve 95 percent of criminal cases.

But there still remained that other 5 percent, whose thousands of case file pages filled the garret offices of Homicide. A handful of especially crafty killers who'd managed to slip through the meshes of the net. They were the hardest to track down; you had to be worthy of arresting them.

As if to defy authority, Sharko trampled on the crime scene one more time, even allowing himself a quick inspection of the vehicle, then disappeared without a word to anyone. Everyone watched him go with lips pressed tight, except for Manien, who was still shouting.

No matter. For the moment, Sharko was having a hard time seeing straight and needed to sleep . . .

Middle of the night. Sharko was standing in his bathroom, feet together on a brand-new electronic scale, accurate to a hundredth of an ounce. No mistake or faulty adjustment: it indeed read 154.76 pounds. The same weight as when he was twenty. His stomach muscles had reappeared, along with his solid collarbones. From the height of his six feet and almost one inch, he palpated his unwell body with disgust. On a sheet taped to the wall, he marked a dot at the bottom of a grid drawn several months earlier. A straight downward line representing the evolution of his weight. At this rate, it would soon dip below the sheet and continue down the wall tiles.

Bare-chested, he went back into his lifeless room. A bed, a closet; in the corner, a pile of disassembled miniature train tracks. The radio alarm whose music he hadn't heard in an eternity said 3:07.

Soon it would be time.

Sitting cross-legged, he positioned himself in the middle of the mattress and waited. His eyelids fluttered. His eyes stared at the glaring red numbers.

3:08 . . . 3:09 . . . In spite of himself, Sharko began counting down the seconds in his head: fifty-nine, fifty-eight, fifty-seven . . . A ritual he was powerless to stop, that returned night after night. The hell buried deep within his scorched brain.

The digital display on the clock changed.

3:10. The feeling of an explosion, like the end of the world.

One year and sixteen days earlier, to the minute, his telephone had rung. He hadn't been sleeping that night, either. He remembered the male voice, from the forensic lab of the CSI unit in Poitiers, delivering the worst news possible. Words from beyond the grave:

"There's no doubt about the results. Comparative analysis of Lucie Henebelle's DNA with that of the burnt victim in the woods came out positive. It's either Clara or Juliette Henebelle, but we don't have any way of telling which for the moment. I'm sorry."

Wearily, Sharko slid under the sheets and pulled them up to his chin, in the dismal hope of dozing for two, maybe three hours. Just enough to survive on. Only true insomniacs know how long the nights can be, and how loud the phantoms scream. The sounds of the night echoing, the thoughts scorching one's head . . . To combat this torture, the old cop had tried nearly everything—lying still, synchronous breathing, sleeping pills, even exercise until he was ready to drop from exhaustion—all in vain. His body gave in but not his mind. And he refused to see a shrink. After years of being treated for schizophrenia, he'd had his fill of doctors.

He closed his eyes and imagined yellow beach balls bobbing lazily atop the waves—his personal soporific imagery. After a while, he finally began feeling the ebb and flow of the sea, the murmur of the wind, the crunch of sand. His limbs went numb, torpor settled over him, he could even hear his heart feeding his exhausted muscles. But, just like every time sleep was about to arrive, the froth of the waves suddenly turned bloodred, tossing the half-crushed beach balls onto the sand, where all that remained were the black shadows of children.

And he thought about her, again, and always. About Lucie Henebelle, whose image came down to a face, a smile, tears. What had become of her? Sharko had quietly learned that she'd resigned from the force a few days after the killer's arrest. Had she managed to keep her head above water since then, or had she, like him, sunk deeper into the pit? What were her days like, her nights?

His swollen heart began pounding faster. Much too fast for any hope of sleep. So Sharko turned over and started again. The waves, the beach balls, the warm sand . . .

On Monday, September 6, his telephone rang at 7:22 a.m., while he was drinking his decaf, alone, in front of a crossword puzzle less than one-third finished. For the clue "God of violence and evil," he had written "Seth," then had silently abandoned the game, his mind too distracted. Once he would have finished a puzzle like this in no time flat; but now . . .

At the other end of the line, Nicolas Bellanger, his new chief, was asking him to go to the primate research center in Meudon, about two and a half miles from Paris. A woman had just been found dead in a cage, apparently attacked and mutilated by a chimpanzee.

Sharko hung up sharply. He was nearing the end of his career, and here he was investigating monkeys. He could easily visualize his colleagues sticking him with the dud case. He imagined the sarcastic remarks and mocking looks behind his back, the "Hey, *Chief Inspector*, you got the hots for a baboon?"

From the depths of his sorrow, he told himself that he'd sunk awfully low.

2

After passing the Meudon Observatory, Sharko sped down a narrow road in the middle of the forest; he was seated next to his new partner on Bellanger's team, a thirty-year-old named Jacques Levallois. Face like a teacher's pet, muscular build, Levallois had joined Homicide the previous year, benefiting from excellent scores on his lieutenant's exam and a boost from his uncle, the deputy chief of Narcotics.

That morning, the chief inspector wasn't feeling especially talkative. The two men had never worked together, and Levallois, like everyone else, was well aware of his partner's turbulent past. The endless manhunts for violent killers, the plunge into the most twisted cases, wife and daughter killed in tragic circumstances several years earlier . . . and that weird illness that had gone off in his head, then just disappeared without saying boo. Levallois looked on him as a real survivor, one of those fallen heroes that you either admire or despise. For the moment, the young lieutenant wasn't sure which attitude to adopt. One thing for certain, Sharko had been a great investigator.

Though very near Paris, the place the two cops were driving through seemed cut off from the rest of the world: trees ad infinitum, muted light, overgrown vegetation. A discreet sign read PRIMATE RESEARCH CENTER, UMR 6552 EEE.

"EEE, that's Ethology-Evolution-Ecology," Levallois explained to break the ice.

"And what's that supposed to mean?"

"To tell the truth, I have no idea."

Sharko turned off at a recess and parked in the lot, where there were already a dozen cars belonging to staff and a police Emergency Services vehicle. Located in the middle of the forest, the center looked like a small entrenched camp, protected by tall, solid wood fences squeezed into a circular enclosure. The entrance was through a gate that at the moment stood wide open. Without a word, the two officers headed into the enclave, toward a group of men and women in mid-conversation at the end of a dirt path.

There was nothing especially remarkable about the center. All around them, huge man-made environments made it look as if the animals roamed freely, but in reality they were held captive by thin wire mesh, and the tall branches of the trees were covered in green netting. Monkeys of all sizes played or hung by their tails and screeched; clusters of lemurs stared at the two intruders with wide jade-colored eyes. A pale copy of the Amazon rain forest, refitted Parisian-style.

A woman with brown hair and drawn features came away from the group and approached them. She must have been around fifty, looking vaguely like Sigourney Weaver in *Gorillas in the Mist*. Levallois proudly held out his police ID.

"Paris police, Homicide. I'm Lieutenant Levallois, and this is . . ."

"Chief Inspector Sharko," said Sharko.

They exchanged handshakes. The woman's was surprisingly firm.

"Clémentine Jaspar. I run this center. It's terrible what happened."

"One of your monkeys attacked an employee?"

Jaspar shook her head sadly. A woman in touch with nature, thought Sharko, noticing the cracks on her fingers, her skin tanned by a different sun from the one over France. A wide scar ran along her forearm, the kind a machete might have left.

"I don't understand what happened. Shery would never hurt a fly. It's just not like her to commit such an atrocity."

"Shery is . . ."

"My West African chimpanzee. She's been with me for years."

"Can you show me where it happened?"

She pointed to a long one-story building, white and modern looking.

"The animal housing facility and the laboratories are in there. Two men from Emergency Services have already arrived. One is inside and the other . . . I don't know, he must be walking around the pathways on his phone. Come with me."

The cops greeted the employees with a nod, the latter visibly shaken by the tragedy. There were five or six of them, mostly young, squeezing plastic coffee cups in their hands and talking animatedly among themselves. Sharko took note of each face, then turned back to Jaspar.

"What exactly do you do here?"

"Mainly ethology. We try to understand how the social organization of primates and their cognitive faculties were shaped over the course of biological evolution. We study their movements, their way of using tools, how they reproduce. We have about a hundred primates on these twenty acres, spread over six different species. Most of them come from Africa."

Neither Sharko nor his partner took notes. Why bother, since the case was practically open-and-shut? In the tops of the trees, like a synchronized ballet, balls of reddish fur swung languidly from branch to branch: a family of orangutans, with the baby in front of its mother.

"And the victim? What was her job?"

"Eva Louts was a grad student at Jussieu. Her specialty was evolutionary biology, and she'd been working here for three weeks, doing research for her thesis."

"Evolutionary biology, what's that?"

"Before I explain, do you know what the genome is?"

"Not exactly."

"It means putting end to end the DNA that composes our twenty-three pairs of chromosomes. It gives a sequence of more than three billion bits of data, which you might call the assembly instructions for our organism. Well, with this genome, we're reconstructing the history of life itself. Evolutionary biology aims to understand why and how new species appear, or new viruses like AIDS or SARS, while others die out. And also to answer questions about the evolution of life—such as why we grow old and die. You've surely heard of natural selection, mutations, and genetic heritage?"

"Darwin and those guys? A bit."

"Well, that's the heart of what we do."

They entered the animal housing facility. After passing a small desk with only basic computer equipment, they reached a large room where cages of different sizes were lined up one after another, most of them empty. A few lemurs were gesticulating to each other. On the shelves sat a huge quantity of plastic toys: colored geometric shapes, puzzles with large pieces, containers. The place smelled unpleasantly of old leather and excrement. Visibly overcome, Jaspar stopped short and pointed.

"Over there is where it happened. You can go see. Forgive me for staying back, but I'm feeling a bit sick."

"We understand."

Sharko and his colleague went closer. The two men shook hands with a third, a cop from Emergency Services with a mustache, who was guarding the crime scene. In the last cage, a large cube three yards on each side and made of bars, the victim was casually sprawled in the straw and woodchips, her arms raised above her head as if she were taking a sunbath. Blood had flowed from the back of her skull. A large wound—apparently a bite mark—ran from her right cheek down to her chin. The girl must have been twenty-three or twenty-four. Her blouse was ripped and her shoes had been thrown several yards away, toward the center of the cage. In the middle of the blood pool lay a fat metal paperweight, perhaps made of copper or bronze.

In the right-hand corner, in the back of the same cage, a chimpanzee was huddled, its fur gleaming with blood around the forearms, hands, and feet. It was tall and black, with a powerful back and long, thin, hirsute arms. It turned its eyes toward the new intruders. In its pupils, Sharko could read, in a fraction of a second, an expression of deep distress. Shery, the great ape, resumed its prostrate position, turning its back to the observers.

The Emergency cop with the mustache twiddled an unlit cigarette between his fingers.

"Nothing we can do. That filthy baboon hasn't budged an inch. Our orders are to wait for you before putting it to sleep."

Sharko turned to Jaspar, who had kept her distance.

"Who discovered the body?"

The primatologist ignored the question. She walked up quickly and stared at the mustached cop with a dark look on her face.

"Shery has nothing in common with a baboon! She's a female chimpanzee who I've been taking care of for almost thirty years!"

The cop shrugged.

"Baboon or not, they all end up turning against us sooner or later. Case in point."

Lieutenant Levallois suggested that the other man go outside for a breath of air. The tension was palpable, the atmosphere charged. Sharko calmly repeated his question.

18

"Who discovered the body?"

Jaspar was now standing next to him. Short and stocky, she nervously twisted her fingers and tried to keep her eyes from meeting the empty gaze of the victim. Sharko knew that, once the initial curiosity had passed, it became impossible for most people to look death in the face. The sight of the partially undressed young woman made it especially unbearable.

"Hervé Beck, our animal keeper. He comes by every day at six to clean the cages. When he got here this morning, he immediately called the police."

"So the door to the cage was closed when he arrived?"

"No, it was wide open. It was Hervé who pushed it shut when he saw the body, to keep Shery from escaping."

"Where is this Hervé?"

"Outside, with the others."

"Fine. That paperweight next to the body . . . any idea where it came from?"

"The desk where Eva worked."

"Your thoughts on what might have led her to open the cage and go inside holding a paperweight?"

"Shery's our center's mascot. Unlike the other animals, she uses her cage only for sleeping and walks around freely the rest of the time. Now and then she spirits away an object, especially if it's shiny. Eva must have been bringing her back inside her cage once she'd finished her observations. As she was often gone during the day, she came in to work fairly late and was the last to leave. We trusted her."

The primatologist gazed at the distressed chimpanzee.

"Shery is completely harmless. She's known to every primatologist in France for her gentleness, intelligence, and especially her ability to express herself."

"Express herself?"

"She speaks ASL, the American sign language system. She learned it decades ago, at the Chimpanzee and Human Communication Institute in Ellensburg, Washington. For years I've been in awe of the progress she's made in sharing her emotions. I'm telling you, she couldn't have . . ."

Jaspar suddenly fell silent, crushed by the overwhelming evidence: the chimpanzee covered in blood, a victim at her feet, struck repeatedly with a paperweight and bitten in the face. What could possibly have happened? How could Shery have committed such an abomination? Clémentine tried to communicate with the animal, but despite her urgings, her appeals through the bars, Shery would not respond.

"She refuses to say anything. I think she's really been traumatized."

Sharko and Levallois exchanged a knowing glance. The young lieutenant took his cell phone and went out.

"Ma'am, an investigation will be launched and the case referred to a judge. My partner just left to call in a team of technicians who will collect samples, and some colleagues who will take statements."

The prospect appeared to set the primatologist's mind at ease. But it was purely routine. Even a guy hanging from a rope in the middle of a locked room required opening a case file. They had to determine whether it was a suicide, an accident, or a staged crime. Sharko stared at the primate. For a few seconds, he wondered if these animals had fingerprints.

"You understand they'll have to enter the cage, and also take samples from your . . . companion, especially from her gums and nails, so they can tell if the blood belongs to the victim, which might prove the attack thesis. They're going to have to put her to sleep."

After not moving for an instant, facing the solid bars, Clémentine Jaspar nodded without great conviction.

"I understand. But promise me you won't harm her as long as you don't know the facts. This chimpanzee is much more human than most of the people we see around us. I found her dying in the jungle, wounded by poachers. Her mother had been killed right in front of her. She's like my own child. She's my entire life."

Sharko knew better than anyone what it meant to have a loved one torn away, whether animal or human. He labored to find the most neutral response possible.

"I can't promise you, but I'll do everything in my power."

Clémentine Jaspar sighed sadly.

"Very well. I'll go get the hypodermic gun."

She had spoken in a murmur. Sharko moved nearer the cage and squatted, being careful not to touch the bars. There could be no doubt about it: the outline of animal jaws on the victim's face was clear. The chimp was guilty; the situation was cut and dried. The animal had bashed her with the paperweight, bitten her face, and there would probably never be an explanation for why she did it. The inspector had already heard about sudden outbreaks of violence in these primates, who become capable of massacring their own offspring for no apparent reason. Eva Louts had probably just been careless; maybe she'd approached Shery at the wrong moment. One thing was sure: the future of this poor animal with its wide-set ears and sweet face didn't look good.

"You're practically the same age as a woman I loved, you realize that? Never too late to blow a fuse, I guess. Why don't you just tell us what happened?"

Jaspar returned with an object that looked oddly like a paint gun. Sharko stood up and glanced at the ceiling.

"I see surveillance cams all over the place. Have you thought of . . ."

"No use. Eva was supposed to turn on the alarm system and put on the lights when she went out."

With a sigh, the director aimed her weapon at the monkey.

"Forgive me, my angel . . ."

At that moment, Shery turned around and looked the woman in the eye. With clenched fists on the ground, she walked limply up to the front of the cage. Jaspar's finger trembled on the trigger.

"I'm sorry, I just can't."

Sharko took the weapon from her.

"Let go. I'll do it."

Gripping the bars, the chimpanzee straightened up a bit more, put its hands together, palms outward, then brought them to its throat, moving slightly backward. Just as Sharko was aiming the gun at the animal, Jaspar blocked his arm.

"Wait! She's talking."

Shery made other signs: hands on either side of her head, waving them palms downward, like a ghost trying to frighten children. Then her right hand on her lips, before dropping it sharply toward the ground. She repeated this series of gestures three or four times, then approached Eva's body and gently caressed her shredded cheek. It seemed to Sharko he'd never seen so much emotion in a living creature's eyes.

"What's she saying?"

"She keeps repeating the same thing: 'Fear, monster, wicked . . . fear, monster, wicked . . .'"

Jaspar regained hope.

"I told you, Shery is innocent. Someone came here. Someone else hurt Eva."

"Ask Shery if she knows this 'wicked monster.'"

With her hands and lips, the woman executed a series of signs that the chimpanzee watched attentively.

"Her vocabulary contains more than four hundred fifty words. She'll understand, as long as we express ourselves clearly."

After a moment, Shery shook her head no. Sharko couldn't get over it: the woman standing next to him was talking with a chimp, our great cousin on the evolutionary scale.

"Ask her why the monster came here."

More signs, to which Shery responded. Index and ring fingers of the right hand forming a V, rapidly crossed by the wide-open left. Then a sharp movement of the arm toward the corpse.

"'Kill. Kill Eva.'"

Sharko rubbed his chin, skeptical and stupefied.

"In your opinion, what does 'monster' mean to her?"

"A violent, destructive creature, intent on causing harm. What's certain is that it can't refer to a man, because she would have used the term for that. It's . . . it's the part I'm having trouble understanding."

"Can monkeys make things up or lie?"

"When it's a survival reflex, they might occasionally 'mislead.' If a group of monkeys is in mortal combat, the sentinel might give a cry signaling an attack from the sky, just to make the others flee. But if Shery says she saw a monster, she really did see one. Maybe another chimpanzee, larger and more aggressive, that she interpreted as a monster."

Sharko no longer knew what to think. Fatigue weighed on him; his mind was bogging down. A monkey, a cage, a body with its face bitten, and even the blunt instrument typical of so many crime stories: it all seemed so simple. Almost too perfect, in fact. But a "monster" might have been here. And in that case, the talking chimpanzee had been witness to a murder.

He needed more coffee, something in his gut. As he pondered the situation, the chimpanzee went back to her corner, turning her back on them again. The cop aimed his pistol once more.

"I'd like to believe you, Shery, but for the moment I have no choice."

He fired. A small dart with a red tip sank into the primate's back; she tried to pull it out, then tottered to the side and fell over, just a few inches from Eva Louts's corpse. Jaspar's lips tightened.

"We didn't have any choice. I'm so sorry, my sweet . . ."

Sharko handed her back the hypodermic gun and asked, "In your opinion, why would a 'wicked monster' have hurt Eva Louts?"

"I don't know. But I discovered something very strange about Eva the day before yesterday. It might be related . . ."

"What was it?"

Jaspar looked one last time at the corpse, then at Shery's inert form. She gave a long sigh.

"Let's go get some coffee, you can't stop yawning. Then I'll tell you. In the meantime, I . . . I should go notify her parents."

Sharko touched her wrist.

"No, leave it. Their lives are going to be shattered. You don't announce the death of someone's child like that, on the phone. Our people will take care of it. This is just one of the sadder aspects of our job."

3

The first day of school is a happy time for most children. After two months apart, everyone is reunited with his or her friends, tells what happened over the holidays, shows off the new Spider-Man backpack or *Dora the Explorer* lunch box. Gleaming sneakers, brand-new pens and erasers . . . The kids greet one another, tease one another, size one another up. The world of childhood explodes in a thousand colors and pieces.

When Lucie arrived at the schoolyard fence that Monday morning, the pupils were assembling in the courtyard. Shrieks, shouts, a few tears. In several minutes, roll would be called; girls and boys would find themselves mixed together in their new classes for another year of apprenticeship. Some parents accompanied their offspring, especially the youngest ones just out of kindergarten.

The Sainte-Hélène private school was not the one where Lucie used to bring Juliette before the tragedy. She had learned from a child psychiatrist that there were no set rules on how to survive the loss of a sister, and it was even more complicated in the case of twins. Because of this, Lucie had preferred to make a clean break with the old school. The little girl would have new friends, new teachers, new habits. And for Lucie, too, severing the umbilical cord with the past was for the best. She didn't want to be the one they looked at strangely, the one they didn't dare approach without dragging out the hackneyed sentiment, "I'm so sorry for what happened." Here, no one knew her, no one looked at her . . . She was just another mother among many.

Pressed against the fence, Lucie watched the children in the courtyard and spotted Juliette in the colorful jumble. The little girl was smiling, stamping her feet impatiently. She showed a real eagerness to return to school. She remained alone for a few seconds in the midst of the indifferent crowd, then joined the line, pulling her spanking new wheeled backpack. No one paid any special attention to her; the other children already knew each other, were talking and laughing. The teacher raised her eyes toward the fence and the parents, her expression suggesting that everything was under control, and went back to her job. The earth did not stop turning; everywhere life went on, come what may.

At the end of the roll call, as most of the parents headed off, Lucie rushed into the courtyard and toward the classrooms. She called after the teacher once all the children had disappeared into the hallway.

"Excuse me, Miss, there's something very important I forgot to ask. It's about recess. Do the teachers come out to watch the children? Do you keep that gate locked?"

"The minute the last parents have left the courtyard. Please don't be concerned for your child. If there's one place he'll be safe, it's here. You are Ms. . . . ?"

"Henebelle. Juliette's mom."

The teacher appeared to think.

"Juliette Henebelle . . . Sorry, I don't recognize the name, but I haven't learned them all yet. It takes a little time. And now, if you'll excuse me . . ."

She walked up the stairs and vanished into the hallway.

Lucie left the courtyard, feeling reassured. The teacher was right, there was no reason to worry. The establishment had one of the best reputations in Lille for safety and the care it took of the children.

Alone, her head sunk into her shoulders, hands in her pockets, Lucie slowly walked back up Boulevard Vauban, a part of the city filled with students from several nearby universities. The sidewalks were crowded with young people, business executives in suits, assorted deliverymen. After two months of summer doldrums, the capital of French Flanders was perking up. Lucie thought it was about time.

She looked at her watch. Eight thirty-five. She had more than an hour to kill before going to work, in a call center near Euralille, barely a mile from her home. Nine-forty-five to six thirty, with a forty-five-minute lunch break at noon. An asinine six-month term contract that consisted of being insulted all day long, but mind-numbing enough to keep Lucie from having to think. The ideal job, under the circumstances.

She hesitated. Should she sit around in a café and waste a few euros killing time, or go home and walk the young Labrador? She chose the second option: better to avoid unnecessary expenditures. And besides, if she organized her time well in the coming days, she could get back to working out a bit, running with the dog at the Citadelle for half an hour every morning. Getting some oxygen into her mind and muscles would do her a world of good. The roots of her body needed to revive.

Lucie veered off toward her building, a group of apartments split between permanent residents and students. A building with some character, in the Vauban tradition: dark brick, tidy architecture, solid and without needless flourishes. For a long time, Lucie had considered leaving it all behind. Change city, faces, surroundings. Set the dials at zero. But ultimately, what was the point? Where would she go? On what money? And leaving Lille also meant leaving her mother—something that Lucie, at thirty-eight, felt incapable of doing.

"Lucie?"

She stopped in the pathway at the sound of her name. That voice—hard, granitelike, as if from beyond the grave. She turned around and froze. It was he, her former boss at Criminal Investigations in Lille.

She didn't hide her amazement.

"Captain Kashmareck?"

One year later, and he hadn't changed a bit. Still the same regulation buzz cut, the same wide mug, the same pit bull jaws. He was wearing black jeans, his indestructible Doc Martens with reinforced toes, a striped blue shirt that gave him a certain elegance. He came toward her; then they felt a bit stupid when she held out her hand while he leaned forward to kiss her cheek. They settled on a handshake and awkward smiles.

Kashmareck, about ten years her senior, stared at her without opening his mouth. You couldn't say she was looking in the pink, but the police captain had expected worse. Her blond hair had grown and now fell to the middle of her back. Her slightly sunken cheeks and sharp features brought out her blue eyes, which she hadn't made up. A pretty, natural-looking woman, who could melt into the workforce crowd without anyone detecting the sorrow of her private story. More or less the same Lucie he'd always known.

"Can I come in for coffee?"

"It's just that . . . I have to be at work soon and . . ."

"I won't take long. There's something important I have to tell you, and I'd rather not do it here."

Lucie's heart contracted, her senses went on alert: the presence of her former police captain was surely no mere coincidence.

"Is it about Carnot?"

"Please, let's go inside."

Lucie could have gone to pieces right then and there. Just hearing the name of her daughter's murderer made her feel sick. She did her best to appear strong and ushered her ex-boss into the small apartment, her brain whirring at top speed. What could he possibly have to tell her? Grégory Carnot had got thirty years, twenty-five of them without parole. The piece of shit was rotting behind the bars of Vivonne Penitentiary, almost four hundred miles away. Was he getting transferred? Married in jail? Writing a book about his miserable life?

Kashmareck entered the apartment in silence. In the several years they'd worked together, he had never set foot in his subordinate's home. They had both respected the hierarchical boundaries.

A young sand-colored Labrador came to say hello. The captain petted it energetically; he liked dogs.

"What's his name?"

"Klark. With two k's."

"Hey, there, Klark. How old?"

"Almost one."

The entry led to a living room containing piles of children's things: toys, coloring books, clothes, and the kinds of study guides kids get quizzed on over the holidays.

"Excuse the mess," said Lucie.

The captain gazed at these objects with a sorrowful sigh.

"No need to apologize."

On the dresser rested dozens of framed photos. The twins, shoulder to shoulder. Impossible to tell Clara from Juliette without squinting. Lucie had once explained that one of them—he didn't remember which—had a flaw in her left iris, a small black spot shaped like a vase. Kashmareck clenched his jaws, feeling uneasy. He had seen so many grieving parents come through his office, so much distress on their faces. Was Lucie inflicting this daily confrontation with the photos on herself as a torture, a punishment, or had she resolved to face the tragedy head-on, and so move past it?

In the kitchen, Lucie turned on the coffeemaker.

"Before you ask me how I'm doing, I'll save you the trouble: there is not one second when I don't think about what happened. Since the tragedy, I've crossed to the other side, Captain. I'm now one of those people we used to deal with without really caring: the victims. But victims continue to breathe, and occasionally they might even laugh. Life has to go on. So, I'm doing as well as can be expected."

Lucie nodded toward two dolls in a corner of the room, identically dressed and coiffed.

"And besides, I still have Juliette . . . I have to give her everything I can now."

The captain gazed at the dolls, then at Lucie, looking somber. She noticed and thought it best to explain:

"It's the two dolls you find shocking, is that it? Two dolls, just one daughter . . ."

She went to pick one up, carefully straightened its miniature gray vest.

"For Juliette, Clara is still alive. The psychiatrist says it will take time, perhaps years, before Juliette can separate *physically* from her sister, but she'll get there eventually. Something is protecting her in her head, a mechanism that makes Clara appear when Juliette needs her."

The police captain pulled up a chair and sat down, elbows on the table, clenched fists supporting his chin. He watched Lucie in silence, then briefly glanced around him. Not a single bottle of alcohol, no trace of medications. No sign that she was letting herself go. Dishes washed and put away. A nice lemony smell floating over the room.

"And what about you, have you gotten any help? From a shrink, I mean?"

"Yes and no. I saw one at first, but . . . I felt it wasn't doing any good. The fact is, I don't remember much about our sessions. I think my mind put up a barrier."

She shut herself up in silence. Kashmareck deemed it better to change the subject.

"We miss you a lot at the squad. It was hard for us, too, you know?"

"It was hard for everyone."

"How are you making out, financially?"

"I'm okay . . . It's not hard to find work when you're prepared to do pretty much anything."

After setting a coffee packet in place, Lucie pressed a button. The machine quickly filled two cups. Time was passing; they could hear the hand heavily ticking off the seconds. Eight-fifty. In one hour, the phone calls would start, angry voices would shout, ears would buzz. Lucie sat down in front of the police captain, handed him a cup, and cut to the chase.

"What's going on with Carnot?"

"They found him stone dead in the back of his cell in solitary, completely bled out."

4

Four CSI techs and the assistant prosecutor who would order the removal of Eva Louts's body had just arrived. Suit and tie for one, coveralls for the others, to preserve the clues of the crime scene as best they could. The center's veterinarian, other investigators, and the boys from the morgue would not be long in coming. Soon around a dozen men would be hustling around the place with a single objective: to find the truth.

While Levallois questioned Hervé Beck, the animal keeper, Sharko and Clémentine Jaspar wandered through narrow dirt alleyways, between colored colonies of monkeys. Around them, leaves shook on the trees, the branches waved. Shrill, exotic cries pierced the dense foliage. Indifferent to the tragedy, the primates went about their morning business: picking nits, harvesting termites from tree trunks, playing with their progeny.

The primatologist stopped at a small artificial belvedere, which allowed them to observe several colonies from above. She rested her elbows on a section of wood, a document folder in her thick, calloused fingers.

"Eva was working on her doctoral thesis. Her subject was the major principles of biological evolution, and particularly laterality—hand dominance—in primates. She was trying to understand why, in humans, for instance, most people are right-handed and not left-handed."

"Is that why she was studying here, in your center?"

"Yes. She was scheduled to stay until the end of October. She started her project in 2007, but she really started concentrating on hand dominance in late summer 2009. At that point she became interested in the five great primates: men, bonobos, chimpanzees, gorillas, and orangutans. Her main job here was to gather statistics and fill charts. Observe the different species, see what hand they used when holding a stick to dig up ants, make tools, or shell nuts. Then draw conclusions."

Sharko sipped his fourth decaf of the morning.

"Did she work alone?"

"Absolutely. She moved around here like a free electron. A kind, gentle girl who loved animals."

Jaspar, too, must have loved animals, Sharko thought. She looked at her primates with a special affection in her eyes, as if each one was a child to love.

She handed him the file.

"And now, look at this. Here are the results of her observations since the time she started at the center, three weeks ago. They were on her desk. She probably meant to take them with her before she left yesterday . . ."

Sharko opened the folder.

"What are these results supposed to represent?"

"For each primate in each colony, Eva was supposed to take precise notes about a set of parameters. The repetition of certain gestures for the same individual would presumably prove that individual's hand dominance."

Sharko opened the folder and looked through the various sheets. The preprinted boxes of the tables were uniformly empty.

"So . . . she wasn't working after all?"

"No. At least, not on the topic her thesis adviser had given her. And yet, she swore the opposite was true. She told me that in three weeks, her work had advanced considerably, and that she'd be able to finish her research on schedule."

"Why would she come here if she wasn't doing anything?"

"Because her thesis adviser required it, and she would have had him on her back if he knew she wasn't following his directives. Olivier Solers isn't easy on his students, and not one to tolerate deviations. If he'd had it in for her, Eva would have lost any hope of earning her doctorate."

"So she was ambitious."

"Very. I already knew her by reputation before she came here. Despite her young age, she had conducted noteworthy studies on laterality in certain birds and fish. The precision and depth of her work got her published in several well-respected scientific journals, which is extremely rare for a student of twenty-five. Eva was brilliant; she was already dreaming of her Nobel Prize."

Sharko couldn't help smiling. He, the most down-to-earth of men, felt overwhelmed by the ridiculousness of the subjects these researchers studied.

"Forgive me, but . . . I'm having a hard time getting the point of this. What good does it do to know if a fish is right-handed or left-handed? And frankly, I can't quite imagine what a right-handed fish looks like. A monkey, maybe, but not a fish."

"I understand your confusion. You spend your time hunting down and arresting murderers, you fill prisons. It's concrete."

"Sad but true."

"*We're* trying to discover where we come from, the better to understand where we're going. We follow the current of life. And observing species, whether plants, viruses, bacteria, or animals, helps us do that. Laterality in certain fish that live in communities is extremely significant. Have you ever watched the behavior of a school of fish when faced with a predator? They all turn in the same direction, so as to remain united and fend off attacks. They don't think about it and say, 'Oh, now I have to turn left like my buddies.' No, this social behavior is a true part of their nature, of their genes, if you like. In the case of those fish, lateralization allows for the survival of the fittest, and that's the reason it exists, that it was selected."

"Selected? By who—a higher intelligence?"

"Certainly not. All those creationist claims, all that 'God created Man and all the living creatures on the planet' stuff, has no place in our center, or in any scientific community. No, it was selected by Evolution, with a capital E. Evolution favors the propagation of whatever benefits the spread of genes, the spread of the best genes, and does away with the rest."

"The famous natural selection, which gets rid of lame ducks."

"You might say that. Sometimes, when schools of fish veer in one direction, some individuals turn the other way, because they don't have the aptitude to follow the group's behavior. Is that a genetic flaw? 'Lame ducks,' as you say? Whatever the case, the fact is that they're the ones who die more quickly, by getting themselves eaten, for example, because they aren't well adapted, or weaker than the others. It's one of the expressions of natural selection. In humans, if there had been a real advantage to being left-handed, then we'd probably all be left-handed; we'd function a bit like that school of fish. The problem is that it's not the case, and yet left-handers exist. Why has evolution favored this asymmetry between right-handers and left-handers? And why in such proportions? Why is one human in ten still born left-handed in a world entirely geared toward right-handers? The substance of Eva Louts's thesis was to try to answer those questions."

Sharko had to admit he'd never wondered about these things: at bottom, he didn't find this kind of scientific navel-gazing very useful. To his mind, there were other things to worry about, much more serious and important things, but to each his own. He turned back to what interested him.

"So Eva Louts came here every day toward the end of the afternoon?"

"Yes, at about five p.m. Around when the center generally closes. She claimed she wanted to work in peace, to observe the primates without disturbing their habits."

"So, based on these empty tables, she spent her evenings here just to put in a token appearance . . . so that nobody, especially her thesis adviser, would notice the subterfuge."

"Or else, she spent her time doing something else. I was very surprised when I discovered these empty grids. Why would such a driven girl suddenly start lying? What could possibly have led her to put her entire future at risk?"

"Do you have any ideas?"

"Not really. But she was conducting research into hand dominance in human populations, past and present, and she'd been working on this particular subject for more than a year. She must have looked into some highly diverse areas. Just two or three days ago, she confided to me that she was on to something big."

"Such as?"

"Unfortunately, I don't know. But she was excited about it. I could see it in her eyes. When she first started her studies, Eva sent her adviser regular reports. Then around June, from what Olivier Solers told me, her reports started becoming more sporadic. This isn't uncommon and at first he didn't think much of it. The thesis adviser wants to hold the reins, and the student wants to shake off his influence, gain some autonomy. But as of mid-July, a month before coming here, Eva refused to send the slightest bit of information to her lab; she began hiding her work, making vague promises about some future colloquium, and guaranteeing that it would be 'a huge deal' if her research panned out."

Sharko nervously fingered his empty cup; there was no wastebasket in which to toss it. Mentally, he tried to envision the case from another angle. Louts, through her research, makes new contacts, meets new people. Somehow or other, just like a reporter, she gets hold of something hot and pulls up the drawbridge.

The sound of slamming doors brought him back to the present. In the distance, near the animal housing facility, two guys from the morgue were carting away Louts's corpse on a stretcher. The black plastic body bag looked like charcoal. *To dust you shall return . . .* Then the men went back inside with the empty stretcher. Clémentine Jaspar brought her fists to her mouth.

"They're going for Shery. Why are they taking her to the morgue?"

"The medical examiner is just going to take a few tissue samples, nothing to worry about."

Sharko didn't leave her time to feel anxious.

"Did Eva have any boyfriends?"

"The two of us talked about it a bit. It wasn't a priority of hers. Career first. She was pretty solitary, and very ecologically minded. No cell phone, no TV, from what she told me. On top of that, she was very athletic. A fencer who had competed in a number of championships when she was younger. A sound mind in a sound body."

"Was there anyone she could confide in?"

"I didn't know her that well. But . . . I don't know. You're a policeman, you'll search her place. The results of her research must still be there."

Faced with Sharko's silence and evident skepticism, she pointed to the chimpanzees, those great primates she seemed to love more than anything in the world.

"Look at them one more time, Inspector. Look closely, and tell me what you see."

"What I see? Families. Animals who live in harmony, peacefully."

"You must also see apes, creatures who are like us."

"Sorry, I only see primates."

"But we *are* primates! Chimpanzees are closer to us genetically than they are to gorillas. It's not just that we have similar DNA: a full ninety-eight percent of our DNA *is* chimpanzee DNA."

Sharko thought about the remark for a few seconds.

"That's a provocative image. When you look at it that way . . ."

"There's nothing provocative about it, it's just the facts. Now, suppose someone took away your ability to speak and put you naked in a cage. You'd be taken for what you are: the third chimpanzee, next to the pygmy chimpanzee and the common African chimpanzee. A chimpanzee almost lacking in fur and who walks erect. The only difference is that none of your cousins knowingly destroys his environment. Our evolutionary advantages, like language and intelligence, our ability to colonize the entire planet, also have a cost in Darwinian currency: we are the animals who can spread the greatest misery. But evolution 'judged' that these drawbacks were smaller than the benefits gained. For now . . ."

Her voice betrayed both conviction and resignation. She gripped the wooden sill that encircled the belvedere.

"Do you have children, Inspector?"

Sharko nodded, lips pressed tight.

"I had a little girl. Her name was Eloise."

There was a long silence. Everyone knows what it means to talk about a child in the past tense. Sharko looked at the monkeys one last time, took a deep breath, then finally said, "I'll do everything in my power to find out what happened. I promise you that."

5

Floored by her captain's announcement, Lucie dropped her sugar cube on the kitchen table. She joined both hands over the bridge of her nose and took long breaths.

"Carnot, dead. I can't believe it. How did it happen?"

"He ripped open an artery in his throat with his bare hands."

"He committed suicide? Why?"

Kashmareck didn't touch his coffee. There was nothing pleasant about delivering this kind of news, but Lucie would have heard sooner or later and he preferred it be from his own lips rather than by phone.

"He had become extremely violent."

"That I know."

"It was more than that toward the end. He attacked anyone who came near and almost beat another inmate to death in the exercise yard. Carnot was no stranger to solitary. He was the bane of the guards' existence. Except that this time, they found him lying in his own blood. It must have taken a . . . an incredible amount of willpower to do something like that."

Lucie stood up and went to look out the window, arms folded as if she were cold. The boulevard, the people walking around carefree.

"When? When did it happen?"

"Two days ago."

A long silence followed those words. The news had been so brutal that Lucie felt wrapped in a gray fog.

"I don't know if I should feel relieved or not. I wanted so much for him to suffer. Every hour of every day. For him to fully realize the pain he caused."

"Guys like that don't work the same as you or me, Lucie, you know that better than anyone."

Oh, yes, she knew that. She had studied them so closely in the past. The sociopaths, the serial killers, the vile refuse who stood way outside the norm. She remembered the days when she was just a police sergeant back in Dunkirk, when she would listen to the waves slapping against the pleasure boats across from her office. The newborn twins babbling in their crib. Days spent dealing with paperwork, when the term "psychopath" was merely an abstraction. The idle hours she spent absorbing books about scum like Carnot. If she had known . . . if only she'd known that the most abject evil can strike anywhere, at any time.

She returned to the table and took a tiny sip of coffee. The black surface was rippling from the way her hand shook. Little by little, talking with her captain was helping loosen the knot in her throat.

"Every night I've tried to imagine how that piece of garbage was spending his days in prison. I imagined him walking, talking, even laughing with the others. I pictured him maybe telling someone how he had stolen my Clara from me, and how he nearly stole Juliette. Each day, I told myself it was a miracle they found Juliette alive, after thirteen days locked up in that room . . ."

The police captain read such tenderness in Lucie's eyes that he didn't dare interrupt. She kept talking, as if her words had remained buried far too long in the depths of her heart.

"The moment I shut my eyelids, I saw Carnot's beady little black eyes, the wretched hair plastered over his forehead, his huge body . . . You can't imagine how much time his face spent spinning around in my head. All those days, all those nights, when I could practically feel his breath down my neck. You can't imagine the hell I went through, from the moment they identified the body of one of my girls to when they found the other one alive. Seven days of hell, seven days when I didn't know if it was Clara or Juliette. Seven days when I imagined everything possible, and they shot me full of medications to keep me going and . . . to keep me from going crazy."

"Lucie . . ."

"And she was alive. Dear God, my precious little Juliette was alive when I went into Carnot's house with the other cops. It was so . . . unhoped for, so extraordinary. I was so happy, even though my other daughter had been found burned beyond recognition only a week earlier. Happy, even though the worst possible tragedy had punched me in the face . . ."

Lucie slammed her fist on the table; her fingers clenched the tablecloth.

"Sixteen stab wounds, Captain! He killed Clara in his car just a hundred yards from the beach, stabbed her sixteen times in some kind of violent frenzy, and then he calmly drove for sixty miles before dropping her in the forest. He poured gasoline on her, lit it, spent long minutes watching while Juliette was screaming in the trunk. Then he headed off again, shut the surviving twin up in his house, didn't touch her, gave her food and water. As if nothing had happened. When they arrested him at his home, there was still blood on the steering wheel. He hadn't even bothered washing it off. Why? What caused all that?"

Lucie was stirring the spoon around her cup, even though the sugar was still on the table.

"Now that he's dead, he's deprived me of the most important thing: answers. Just some goddamn answers."

Kashmareck was hesitant about pursuing the conversation. He should never have come here and revived this horror. But since she was staring at him intently, waiting for his reaction, he replied:

"You never would have got any. That kind of behavior is inexplicable, it's not even human. One thing for certain is that Carnot hadn't really been in his right mind for the past year, and apparently it was getting worse. His bouts of violence were totally unpredictable. According to the prison shrink, Carnot could be gentle as a lamb, and the next second he'd go for your throat."

The captain sighed, and seemed to be weighing each word.

"I probably shouldn't tell you this, but I know you'd find out sooner or later. The shrink had requested a psychiatric reevaluation, because his patient's behavior had so many earmarks of mental defect."

He saw Lucie react; she was on the verge of a breakdown. He grabbed her wrist and held it against the table.

"Between you and me, it's a good thing that piece of shit is dead. It's a good thing, Lucie."

Lucie shook her head. She jerked her hand away from the captain's grasp.

"Mental defect? What do you mean, mental defect? What kind?"

Kashmareck reached into the inner pocket of his light jacket, taking out a packet of photos that he set on the table.

"This kind."

Lucie picked up the photos and studied them. She squinted.

"What is this nonsense?"

"It's something he drew on a wall of his cell, with colored markers he borrowed from the prison art room."

The photo showed a magnificent landscape: sun setting in the water, radiant boulders, birds in the sky, sailboats.

But the drawing, which began about a yard off the floor, had been done upside down.

Lucie turned the photo in all directions. The police captain took a large swallow of coffee. The taste stuck in his throat.

"Weird, isn't it? It's as if Carnot had hung himself from the ceiling like a bat and started to draw. Apparently he'd begun making drawings like this since shortly before he landed in jail."

"Why did he draw upside down?"

"He didn't just draw upside down. He also said he saw the world upside down, more and more often. According to him, it lasted for a few minutes, sometimes more, as if he'd put on special glasses that flopped images from the real world. When that happened, he'd lose his balance and often keel over."

"Pure ravings . . ."

"You said it. His psychiatrist naturally thought they might be hallucinations. Perhaps even . . ."

"Schizophrenia?"

The captain nodded.

"Carnot was twenty-three. It's not uncommon for psychiatric illnesses to become manifest or be developed in prison, especially around that age."

Lucie let the photos fall from her hands. They scattered over the tabletop.

"Are you telling me he might have had a mental disease?"

She squeezed her lips tight, clenched her fists. Her entire body felt like screaming.

"I refuse to let the cause of my child's death be pushed off on some miserable shrink's suppositions. Carnot was responsible for his actions. He knew what he was doing."

Kashmareck nodded without conviction.

"I agree. That's why he was judged guilty and ended his life in prison."

He could tell she was stunned, overwhelmed, even though she was trying her best to dominate her feelings.

"It's over, Lucie. Crazy or not, it doesn't matter. It doesn't go any farther than this. Tomorrow Carnot will be buried."

"It doesn't matter? Is that what you think? On the contrary, Captain, nothing could matter more."

Lucie stood up again and began pacing across the room.

"Grégory Carnot ripped the life from my little girl. If . . . if even the slightest hint of hidden madness had anything to do with that, I want to know."

"It's too late."

"That psychiatrist—what is his name?"

The police captain looked at his watch, finished his coffee in one gulp, and stood up.

"I won't keep you any longer. And besides, I have to get to work."

"His name, Captain!"

The cop heaved a sigh. Shouldn't he have expected this? During the several years they had worked together, Lucie had never backed away from anything. Deep down inside, buried somewhere in her brain, she must still have retained the purest predatory instincts.

"Dr. Duvette."

"Get me a visitor's pass there. For tomorrow."

Kashmareck clenched his jaws, then nodded limply.

"I'll do my best, if it'll help you see things straight and set your mind at ease. But you be careful, all right?"

Lucie nodded, her face expressionless, now devoid of feelings. Kashmareck knew that expression so well on the ex-cop's face that it made him shiver.

"I promise."

"And don't hesitate to come by the squad room whenever you like. We'd all be very happy to see you."

Lucie smiled politely.

"I'm sorry, Captain. I have to keep all that far away from me from now on. But tell everyone hello for me, and let them know that . . . that I'm okay."

He nodded and moved to gather his photos, but Lucie snatched them up.

"I'm keeping these, if you don't mind. I'm going to burn them. It's a way of telling myself that all this is almost over. And . . . thank you, Captain."

He looked at her as he would look at a close friend.

"Romuald. I think we're at the point where you can call me Romuald."

She accompanied him to the door. Just before leaving, he added:

"If someday you ever want to come back, the door is always open."

"Good-bye, Captain."

She closed the door behind him, resting her hand on the knob for a long time.

Back in the kitchen, she used a chair to climb up next to a cabinet and ran her hand over the top. Hidden there were a brown envelope, a Zippo lighter, and a 6.35-mm Mann semiautomatic pistol. A collector's firearm, in perfect working order. She didn't touch it but grabbed up the rest.

In the envelope were two recent photos of Carnot. Front and profile. The brute had a slightly flattened nose, bulging forehead, and eyes sunken in their sockets. Six-foot-five, an ominous face, and the build of a giant.

He ripped open an artery in his throat with his bare hands. The words were still echoing in Lucie's head. She could perfectly well imagine the horror of the scene, in the depths of the solitary wing. The young colossus lying in his hot, black blood, hands still clutching his neck . . . Did madness really have something to do with all this? What kind of frenzy had seized Carnot that it could drive him to mutilate himself so drastically?

Looking at the photos, Lucie felt only bitterness. Since Clara's death, she couldn't see Carnot as a human being, even if, for some incomprehensible reason, he had spared Juliette. For her, he was nothing but a mistake of nature, a parasite whose only purpose in life had been to cause harm. And try as they might to come up with some sort of explanation, to pass this off as sadism, perversion, uncontrolled impulse, when you got down to it there was no satisfactory answer. Grégory Carnot was different from the rest of the world. Clara and Juliette had had the misfortune to cross his path at that particular moment, the way some people get bitten by a disease-carrying mosquito as they leave the airport. Chance, coincidence. But not madness. No, not madness . . .

The photos of Carnot had already been ripped up and taped together again, several times over. Lucie placed them in the sink, along with the ones showing the upside-down drawings.

"Yes. It's a good thing you're dead. Go burn in hell with all your sins. You are completely responsible for your actions, and you are going to pay."

She turned the flint on her lighter.

The flame devoured Carnot's face first of all.

Lucie felt no satisfaction or relief.

At most, the vague sensation of spreading ointment on a third-degree burn.

6

Checking in at Quai de la Rapée is a required step in any criminal investigation assigned to the sleuths of 36 Quai des Orfèvres. The cops rarely go there to admire the Seine and the barges: the sights they see are much less picturesque.

Arms folded, Sharko stood between two autopsy tables in one of the large rooms of the Paris forensic institute. Around him were solid walls, endless corridors, and neon lights giving off late autumn hues. Not to mention an odor of dead game that, over time, impregnated even your chest hairs. Levallois was leaning against a wall just behind the inspector, looking a bit pale: before going in, he'd confessed that autopsies weren't really his thing. The opposite would have been worrisome.

Paul Chénaix, the medical examiner, had seen some weird stuff in his day, but this was the first time he'd had a chimpanzee on his table. The unconscious animal was lying on its back, arms and legs splayed. Its huge fingers were slightly bent, as if clutching an invisible apple. To the right, the nude body of Eva Louts was devoured by the interrogating light of the scialytic lamp, the same kind they used in operating theaters, which had the peculiar property of creating no shadows.

Sharko rubbed his chin without a word, impressed by the sight of the two inert bodies lying side by side, in more or less identical positions, and showing distinct morphological similarities. *Ninety-eight percent of our DNA is chimpanzee DNA*, the primatologist had said.

Just as the two cops arrived, Chénaix had been finishing the external examination of the human subject. Her skull had been shaved, very clearly revealing a fracture and a large hematoma at the occipital level. Rudely splayed on the steel surface, poor Eva Louts had lost the little bit of humanity left to her.

"It's anything but an accident. If you don't mind my horning in on your territory, Cheetah here had nothing to do with it."

First good news of the day. Clémentine Jaspar would get back her chimpanzee, her "baby," safe and sound. On the other hand, it meant there had indeed been a murder, announcing what looked to be a diabolical case.

"Cause of death was the blow to the skull. The victim was probably struck, and blood loss from the scalp wound did the rest. Death occurred between eight p.m. and midnight. Lividity on the shoulder blades and around the buttocks suggests the body was not moved postmortem. As for the bite, hard to tell if it was made before or after death."

In fifteen years, Chénaix had carved up several tons of cold meat. Neatly trimmed goatee, small round glasses, tough exterior: in his white lab coat, he could easily have been mistaken for a university professor, especially since his knowledge of various spheres of medicine was staggering. The man was a fount of science and had an answer for everything. He and Sharko knew each other well.

In silence, the inspector walked around the table, studying the victim from every angle. After the first contact, which was always hard, he now saw not the body of a nude woman but an investigatory landscape, from which clues jutted like little flags to be plucked.

"Did they show you the paperweight?"

"Yes—it matches."

"And why rule out the monkey right off the bat? There's still the bite mark. And just before coming here, we learned it had handled the paperweight. Couldn't it have picked it up and hit her?"

"It might have handled it postmortem. In any case, the size of the bite mark doesn't correspond to what the chimp could have left. The traces are very clear. The diastema, the gap between the upper incisors, is different. Same for the spread of the jaws. Besides, the chimp's molars don't show any traces of blood. And the blood on her limbs and fur is no doubt from touching the victim after death. The killer tried to commit a perfect murder and he was very sly but not enough to fool us."

Chénaix turned toward the anesthetized chimpanzee.

"Shery, my *chérie*, I'm happy to report you'll be eating bananas for some time to come."

His comment lightened the atmosphere for a few seconds, before they got back to business.

"So in that case, who or what caused the bite?"

"Something a bit bigger than this critter. The shape of the jaws is distinctly simian, probably of the family of great apes, according to the vet. He ruled out gorillas and orangutans. He's leaning more toward another chimpanzee, just larger. In any case, an animal that the situation made very aggressive."

The ME nodded toward some stopped-up glass tubes near the sink.

"The blood samples from the wounds are going to the lab. I asked for a saliva analysis. That way we should be able to get the DNA of the attacking animal, and its exact species."

"Can you do that—tell an animal species from its DNA?"

"With genome sequencing, sure. It's all the rage these days. We unspool the DNA molecules of plants, bacteria, dogs, toss them into huge machines, and we get a genetic cartography specific to each species. To put it another way, it's the complete, detailed listing of all of its genes."

Levallois had moved toward the tiled floor. He lifted a flask that looked almost empty.

"You can't stand in the way of progress. What's in here?"

"Looks like a minuscule piece of enamel. I found it inside the facial wound. There's also DNA there that could be analyzed, in case the saliva is too diluted by the blood. At this point, it's up to the biologists."

"Anything else?" said Sharko.

The ME flashed him a little smile.

"Give you an inch . . ."

"You know me."

"I've already told you quite a bit, don't you think? Now comes the internal exam."

Sharko held out his hand to the ME, who shook it out of reflex.

"What, you're not staying to watch?" said the doctor.

Behind him, Levallois's eyes flashed. Sharko didn't leave him time to react and headed for the exit.

"Not in the mood for innards today. My colleague can get along fine without me. He's crazy about autopsies."

"And what about our little lunch? You've owed me for years."

"Soon, I promise. In the meantime, have a beer for me."

He pushed through the swinging doors and disappeared without looking back.

Outside, he sucked in a huge gulp of air.

By telephone, he let Clémentine Jaspar know that she would get her animal back safely and asked her to try, in the coming days, to make Shery talk more. Jaspar promised to call back if she got any results and thanked the inspector warmly. Sharko knew the woman would do everything possible to help him.

Sluggishly, he went to sit on a small metal bench on the banks of the river. Not many people in the area. The proximity of the forensic building and the number of police cars discouraged casual strollers. Nearby was Paris-Arsenal port, with its shuttle boats and massive barges. A light breeze, the early September sun: it was all so pleasant. He mused that Eva Louts would never again enjoy such a view.

Sharko rubbed his temples and, after putting on his sunglasses, one stem of which had been glued back on, he bent his neck and turned his face to the sky. Warm rays gently caressed his cheeks. He closed his eyes, pictured the killer entering the animal housing facility with an aggressive primate. One struck the victim, the other bit her in the face, following its wild instincts. Perhaps the "monster" Shery had witnessed, one of her fellow simians . . .

He started violently when a hand dropped onto his shoulder and it took him a few seconds to remember where he was. He rubbed his neck and sat up with a grimace. Levallois was standing in front of him.

"Nice of you to leave me in the autopsy room. We've just started working together and already you're putting me through the grinder."

Sharko looked at his watch. More than an hour had passed. He stifled a yawn.

"Forgive me—things are a bit difficult at the moment."

"Things have been difficult for a lot of moments, from what I hear. Sounds like you and Manien were at each other's throats until he finally sent you packing."

"Let evil tongues wag. You'll hear a lot of things in the corridors of number thirty-six. Unflattering rumors, most of which are unfounded. So, what about the autopsy?"

"You didn't miss anything. Staying to watch that, honestly . . . it's just nauseating, end of story. If there's anything I hate about this job, it's that."

"Was the victim raped?"

"No."

"Not a sex crime, then."

"Guess not."

Nervously, Jacques Levallois stuck a stick of mint chewing gum on his tongue, putting on his own sunglasses. The guy had a handsome face, a bit like Brad Pitt in the film *Se7en*.

"Shit . . . This isn't the kind of case I want to tell my wife about."

"Then don't."

"Easy for you to say. Tell me, there's something your colleagues and I can't figure out . . . You must have been making twice the salary in Nanterre, with half the grief. In less than ten years, you'd have been eligible for a pension. What made you come back to muck around at Homicide? Why did you ask to be demoted to lieutenant? No one's ever done that—it doesn't make any sense. What's the matter, you don't like money?"

Sharko breathed in, forearms between his thighs like some derelict who feeds crumbs to birds. His colleagues knew almost nothing about his last case at the Bureau of Violent Crimes, which he'd conducted from the offices in Nanterre. Given the political, scientific, and military repercussions, the Syndrome E case had been kept under wraps.

"Money's fine. As for my reasons, they're private."

Levallois chewed his gum while gazing at the river, hands in his pockets.

"You're kind of a bitter sort, aren't you? I hope we're not all destined to become like you."

"None of it's up to you. You'll become what fate intends you to become."

"Wickedly fatalistic."

"More like realistic."

Sharko watched a barge for a few seconds, then stood up and headed to their car.

"Come on, let's go. We can grab a bite to eat, then have a look around Eva Louts's place."

"If it's all the same to you, let's skip the bite and go straight to Louts's. This shit has spoiled my appetite."

7

It was the typical apartment of a single grad student. An extensive book collection, volumes piled up by the dozens, crammed shelves, a corner desk that ate up half the living room, cutting-edge computer equipment: huge CPU, printer, scanner, disc burner, turret of CDs. Eva Louts's one-bedroom was located a few steps from the Bastille, on Rue de la Roquette: a narrow paved street that looked as if it were shoved into the back end of some medieval village.

Armed with a warrant, the cops had had a locksmith let them in. For the past few hours, cell phones had been ringing, information had been pinging back and forth among the investigators. Now that it was ruled a homicide, the four men from Bellanger's team and a number of colleagues sent as temporary backup had latched on to the case. While Sharko and Levallois combed through the apartment, others were questioning Louts's thesis adviser, parents, and friends, or going over her bank records. The dragnet was under way; the "number 36 steamroller" was churning forward.

With gloved hands, Jacques Levallois had immediately sat down at the victim's computer, while Sharko looked through the various rooms. He meticulously studied the types of decoration. Over the course of his investigations, he had learned that objects always whispered the reason for their presence to whoever knew how to listen.

In the bedroom, numerous framed photos showed Louts in elastic harness at the edge of a bridge, or parachute jumping, or in fencing gear at various ages. A lean, agile body that seemed to leap off the mat. About five foot seven, the physique of a panther: forest-green eyes; long, arched eyebrows; a lithe, well-proportioned silhouette. Silently, and also with gloved hands, the inspector carefully examined the rest of the room. In a corner were a rowing machine, an exercise bike, and several barbells. Facing the bed, a large colored fresco depicted the family tree of the hominids, from *Australopithecus africanus* to Cro-Magnon. It was as if Louts studied the mysteries of life even in her sleep.

Sharko kept rummaging. He riffled through closets and drawers. He was about to leave the room when something clicked in his head. He went back to the framed picture of two dueling fencers. He knitted his brow, placed his finger on Louts's foils and those of her adversary.

"Now that's very curious."

Intrigued by his discovery, he removed the picture from the wall, tucked it under his arm, and continued his inspection. Bathroom, hall, kitchen, all nicely furnished. Mom and Dad, both white-collar professionals according to the initial reports, must have been helping out financially. The cupboards and refrigerator contained various dietetic products, powdered protein, energy drinks, fruit. An iron will when it came to food. The young woman seemed to have everything going for her, mind and body.

Sharko returned to the living room, near the desk, and cast an eye over the surroundings. No television, as Jaspar had said. He checked the books in her library and the ones stacked on the floor, which presumably were the ones she'd consulted last. Biology, essays on evolution, genetics, paleo-anthropology: a primitive world about which he knew almost nothing. There were also dozens of science periodicals, to which Louts probably had subscriptions. A calendar of training courses and conferences was tacked to the wall, printed on recycled paper. Full days, unenticing topics: paleogenetics, microbiology, taxonomy, biophysics.

For his part, Lieutenant Levallois was ignoring the universe of paper around him. Absorbed in his task, he was navigating through the computer's programs. Sharko watched him while snapping the latex of his gloves.

"So?"

"She's got a left-handed keyboard. It's a pain, but I was still able to do a full-disc search of her computer by date. The most recent document goes back a year."

"Anything having to do with hand dominance?"

"Nothing. Not a blessed thing. Someone's apparently been here and erased it all. Including her thesis."

"Can we recover the data?"

"Depends on how thoroughly they wiped it. We might only be able to get fragments, or nothing at all."

Sharko glanced toward the entrance.

"We didn't find any house keys on the victim or among her effects at the office, but the entry door was locked. After getting rid of Louts, the killer came here, calmly, to clean up, then locked up after himself. Clearly not the panicky type."

Levallois pointed to the frame under his partner's arm.

"How come you're walking around with that? You like fencing?"

Sharko went up to him.

"Here, look at this. You see anything odd?"

"Apart from two masked girls who look like giant mosquitoes? No, not really."

"And yet it's clear as day. Both opponents are left-handed. When you consider the odds—one lefty out of ten—you can admit it's curious, to say the least."

Jacques Levallois took the frame with aroused interest.

"You're right. And that's exactly what her thesis was about."

"Her thesis which has disappeared."

Sharko left him to mull it over and opened the drawers. Inside were office supplies, reams of paper, and more science magazines. One of the cover headlines caught his eye: "Violence." It was on the American magazine *Science*, an issue from 2009. Sharko glanced through the table of contents. The articles were about Nazis, high school shootings, the aggressive behaviors of certain animals, serial murderers. The editorial was very short: Where should we look for the causes of violence? In society? Historical context? Education? Or in our genes?

Sharko shut the magazine and sighed. He might have been able to furnish an answer, after all the horrors he'd uncovered during his investigation the previous year. He finished looking around and nodded toward the computer.

"What about in her Internet bookmarks? Did you check?"

Levallois put down the framed photo and shook his head.

"No bookmarks, no history, no cookies. I didn't find anything of note in her e-mail, either. We'll have to check with her service provider."

Sharko noticed traces of glue scattered over the large blotter that depicted a map of the world. No doubt Post-it notes that had been torn off. The killer might have taken them.

His gaze stopped at the tower of CDs, which he pointed to.

"I'd be very surprised if Louts didn't make backup copies of her hard drive."

"I've already had a quick look around. If she burned any discs, they aren't here now."

"Let's bring in a full team for a complete search and take the computer with us."

A phone rang and Levallois answered his cell. Two minutes of conversation, after which he returned to Sharko.

"Two bits of news. The first has nothing to do with us, it's about the body in the Vincennes woods, Hurault. The boss asked me to give you this message: your former chief wants to see you in his office, pronto."

"See me? Fine . . . and the other news?"

"Robillard started by checking through the police files. Apparently, less than a month ago, Louts requested her police record—which is clean, by the way—to obtain authorization to visit penitentiaries."

"Penitentiaries?"

"At least a dozen of them. It's as if our victim was out to meet the great jailbirds of France. So I can't help wondering: what was a student who spends her time watching monkeys hoping to find in those hellholes?"

8

Once the door of the Homicide office had closed behind him, the inspector found himself opposite two men, Bertrand Manien and his right arm, Marc Leblond. One was seated, stiff as a rod, the other casually leaning against the rear window that looked out on the Seine. The atmosphere was tense, the furniture from another era.

"Have a seat, Franck."

Sharko took a seat. Rudimentary wooden chair: his ass hurt and his bones ached. Too thin, way too thin. Normally that room, arranged as an open space, held an average of five or six officers working at their computers. Now, either the men were in the field or they'd been told to vacate the premises long enough for the "interview." Marc Leblond walked toward Manien and sat down in turn. Tall guy, also thin, about forty, never seen without his cowboy boots or pack of generic cigarettes. Face like a reptile, narrow eyes that shone with malice. Before Homicide, he'd pulled five years in Vice, cuffing prostitutes and sometimes helping himself to the fringe benefits. Sharko had never liked him, and the feeling was mutual.

The blond reptile fired first. Hoarse voice that brooked no argument: the guy was enjoying the situation.

"Tell us about Frédéric Hurault."

Frédéric Hurault. The murder victim found in his car in Vincennes. Facing the two cops, Sharko adopted a falsely relaxed posture. Arms folded, slouching a bit in his chair: he was in his former office, no more, no less.

"What do you want to know?"

"How you nabbed him, and when."

The inspector knit his brow. He tried to stand up, but Bertrand Manien leaned over the desk and pressed down on his shoulder.

"Sit a while, *Chief Inspector*, what's your hurry? For two days we've been drawing blanks on this case. No witnesses, no apparent motive. Hurault wasn't big on whores—he couldn't even get it up anymore with all the meds they'd shot into him at the psych hospital. So what was it, a date? A sudden impulse? But why there, in such a secluded spot? So you see, we've hit a dead end for the moment."

"You fired me from your team, and now you want my help?"

"I did you a favor by letting you go, didn't I? It was . . . how shall I put it, one good turn for another. Listen, this killer isn't exactly your average moron. We're only asking questions that will help us make headway. You're the one who hunted down Hurault, back when. You're the one who put him away. You know the guy—who he is, who he hangs out with."

"There are files full of that stuff."

"Files are heavy and dusty. Nothing beats a good face-to-face. We'd appreciate it if *you* gave us the pertinent info. Soon all my men might be on that monkey thing, and I have to show results on this case no one gives a shit about, you understand?"

Sharko regained his calm.

"Not much to say that you don't already know. It was the early 2000s. Hurault had recently divorced after about a dozen years of marriage, at his wife's instigation. The divorce was messy—Hurault didn't appreciate being left. He was about thirty, a worker at Firestone. Lived in a small apartment in Bourg-la-Reine. The day of the incident, he had custody of his daughters for the weekend."

The cop swallowed, took a breath, tried to keep his voice neutral, emotionless. Still, he had never forgotten the horrors he'd seen that day, on the fourth floor of that nondescript apartment building.

"The little girls were found by their mother on Sunday evening. They were in their pajamas, drowned in the bathtub. You want me to describe the scene for you?"

"No need."

"Through his bank records, we traced Hurault two weeks later to Madrid, in some fleabag hotel. He claimed he'd gone temporarily insane when he committed the crime, and that he didn't remember killing the kids. The psychiatric expert testified that he'd suffered a psychotic episode brought about by the strain of his divorce. When he saw the bodies drowned in the tub, he panicked and fled. His lawyers cited Article 122.1 of the Penal Code, the clauses about not being responsible. After a long, drawn-out trial, they got their way. Sainte-Anne psychiatric hospital, for an indeterminate amount of time. After that the mother made several suicide attempts. She's never gotten over it."

Manien fiddled with a ballpoint pen, not once taking his eyes off Sharko. His movements were nervous, staccato.

"And what did you think? Did you feel he was responsible?"

"What I felt didn't count for much. I'd done my job. The rest wasn't my business."

"Not your business? And yet you were seen at the trial. A trial you followed closely, as if you were personally involved."

"I've often sat in on the trials for my larger cases. And I was on vacation."

"When I'm on vacation, I go fishing or to the mountains."

He turned to Leblond.

"What about you?"

The reptile just stretched his lips in a grimace, without answering. Manien turned back toward Sharko, looking a bit more relaxed, even a bit mocking.

"And you prefer to go watch trials. Whatever gets you off, I suppose. Did you know of any enemies Hurault might have had?"

"You mean aside from every parent in France?"

Silence. Eyes gauging each other. Manien dropped his pen and leaned forward, fist under his chin.

"Did you know he was out?"

Sharko's reply, frank and without hesitation:

"Sure. A few years ago he'd been transferred to La Salpêtrière, to prepare him for his eventual release. I'd been in treatment there for several months. You know what for, I presume."

Leblond gave an unpleasant smile.

"Did you run into each other over there?"

"In the padded cell, you mean?"

"Don't take it like that. You're looking awfully nervous."

Sharko rubbed his forehead. The sun had been beating on the window all day; humidity had seeped into the walls like ringworm. The old impregnated odors oozed from all sides: cigarettes, sweat, worn-out wood. It stank of men.

"No, ya think?" he retorted to the reptile. "You were still scooping out army latrines when I was already doing exactly what you're doing now. Putting guys on the grill. What do you take me for, an idiot? Are you trying to trip me up? Make my life miserable just because I knew the victim? Why, because I did everything I could to get assigned to another squad?"

"Can the paranoia. We're just asking for your help. We're all friends here, *Chief Inspector*, don't forget. So—did you run into each other at La Salpêtrière?"

"It happened once in a while. We were being treated in nearby departments."

"And did you see Hurault after he got out?"

"Two days ago, in the Vincennes woods. Not looking too hot."

"You aren't looking too hot yourself," went the reptile. "Since you lost your wife and daughter, you've been seeing little blue devils all over the place. I can't understand why they allow head cases to stay on the force."

It took barely a second for Sharko to leap from his seat and throw himself on Leblond. The two masses of bone and muscle slammed violently against a partition, sending a tray of paperwork flying. A chair fell over. His face tense, Manien managed to separate the two men before they came to blows.

"Cut it out, goddammit! What the hell's the matter with you?"

Hateful looks, saliva on lips, veins bulging. Finally, each man sat back down. Sharko could feel his temples pounding, his blood boiling. Leblond went to light a cigarette at the open window while Manien cooled things down, at least on the surface.

"Don't mind him. All that stuff people say about you drives you out of your gourd, that's understandable. You were a chief inspector, nice and comfy, and now you're back shoveling shit. If I were in your shoes, I'd act the same."

"You're not in my shoes."

Manien ignored the remark and continued working on Sharko.

"So, since the hospital, you never saw Frédéric Hurault again until Saturday."

"Unless my memory's faulty, no. But you know, Bourg-la-Reine and

L'Haÿ-les-Roses are pretty close. It's not impossible that I passed by him one day without really noticing. You always said I was capable of forgetting where I'd left my piece."

Manien turned toward Leblond, pondered him with amusement, then struck a still calmer pose. He was almost smiling.

"Without really noticing . . . okay. Let's get to the real reason for you being here. You know we found an eyelash on the victim's clothes?"

"No, I didn't. It's not my case."

"It's so hard to avoid leaving *any* traces of oneself, with all our technical know-how. I'd even say it's become impossible. Wouldn't you say so? Skin cells, sweat, flakes, fingerprints . . ."

"So what?"

"The DNA we extracted from the eyelash was fed through the national database. We got a match. If we were basing our case on science alone, leaving aside our instincts as cops, we could say we'd got our man."

"That DNA wouldn't happen to be mine, would it?" Sharko saw Manien's throat tighten, his eyelid quiver. "That's exactly why our info is now in the database, too," he added. "We too are contaminants of the crime scene. It happens all the time, and it's going to happen again in that monkey case I'm working on. DNA from the first responder cops, from the chimp, the animal keeper, the primatologist. Tons of fingerprints on the bars of the cage. Shit, you didn't drag me over here just to accuse me, did you? What's your point? To fuck up the few years I have left in this joint?"

Manien hesitated for a moment, before regaining confidence.

"That has nothing to do with it. The problem is the way you conducted yourself on the crime scene. You manhandle the body, you get all over everything. Were you out to pollute the scene so they couldn't find the killer? Or did you just want to break my balls and make sure I'd can you? Be honest, *Chief Inspector*, and don't forget we work in the same shop."

"I hadn't slept a wink. I had a hundred things on my mind. The car window was wide open, and I wanted to see what kind of clown would go hang around that area at night. I leaned inside the car. I forgot to take precautions. I fucked up."

At the back of the room, Leblond was silently blowing smoke out the window, one foot flat against the wall. Manien returned to the charge:

"You know, the guy who offed him in cold blood might not have been wearing a face mask . . . He probably wanted Hurault to see his face just as he shoved the screwdriver into his guts. Because . . . I don't know, because maybe he wanted to show him he hadn't forgotten, that he knew he was responsible for his actions? Thanks to the noncompetency ruling, Hurault served only nine years in psych; he would have spent at least twice that in the slammer if he'd confessed. Cops like us hate people like that, because they make us feel we're doing all that work for nothing. What do you think?"

Sharko shrugged. But Manien wouldn't let it drop.

"A little more than a year ago, you were still a behavioral analyst. You must have *some* answer."

"There are other analysts who are still active. Go ask them."

Sharko looked at his watch, then stood up, gently this time.

"I've put in almost thirty years in my career. Thirty flippin' years of good and loyal service, locking up guys ten times worse than Hurault. I sweated out this job like you'll never know, no matter how much shit you've seen. And you, you get it into your head to have my hide. You're out to destroy me the way you've already destroyed so many others. Apart from the DNA from the contaminated crime scene, you don't have squat against me. I crapped all over your crime scene, so why don't you report me to Internal Affairs? Is it because they can't stand you either? Maybe because you've already been too heavy-handed with suspects and even with your own colleagues? I already know you're going to keep after this; you're worse than a tapeworm. Are you really that bored?"

He leaned toward the desk, his face just inches from Manien's.

"I'm going to say this once and for all: I had nothing to do with Hurault's death. I'm a cop, just like you. I came back to Homicide because I was climbing the walls at my desk job in Nanterre, simple as that. And in case you still have any doubts, I've got a little piece of advice for you—you and that other moron over there: watch where you stick your flat feet."

"*You* watch. I need to find the guilty party, and you can bet I'm going to find him."

As Sharko was walking away, Manien added:

"For now, this business stays between us. Nobody else knows about it. As for the DNA—the contaminant, like you said—piece of cake. I'm not out to cause you any trouble about that. You see how we're looking out for your interests?"

Sharko went out, slamming the door behind him, and walked quickly to the water cooler at the end of the hallway. He needed water, with a coffee chaser. Strong, black, and full of caffeine this time.

Gripping a plastic cup, he veered toward his desk, where Levallois was sitting. Outside, on the roofs of the buildings, the setting sun spread its gilded pigments. In that unbearable humidity, Sharko set down his hot drink and dropped into a desk chair, beat. The day, and that kangaroo interrogation, had sapped him of the little energy he had.

He nodded toward a leave of absence slip.

"Give me one of those, I'm taking a day off."

"Anything wrong? What happened with Manien?"

"Oh, nothing. I just need sleep, sleep, and more sleep."

Levallois passed him the form, which Sharko filled out sloppily. Bellanger, his boss, would find the request on his desk when he got back that evening or the next morning. He'd probably pitch a fit, but too bad: it was the least of his worries.

"Any news about Louts?" asked the inspector.

"I've just seen Robillard, who's been on it since morning. He gave me the list of prisons and inmates the student visited. No less than eleven convicts, long-timers only."

Sharko signed the absence slip with a sigh and held out his hand. Levallois gave him the list.

"Do we know why she went to see them?"

The lieutenant was now standing, an empty thermos of coffee in his hand.

"Not yet, we just got the list. Robillard will deal with it tomorrow. We have to continue sifting through her accounts and bills. Robillard made some good progress. Anyway, I've got to be home by eight, sorry. See you Wednesday, then—get some rest on your day off."

He disappeared in a flash, the door slamming behind him. Alone, Sharko let himself enjoy the calm in the room for a moment, eyes half closed. His temples were throbbing; the evil faces of Manien and Leblond floated beneath his eyelids. Two mad dogs snapping at his heels, who could easily make his life a living hell. If they started leaking information, rumors would start circulating around the hallways, and people would look at him even more strangely. Sharko, the ex-schizo. Sharko, the guy who saw shrinks, who wasn't entirely right in the head. Was the *Chief Inspector* protecting a killer, or had he actually offed someone himself? Had he cracked up, blown a gasket, just when he was slowly getting toward retirement? This kind of breakdown happened so often. How many cops ended up alcoholics or depressives, drowning in the shit of their past years?

With a last-ditch effort, he opened his eyes and quickly glanced down the list of prisoners. He looked without really reading—impossible to concentrate, to stay in the rhythm of the investigation. Too severe a headache, too exhausted, too everything.

Only one solution: go home. Fall into bed. Try to sleep for an hour, maybe even two, before moping about at around 3 a.m. Like every night.

As he was about to put down the paper, his eyes were suddenly drawn to a particular line in the list. The last one. Date of the meeting between Eva Louts and the inmate: Friday, August 27, 2010. Ten days ago.

The institution and the convict's name froze his blood.

Vivonne Penitentiary.

Grégory Carnot.

9

Everything had suddenly changed.

No chance of going home now.

Just ten days before her death, Eva Louts had been in touch with Grégory Carnot. The man who had destroyed everything.

Sharko downed another cup of coffee. A taste of scorched earth clung to the back of his throat.

Stoked by adrenaline and caffeine, he now paced the nearly deserted corridors of the Homicide unit. At that hour, only a few shadows remained, bent over their urgent cases: the duty officers, the guys from Narc who never left and watched over junkies in their cells, or else the ones who simply didn't want to go home, devoured as they were by the job.

He went into Robillard's empty office, the lieutenant who was going through Eva Louts's computer records: bills, various receipts, subscriptions. Behind him, through the small window, Paris was fading into night. The police station looked out over the city from here, like a bogus promise: *Sleep tight, dear citizens, we're watching over you.*

Sharko got down to the task: go back in time, note the possible blips in the victim's life patterns. In front of him were two stacks of paper: the ones Robillard had already sifted through, and the others. He started reading through the first batch, the ones already analyzed. Very quickly, Sharko raised an eyebrow at photocopies of airplane reservations, issued by an Air France travel agency. On July 16, 2010, a little less than two months earlier, Eva Louts had taken an economy-class flight to Abraham González International Airport in Ciudad Juárez, Mexico; she'd stayed five days, with a return dated July 21.

Then, eight days later, on July 29, Louts flew from Orly airport to Manaus, in Brazil. She'd returned from Manaus to Paris on August 5.

Sharko rubbed his chin, lost in thought. Two successive trips to Latin

America, before ending up at the primate center. And from what he could tell, these didn't look like vacations. The inspector knew Juárez by reputation: it was one of the world's most dangerous cities. The murders of Juárez women had contributed to the dark reputation attached to Mexico's sixth-largest population center. Between 1993 and 2005, nearly five hundred women had disappeared, and three quarters of them had been found, all killed in the same way: torture, sexual abuse, mutilation, and strangulation. One of the most horrendous criminal cases of all time, never solved.

Why would a twenty-five-year-old biology student want to go there?

Intrigued, Sharko pushed the papers aside and had a look at the bills just beneath them. Lieutenant Robillard had already cross-referenced certain facts: the data showed that in Mexico, Louts had stayed at one hotel, Las Misiones, in the center of town, and had eaten dinner every night in the same place, probably the hotel restaurant.

In Brazil, it was a different story. The student had used her Gold Card on the first day to withdraw a hefty sum of cash from a bank machine in Manaus—more than four thousand reais, or about two thousand euros—then had probably paid her hotel and restaurant bills and other expenses with that money, since there was no computer trace of her presence there.

Robillard had highlighted another curious fact: she was planning another trip to Manaus. The reservation had been made the week before, with departure scheduled for two days later.

Paris–Juárez–Paris, mid-July 2010. Five days in Mexico.

Paris–Manaus–Paris, late July 2010. Seven days in Brazil.

And again, Paris–Manaus–Paris, scheduled for September 8–15, 2010. A trip the student would never take.

Faced with this mystery, Sharko recalled the words of the primatologist Clémentine Jaspar: "Eva confided to me that she was on to something big."

"Yes, but what, exactly?" the cop said aloud. "Is there even a relation between those trips and your murder?"

He switched on the computer and Googled the map of Brazil. Twenty-five times the size of France, it was separated from Mexico by Central America and Colombia. The cop didn't know exactly where Manaus was located, but the map showed that it was tucked away in the northern part of the country and was the capital of the state of Amazonas.

Searching further, he discovered that Manaus was situated at the confluence of the Rio Negro and the Rio Solimões, just before their waters join to form the Amazon River. A huge city of nearly two million inhabitants, which had long subsisted on rubber and which today was becoming westernized: cars clogging the streets, industry, McDonald's and Carrefour, commercial port with cargo ships. One of the most popular tourist destinations in Brazil.

Sharko rubbed his eyes. They were burning, but no matter. His curiosity was piqued and he wanted to follow his research, his deductions, to the end. In any case, he probably wouldn't sleep that night.

He moved on to the other stack, the one Robillard hadn't yet had time to look through. Again, numbers on bank statements. His eyes slid quickly over the figures. Nothing very useful. Withdrawals, everyday expenses . . . the next sheet, and the next . . . Then, suddenly, a particular line drew his attention: a withdrawal on Eva Louts's bank card from an ATM in a French town called Montaimont, in the Savoie region . . . Two hundred euros, on Saturday, August 28, 2010, at 9:34 p.m.

The day after her interview with Grégory Carnot.

The cop sat back in his chair, brushing his hair off his forehead. Just after Vivonne, Eva Louts had gone straight to the heart of the Alps. More than four hundred miles. What if the student was on the trail of something—an invisible breath that had driven her from the cities of Latin America to the highest mountains in Europe, when she was merely supposed to be studying lefties and righties from behind a desk? How had a simple study of hand dominance caused her to travel so much, and how had it led to such a violent death? What had pushed her to get close to scum like Carnot? And why was she planning to go back to Brazil?

Carnot. Sharko hated him more than anything in the world, and now, thanks to his investigation, he had the chance to confront him face-to-face. He wanted the murderer for himself, and for himself alone . . .

He clenched his teeth and let the bank statement fall to the floor. Then, with the tip of his shoe, he slid it under a file cabinet.

10

The sky was the color of mourning.

It was raining when the car with northern plates arrived in Vivonne—rain black as a swarm of flies, which had been hammering the windshield of the Peugeot 206 for a good fifteen miles and gave the illusion of a landscape with no end and no hope.

Lucie had stopped once to down a bitter coffee in a rest area and nibble on a few biscuits.

She looked at her watch. At exactly 4 p.m., they'd be burying a piece of garbage in the town cemetery of Ruffigny, about six miles from Poitiers. The town where Carnot had lived much of his life, going about his simple existence as a factory worker. Lucie wanted to see the ground swallow up the casket; she had a visceral need to see it. Her mother couldn't understand it. She'd tried everything in the book to keep Lucie from coming to the burial, but too bad.

First, though, she needed some answers, and they were to be found behind these high walls in front of her, with their barbed wire and depressing gray tones. In the ultramodern prison where Grégory Carnot had killed himself.

True to his word, Captain Kashmareck had come through with the pass. At the reception check, where she was relieved of her keys, cell phone, and wallet, a guard pointed Lucie to the prison psychiatric ward. This was a special wing of the complex, its main functions being to detect psychological disturbances and provide the most troubled inmates with treatment. In recent years, the prisons of France had become veritable incubators of mental illness.

In silence, Lucie walked up a corridor lined with clean, modern individual cells, each one occupied by an inmate sprawled on his bed or sitting on the spotless linoleum. A rather calm atmosphere for a place tainted by madness; at most a few murmurs and groans. Indifferent eyes watched her pass; some prisoners dragged themselves to the bars of their cells to check her out and remind themselves what a woman looked like. Whatever their crimes, the circumstances of their imprisonment, they repulsed her. Every one of them, without exception, deserved to rot in hell.

She halted abruptly in front of an empty cell. Her chest tightened. Slowly she approached; her hands gripped the cold iron bars. The upside-down drawing Carnot had made was even more striking in real life than on the photos. It was a good five feet wide. A veritable colored fresco of clocklike precision. The sea, the foam of the waves, the sun . . . Lucie wondered if that filth hadn't pushed perversity to the point of drawing the beach at Les Sables d'Olonne. The guard shoved his key into the lock of the heavy door in front of him.

"The doctor let him finish his drawing. We'd never seen anything like it here. He didn't even bend his head over to draw upside down. It was more like . . . natural. Facilities will be here soon to paint it over. We want to forget all about Carnot, the quicker the better."

He stood waiting. Lucie didn't move.

"Well, uh, will you follow me, ma'am?"

Lucie spent a few more moments staring into the void, at the floor, clean as a hospital. It was easy to imagine Carnot in there, his monstrous body, his little sadist's eyes. Easy to see him handling his felt markers, laughing or entertaining himself within these few square feet.

"Did he cry a lot? Did Grégory Carnot cry a lot?"

"No idea, ma'am. Why do you ask?"

"No reason."

Lucie slowly started walking. Through an airlock, the sharp clang of security bolts. Sounds that made you jump, that echoed on all sides, to the far corners of those endless hallways. Administrative offices in a row, all identical, before reaching the one for Francis Duvette, one of the psychiatrists in charge of the prisoners' mental health. He was a man of around fifty, bald, with sallow skin and sunken cheeks. His workspace was buried under files and papers. Stacks and stacks up to the ceiling—the joys of French bureaucracy. Wearing a tight-fitting lab coat, he greeted Lucie and motioned her toward a chair.

"We've never met, Miss Henebelle. I wanted first and foremost to let you know that I was not trying to exonerate my patient from the horror of his crimes. But Grégory Carnot was in mental distress, and it was my duty to find the causes of that distress."

Lucie nervously readjusted the hem of her suit. Before the tragedy, she had felt great respect for these psychiatrists, doctors, and caseworkers who dedicated their lives to improving those of others, and who were perhaps even more imprisoned than the prisoners themselves. But today, her view had changed: she would have preferred that this type of person didn't exist.

"What kind of distress?" she asked.

"The kind that schizophrenics can feel when they cycle into delirium. Powerful hallucinations, spontaneous, uncontrolled acts of violence, of the most horrific sort. It was probably why he committed suicide. He'd become too aware of his suffering and was complaining of abominable head pain."

"Carnot was schizophrenic?"

"I don't think he was, that's the strangest part. My patient had no bouts of depersonalization, the feeling that your body is breaking up. He had no hallucinations, didn't see nonexistent people. The diagnostic I drew up didn't really correspond to schizophrenia, more like a succession of delirious episodes. Despite everything, I remain convinced that his experiences of 'seeing the world upside down' were quite real, not hallucinations. His drawings are too detailed, too meticulous. Try drawing even a simple tree upside down, and you'll see how hard it is."

"If they weren't hallucinations, what were they?"

"I'm not sure. To my knowledge, these symptoms are completely unknown in the medical literature. I was going to take MRIs of his brain activity. There might have been a real organic dysfunction, perhaps in the visual cortex or optic chiasma, the part of the brain where the optic nerves cross. Neurologists have already come across problems like hemianopsia, where the patient sees only half an image, for instance, but never anything like this."

"Did they do an autopsy?"

"I'm sorry to say they didn't. There was no question about the suicide. And you know, the rules are a bit different in prison. Carnot had been sentenced to thirty years, twenty-five of them in solitary. He didn't exist anymore. And his adoptive parents . . . they didn't request an investigation."

He took a sheet of paper and sketched a diagram.

"The eye functions like a lens. The image of the outside world as it hits the retina is upside down. Then it's the brain, in particular the visual cortex, that turns it right side up, in the direction of gravity. It's quite possible that Carnot's brain presented a real neurological dysfunction in that regard, which would have begun imperceptibly a little more than a year ago."

"So before he kidnapped my children."

"Indeed. He claimed he'd already made upside-down drawings on paper before he committed his acts. But as you know, a sheet of paper can be turned in any direction, so it's hard to say if he was telling the truth. The fact remains that his headaches were growing worse exponentially over the past weeks."

"And could the . . . the fact that these images were upside down, could that somehow have been related to his acts of violence? His brutality?"

Duvette seemed to be weighing every word.

"You know as much about Carnot's past as I do, I imagine. Loving adoptive parents, both Catholic. A childhood as normal as any other kid's. Mediocre student but generally well behaved. No psychiatric history, not many fights. In any case, given his size, no one bothered him much. At thirteen, he was already five foot eleven, a real force of nature. As his birth records are sealed, I wasn't able to check his biological family's medical history. That's the only gap in the file. All we know is that Carnot was lactose intolerant: he couldn't drink a drop of milk without experiencing intense vomiting and diarrhea. Often other inmates would slip a bit of milk into his food, just for the fun of seeing him suffer."

"His suffering is the least of my concerns."

Lucie couldn't unwind. Her hands kneaded her thighs. Surely because of this prison, the atmosphere of madness and death floating over everything. She, too, had checked the past of the man who had killed her daughter. Born in Reims on January 4, 1987, and given up for adoption; taken in by a local couple, devoutly religious, around thirty years old at the time, who had later moved to the Poitou region because of a job transfer. When he was old enough, Carnot had taken a job in a factory in

Poitiers that made ice cream cartons. A regular guy, always on time for work, everybody liked him. Until he committed his atrocity.

Lucie returned to the present, biting the insides of her cheeks. Every time she thought about the killer's squeaky-clean past, she flew into a rage. She did not want Carnot's responsibility for his crimes to be reduced in any way. Even dead, she wanted him to bear the weight of his actions, to carry it with him to the shores of hell.

"Even individuals with the nicest childhoods can become sick perverts," she said sharply. "We've seen that enough times. You don't need any anomalies in the brain or family history. You don't need to have tortured little furry animals when you were young. Some of those murderers were ideal neighbors, the picture of innocence."

"I'm well aware of that. But given the situation, I can only tell you what I know. Carnot had episodes of extreme aggressiveness, as well as visual disturbances and loss of balance, accompanied by severe head pain. Recently the two symptoms had been increasing in the same proportion. They might well be related. The brain is a complex machine and there's still a lot about it we don't know."

Resigned, he lifted a thick sheaf of paper and released it like a brick.

"It's all here in black and white. Carnot was suffering from *something*, which was getting worse every day, sort of like a cancer. If this had happened on the outside we probably would have had more clues, more sources of information. No doubt Carnot would have been given an MRI and a complete diagnostic workup a long time ago. But you know, in the prison system, everything gets slowed down by this damned paperwork and a crippling shortage of equipment. And now my patient is dead."

Lucie leaned firmly over the desk.

"Let me ask you straight: do you think Grégory Carnot could have committed such horrors under the influence of some kind of mental disturbance? Do you think, a year after he went to prison, that we can question his responsibility? Do you believe the twelve jurors who judged him responsible for his actions were wrong?"

The man cleared his throat. His eyes left Lucie's for a moment, then returned and held her gaze.

"No. At the time, he was fully aware of what he was doing."

Lucie sat back a little in her chair, a hand to her lips. His answer didn't satisfy her. Limp tone. No conviction. He was lying to avoid challenging the verdict and so that she'd leave mollified—she was sure of it.

"'At the time' . . . Are you just saying that to make me feel better? Is that really what you believe?"

He began moving stacks of papers, as if arranging his desk. He was doing everything he could to not meet her gaze.

"Absolutely. I'm telling you exactly what I told the cop who was here this morning. Carnot was responsible."

Lucie knit her brow.

"A cop was here this morning? When?"

"Not two hours ago. Some cop from the Homicide bureau in Paris. He looked like he hadn't slept in ages. I've got his card here—well, if you can call it a card. More like a piece of cardboard."

He pulled open his drawer and took out a white rectangle, which he handed to Lucie.

It felt like a kick to the stomach.

On the card, written diagonally in ballpoint across the blank surface, was a name: Franck Sharko.

"Are you all right, Miss Henebelle?"

Lucie handed back the card with trembling fingers. She no longer had Sharko's number in her cell phone. She had erased it a long time ago, along with any feelings she'd had for the detective. Or so she'd thought. Seeing that name again, here, now, so abruptly, under such circumstances . . .

"Homicide? Are you sure?"

"Absolutely."

A pause. Lucie couldn't believe it.

"What did he want? What was Franck Sharko doing here?"

"Do you know him?"

"I used to."

A curt answer that left no room for further comment. The psychiatrist let it drop and returned to the subject at hand.

"He asked me questions about Eva Louts, a student who had come to visit Grégory Carnot about ten days ago. From what the inspector told me, she'd been murdered."

Everything was spinning too fast in Lucie's head. Carnot was dead, but his ghost was still prowling around her. She thought of Franck Sharko. So he was still on the job but had left his position at the Violent Crimes unit and gone back to Homicide . . . Why hadn't he just quit the whole damn thing, the way he'd promised before the twins were kidnapped? Why this return to the streets, guts, blood, starting over at point zero?

Shaken by the abrupt revelations, Lucie took a deep breath. She had to proceed calmly, methodically, like the cop she once had been.

First she asked questions about the circumstances of the crime. The psychiatrist passed along what the police inspector had told him: Eva Louts, found murdered in a primate research center near Paris. The bite mark on her face, the theft of files from her apartment. The fact that she'd requested meetings with violent criminals in different parts of France. Lucie tried to store away as much information as possible, to link various facts. In spite of her, her ex-cop's brain had started working at top speed, and certain reflexes were already returning.

"Why? Why did Eva Louts want to meet these criminals?"

"Because they were all left-handed."

He noticed how deeply his answer had troubled the woman, and explained further:

"Not to say that all criminals are left-handed, obviously, just that Louts had chosen only left-handers. And the most violent ones, who had killed under murky circumstances that they themselves usually couldn't explain."

"But . . . but why? What was the point?"

"For her thesis, I presume. When she came here, she wanted to question Carnot in detail, but he wasn't really up for it, so I acted as intermediary. She wanted to know if his parents were left-handed. If they had made him use his left or right hand when he was a child. And a bunch of other questions that were only meant to establish statistics and form hypotheses. Did you know that most of the time Carnot was right-handed?"

"I couldn't care less."

"He ate and drew with his right hand, because his adoptive parents had forced him to be a right-hander, from what Louts told me. Since the dawn of time, being left-handed has always been considered a flaw, a curse or a mark of the devil, especially in the Middle Ages. Carnot was a false righty, made to become one by the education his Catholic parents had given him."

Lucie was silent a moment, lost in thought.

"And yet . . . he stabbed my daughter with his left hand. Sixteen stab wounds and not a trace of hesitation."

Duvette stood up and poured them both some coffee in tiny cups. Lucie thought aloud:

"As if the fact of being left-handed was buried deep within him and had never left."

"Precisely. That was the sort of detail that interested Eva Louts. It's possible that left-handedness is ultimately genetic, and in certain circumstances there's nothing education can do about it. I think that's what the student was looking for when she came here."

Lucie shook her head, eyes staring into the void.

"None of that sounds like a reason for her murder."

"No, probably not. But there are two more things I can tell you. The first is that Louts wanted very badly to take away photos of Carnot's face, supposedly to 'remember him by' when it came time to write her thesis. I gave her the mug shots from his file—they weren't restricted. The second thing—and I don't know if this has anything to do with left-handedness— but when Louts discovered the upside-down drawing on the wall of his cell, her behavior changed. She started asking me tons of questions about the genesis of the drawing. When had Carnot done it? Why? Was there some explanation? The fresco seemed to excite her."

"Do you know why?"

"I don't. But from then on, her attitude toward Grégory Carnot changed. After seeing the drawing, she looked at him with a kind of . . . fascination."

Lucie shivered. How could anyone be fascinated by such a monster?

"She left without telling me much, and I never saw her again. Today I learned she's dead. The whole thing is very strange."

Lucie finished her coffee in silence, floored by these revelations. There was nothing more for her to say or do. She asked a few more routine questions, then thanked Duvette and left the prison. Outside, she collapsed onto the seat of her car and fished out the little semiautomatic pistol that she'd stashed in the glove compartment, next to an old pair of wool mittens and a handful of CDs she never listened to anymore. Handling the weapon did her good. The coldness of the barrel, the reassuring weight of the grip . . .

She'd come for answers, but she was leaving with only more questions.

What had been going on in Eva Louts's head? And in Grégory Carnot's? And in Clara's, at the moment when that 220-pound piece of filth had leaned over her? So many unknowns, so many things not understood, which threatened to remain unanswered forever.

She put away the pistol. She had bought it because, deep down, she had always hoped to use it against her daughter's killer. To somehow slip it into the courthouse and put down the bastard with a clean shot to the head. But she'd never had the guts to go through with it. Because she still had Juliette, and her duty as a mother was to watch over her child.

As she started driving, Lucie looked at herself in the rearview mirror and realized she was on the verge of tears. So she slammed on the brakes and dialed the number of the cell phone that she'd bought for Juliette, which should have been in the little girl's backpack. It didn't matter if the child was in class. She had to talk to her daughter, hear her voice, reassure herself that everything was all right, even if it meant interrupting the teacher's lesson. That was why she had bought the phone in the first place, so she'd always be able to reach her daughter, so she could stay close to her and know where she was at any moment.

But the call went to voice mail, so instead she left a long, affectionate message.

11

Franck Sharko walked bareheaded in the pouring rain. The wind had risen, a cold slap that reddened your cheeks. He raised the collar of his overlarge raincoat and, hands thrust in his pockets, entered the cemetery.

The procession had halted at the end of the sixth alley. A line of black, motionless silhouettes, who fought against the wind to keep their umbrellas from shredding. Possibly Grégory Carnot's adoptive parents, a few relatives. People for whom the murderer still retained a semblance of humanity. Individuals come to seek answers they'd never find. Soaked, the men from the funeral parlor were lowering a wooden box into its pit.

As the cold was drilling into his back, Sharko noticed another static form, standing apart as he was, but on the other side of the cemetery. No umbrella, only an ample hood that devoured his left profile, leaving only the tip of the nose visible. The silhouette had taken care to place itself in a blind spot in relation to Carnot's grave. To see without being seen.

Intrigued, the inspector decided to go meet the figure, but by surprise. First, he made sure his Sig Sauer was ready in its holster. He quietly worked his way back along the alleys, skirting the sepulchers to position himself behind the individual's back. The wind and rain covered the sound of his footsteps on the gravel. Firmly, he rested his large hand on the observer's right shoulder, who spun around with a start.

Sharko felt the ground shift under him.

The face appeared to him in the half darkness, soaked and numb with cold, but instantly recognizable.

"Lucie?"

It took Lucie a fraction of a second before she realized who was in front of her. Could it really be the same man? The strapping fellow she'd known only a year before? Where was the flesh on his cheeks, the imposing breadth of his outline? Was she talking only to a shadow, or really to . . .

"Franck? Is that . . . you?"

She fell silent, with something powerful and gnarled rising in her chest. Good God, what could have changed him so drastically? Was it Clara's death? Their abrupt separation? What hell had he gone through? In the depths of his eyes, he wore all the guilt of the world, a suffering as prominent as his cheekbones. Heavy rings devoured his stonelike face. Without thinking, acting on impulse or from too much emotional buildup, she crushed herself against him, slowly running her hand along his back. She felt his heart beat, the sharp edges of his shoulder blades along her fingers. Then she abruptly pulled away. Her hood had slid back, revealing her long blond hair. Sharko looked at her tenderly. She was as beautiful as he was damaged. He was hurting so, so badly. The wound had reopened.

"I shouldn't have come here."

Slowly, he again plunged his dripping hands in his pockets and turned away. He was grateful to the rain for hiding his sadness, his obvious feelings—he who, in his entire life, had cried so little. He was walking away when a word, the word he both desired and dreaded, echoed behind him:

"Wait."

He halted, clenching his fists. She came up to him, ignoring the puddles.

"One year ago, Carnot tore us apart, and today he's brought us together again. I don't know what for. But I think we have to talk. If you're willing."

A long silence. Too long, to Lucie's mind. Why? What was he thinking about? Did he hate her for the way she'd left him? Finally, his hoarse voice sounded in the rain.

"Okay . . . but not too long."

Lucie turned back toward Carnot's distant gravesite. Water was running down her face and her lips trembled; she felt abnormally cold.

"I have to see the earth swallow up his coffin," she finally said. Sharko nodded without moving, so she added, "Alone."

12

He was waiting for her in a dark corner of the café, not far from the graveyard, his hands wrapped around a large, steaming cup. Furious volleys of water slammed against the window, isolating the place from the rest of the world. Two or three shadows were idling near the beer taps, regulars who'd come to damage their livers at the bar. In the shadows, Lucie removed her soaked jacket and wrung it out on the mat before going to join the man sitting alone at a table. She pulled up a chair and sat down opposite him, wiping a handkerchief over the droplets that were still running down her face.

They sized each other up for a moment with timid glances. Both opened their mouths at the same instant, the words fluttering on the threshold of their lips; finally, it was Lucie who broke through the awkward silence.

"I've sometimes thought about you, Franck, after . . . after what happened. I always imagined you impeccably dressed, standing firm on your feet, your face hard and assured." She nodded toward the cemetery that they could barely see from there. "I imagined you so far away from this filth. I thought you'd maybe forgotten all about it."

Sharko gave Lucie a sad smile, which made her sadder still. What shadows had he been wallowing in?

"The more time goes by, the deeper the wound grows. How could I forget?"

Lucie was surprised to feel a pain in her heart. No sense asking how he was doing, what he'd been up to these past months: everything was etched into his bony face, in the empty eyes that had lost all their sparkle. No doubt he had wandered from case to case, soaking up his days and nights. Submerged in work, in blood. Just another way of numbing yourself, of not having to think, like Lucie at her call center. In spite of herself, she couldn't help feeling sorry for him. She forced herself back to the reason for their meeting.

"I stopped in at Vivonne. The prison psychiatrist told me everything. Your visit, the investigation into this Eva Louts. You have to talk to me, let me know everything you've got on her."

Sharko tried to check her enthusiasm. He had to calm her down, quickly, convince her to go back up north and put all this behind her.

"Grégory Carnot is dead, Lucie. Dead and buried. There's nothing left for you here. Go home. Forget this stuff and get on with your life."

"I hear you're back at Homicide now. Where's your partner? Why did you come here alone? This isn't an official visit, is it?"

Sharko ran his finger pointlessly around the rim of his cup. He didn't dare look at her.

"I see you haven't lost your observational skills."

"Why are you here, Franck?"

The inspector looked vainly for a distraction that wasn't coming. He'd handled himself ten times better in his run-in with Leblond and Manien. But in front of Lucie, all his inner barriers collapsed. He paused a bit too long before blurting out the truth:

"I came here to look Carnot in the eye. To see how that creep was getting along. But he's dead . . ."

Lucie tried to repress the shiver running up her spine. She had fallen in love with this man. Then she thought she hated him more than anything in the world. And now her certainties were being shattered. Deep inside of her, a small flame still flickered. So Franck Sharko had never forgotten them—her, Clara, Juliette. He lived with their ghosts in the depths of his heart and it was eating him up inside, like a disease that would inevitably prove fatal. A waiter arrived at their table; Lucie shooed him away and turned back to the inspector.

"You won't get there alone. Let me help you. I need to know. I need to . . . do something!"

"You're not a cop anymore."

"I'm still a cop deep down. You can't deny your true nature, no matter how hard you try. Anything, Franck, just one clue. I'm begging you. Give me a trail to follow. The fact that you're here proves Carnot isn't really dead yet, and you know it."

Sharko crushed his fist against his lips, as if he were about to make a decision of vital importance.

"I'm sorry, I can't. It's too risky. My colleagues will be making calls to the eleven prisons on the list, trying to learn more about Louts's visits. Sooner or later they'll call Vivonne and find out you were here."

"Unless you tell them they don't have to because you called Vivonne yourself."

Sharko remained imperturbable. Anger flashed in Lucie's face and she stood up.

"How can you just let me walk away empty-handed? Without giving me a chance to get any answers? What am I supposed to tell Juliette when she gets older? How can I explain what happened?"

She stormed off toward the coatrack, while Sharko stared after her, unable to breathe. He rubbed his hands over his face, feeling as if his entire world was crumbling around him.

"Oh my god . . ." he murmured.

At that moment, everything rushed through his head. As she was about to leave, he called out:

"All right."

Somber faces turned toward him. Lucie sat down again at the table. He got up, went to the bar, and returned with paper and a pencil.

"Can you leave right away? For maybe two or three days?"

Lucie felt a pernicious impulse rising in her, one she thought she'd left behind forever: a dangerous excitement that annihilated all her promises. Especially the one to take care of Juliette, never leave her alone again, bring her to school every day of every week and wait for her in the afternoon. To act like a mother. The predator she'd thought dead and gone was still lurking deep inside her, and today it had reawakened.

"Yes."

"I was hoping you'd say no."

"So was I. But I said yes."

A silence. A final hesitation that might have changed everything.

"In that case, listen carefully. I spent a good part of last night at number thirty-six going through Eva Louts's bills, account statements, and credit card charges. And I discovered something peculiar. On August 28, a bank slip says she withdrew money in Montaimont, not far from Val Thorens, in the Savoie. The day before, as if by coincidence, she had met with Carnot and the prison psychiatrist."

The inspector continued his rundown. He chose not to mention the part about the two trips to Latin America. Too far away, too complicated, and for the moment too incomprehensible. Lucie had to stay on the outskirts of the investigation, just close enough to make her feel she was doing something useful . . .

"She withdrew two hundred euros, late in the evening. Montaimont is a backwater. Did she use the money for a place to stay that night? Given the amount, she couldn't have stayed much more than the weekend, and they didn't note any absence at the primate center. So why did she make such a rush trip to the middle of the Alps? The prison psychiatrist said that neither he nor Carnot had made any mention of that area."

He jotted down the name of the village and slid the paper toward Lucie.

"Just do a quick round-trip. I'm to remain your sole contact. No one, and I mean no one, must know we're working together on this. We haven't been in touch."

"Got it."

"As you said, I'll tell my colleagues I called Vivonne because I wanted to know what Louts was after. Meanwhile, you try to pick up her trail, call me with the info, and then go home to Lille. Are you in?"

"More than ever. The mountains will make for a nice change of scenery from my day job. It's been a year since I took a break. It might be about time. I'll head straight there—I've got a change of clothes in my bag."

"Remember, you're not a cop anymore."

"Do you have a photo of the vic?"

The cop pulled an ID photo from inside his raincoat and handed it to her.

"Louts was a pretty girl, barely more than a child. A loner like you, with a real zest for life. She did bungee jumping, fenced, worked hard, and had serious plans for her future. I want to find the scum who did this to her. I'll make him pay his debt."

Lucie felt a slight shiver. Sharko tossed some money on the table. He also held out three hundred-euro bills to Lucie, which he peeled off a thick wad.

"For expenses. It's my investigation, no reason you should have to pay for it."

Lucie wanted to refuse the money, but he crushed it into her hand and closed her small fist over it. A sensation of warmth crept over her at his touch.

"Take it. At least there's no shortage of cash."

He stood up. He had so many questions for her—especially about Juliette—but he couldn't bring himself to ask them. Keep his distance. Stay away from Lucie at all costs, and push away the dangerous feelings that were already taking hold of him.

He plucked his wet raincoat from the rack just behind his shoulder.

"Okay, then. I have to get home. Tomorrow's another workday. One more time: the Vivonne business stays just between us."

Lucie remained seated. She ended up pocketing the cash, then ran her finger over the photo of Eva Louts.

"Your phone number, Franck. I don't have it anymore."

He gave it to her and buttoned his gray coat to the top. Still shaken by his unexpected run-in with Lucie, he couldn't keep himself from asking in a low voice, "Tell me what Juliette says to you, Lucie. Does she whisper what happened to her during those thirteen days of captivity? Does she come wake you in the night? Does she resent you for it? Is she good to you?"

Lucie paused before answering.

"Juliette is my little angel. No matter what she says or does, I'll always love her."

Sharko felt a surge of anger against himself, and he already regretted having implicated Lucie in this business. She needed to go home, to rest. He tried to take back the sheet of paper, but Lucie flattened her hand over it.

"Why, Franck?"

Sharko didn't answer and contented himself with nodding good-bye. He was disgusted by his sudden emotional weakness.

"Call me only if you get some answers," he finally said. "And afterward, go back home."

He headed toward the exit and stepped out into the downpour. The storm was raging; lightning tormented the horizon. The cop felt as if he were at one with nature. Once he was alone inside his car, he let out in a murmur:

"Why? Because we're both cursed, Lucie, that's why."

13

The feeling of rolling through nothingness.

Since passing Chambéry, at around midnight, Lucie had trusted only the readings from her GPS. From what the indicator said, she had about thirty miles to go.

Alone, exhausted by the constantly winding road, she felt lost in a void. She had only one fear: that her car might break down. All around her was an apocalyptic landscape that no stars could brighten. While the mountains were probably beautiful in daytime, at night they looked like angry titans—frozen monsters with bodies of ice, which tore the horizon to shreds and absorbed the slightest ray of light. Lucie imagined Eva Louts in the same situation, driven by a force that had pushed her to travel all those miles, toward the far edge of darkness.

Finally, she arrived in Montaimont. Eyes burning, jaw aching, neck in tatters. On her dashboard was Eva's photo, and next to it an empty water bottle and a sandwich wrapper, along with Franck Sharko's phone number. Lucie could still see his scarecrowlike frame in the gloom of the café. *I want to find the scum who did this to her. I'll make him pay his debt,* he'd said in a cold voice, with no trace of feeling. She had also seen all that money in his wallet. Large bills, at least two thousand euros, she'd estimated. She knew he'd received a huge life insurance settlement following the deaths of his wife and daughter. He could have taken an easy retirement somewhere in the sun, but instead he kept on scraping the worn-out streets, his wallet stuffed with unused cash. Why would he inflict that daily torture on himself?

Back to the narrow road. Fewer than five hundred lost souls here, scattered across the foothills. The streetlamps struggled to diffuse a coppery glow.

The GPS told her she'd reached the street with the bank machine.

Under her headlights, the village center revealed a few sorry-looking shop windows. Louts must have driven up by the same route, arrived late, and withdrawn some cash, no doubt for a night's lodgings. Lucie began exploring the nearest streets. After about ten minutes of driving around, a lit sign caught her attention.

The Ten Marmots hotel was set back slightly from the road, at the other end of the village. An unpretentious structure, white façade, little wooden balconies, carriage entrance. A dozen rooms at most. Lucie stopped at a gravel-covered parking area and, once out of the car, stretched lustily. The fresh, sharp air made her quickly put on her jacket. Finally, she pulled her meager bag from the trunk: a pair of jeans, two T-shirts, underwear . . .

It was almost two in the morning when she walked up to the receptionist, a sixty-year-old in a sweat suit, with a mountain-man beard, graying hair, and black eyes. He was watching a nature show on Rai Uno, though "watching" might be pushing it.

"Evening. Have you got a room?"

He gauged the woman with a dull eye, then turned toward a board still containing more than three quarters of its keys.

"*Sì, signora.* Number eight. Your name?"

An Italian, with an accent you could cut with a fork and r's you could roll uphill. Lucie improvised:

"Amélie Courtois."

He wrote the name in the register.

"For how many nights?"

"One or two. It depends."

"Tourist?"

Lucie slid the photo of Eva Louts across the desk.

"This woman might have come here about ten days ago. Saturday, August 28, to be precise. Do you recognize her?"

He looked at the picture, then at Lucie, with an anxious face. She saw a dull light in his eyes: a workaday type who didn't want any trouble.

"Are you with the police?"

"No, Eva is my half sister. She went abroad without leaving me her address and I need to find her. I know she probably stayed in a hotel. Is this the only one around here?"

"Yes."

Dubious, he put on a pair of glasses and looked more carefully at the picture. Then he opened the register, turned a page, and pressed his finger onto a line written in spidery scrawl.

"That's it. Eva Louts, right."

Lucie's fists clenched: that was one obstacle passed. The man kept silent, as if digging into his memory. Another glance at the photo. Then he pointed to a phone number written on the register, just underneath the young woman's name.

"Is that Eva's phone?" asked Lucie.

He took a cell phone from his pocket, scratching his head.

"*Pazienza, pazienza.* I think this number . . . is in *my* contacts list. *Curioso . . .*"

For a brief moment, Lucie forgot all about her fatigue and her troubles, or that she had set off on the trail of a girl she'd never met.

"Here we are. It's him. It's his cell number."

He showed her the screen of his phone, with a name and number: Marc Castel. Lucie felt her throat tighten.

"Who's that?"

"He's a kind of guide for the upper mountains. I often recommend him for tourists who want to do some climbing or hike up top. I must have jotted down his number here so she could copy it—something like that, I don't really remember."

Lucie knit her brow.

"What did Eva need a guide for? Where was she going?"

"I have no idea. All I can tell you is that she stayed here two nights, then left early Monday morning. The best thing would be to ask Marc. He lives in Val Thorens. I'll tell you how to get there."

"Terrific."

"Be sure to get to his place early. I'd say seven at the latest. After that, Marc heads up to the summit and you won't see him again until after dark."

He scratched out an approximate map with an address and handed it to Lucie, who thanked him and gave him back the room key.

"Could you give me number six instead? According to the register, that was Eva's room."

Room 6 was pleasant enough but awfully small. A bathtub that could crack your spine, narrow single bed, miniature television. The one window looked out on something dark and infinite, probably a mountainside. Beneath the wan luster of a nightlight, Lucie sat on the mattress and removed her shoes with an *ahhh* of relief. She massaged her feet slowly, pensive.

Delicately, she pulled a small, transparent medal from the pocket of her jeans and slid it under her comforter. It was a plastic oval, with a small loop for hanging on a chain, that contained the last photo she'd ever taken of the twins together. The living one on the left, the dead one on the right. She'd had medals of this type made by the dozens, and had put them everywhere. In her car, her house, her clothes. Her children were always with her, no matter where she went.

Lucie spent ten minutes composing a text to her daughter. Juliette would find it tomorrow morning at breakfast, when she put the phone inside her schoolbag.

Once she had washed, undressed, and set her cell phone on "alarm," she sat on the bed, handling her Mann pistol. She ran a finger over the grip, brushed the trigger with a sigh. Through this object, she recalled the smells of the squad room, of black coffee, ink on freshly printed reports, the cigarettes some of her colleagues smoked.

After setting the pistol on the nightstand, she lay back on the mattress, hands behind her head, eyes to the ceiling. Lucie could hear the mountain breathing. A lugubrious lung with granite alveoli, which seemed to be pumping all the air out of her. She turned onto her side, shut off the light, and curled up like a child. Sleep enfolded her in its thick, warm blanket.

Lucie was dazzled by the beauty of the countryside closely surrounding her. At the foot of Marc Castel's chalet, set into the heights of Val Thorens, she enjoyed a panoramic view of Vanoise National Park. Snowy peaks as far as the eye could see. Powerful, hieratic crests assaulting a crystal sky. Closer in, so near it almost seemed you could touch them, were smaller mountains of red, green, and yellow that were already playing with the tints of morning light. In this early dawn, nature offered up its freshest and most gorgeous spectacle: wrapped tightly in her thin jacket and black woolen gloves at an altitude of more than sixty-five hundred feet, Lucie was shivering.

Beautiful as it was, the landscape had nothing on the man who opened the door. Eyes of a troubling green, short brown hair, a compact, angelic face that made him look like Indiana Jones. He was a head taller than Lucie and, beneath his tight-fitting undershirt, showed a climber's fine physique. Apparently the woman from the North was catching him fresh from bed.

"Forgive me for intruding, but . . . the owner of the Ten Marmots suggested I come find you here before you headed up the mountain."

He looked her over from top to bottom, as if she had disembarked from another planet.

"Do you know what time it is? It's not even seven! Who the hell are you?"

Lucie again pulled out the ID photo, holding it out in front of her, and adopted an authoritative tone. Given how rude the guy was being, enough with the politeness.

"Amélie Courtois, Paris police. I need to know what this woman was doing here."

He accepted the photo mechanically, without taking his eyes off Lucie.

"Come inside a minute. I'm freezing my balls off."

Lucie entered the wooden lodging and shut the door behind her. She loved the ambiance of these large mountain chalets: the honeyed tones, the softness of the wood floors, the brute force of the exposed beams. In the living room, a large bay window offered a picture postcard view. It must have been so nice to wake up here every morning, head in the clouds, far away from the blackness of the big cities, the pollution and honking horns.

The man stared at her questioningly.

"The police? So what do you want with Marc?"

"Wait—you're not Marc?"

"No, just a friend."

Lucie clenched her teeth. Couldn't the idiot have said so sooner?

"I just want to ask him some questions about one of his customers. Where is he?"

The man nodded toward the summit, through the bay window.

"Up there. Didn't you see the helicopters as you were coming up?"

"Sure. They seem to be making round trips from the top, carrying large rolls of something."

"They've been at it since six thirty. Marc was in one of them. For the last few days he's been helping cover the most vulnerable parts of the Gebroulaz glacier with tarps, in preparation for next summer. The choppers regularly bring men and materials up there."

"They wrap up glaciers these days?"

"Just a small part. With climate warming these past years, all the glaciers on the planet are starting to sweat, especially in the Alps. In the last century, some of them have lost eighty percent of their volume. This year, they're trying to see if they can slow down Gebroulaz's melt rate, the way they did last year at Andermatt. Sixty-five thousand square feet to wrap in two layers of film barely an eighth of an inch thick, to protect them from UV rays, the heat, and the rain."

"So, this girl?"

"I'm not the one you should ask—I've only been here a few days."

"And when will Marc be back?"

"Not before evening. He spends all day up on the glacier. Sorry."

Lucie pocketed the photo and thought a moment. There were only two solutions she could see: wait patiently for his return or . . .

"Take me to the helicopters."

14

In the elevator of his building, Sharko turned the key in the lock and pushed Sub 1, a restricted floor that gave residents access to the underground parking lot. He hadn't slept a wink, having spent the entire night thinking of Lucie. He'd been so worried about her that he hadn't been able to resist sending her a text at 3:10 a.m.: "Is everything all right?" To which she'd answered simply, at around 6, "All ok."

Heading down, he looked at himself in the elevator mirror. For the first time in ages, he'd put a little gel in his long salt-and-pepper hair, brushing it back off his forehead. He hadn't used the stuff in so long that it had practically hardened in the tube. On an impulse that morning, he had also donned his old charcoal-gray suit, one of the ones he'd worn for his big criminal cases. Every cop has a fetish object—a pipe, good luck bullet, or medal. For him, it was these clothes, and he couldn't have said why. To keep his pants from falling, he'd had to pierce another hole in his black belt, using a fruit pitter because he didn't have a screwdriver. He floated in the jacket, its shoulders drooping. It was as if Hardy had lent Laurel his outfit, but no matter: in the well-tailored suit, he felt better and looked better.

He jumped when he reached the parking spot for his Renault R21. A shadow emerged from a recess in the garage stacked with piles of junk.

"Shit, you gave me a start!"

The shadow was Bertrand Manien. Harsh face, molelike black eyes. He stuck a cigarette in his mouth and flicked his lighter. The click echoed in the concrete cavity, and a yellowish glow haloed his flinty face. Of all the captains in Homicide, Manien had the darkest, murkiest past. He had been around every squad, from Vice to Narc, and knew the underbelly of Paris like the back of his hand. Secret brothels, S&M clubs, shady joints where he'd sometimes been seen off-duty. Not to mention his long stint in the human trafficking detail. A squad that no one came out of unscathed: the vicious way people treated one another—especially minors—defied the imagination.

No one, except Bertrand Manien, who often boasted of his service record.

"Nice suit. And I see you got a haircut. There been a change in your life, Sharko? Maybe a girlfriend, after all this time?"

"What do you want?"

"I was just at Frédéric Hurault's place. The poor guy lived not two miles from here. You two were practically neighbors, fancy that. So I figured I'd drop by."

How long had he been waiting? How had he got in? Why had he come alone? And why the allusion to a girlfriend? Sharko tried to open his car door, but Manien flattened his palm over it.

"Two seconds. Why are you always in such a rush?"

The inspector felt his throat tighten. If Manien had camped out here, someone else could easily have followed him yesterday to Vivonne Penitentiary, or even broken into his apartment to look around. There was nothing more rotten or twisted than one cop pursuing another.

"What do you want?"

"You've scored a prime parking spot for this rust heap. I didn't know you could still get an R21. Why don't you keep it outside?"

"Because this spot exists and it's mine."

Manien played with silences, looks. He walked around the vehicle, as if he were about to strip it to nothing.

"Can you tell me where you were last Friday night?"

Sharko greeted a neighbor with a nod of his chin and let him move away. He lowered his voice:

"You keep coming after me. You're here alone, at my house, at not even eight in the morning. This is becoming personal with you. Why aren't you out questioning the whores and pimps who were in that neck of the woods? Why don't you just do your job?"

"On the contrary, I am doing my job. So, I suppose you were in your apartment on Friday night, around midnight?"

"Nothing gets by you, that's for sure."

"And no one to vouch for you?"

"I'll say it again, nothing gets by you."

With a malicious smile, Manien pulled out a small notepad.

"You know what's in here?"

"Search me—the address of your last pickup? Who was it this time, some Romanian teenager?"

"Don't be obnoxious. You know, I've gotten hooked on quite a little game since you intentionally fucked up my crime scene. I said to myself, 'Well, now, what if I tried to find out exactly who this *Chief Inspector* is, with his dark, mysterious past?' The Hurault case was the perfect opportunity for me to look into you."

"If you've got nothing better to do, I feel sorry for you."

"Not at all. I've rather enjoyed it. So I chatted a bit with your building superintendent, and he told me something really interesting."

He let linger an unwholesome silence, hoping to rouse Sharko's curiosity and reveal a sign of weakness. But the inspector didn't flinch. It was like the silent combat of two cobras gauging each other before the final attack. After a while, the detective went on with his story.

"Since he's known you, the good super has almost always seen you use the outside parking lot, in front of the building, just a few yards from your entrance. If you had a BMW, I'd have understood why you'd suddenly want to stick it underground, safe from delinquents and rainstorms. But a clunker like this . . ."

Manien squatted down, touched the brushed concrete floor with the back of his hand.

"This concrete is like new. The guy in the next spot assured me the space had always been empty, so he parked on a diagonal because it was so narrow. But you went to see him last week and told him from now on you'd be taking the spot, and he had to keep off."

Voices echoed in the underground lot. In the distance, a squeal of tires, a hiss of rubber. People were going to work. Sharko could again feel the tension mount.

"And?" he replied. "Would you like the results of my last physical? Given my condition, I have to avoid carrying anything heavy, and packs of milk or water are heavy. Look behind you, the elevator is right there, and it lets me out just opposite my door. If I park outside, I have to walk at least two hundred yards and climb a bunch of stairs to reach the building.

I confess I'm having a hard time seeing what you're getting at. It's like you're trying to drag me down, no matter what I do."

Manien let out a huge puff of smoke, despite the detectors just a few feet away. The guy was dangerous, even crazy; Sharko had seen him bust suspects with hard kicks to the shins.

"The super was positive: your car didn't budge from its spot on the night of the murder."

"Not surprising, since I was at home."

"You created the perfect alibi for yourself. Even days later, you continue to park here. You're a genius, a real genius. To change your habits so thoroughly. Open the garage with the remote, wait, cruise around these narrow aisles in this boat that barely has power steering. When were you planning to drop the charade and start parking out in the fresh air again?"

Sharko finally opened his door. He kept his voice calm, assured.

"You didn't hear what I just said, but no matter. It's possible I'm mistaken, that I still don't understand how cops work, but since when does having an airtight alibi make you guilty?"

Manien didn't let go. Worse than a starving dog let loose on a bone.

"It's a long way to the Vincennes woods. Since you left your heap here the night of the murder, you must have taken a cab or bus, or better still, the subway. There are surveillance cams in the subway."

"That's right. Go look through every camera in town. It'll give you something to do."

Puffing on his cigarette, Manien stepped back until he was in the middle of the aisle. Then he flicked away the butt, just under the Renault's rear tire.

"Don't bother seeing me to the door. Anyway, we'll catch up at number thirty-six. And don't worry, this whole business is just between you and me. I reassigned Leblond—he should be helping out with your investigation in just a few days. I certainly wouldn't want my little conjectures to sully your . . . troubled reputation."

His steps echoed in the silence, then faded away for good.

Sharko remained still for a long time, feeling as if he'd received a sock on the jaw.

As every Wednesday, he went by the cemetery, where he meditated for a while at his family's grave. He couldn't keep from thinking about what had just gone down with Manien.

A half hour later, he met Jacques Levallois at a café on the corner of Boulevard du Palais and Quai du Marché-Neuf. The place was hopping at that time of day. Pedestrians, cars, hordes of scooters rushing to work. The young lieutenant was a regular of the establishment, which he frequented just before going on duty. He was seated at a sidewalk table, in his thin tan cotton windbreaker, dipping a sugar cube into his espresso while watching the barges drift by along the Seine. His large scooter, a 250-cc with two front wheels, was parked at the curb. Sharko ordered a juice for himself and took a seat across from his partner, who gave him a quizzical look.

"Where'd that suit come from?" asked Levallois. "You *did* notice it's a bit big on you, right?"

Sharko's gaze was absorbed by the police vehicles already circulating around the front of the Palais de Justice, right next to number 36. Cops in uniform, judges in robes, suspects in handcuffs. A constant round, tons of cases to handle, solve, and stash in the archives. Overcrowded prisons, ever-increasing and ever more violent delinquency. What was the solution? Sharko snapped back to the present when he saw a hand waving in his field of vision. Levallois was leaning across the table.

"You've got a real problem, you know? It's eight in the morning and you're already asleep on your feet. Robillard told me yesterday evening that you'd been in touch with him. That you'd also called some of the prisons, the last ones on the list. Pretty ambitious for a day off . . ."

Sharko took a large swallow of coffee. Activate the internal machine, restart the boiler, whatever it took.

"I needed to know what our victim was hoping to get from those convicts. So, what's new with the Louts case?"

"Okay, so, the tech guys struck out with the computers. Nothing interesting on the one at the animal center. On the other hand, they managed to find the thesis on the girl's PC. The file was fragmented on the hard drive, but nothing permanently lost since the killer didn't reformat the disc. They've given Clémentine Jaspar a complete copy of the text."

"Excellent. Did you have a chance to look through it?"

"Not really, it's more than a hundred pages, with all kinds of graphs and incomprehensible blah blah about biology. I'm meeting with Jaspar this morning so she can explain it to me. She's had it since noon yesterday."

"You're learning to delegate, that's good. And I can see from your eyes that that's not all."

Levallois flashed him a smile. Sharko wondered what his wife was like. Did he have kids? What were his hobbies and interests? The inspector had never asked, not wanting to get close to anyone. The less he knew, the better.

The younger man skimmed through his notepad.

"Not a whole lot of info on Louts herself. Something of a loner, as we'd figured. Her neighbors didn't notice anything out of the ordinary; her friends said she'd dropped out of sight. For the last year, she'd cut herself off from the world to do her work. Her thesis adviser didn't tell us much we didn't already know. On the other hand, he practically fell off his chair when we told him about Louts's trips to South America. He had no idea. As for her parents . . . you can imagine. They're completely devastated, they don't understand any of it. Eva was their only child."

Sharko sighed sadly.

"They've lost everything and won't ever get over it. Did they know about the trips?"

"Not even. They only saw her once or twice a month, for brief visits. Louts was very independent. And thanks to her parents, her bank account was always full. She was plenty able to indulge that kind of whim."

He leafed through his notes.

"For the prisons, you checked with Robillard, you're already up to speed . . ."

"Yes. Louts only interviewed violent criminals, all young, with large builds, who'd committed child murders or massacred people with knives— who had succumbed to murderous impulses that no one could explain. She always asked the same questions: did they use their left hand, were they born left-handed, and so on."

"She was trying to determine if the fact of being left-handed had an influence on their life, their actions. Each time, she came away with photos of the prisoners' faces. She claimed it was so she could reconstruct the interview later on, but it's curious all the same. We haven't found those photos. The killer might have taken them."

"What about the lab tests?"

A sudden glint appeared in Levallois's eyes.

"They called me late last night. It was about the tiny shard of enamel we found in the victim's wound. DNA analysis confirmed that it was indeed from the tooth of a common chimpanzee."

Levallois grabbed a paper napkin and wrote something down.

"You like puzzles, right?"

"Not first thing in the morning."

He pushed the napkin toward the inspector. Sharko looked at what he'd jotted.

"'2,000.' What's that mean?"

"It's the age of the tooth fragment."

Sharko, who was lifting his coffee cup, stopped short and put it back down.

"Are you saying that it was . . . ?"

"A fossil, exactly. The killer probably showed up at the primate center with a monkey skull from way in the past. He killed the victim after knocking her out with the paperweight, then pressed the jaw into her face. That's what created the bite mark. It's confirmed by the fact that the lab found no animal saliva mixed in with Louts's blood."

Sharko rubbed his chin. The setup was worthy of a horror film and told him they were after a killer who was precise, cunning, and perverse.

"That's why Shery kept talking about a 'monster,'" he deduced. "A terrifying monkey skull, which gradually became covered with Eva Louts's blood."

Levallois nodded.

"No doubt. The killer tried to disguise his crime by making us think it was an ape attack, and that might be where he slipped up. He probably had access, probably even owned, jaws, a skull, or perhaps even an entire fossil of a chimpanzee. He didn't leave any fingerprints, but that scrap of tooth enamel gave him away. So we're dealing with someone who has access to the world of paleontology. Maybe a conservator, collector, a scientist, or a museum employee. There can't be that many places around here where someone can get information about this type of thing. You don't find two-thousand-year-old skeletons on every street corner."

"The natural history museum . . ."

"Precisely, in the Botanical Gardens. I was planning to go when it opens, right after I finish my java. I've arranged to meet Clémentine Jaspar. After the live monkeys at the primate center, it's on to the fossilized mammoths at the museum."

Sharko was beginning to develop a liking for this young fellow he barely knew. He downed his coffee in one gulp, then nodded toward the scooter.

"Finally, something solid. You've got an extra helmet, I hope?"

15

From way up high, the Alps were even more dazzling than usual. They looked like sheets of aluminum thrown together, crumpled by the rough contact. Aggressive gneiss, jutting schist, sparse vegetation clinging to sheer drops.

The helicopter that ferried her, a red-and-yellow EC145 belonging to the Civil Defense authorities, was also carrying thick rolls of special film from a winch. To get herself on board, Lucie had relied on a fair amount of nerve buttressed by huge dollops of procedural jargon, and the trick had worked: broadly speaking, as part of a criminal investigation conducted by the DA's office in Paris, she had to question Marc Castel as soon as possible. To protect herself, she'd kept her fake identity, Amélie Courtois. No one had dared ask to see her ID, and no one would be checking out her story. They'd flown her up with the supplies, period.

Jordan, the pretty face with the green eyes, had gone with her to a sporting goods store run by a friend of his, who'd lent her a fur-lined jacket, ski pants, and hiking boots, along with gloves and protective goggles, and had thrown in some cocoa butter for her lips. From pure city girl, Lucie suddenly looked every inch the athlete. The change in physical appearance wrested her from her dull routine and did her a world of good.

The Gebroulaz glacier surged abruptly at a bend in the cliff. A gigantic tongue of frost, trapped in a granite bed. It was as if time itself had frozen, as if a volcano had spewed up cold lava, captured in all its climactic fury. Colorful silhouettes moved about on its virgin flanks, stretching tarpaulins and lugging equipment. Farther on and lower down, they could see Val Thorens, an absurd blip of cement surrounded by a lake of vegetation.

The twin turbine veered west and then hovered about twenty yards above a relatively flat area. Below, firm hands gripped the roll and unfastened the spring hooks. Masses of film crashed into the snow, sending up silky clouds. Once the ropes had been pulled back up, the copilot spoke into his walkie-talkie, then solidly harnessed Lucie into the winch. After giving her a few technical instructions, he fitted her shoes with steel crampons. Finally, he handed her a black wool cap, which she put on.

"Good luck! See you later!"

He had to shout. The propeller thrummed, the air howled in their ears. Lucie gave a thumbs-up and the descent began. Slowly, her small body, insignificant in such an outsized space, rolled in the void. Dizzy with vertigo, Lucie felt drunk, overcome by a futile sense of freedom. The altitude weighed on her muscles, her breathing, her organs, and the dry air burned her lungs, but she felt immersed in an incredible state of well-being.

The contact with the ice crust was hard—a shock to her knees and ankles—like landing in a parachute. Hands took hold of her, pulled her back and forth; in an instant, the spring hooks flew up before her eyes and the helicopter instantly rose into the sky. The roar of the propeller blades faded into nothing.

"I hear you're looking for me."

A tanned face was staring straight at her. A dry, leathery face, lips white with sunblock, eyes hidden behind round, opaque lenses. Lucie went to remove her own sunshades: in a fraction of a second, she felt her retinas burning and squeezed her eyes shut.

"Don't take your goggles off! Haven't you ever walked in snow? You heard of solar reflection?"

"Where I come from, the snow looks more like charcoal."

Her pupils took a while to adjust to the light again. Colors and shapes gradually reappeared.

"Am I speaking to Marc Castel this time?"

"That's me."

Lucie turned around. Ice crystals crunched under her feet. The glacier breathed, palpitated, like a living artery.

"I'd rather have met you under less dangerous circumstances. In the North, the terrain is a bit flatter than here."

"The North? On the radio, they told me you were from Paris. Amélie Courtois, from Paris."

Lucie improvised.

"I work in Paris, but I live in the North. I came to ask you about . . ."

She bit onto a glove, pulled it off with her teeth, and dug into her pocket.

"Eva Louts," Castel finished the sentence.

Lucie didn't bother pulling out the photo, and quickly pulled her neoprene protection back on.

"What crime can she have committed for you to come all the way up here?" asked Castel.

"She was murdered."

The guide absorbed the news. His blond eyebrows lifted slightly. After a long moment of immobility, he pulled out a bottle of water and took several gulps. Behind him, men had begun unrolling the thick film and cutting it with large shears.

"How? Why?"

"For how, let's just say in circumstances that I'd rather not go into. As for why, that's the reason I'm here. Tell me about her."

The guide began climbing higher. He was tall and well built.

"Come with me. There aren't any crevasses up there. Dig your crampons firmly into the ice. You wouldn't think so, but it can play real tricks on your eyes, and it's a steep climb."

Lucie did as told. Her boots seemed to weigh a ton. She breathed hard, while Marc Castel talked with irritating ease. The guy must have been carved from stone and raised on pure oxygen.

"The girl was full of pep. Small, high-strung, independent, and cute as hell. She'd come to my chalet on Mario's recommendation."

"The manager at the Ten Marmots . . ."

"Right. She had all the right gear: hiking boots, fancy backpack, and even the photo equipment around her neck—a Canon EOS 500, nice camera. She told me she was a scientist doing research into Neanderthal man."

"Research into . . . Neanderthals? That's what . . . she told you?"

He walked with large, surefooted strides. Lucie struggled to keep up, and she was panting hard. At higher than nine thousand feet, the air was getting thinner, and every step felt like lifting weights.

"That's right. She was trying to understand why that race of men died out thirty thousand years ago and why *Homo sapiens* continued to live and evolve. She seemed to know a hell of a lot about it."

Lucie might not have got all of it right, but hadn't Sharko talked about research into left- and right-handedness? What did Neanderthals have to do with any of this? Castel nodded toward the endless twisting path rising ahead of them.

"The entire reason for her visit was for me to bring her up there, near the Col du Soufre, on the glacier's accumulation zone. There's a place there, a cave, discovered about six months ago. A grotto that the melting ice revealed, because of . . ."

"Global . . . warming . . . I know . . ."

Behind his dark glasses, he looked at her with a smile that showed dazzling white teeth. The only thing missing was the little sparkle they use in toothpaste ads.

"We went up fast. The girl was in terrific shape and she climbed like a gazelle."

"Let's just say . . . that's not me."

"I can sense you've got a fair amount of pep yourself, somewhere in there. We've got about an hour of climbing, with a difficult passage over ladders across a wide crevasse."

After Marc Castel notified his colleagues and picked up some equipment, he roped himself to Lucie, giving her the basic instructions for attacking the glacier. He explained with an ease mixed with firmness. This was his territory here, his oxygen, his rock face.

The climb began. Ice ax in hand, a coil of ropes and spring hooks around her waist, Lucie pulled on her calves, pushing her dormant muscles. The ice snapped and cracked. The sun's rays danced, and translucent blues ricocheted beneath her shoes. After they'd passed the tarpaulin-covered areas, the walls of gneiss stretched out, the dimensions around them expanded, extending beyond measure.

Finally a kind of natural crater appeared, level with the ice. A horizontal half-moon sunken into the mountainside. While Lucie gulped down water from her bottle, Marc pulled two flashlights from his backpack.

"This is it."

Lucie caught her breath, hands on her knees. From that spot, she felt as if she were overlooking the world and its verticality.

"How could Eva . . . have known about . . . the existence of this . . . this cave?"

"It was written up in the scientific journals when they discovered it."

The guide stood at the edge of the grotto. Floes of ice spilled inside and disappeared in the shadows. Marc pointed to a dark spot on the rock, above the cave entrance whose lower portion was still obstructed by the glacier.

"You see this line? It's how high the glacier used to be. Glaciologists estimate that it goes back less than half a century. Fifty years ago, the cave we're about to enter was covered over by ice and completely inaccessible."

"That's amazing."

"I'd say instead that it's catastrophic. Glaciers are the thermometers of our planet. And our planet has a fever."

Marc removed the rope tying them together and rolled it in his bag. Lucie cast a prudent eye toward the peak. In front of her were countless striations, clouds you could practically touch with your hand, the blue of the sky competing with the blinding white of the reliefs. The young man called to her.

"A small jump a yard down will get us below the level of the glacier. Then a few steps on the ice, and then we'll reach a flat surface made of rock. I have to warn you, it's extremely cold in there. And it was worse when the whole thing was blocked up and not a drop of sun got in. In a word, this cave hasn't seen daylight in thirty thousand years."

"Thirty thousand? That's fantastic!"

"Very soon, access will be strictly regulated, or even prohibited, so let's take advantage while the local politicians are still squabbling over who gets jurisdiction."

He headed in first. Sitting on a step of ice, he let himself slide toward the fearsome maw. Standing a level below the young woman, he reached his hand up.

"Come on."

In turn, Lucie jumped into the time machine. Behind her, bluish strata, accumulated and compressed for centuries, overlapped like layers of phyllo dough. The cold immediately pressed against her face, neck, on the smallest bit of unprotected skin. The fog that her body and mouth exhaled traced swirls in a swath of harsh light. Marc had removed his glasses. His eyes were pure blue, even lighter than Lucie's. In the intimacy of this place removed from history, their gazes met for the first time.

"I always imagined policewomen to be ... fairly unattractive and built like tanks."

"And I always imagined guides having blue eyes. You don't go against the stereotype."

"Fortunately, you do. Why would someone so pretty become a cop?"

"So she can get a guide's services for free and go where no one else gets to go."

He gave her a frank smile.

"Okay, back to business. So this place is a sanctuary that appeared even before the birth of the glacier. A place where modern man had never set foot."

Despite her layers of clothing, Lucie couldn't help shivering. The skin of her face felt hard as stone.

"And yet, here we are," she said. "Nothing escapes the conquest of our world."

Marc nodded, then pointed his beam toward the dark entrance.

"The cave is fairly large, about thirty yards deep. It's in there, all the way in back, that some Italian mountain climbers found the ice men."

Lucie narrowed her eyes. Had she heard right?

"Ice men? How many?"

"Four. Remarkably well mummified and preserved by the subzero temperatures. From what I've been told, it was as if they'd been in a freezer for thirty thousand years."

"That all?"

"That's a drop in the bucket on the evolutionary scale."

"Still . . ."

He took a slug from his water bottle.

"With the dry air, all the water had evaporated from their bodies, their eyes were gone, but the muscles had barely receded, just become black and desiccated. The near absence of oxygen prevented decaying. They still had their hair, remains of furs, some hand tools nearby. It was as if they'd dried out . . . like raisins."

They moved forward, bending down to enter a low passageway.

"If I recall my history right, these would have been Cro-Magnons?"

"It's more complicated than that. I'm not an expert and I wasn't there when they were discovered, but the paleoanthropologists who came here almost certainly identified one Cro-Magnon male and a family of Neanderthals: a man, woman, and child. Unfortunately I can't tell you much more than that. The scientists acted fast, doing their best to preserve the area so as not to damage the mummies. All I know is that the mummies, the remains of clothing, and the tools gathered here were carefully wrapped up and airlifted out under strict hygiene and temperature conditions. Then they were brought for analysis to the paleontology lab at the college in Lyon."

"Lyon isn't exactly next door. Why not Chambéry or Grenoble?"

"I think Lyon's the only facility in France that handles this kind of situation and has equipment advanced enough for this type of study. The scientists took photos of the site at the time, which you can see if you go there."

His words echoed strangely against the cave walls. Lucie felt as if she were intruding upon a narrow crypt, violating some ancestral secret, one buried in layers of ice in the heart of the mountains.

"I didn't remember, or actually, I hadn't known that Cro-Magnons and Neanderthals had coexisted."

"They did for several thousand years. The Neanderthals died out while *Homo sapiens* continued to evolve. We're not sure exactly what the reasons were for the Neanderthals' extinction, though there are theories. Mainly having to do with his inability to adapt to the cold. But Eva Louts had her own belief. She was convinced the Neanderthals had been exterminated by the Cro-Magnons."

"Exterminated? You mean like genocide?"

"Exactly."

Genocide . . . The word came surging forward again, in the middle of a new investigation. The expression of human folly, which Lucie was encountering once more, a year later. She banished the memories that tried to flood in and made an effort to concentrate.

"A prehistoric genocide . . . Is that plausible?"

"It's a theory among others, upheld by certain paleontologists. For Louts, Cro-Magnon was taller and more aggressive. And the more aggressive ones naturally reproduce better, because they eliminate the competition as fast as they can."

They passed by small heaps of black ash, which seemed about to scatter at the slightest breath of wind. The vestiges of a fire as old as eternity. Lucie imagined the reddened, almost simian faces, the bodies with their wild beast stink, covered in animal pelts, gathered around the flames and uttering guttural grunts. She could see the fat beads of sweat covering their gnarled bodies, their grotesque shadows stretching across the cave walls. In a moment of anxiety, she turned around: the translucent wall from the glacier had vanished, along with all traces of light. A veritable leap into prehistory. Her imagination was on overdrive. And what if some sudden landslide trapped them here, her and Marc? What if she were never to see her daughter again? What if . . . ?

She rushed forward, close behind her companion, who had already gone ahead. She had to talk.

"Excuse me, Marc, but I assume those ice men are no longer here?"

"No, of course not."

"In that case, what are we doing here? Why did Eva come all this way to see a place she knew was empty?"

Marc turned around and looked her in the eye. Small white clouds drifted from his mouth.

"Precisely because this cave isn't exactly empty."

Lucie felt a chill invade her throat and occupy every one of her arteries. Her head began to spin. The effort, the altitude, the enclosure . . . She would give herself just ten more minutes in here, because images of burial were beginning to stifle her. Marc noticed her discomfort.

"Are you all right?"

"Yes, fine . . . Let's keep moving."

Finally they reached the back of the cave. A large, circular area, like a dome. The guide aimed his flashlight toward a side wall.

Lucie's eyes widened.

Hands painted in negative appeared. Dozens of thick, frightening hands, transferred in red and ochre pigments. Marc went up to one of them and placed his own hand over the print.

"This is the first thing Eva Louts did when she got here."

"Right hands . . . tons of right hands . . ."

"Indeed. Prehistoric men spread out their right hand and blew out pigments from a tube that they held in their dominant hand. The ones here were therefore left-handed."

Lucie stared at the depictions, her nose buried in her jacket, arms folded to keep warm. She imagined these Stone Age, primitive men, already moved by a desire to transmit their knowledge, their tribal culture, by leaving a trace of their passage. A collective memory, dating from tens of thousands of years ago.

"Louts just took a few photos. But this discovery was only the appetizer, so to speak. What really interested her is what's behind you, on that other wall."

Lucie turned around.

Her flashlight beam revealed something unimaginable.

The rock fresco depicted a troupe of aurochs. Twelve galloping animals, in red, yellow, and black hues, apparently fleeing some hypothetical hunter. The line quality was clear, precise, very different from the archaism often associated with prehistoric man.

The aurochs had all been painted upside down.

Just like in Grégory Carnot's prison cell.

Dumbstruck, Lucie moved forward and slid her fingers over the smooth surface. Those primitive beings, located at the other end of the human scale, suddenly seemed much closer to her. As if they were whispering in her ear.

"When did you say this cave was first discovered?"

"During ski season. January of this year. Those paintings are curious, aren't they? How could a Cro-Magnon or some Neanderthal—I'm not sure which—have had such lucidity of mind? And especially, why paint them upside down? What was the point of that?"

Lucie thought with all her might. The cave had been discovered in January 2010 . . . Grégory Carnot had been jailed in September 2009. And according to the psychiatrist, he'd already been making upside-down drawings. There was no way he could have known about this fresco.

She had to face the facts. Two individuals, more than thirty thousand years apart, had been afflicted with the same symptoms. And both, at first glance, appeared to be left-handed.

A strange case, never before seen in neurology, the hospital psychiatrist had said. Lucie had discovered two in less than two days. Two cases separated by thousands and thousands of years.

Full of questions, Lucie went back toward Marc.

"Did Eva Louts tell you anything further?"

"No. She took pictures of the drawings, then we went back down. She paid me and went on her way. I never saw her again."

Lucie thought for a few moments, feeling doubtful, trying to put herself in Louts's shoes. Would she have gone directly back to Paris after just this visit and a few photos? Wouldn't she have been curious enough to go instead to the paleogenetics lab to see these prehistoric creatures? Especially since Lyon was on the way back?

As far as she could tell, the student had engaged in a sinister face-off with the four beings from another age, who had crossed through eternity and buried their secrets in the shadows of a cave that was never meant to see the light of day.

16

The Paris Botanical Gardens, at the edge of the fifth arrondissement, afford a magical spectacle on September mornings. Reddish light, the kind that spells the end of summer, falls obliquely on the foliage of thick, venerable cedars and drips onto the leaves. Joggers disappear down paths still damp with the previous evening's rain, while gardeners begin trimming shrubs in preparation for the harsher seasons. Everything is conducive to calm and relaxation. At that time of year, school groups haven't yet taken over the park and its museums.

Sharko and Levallois entered the foyer of the Hall of Evolution, a massive building straight out of another era. Above them, the huge glass roof filtered an orangey light, which spread across the three levels organized around a central nave. Without even penetrating into the center of the museum, one could discern strange skeletons, stuffed giraffe heads, hundreds of display cases harboring animal species. Here in particular, life was laying itself bare.

Clémentine Jaspar was waiting at the reception desk, a thick folder in her hands. In her brown pleated trousers and a khaki shirt with large pockets, the primatologist could easily have been mistaken for a guide or some hiker lost in the middle of the capital.

The cops greeted her. Sharko gave her a sincere smile.

"How's Shery?"

"She's still having trouble expressing herself. It will take her a while to fully recover, at her age. And there aren't any shrinks for chimpanzees."

She quickly changed the subject.

"And how's your investigation coming?"

"Not bad for the moment. We're gathering up as much information as we can before drawing any conclusions."

The inspector nodded toward the folder.

"I'm especially counting on what you can tell me about this thesis."

Jacques Levallois, who had remained a few steps back, gave his colleague a light tap on the shoulder.

"I'm going to go find the director or someone who can clue me in about the fossil. See you in a bit."

Jaspar watched him walk away, then headed toward the turnstiles.

"Let's go into a gallery, if that's okay. I can't think of a better place to explain all this to you."

As Sharko reached for his wallet to buy a ticket, she handed him one.

"I've got a few privileges here. It's a bit like my second home."

The inspector thanked her. He had lived in the area for more than thirty years and yet he'd never set foot in the museum, or in most Paris museums, for that matter. His habits ran more toward prisons, courtrooms, psychiatric wards. A macabre round of institutions that had punctuated his life.

They went through the turnstile and entered the nave. They wandered among life-size reproductions of sharks, elephant seals, giant rays. Most impressive was the hanging, outsized whale skeleton, which clearly exhibited the mysteries of nature. By what magic secret had those giant ribs been formed, until each was almost as big and heavy as a man?

Jaspar climbed a flight of steps to the first level, devoted to land species. In the middle, scores of jungle animals seemed to be fleeing an imaginary fire. Buffalo, lions, hyenas, antelopes, all frozen in flight. The primatologist skirted several cases, then stopped in front of the one containing *Lepidoptera*. Hundreds of flying insects, pinned to cork, numbered and precisely identified: phylum, class, order, family, genus, species. She sat on a bench, inviting Sharko to join her, then opened the fat green folder.

"Here's the copy of Eva's thesis back. You'll find my notes in the margins."

She spoke with gravity, her features drawn and tired.

Sharko focused his attention on his interlocutor.

"Tell me what Louts discovered."

Jaspar thought for a moment. She seemed to be seeking the best way to broach a complex subject.

"She found a relation between hand dominance and violence."

Violence.

The word burst like a firecracker in the inspector's head. Immediately, the image of Grégory Carnot appeared to him. He also thought about Ciudad Juárez, a city of fire and blood, where terror showed itself at its crudest. Violence, everywhere, in every form, that clung to him like a tick.

The primatologist brought him back to earth.

"So that you can fully grasp the essence of her work, I first have to tell you some of the more notable principles of evolution. Listen very carefully."

"I'll do my best."

With a circular movement of her arm, Clémentine Jaspar indicated the species that inhabited the magnificent gallery. Fish, beetles, crustaceans, mammals.

"If these species populate our planet today, if this little dragonfly exists, even though it appears so fragile, it's because it is much more adapted to survive than a dinosaur. Look at these animals, the shape of their shells and tails, their color. These are clear examples of adaptation to the environment, which all have but one function: attack, defense, camouflage . . ."

She pointed toward one particular display case.

"Those two specimens in front of you are birch moths. Look carefully. Do you notice anything?"

Sharko got up and leaned closer to the glass, intrigued.

"Two identical moths, one with white wings and the other with black wings."

"Well, now, you see, in the nineteenth century, in England, the pale form was ultra-dominant. During the day, the pale moths could hide on the trunks of birch trees, which ensured their survival. That's why they were more plentiful: predators didn't see them. You might object that, on the other hand, black moths wouldn't be seen at night, but neither were the white ones, since it was too dark."

"Okay, logical enough. So it was better to be a light moth than a dark one."

"Correct. If nothing had changed, the dark moths would eventually have become extinct, because they were less adapted to their environment, more vulnerable, genetically less efficient, and thus eliminated by natural selection."

"My famous lame ducks . . ."

"Absolutely. But today, we've noticed that the light-colored variety is becoming increasingly rare, while the dark variety is flourishing. In a hundred years, the ratio has completely inverted."

She came up and stood next to Sharko. Her eyes shone in the reflection of the glass.

"What effect of natural selection could have changed the distribution to that extent?"

"You tell me."

"The man-made kind, Inspector. With the advent of the Industrial Age, England experienced a serious problem of air pollution. This pollution caused the color of birch trees to turn from pale gray to dark gray. And so it became increasingly difficult for the pale variety of the butterfly to survive, because its camouflage was no longer effective. You have here a typical example of natural selection influenced by human agency: the better-adapted species, the dark-colored variety, began to increase in number, while the light-colored variety was being eaten by predators. All because of humans."

"So man and industrialization are able to influence nature's choices— or even to change them."

Jaspar pointed toward a graph that charted population growth over time. In the space of several centuries, it went from thousands of individuals to several billion. A veritable human virus seemed to be spreading over the planet. Sharko felt a chill in his spine.

"The second point to keep in mind is, every human being alive today is a pure product of evolution. You are incredibly well adapted to your environment, as am I."

"I really didn't think I was all that well adapted."

"But you are, I guarantee it. If you're alive today, it's because none of your ancestors died before reproducing, and this has been so since the dawn of time. More than twenty thousand generations, Inspector, who sowed their seed all the way down to you."

Sharko pondered the profusion of shapes, sizes, and colors. Bound by the intrinsic power of Mother Nature, one couldn't help feeling humble. Little by little, the cop grasped the stakes that biologists grappled with, and could get an inkling of their obsessions: to understand the how and why of life, just as he tried to get inside the minds of his killers.

Comfortably in her element, Jaspar spoke with increasing ardor:

"Your forebears went through wars, famines, natural catastrophes, plagues, the great scourges but still brought babies into the world, who grew up and themselves propagated those extraordinary genes, all the way to you. Do you realize what a hidden combat our ancestors waged, just so you and I could be talking about this today? And it's the same story for each of the seven billion men and women who populate our planet. Incredibly well-adapted individuals . . ."

Her words echoed particularly loudly in that spot. The cop felt perturbed, touched. He thought of his little daughter, of Eloise, who had been struck by a car and killed. Her blood, her genes, the thousands of years of effort by his ancestors, just to hit a dead end in his lineage. He would die leaving no one behind, without furthering his own flow of life. Was he a failure, ill adapted, the result of exhaustion, which nature, chance, or coincidence had deemed fit only for the trash dump?

Listlessly, he tried to latch on to the primatologist's words, to his investigation. Only the taste of blood and the smell of the manhunt could still calm him and make him forget everything else.

"Where are you going with this?"

"To Louts's thesis. If left-handers exist, there is a reason, like the light or dark moths have reasons to exist."

The inspector thought of the framed picture they'd found in the student's room. Two armed panthers, challenging each other with thrusts of the foil. Both left-handed . . . Jaspar had begun walking again, toward the Arctic exhibits. Animals with white fur that allowed them to move about unnoticed and be protected from the cold; mammals endowed with a thick layer of blubber . . . more examples of environmental adaptation.

"Eva Louts drew up some very precise statistics. References, sources of information, and the dates when portions were written were all inscribed in her thesis: in highly interactive sports, in which close contact is an intrinsic part of the combat, the frequency of left-handers reaches nearly fifty percent. No matter if it's boxing, fencing, or judo. The farther apart the adversaries stand from each other, the more this ratio diminishes. It remains high in Ping-Pong, for instance, but falls back into the normal range for tennis and group sports in which there's less one-on-one contact."

Jaspar opened the thesis. She turned a few pages, to photos of hand-prints painted on a cave wall.

"With these data, Eva attempted to trace hand dominance throughout the ages. She discovered that most cave paintings dating from the Paleolithic or Neolithic Era had been done by left-handers. The handprints, made from pigments blown from the mouth, are of left hands in 179 cases, against 201 cases of right hands, or around forty percent. Which suggests that, long ago, in the time of the first humans, there were many more left-handers than today, and that over the course of the centuries, evolution tended to weed them out, just as it did with the dark moths."

She continued to leaf through the thesis. More photos appeared.

"After that, Eva went into museums and archives, copying down ancient documents concerning the reigns of the Goths, Vikings, and Mongols. In other words, peoples that have gone down in history as particularly violent . . . Look at these photos of their tools from back then, their weapons. Louts concentrated on their configuration, the rotational direction of drill bits in the materials, the signs of wear from teeth on wooden spoons, which are different depending on whether you bring the spoon to your mouth with your left or right hand."

She pointed to the characteristic traces.

"By studying these collections, she was able to gauge the proportion of left-handers in these violent populations, and realized that it was much higher than in other populations during the same period. The student accomplished a major piece of work. No one else had noticed such a thing or delved into it like that. I can understand why she broke off relations with her thesis adviser. She was on to something huge, a major discovery for evolutionary biology."

Sharko held out his hand, and Jaspar gave him several photocopies. He looked through the graphs, figures, and photos. As he turned the pages, Jaspar commented:

"Here's another long section, just as interesting, which takes Eva's research all the way up to contemporary society. This time, she based her conclusions on murder rates over the past fifty years in a city that's considered one of the most violent in the world, Juárez, Mexico. I'm not sure how she obtained this information, but it seems to have come straight from the files of the Mexican police."

Sharko ran his hand over his mouth. A piece of the mystery was becoming clear; no doubt this was the reason for her trip to Mexico.

"She went there barely a week before coming to your center, in mid-July," he confided. "We found her plane reservations."

Jaspar paused in surprise for a few seconds.

"To go so far just to get that information. She truly was remarkable."

"What was she looking for in those records? More left-handers?"

"Exactly. She wanted to know the proportion of left-handers among extremely violent criminals living in very violent surroundings. Were there as many as in the time of the barbarians? Would you get statistics that showed, globally, in contemporary civilization, one left-hander for every ten right-handers?"

Sharko looked through pages and pages of documents with a questioning eye, and spoke before she could continue.

"So tell me—how does violence figure into all this?"

"Eva discovered that in violent societies, where combat is the dominant factor, being left-handed offers a huge advantage for survival."

Jaspar paused to let Sharko digest that information, then went on.

"According to what she wrote, if left-handers exist, it's because they're better fighters. They enjoy a strategic advantage in combat, which is the effect of surprise. When two individuals confront each other, the left-hander has the advantage because he's used to fighting right-handers, whereas the right-hander is disoriented by someone who favors using his left hand or foot. He doesn't see the blows coming. And therefore, it's because they are less numerous, less common, that left-handers have an advantage."

"In DNA, you mean?"

"Yes. That might seem simplistic, but it's really the way nature works: everything favorable to the propagation of genes is selected and transmitted, while the rest is eliminated. Obviously, this doesn't take place over just a few years, it often takes centuries for this information to be inscribed in our DNA."

Sharko tried to summarize.

"So, from what you're saying, the more violent the community, the higher the proportion of left-handers?"

"That was the evolutionary phenomenon Eva highlighted. The 'left-handed' trait is spread via DNA in violent societies, while in other societies it gradually fades out, leaving more room for right-handers."

"I know a number of lefties. They're not particularly athletic or violent. So if nature tends to eliminate anything that isn't useful, why aren't they right-handers like everyone else?"

"Because of genetic memory. Our modern culture will end up eliminating it, as it will end up eliminating white moths."

She nodded toward the thesis.

"That's why, among the violent criminals in that Mexican city, Eva didn't find a higher proportion of left-handers than anywhere else. She must have been extremely disappointed by those findings, but all things considered, it's logical: no question that, in a world where you only need press a button or pull a trigger in order to kill, being left-handed doesn't do you any good, because we no longer have to engage in hand-to-hand combat. Consequently, the gene pool of left-handers will eventually die out. One day there will no longer be any more left-handers in any society, whatever its level of violence."

Sharko took time to assimilate this information. It all struck him as implacably logical and extremely interesting. Culture modified the environment, which in turn affected the selection of the fittest . . . He returned to his questions.

"A week after Mexico, Louts traveled to Manaus, in Brazil. Did she make any mention of that in her thesis?"

Jaspar's eyes widened.

"Brazil? No, no . . . nothing to explain a trip down there. No statistics, no data. Is Manaus also a violent city?"

"No more than any other, apparently. In any case, after her quasi-failure in Mexico, Eva seemed to be conducting very focused research. And does the thesis talk about her studies of French prison inmates? A certain Grégory Carnot, for instance?"

"No, nothing like that either."

Sharko placed the sheet of paper on the others, skeptical. Nothing about her trip to Brazil, nothing about Carnot or her prison visits. After Manaus, Louts had moved squarely outside the parameters of her thesis. The inspector probed further:

"She visited prisons during the day, when she was supposed to be at your center. That's why she wanted to start at five o'clock—she didn't want anyone knowing about her visits to penitentiaries. She interviewed inmates and collected their photos. From what you've read, and from what you know, why would Eva have gone to visit prisoners who were all young, left-handed, and had committed violent murders?"

She thought for a moment.

"Hmmm ... Her approach this time seems rather different from in Mexico. She was not looking for a left-hander behind the crime, but for a crime behind the left-hander. She might have been trying to determine if hand dominance and violence could be related in isolated cases of individuals who lived in civilized environments ... Did these men have any points in common? Was there something that made them stand out? I'm sorry, that's the only line of inquiry I can think of."

Which didn't explain much of anything, Sharko thought to himself. Lower down, he saw Levallois climbing the steps two by two. He asked the primatologist one last question:

"Is there anything else about the thesis I should know?"

"I don't believe so, but you can read it for yourself. Apart from the graphs and some mathematical data, most of it should be fairly accessible. Eva had written an incredibly thorough and careful study, one that would certainly have caused a stir in scientific circles. And still will if her work gets published."

The young lieutenant was catching his breath on the top step. He spotted Sharko and waved, then gazed at a large poster that explained how viruses work. The police inspector warmly thanked the primatologist.

"Naturally, I have to ask you to keep all this confidential until we're finished with our investigation."

"Of course. I'm going to wander around the galleries a bit more. Please keep me posted on the case. You can call whenever you like, even at night. I don't sleep much. I'd really like to understand this and help you out as much as I can."

"I will."

She gave him a shy smile, shook his hand, and walked off. Sharko gazed after her a few seconds, then headed toward his partner.

"So, what about the fossil?"

"It's not from here, for the simple reason that they don't have any chimpanzee fossils that old in their collection."

"So, wild goose chase."

"Not at all, we've got a huge lead. The director told me that for the past week there's been an exhibit on mineralogy and fossils at the Drouot auction house, which ends tomorrow. A sale of mammal skeletons several thousand years old was held last Thursday. No doubt there were monkeys in the batch. I've got the name of the auctioneer who handled it. He'll be at Avenue Montaigne tonight at nine for another sale."

"Can we reach him right now?"

"I called Drouot, but no luck. He doesn't show up until about a half hour beforehand."

Sharko headed for the stairs.

"In that case, I know where we'll be spending our evening."

"Mmmm . . . I had other plans."

"You already went to the movies once this week. Mustn't overdo it, you know."

Levallois greeted the quip with a smile, then grew serious again.

"And what about you, anything new?"

"You might say that. I'll fill you in at thirty-six."

When they stepped outside, the temperature rose sharply. Sharko slapped the thesis into his partner's hands.

"Can you put this on my desk? I want to give it a read-through."

He veered off to the left, toward the main gardens.

"The scooter's this way, Franck."

Sharko turned around.

"I know, but I'm going to walk home and stop in at the barber's. Besides, if I've got this evolution business right, we were given legs to walk on. If we keep taking cars and public transportation, we'll just end up losing them."

17

Lucie had hit the road after lunch. The nice manager of the Ten Marmots had whipped her up a splendid risotto that would surely hold her until evening. She wasn't sorry to be sitting behind the wheel for a few hours: the descent from the glacier had been difficult, including a painful cramp in her calf that had kept her stuck on the ice for an extra five minutes. But the round trip to the summit had been worth it. Lucie was on the trail of *something*, a prehistoric oddity that lit up a fury of little flashing lights inside her.

As she drove, the mountain reliefs overlapped, the gorges widened until they pushed the Alps into the background. Then came small valleys, steeply inclined fields, and nervous streams. Finally, Lyon, in late afternoon, looked like a black boulder on a lake of hot coals. People were returning home from work, clogging the approach roads to a standstill. A life regulated to the quarter of an inch, in which everyone, once back home, would spend a few hours on spouse, children, or Internet, before going to bed, head swarming with tomorrow's stock of woes. Lucie tried to keep patient and took advantage of the traffic jam to call her mother. She knew Juliette was out: the little girl had been taking music lessons for the past two years. She asked Marie to give her a kiss and tell her how much Mommy loved her. Was she looking after Klark? She passed on a bit of news, explained merely that she was resolving an old issue, then quickly hung up. It took her another half hour to get out of that traffic sludge and enter the city's seventh arrondissement.

As Lucie neared her destination, she noticed another message on the screen of her phone. Sharko again, asking for news for at least the fourth time. Vaguely annoyed, she sent back a quick text that all was fine, she was making progress, no further details.

She found a small spot on Rue Curien, near the École Normale. To her left, she could see the Saône, which flowed into the Rhône to form the Presqu'île. The area was bustling with students and filled with modern-design buildings: architecture with receding angles, tinted windows, and pure lines. Unlike Lille, whose brick constructions seemed flat and ruddy, Lyon offered an impression of mastered chaos, in both its relief and its vibrant colors.

During the drive, Lucie had managed to reach the secretary of the Functional Genomics Institute and, still with her cop's hat on, to score an appointment with Arnaud Fécamp, a member of the research unit that had taken in the bodies from the glacier. The scientist worked on the PAL-GENE platform, which was one of a kind in Europe and specialized in the analysis of fossil DNA. On the phone, he confirmed what Lucie already suspected: Eva Louts had indeed visited their lab ten days before.

She quickly found René Descartes Square and entered the building, an impressive block of glass and concrete four stories high, hosting various activities related to the life sciences: biology, molecular phylogeny, postnatal development . . . At the far right of the foyer, two fat blue and red intertwined cables rose several yards into the air—the symbol representing the double helix of DNA. Lucie vaguely recalled her biology courses in high school, particularly the four "bases" of that giant helicoidal ladder, formed by the letters G, A, T, C: guanine, adenine, thymine, and cytosine. Four nitrogenous bases, common to all living creatures, whose complex combinations, which among other things formed genes and chromosomes, could give someone blue eyes, female gender, or a congenital illness. Lucie made out an inscription at the base of that curious construction: DNA HAS BEEN HIDDEN IN OUR CELLS FOR MILLIONS OF YEARS. WE ARE UNRAVELING IT.

Everything was clean, immaculate, flawless. Lucie felt as if she were wandering through a science fiction setting, in which the staff would all be robots. Arnaud Fécamp, luckily, didn't look like he was held together with nuts and bolts—in fact, he was rather well padded. Squeezed into his lab coat, he was shorter than Lucie and wore his flaming red hair extremely short. Round, smooth face, despite pronounced wrinkles on his forehead. Chubby freckled hands. Hard to guess his age, but Lucie figured a good forty.

"Amélie Courtois?"

"That's me."

He shook her hand.

"My boss is in a meeting, so I'll see to you, if that's all right. If I've understood correctly, you're looking into the student who came to visit us about a week ago?"

While they went up in a hyperefficient elevator—with a female voice to call out the floors—Lucie explained the reason for her visit: Eva Louts's murder, her trip to the glacier, her passage through Lyon a few days before . . . Fécamp absorbed the news. His red jowls trembled from the elevator's vibrations.

"I sincerely hope you find the killer. I didn't know that student very well, but no one has the right to do such a thing."

"We hope so too."

"I often watch old detective movies on TV, Maigret and the like. If thirty-six Quai des Orfèvres is on the case, it must be serious."

"It is."

Lucie remained purposely evasive, by the book. She didn't want to say too much about the investigation, and in any case she had very little information to impart.

"Tell me about Eva Louts."

"Like a lot of researchers or students working on evolution, she had come here to see the famous ice men."

"Do you know in what context?"

"Research into the Neanderthal, I believe. The usual stuff. I don't think you'll learn much here, unfortunately."

Once again, Louts had used the pretext of research into Neanderthal man, perhaps hoping to conceal the real reason for her visit. A cautious girl, thought Lucie, who knew not to draw attention to herself. The door opened onto a long corridor with bluish linoleum. A vague odor of disinfectant floated over everything.

"We can use my boss's office, if you like. It'll be more comfortable to talk there."

"It would be a shame for me to come all the way here and not have a peek at the ice men. I'd really like to see what our supposed ancestors looked like."

Fécamp paused a few seconds, then gave her a brief smile. His teeth were especially long and white.

"Well, I suppose you're right—might as well take the opportunity. It's not every day that you come face-to-face with a thirty-thousand-year-old."

They turned off into a cloakroom where dozens of shrink-wrapped coveralls were piled up. The scientist handed a pack to Lucie.

"Put this on, it should fit you. We're going into a white, windowed rectangle more than a thousand square feet, in which the air is filtered five times over, the temperature is kept a constant seventy-two degrees, and the rooms are washed down with bleach several times a day."

Lucie did as instructed. To make an impression and add to her role as cop, she took her pistol from her jacket.

"Can I keep this? Any metal detectors or things like that?"

Fécamp swallowed, staring at the compact weapon.

"No, go right ahead. Is it loaded?"

"What do you think?"

Lucie stuffed the small semiautomatic in the back pocket of her jeans, along with her cell phone.

"The policeman's ideal arsenal." Fécamp sighed. "Pistol and telephone. I hate mobile phones. We're getting too far ahead of nature and changing our behavior because of those miserable contraptions, and one of these days we're going to pay the piper."

The type who likes to spout off life lessons, Lucie thought to herself. Without answering, she pulled on the coveralls and paper overshoes, the latex gloves, and the surgical mask and scrub cap.

"So what exactly *is* paleogenetics?"

Fécamp seemed to be putting on his protective gear very slowly, with precise, inch-perfect movements that he must have repeated day after day.

"We analyze the genomes of past biodiversity, in other words the cartography of genes from ancient DNA that we get from fossils, which sometimes are several hundred million years old. Thanks to the organic parts of bones and teeth, which resist the effects of time, we can travel back centuries and understand the origins of various species, their filiations. I'll give you a concrete example. Because of paleogenetics, we now know that more than three thousand years ago, Tutankhamen died from malaria combined with a bone disease. His DNA revealed that he was not in fact the son of Nefertiti, but rather of his father Akhenaton's sister. Tutankhamen was purely and simply the fruit of incest."

"The tabloids would've eaten that up. And with all this technology, I guess you're not too far away from bringing back the dinosaurs. You just scrape up the DNA from some fossils, a little cloning, and presto, is that right?"

"Oh, we're still light-years away from anything like that. Fossil DNA is often extremely degraded and scarcely available. What can you do with a thousand-piece puzzle when you're missing 990 of the pieces? Each new discovery puts us in front of a real obstacle course. Still, with the ice men, we really hit it lucky, since they were in such remarkably good shape, much better than the Egyptian mummies or Ötzi, the famous *sapiens sapiens* found near the Italian Dolomites in 1991. The fact that the cave was completely sealed off and largely deprived of oxygen slowed down the proliferation of bacteria and protected them from bad weather and climate changes. DNA is a stable molecule, but it doesn't last forever. Its degradation begins the moment the individual dies. It breaks up, and some of the letters that compose the genetic information gradually get erased."

"The famous G, A, T, C."

"Exactly. The rungs of the ladder get broken. For instance, the sequence T G A A C A on a bit of DNA can become T G G A C A through alteration, and this entirely distorts the genetic code, and therefore its interpretation. The same as with words, which can change meaning entirely when one letter gets erased, like 'slaughter' and 'laughter.' In particularly unfavorable conditions, a mere ten thousand years is enough to ruin every last molecule of DNA. But in the present case, it was more than we'd ever hoped for."

Once in their blue coveralls, they proceeded to the laboratory. The entrance door was like the airlock in a submarine.

"You'll experience an unpleasant sensation in your ears. The air in the lab is highly pressurized to prevent contaminant DNA from entering. I can't think of anything more horrible than to spend weeks studying DNA that turned out to be ours! Hence the reason for these sterile garments as well. You sure you want to go on?"

"Of course."

After the scientist had placed his badge over the sensor, they went in. Lucie felt a pain in her ears, then heard a screeching sound, like the kind a train makes when it enters a tunnel. Four lab technicians, bent over powerful microscopes, were filling pipettes or adjusting DNA sequencers, far too absorbed in their work to notice the newcomers. On the benchtops, which were also protectively wrapped, lay various labeled objects: a tooth from a cave-dwelling bear, some Gallo-Roman amber with an insect carcass, ancient excrements from a Madagascan elephant bird. Passing by a freezer with glass doors, Lucie stopped short.

"A baby mammoth?"

"Good eye. That's Lyuba. She was found in the Siberian permafrost by a reindeer breeder. She's forty-two thousand years old."

"She looks like she could have died yesterday."

"She's in an extraordinarily good state of preservation."

Lucie stood agape before the animal that she had seen only in textbook drawings. This place was like an Ali Baba's cave of Prehistory. They walked on. Arnaud Fécamp continued his explanations about DNA.

"Usually, we grind up the bones, teeth, or tissues into fine powder, which we then let incubate for several hours in a buffer that facilitates the degradation of undesirable elements, such as limestone or parasitic proteins. Then we're left with the pure DNA. Since generally it's broken into too many bits for our machines to analyze, we 'photocopy' the fragments in billions of copies, thanks to an amplification technique called PCR, so that we can manipulate them more easily."

He opened the door.

Lucie felt a slap of icy air on her face.

A refrigeration chamber.

Once inside, she opened her eyes wide and paused for a moment, with a curious feeling in the pit of her stomach. Never would she have imagined such a spectacular case of mummification by cold. Completely nude and wrapped in clear plastic film, the three members of the Neanderthal family were lying next to one another, slightly curled up. The small one was between the male and the female. Behind his empty eye sockets, with his limp, emaciated jaws, he seemed to be screaming. The most impressive part was their prominent brow, their skulls pulled back as if into a hair bun, the face receding from the prominent nose. Their bone structure was massive, with short limbs and squat, stocky bodies. Their teeth showed evident signs of wear, and some of them were broken and black. Lucie went closer, shivering uncontrollably, and leaned toward them. She squinted.

On the dead, desiccated bellies, she noticed wide, deep gashes, like furious mouths. Not even the child had been spared.

"Those look like lacerations," she said questioningly from behind her mask.

The scientist nodded toward another table, to Lucie's left.

"Yes. That's the tool the Cro-Magnon used to murder them."

Lucie felt her muscles stiffen and adrenaline whip her blood.

A triple murder.

This family had been massacred. It now seemed so clear. The wounds had been too numerous, too violent. The slashes howled on the dehydrated skin. Lucie was in the presence of one of humanity's oldest crimes, an episode of violence from the most distant ages that had come down through the millennia intact.

Fécamp showed her the weapon, which she examined intently. It was about as long as a forearm and extremely sharp.

"It's a harpoon made of deer antler, with barbs meant for catching and ripping the intestines. It's incredibly resistant, able to pierce thick layers of hide or blubber. You can imagine its effectiveness. Truly formidable."

Lucie looked at the finely honed weapon, which seemed to have been fashioned with only one purpose: violent killing. Was this what had led Eva Louts here, and to the criminals in prison? This expression of violence from the past? And yet, supposedly, she wasn't working on serial killers, or criminals in general, or violence. Just a study of left-handedness, Sharko had assured her.

Disturbed by this ancestral barbarity, Lucie turned around.

"Where's the Cro-Magnon?"

Arnaud Fécamp flinched, then let out a long sigh.

"He's been stolen."

"What?"

"He's gone, along with all the results of his genome sequencing. There's nothing left. Not one scrap of data. It's a disaster—for the first time, we actually possessed an almost complete sequence of the genes of our ancestor from thirty thousand years ago, *Homo sapiens sapiens*. A sequence of A, T, G, C's that we only had to read in order to take his genetic inventory."

Lucie folded her arms, shivering with cold. The more she discovered, the deeper the mystery seemed to grow. Questions crowded to her lips.

"Why didn't you tell me that before?"

"We try not to let the information get around. We were very fortunate that the media didn't latch on to the story."

"How did the thief even get in here?"

"With my badge, I'm afraid. Two guys in ski masks attacked me one night as I was leaving. They forced me to come back here and give them access to our findings on the *sapiens*. They took it all: the hard drives, the backups, the printouts, even the mummy. And when they were through, they pistol whipped me and left me for dead."

"Isn't the building under surveillance?"

"We have cameras and alarm systems. The cameras are always on, but some of the alarm systems are deactivated by the badges, so we can have free access to the laboratory when we work here at night. The two men are on the security tapes, but apart from their masks, there's not much to see."

"When did this happen?"

"About six months after the cave was discovered. The police came—it's all in the report."

"Any leads?"

"None. It remains unsolved."

Lucie went back to the Neanderthals. Their empty sockets seemed to be staring at her. The child had such small hands. How old could he have been—seven? eight? He looked like a wax effigy, hideous, disfigured by the ravages of time. But like her daughter Clara, he had been murdered. Lucie thought of what the mountain guide had said about Eva Louts's theory: the genocide of the Neanderthals by Cro-Magnon man.

"Why didn't the thieves make off with these as well?"

"Perhaps because they aren't modern man's ancestors. They don't have any direct relation to our species, and in that regard their genome is much less interesting. Actually, that's just a supposition. I really have no idea why they didn't."

"Did Eva Louts know about the theft before she came here?"

"No. She was as surprised as you are."

Lucie paced back and forth, rubbing her shoulders to warm up.

"Forgive me if I still haven't understood all the subtleties, but . . . why would they steal Cro-Magnon's genome?"

"It's absolutely essential to understanding the secrets of life and the evolution of *Homo sapiens sapiens*, our species."

He approached the mummies and gazed at them with an odd tenderness.

"Don't you see? We had in our hands the DNA of our genetic forebears. Hundreds of millions of genetic sequences that contain the secrets of prehistoric life. DNA is the fossil map of evolution—like the black box in an airliner. What genes did Cro-Magnon have that we don't? Which ones mutated during those thousands of years and which remained intact? What was their purpose? Did the mummy carry any known or unknown pathogens which would have given us a glimpse into the health levels of the time, for example, or let us discover ancient viruses, which would also have been fossilized in the DNA? By comparing our genome to Cro-Magnon's, letter by letter, we would have had a much better understanding of evolution's grand strategy over the past thirty thousand years."

Lucie didn't yet grasp all the fine points of these explanations, but she could appreciate that the scientific import was enormous. She preferred to get back to concrete matters.

"I'd like to try to put myself in Eva Louts's shoes for a few moments. So she's here, looking at the Neanderthal mummies. What was her reaction? What was she looking for, exactly?"

Fécamp put his fingers on the plastic, passing over the gaping wounds.

"She was just a student, you know, apparently fascinated by morbid things. It was the extreme violence of the scene that grabbed her, nothing more. The discovery was an excellent opportunity to drag a theory about the disappearance of the Neanderthals back into the spotlight."

"Their extermination by Cro-Magnon, you mean. The theory Louts was trying to prove."

Fécamp nodded, then glanced at his watch.

"Yes, but I don't share her view. I think it's too simplistic, and an isolated case shouldn't lead to generalities. Let's say she came here looking for some good material to shore up her work. Unfortunately I can't tell you much more than that. She took a few notes, some photos of the wounds and the weapon, as a way of filling out her thesis and getting a good grade. Then she left. That's all."

"Did she allude to the upside-down drawings? Did she mention a certain Grégory Carnot? Prisoners? Anything about left-handers?"

Fécamp shook his head.

"As far as I can recall, none of that. Well, it's very cold in here . . . Will you also need any photos for your investigation?"

Lucie looked sadly at the massacred family, then back at the scientist.

"No, that'll be all."

She moved away from the group while the researcher opened the door, then halted in the middle of the room, undecided. She couldn't just let herself abandon the trail, leave without an answer.

"You're a researcher into the ancient past. You spend your days reconstructing prehistoric facts. Can you tell me what happened in that cave thirty thousand years ago?"

With a sigh, the scientist walked toward her.

"I'm sorry, but I . . ."

Another voice rose at almost exactly the same moment—female, and harsh.

"*I* can. But first, may I see your credentials?"

18

A woman was standing in the doorway to the refrigerated room. Tall, planted firmly on her feet, wearing square-rimmed glasses. She had put on only a face mask and gloves and was staring at Arnaud Fécamp, whose hands were now joined over his stomach.

"When we get visitors here, I at least expect to be notified."

Fécamp's jaws tightened.

"I thought you were in a meeting until late this afternoon and . . ."

"It's not your job to think, Arnaud."

The researcher remained frozen for a few seconds, a small vein throbbing in the middle of his forehead. *Treated like a dog*, thought Lucie. He gave his boss one final look, lips pressed tight, then left the room. Facing the tall, brown-haired woman, Lucie tried to maintain her self-assurance.

"And you are?"

"Ludivine Tassin, the director of this laboratory. But I should be asking who *you* are."

"Amélie Courtois, Paris Homicide."

Tassin stood waiting, hands on hips. Everything about her radiated unpleasant authoritarianism. Lucie ostentatiously pulled her pistol from her pocket, then her cell phone. She displayed the contacts list on the phone's screen, pressing the buttons with her gloved finger.

"My police ID is back at the hotel, but you can call the Homicide bureau at thirty-six Quai des Orfèvres if you wish. Ask to speak with Chief Inspector Franck Sharko."

The moment of truth. Lucie felt her heart pounding in her chest. The imposing woman finally backed down.

"That won't be necessary. Kindly put away your weapon. What exactly is it you're looking for?"

Lucie explained the reasons for her visit, regaining her footing after the brief exchange.

"What I'd really like to know is what happened in that cave thirty thousand years ago, because I believe it has a bearing on my investigation today."

"Very well. But let's get out of this room before we freeze."

Tassin led the way. Decisive gait: every inch the boss. Arnaud Fécamp was sitting in front of an enormous machine, shoulders slumped. Lucie watched him in silence and noticed, from the reflection in a glass case, that he'd begun staring after her once she'd passed by. The odd look on his face put her ex-cop's senses on alert.

The two women passed through the airlock and headed to the scientist's office.

"Your lab tech says he was hit pretty hard, the night of the theft."

"They didn't go easy on him, that's a fact."

"Is he the one who called the police?"

"From the laboratory. That episode caused us an irreparable loss. We'll never have another opportunity to find such a well-preserved specimen of Cro-Magnon. When I heard the news, it was as if I'd lost an arm. You cannot imagine how it feels."

In the office, the director took a packet of photos from a cabinet.

"I went to the glacier the same day the bodies were found. As the sponsoring agency of a national project, we were contacted within hours of the event."

She looked at the photos she must have seen hundreds of times already, then slid them toward Lucie. Her eyes shone, like those of a pirate with a treasure chest.

"What a magnificent find! The Grail for any researcher who has devoted his life to the study of living things. A complete family of Neanderthals and a Cro-Magnon, in a remarkable state of preservation. It was so incredible that at first we all thought it was a hoax. But the dating process and our analyses left no room for doubt: they were authentic. Look . . ."

Lucie spread out the photos, taken in the very first hours after the discovery. A wide angle showed the three Neanderthals on one side, huddled on the ground, jaws open as if they were screaming. In another corner, the

Cro-Magnon sat leaning against the rock, just below the upside-down fresco of the aurochs. Despite the desiccated state of the flesh, the morphological differences between the individuals were glaring. Cro-Magnon had a prominent forehead, as well as a long, straight nose, a flattened face, and a smaller brow: the same characteristics as modern man.

"Cro-Magnon and Neanderthal cohabited for eight thousand years, and the period in which these individuals lived corresponds to the last years of Neanderthal's existence. What you're seeing here are pretty much the last representatives of the species. Various clues and careful research have allowed us to reconstruct their final hours . . ."

Lucie listened closely, incredulous. She was about to hear the analysis of a thirty-thousand-year-old crime scene. Modern CSI teams couldn't have done better.

"First of all, fossil DNA analyses proved that these were indeed a *family* of Neanderthals: father, mother, and son, whose DNA contained the genetic material of the two creatures next to him. The man was roughly thirty-three years old, which was about the age limit at that time."

"Young."

"They reproduced very early, usually between fifteen and twenty. The characteristics of biological evolution being to . . ."

". . . To perpetuate the genes and ensure the survival of the fittest, if I've understood right."

"Correct. At the time, however, it was rare for an individual to live past the age of seven. Living conditions were brutal, and most illnesses and injuries proved fatal. For each member of this family, we detected traces of rickets, arthritis, dental abscesses, and various bone fractures, and yet they'd somehow managed to survive. They were solidly built. Analysis of pollen fossils found in their intestines showed that it was beech pollen. Combining this result with the isotope analyses, we were able to reconstruct where the family spent much of its life: in the Southern Alps, near the Italian border. We believe they were in migration, perhaps because of the great cold. They had probably taken shelter in that cave to wait out the bad weather . . . and then the intruder came."

"Cro-Magnon."

"Yes. Our future modern, civilized man. *Homo sapiens sapiens* . . ."

Her tone was now tinged with bitterness.

"We don't know what this isolated individual was doing in that place. Had he spotted footprints in the snow and followed them? Was he also in migration, or perhaps fleeing something? Had he been banished from his village, sentenced to exile? The fact is, he had very little equipment with him, unlike the Neanderthals. Just an itinerant. An outsider."

Tassin spoke with passion, as if living her story. Lucie had no trouble visualizing the distant scene: the horrific weather conditions, hunched creatures squaring off against the howling wind and snow. Hunters who often died of hunger or cold, if injuries or infections didn't get them first.

"The fire, the smell of drying meat or freshwater fish, may have attracted him. When he entered the cave, the male Neanderthal stood up and grabbed a weapon. Recent research in paleontology and paleoanthropology has demonstrated that Neanderthal man was not the retarded, grotesque creature we make the butt of our jokes. He buried his dead, played music, and cultivated a certain form of primitive art. We don't believe he started the fight."

Tassin pointed to close-ups of the frozen bodies.

"Look here. The three Neanderthals, including the child, show defensive wounds on their forearms. They weren't taken unaware but were attacked frontally by Cro-Magnon. They were literally massacred, without restraint. Struck again and again with the harpoon. Arms, sides, legs—everything."

Lucie could imagine the scene: A family gathered around the fire. A shadow approaches. A confrontation, then the slaughter: first the man, then the woman. The terrified child is huddled in a corner. The shadow comes closer, raises its weapon . . . She turned away, shaken by the similarity with her own recurrent nightmares.

"Are you all right, Miss?"

"Yes, yes, I'm fine. Please go on."

"For his part, Cro-Magnon showed very few signs of injury. He dominated the fight. And yet Neanderthal was no weakling. Five foot three, a hundred seventy-five pounds of muscle—these were exceptional hunters, very strong, with heavy, powerful limbs, but they were slaughtered by an individual who was taller and much more savage than they. After that comes an episode we're having difficulty understanding. I'm speaking of the upside-down cave painting."

"So it's Cro-Magnon who painted it?"

"Probably after the killings. He used pigments and calmly went about his work while the corpses lay at his feet. I'd never seen such a painting in my life. A pure scientific curiosity. And no one has yet come up with a satisfactory answer."

"Painted by a left-hander, yet again."

Tassin cocked her head.

"Eva Louts said the same thing. You seem to have the same reactions as she did."

"I'm trying to put myself in her head—it helps my investigation."

"I can confirm that he was left-handed, as indicated by the negative handprints he painted on the cave walls. Cro-Magnon clearly wanted to take possession of the cave. But we think that soon after, the avalanche occurred, which trapped the *sapiens* inside and quickly froze the bodies, preventing the DNA from being degraded. The layers of ice that were blocking the entrance are exactly the same age as our mummies. Cro-Magnon died either from the cold or from hunger, in the dark, surrounded by the carnage he'd inflicted for a reason we'll probably never know, but that proves he was already not the peaceful, unwarlike creature that some still maintain. It challenges a fair number of our assumptions and supports the contention that the extinction of Neanderthal was the result of domination by *Homo sapiens*."

She sighed, stacking up some papers.

"At least we know who our ancestors were. While many things have evolved, violence is one thing that's remained unchanged down through the millennia."

"You mean it's transmitted genetically? Like the so-called violence gene, passed from father to son?"

The scientist jerked as if she'd been stung.

"The violence gene is a myth, maintained by the deliria of a few individuals. It doesn't exist."

Lucie knew something about this violence gene: in the 1950s, scientists had advanced the hypothesis that a number of criminals, particularly violent ones, had an extra Y chromosome. These days, the theory had largely been discredited, as evidenced by Tassin's reaction. She let it go.

"Did Eva Louts tell you she'd seen an upside-down drawing in a prison cell?"

"She did mention it. It was apparently what brought her to this laboratory. She too wanted to know the information I've just given you. What captivated her more than anything was the violence and strangeness of the scene, the apparent lack of logic."

Lucie thought again of Carnot's cell, the terror she'd felt when she'd discovered the drawing.

"Things are rarely logical when it comes to crime. And . . . your employee, Arnaud Fécamp, was he present when she told you about the prison drawing?"

"Naturally. We met with her together. Louts was extremely curious. She wanted to know all about the discovery. She even taped our interview. A very thorough investigation. Like yours today."

Lucie sat back in her chair. Fécamp had lied to her about several things. First the drawings, which he claimed not to know about, then Louts's interest in this story. Why? What was he hiding? Lucie thought through everything that had happened since she'd arrived at the institute. The scientist had made sure to see her alone, had tried to give her only a quick tour of the place and a few purely technical explanations to dazzle her, then send her on her merry way without even showing her the mummies. Maybe he'd been caught short by a visit from a cop ten days after Louts's disappearance.

"Arnaud Fécamp told me the results about Cro-Magnon were stolen just before you could start analyzing them, is that right?"

"Sadly, yes. Shortly after the sequencing of his genome."

"The thieves came just at the right time, so to speak."

"Or just at the wrong time."

Lucie didn't add anything, but an idea was forming in the back of her head. She stood up and shook hands with the laboratory director. Before leaving, she asked one final question.

"What time do your employees usually finish work?"

"They don't really have a schedule, but usually around seven or seven thirty. Why?"

"Just asking."

Another hour to wait, concealed in her car. If Fécamp was hiding something, he would probably react.

"One last thing: could you please photocopy those crime scene photos for me, if I can call them that? I'd like to take them with me."

The woman nodded and did as asked.

When Lucie returned to the hallway a few minutes later, she found she wouldn't even have to wait until seven o'clock.

Dressed in his street clothes, at the other end of the hall, the chubby little redhead had just vanished into the elevator.

He looked like he was being chased by the devil himself.

19

An erupting volcano.

Blue-and-red pennants whipped the air.

Sporting scarves in the same bright colors, fans were crowding toward Gerland Stadium for the midweek match, wearing the emblem of the Olympique Lyonnais soccer club. Loud voices, alcohol-laden breath, eyes red with excitement. The area was teeming with men, women, and children choking sidewalks and clogging the streets: amid honking horns and smoking exhaust pipes, the hapless drivers had no choice but to wait.

Fraying a passage through the crowd, Arnaud Fécamp walked quickly. Lucie followed as best she could, first in the same direction as the masses, then against the tide once they'd passed the stadium.

Suddenly, the scientist veered across Avenue Jean-Jaurès just as the traffic light turned green. In the blink of an eye, he vanished into the Stade de Gerland subway stop, which was spewing out further batches of stadium-goers. Lucie began slaloming among the shapes and dodged into the traffic, triggering insults from the aggravated drivers.

Difficult to get down the stairs. She elbowed her way through, mumbling excuses. People were shouting, singing, shoving, indifferent to her small presence. She rushed into the narrow corridor. No trace of the redhead. No chance of finding him in such a ruckus. Distraught, Lucie cast around for signs, burrowed through the tempest toward a subway map. Luckily, the station was at the end of the line. Which meant that Fécamp could only be waiting for one train, the one heading back toward Charpennes. With no time to waste, Lucie crushed in behind a woman entering the turnstile and managed to get through just as the Plexiglas barrier slammed shut behind her. She started running.

The redhead was there, at the edge of the platform. When the subway rolled forward and opened its doors, he rushed in and took a seat. Panting,

Lucie stepped into the next car, keeping her eyes on him. Discreetly, through the windows, she watched his profile: he was looking undeniably anxious. He stared at the floor, eyes vacant, jaws clenched.

The man got off at Saxe-Gambetta and transferred to Line D, toward Vaise. The cars were packed, which for once worked in Lucie's favor. With a rumble, the train entered the tunnel, sinking into a furnace of burning steel. Odors of rancid sweat and burned rubber.

Six stops later, another end of the line. Gare de Vaise, one of six train stations in Lyon. Fécamp got off and resumed his hurried pace. Hidden by the barriers of arms and legs, Lucie again followed in pursuit. She let herself fall farther behind in quieter streets to make sure she wasn't spotted. The moment he turned a corner, she ran to the intersection, then again let him gain some distance. Despite the adrenaline, Lucie began to feel her exhaustion. Sweat poured down her back. The glacier, the highway, running through the streets of Lyon . . . too much for one day, and her muscles were rebelling. In just half a week, her life had made a complete turnaround.

Where was the researcher going? The neighborhood was nothing like the one Lucie had been in only half an hour before. Construction cranes bristled on the horizon. The buildings were crammed together; the rare balconies were littered with laundry and bicycles. Barely any pedestrians. Straight ahead rose a wall of high-rises, looking as if they had burst from the treetops. Lucie had a hard time imagining the scientist living in this squalid neighborhood.

Arnaud Fécamp turned onto Boulevard de la Duchère. Clumps of teenagers dragged their boots along the sidewalks: caps, hoods, the ample outfits of rappers . . . Quickly, without raising his eyes, the scientist clambered up a flight of steps and disappeared into the foyer of one of the dingy high-rises. Lucie quickened her pace and plunged in after him. The hallways stank of stale cigarette and pot smoke. Shadows sized her up with the usual whistles and crudities. Instinctively, she verified that her pistol was in her pocket and caught herself wondering whether she shouldn't turn back, go home, be with her daughter and mother. But her cop's impulses, which she'd tried so hard to suppress, wouldn't be denied.

In front of her was a decrepit elevator. Above the doors, half-broken diodes lit up sequentially to the fourth floor. Lucie took the stairs, running up two at a time. The burning sensation in her calves returned.

Male voices reached her as she was covering the last few yards. She tried to control her breathing, advanced with caution, and flattened against the wall, already out of breath.

She entered the hallway. A door slammed.

Number 413.

Lucie could hear a baby crying somewhere. Then children laughing, doors closing. She crept forward. Images from old memories came flooding back. Stakeouts, manhunts, pursuits. The misery and decay of the city's peripheries.

In apartment 413, she could hear two men arguing. Certain words set off shrill alarm bells: *murder . . . Louts . . . cop . . .*

Suddenly her heart skipped a beat. A cry. Then shattering glass.

Immediately, Lucie yanked the gun from her pocket, turned the doorknob, and gave it a shove, aiming the gun ahead of her.

Arnaud Fécamp was lying on the floor in the middle of the hallway, his head crowned with shards of glass. In front of him, a man was gripping a broken bottleneck. Sweat pants, no shirt, tattoos. About twenty, and all nerves.

"Police! Don't move or I'll blow your head off. Drop that bottle!"

Lucie closed the door with her heel. The man stared at her with gaping eyes. Veins bulged on his thin neck. Caught short, he let go of his weapon and raised his hands to about the level of his pecs. His coke-white torso was completely hairless.

"So what the fuck is all this?"

In the narrow hallway, Lucie tried to control her stress level. She prayed her hands wouldn't shake. Too late to turn back now. She walked forward firmly, straddled the inanimate body, and pushed the young man against the wall.

"Sit down."

The kid gave her a defiant look and didn't obey.

"What do *you* want, bitch?"

Without thinking, Lucie raised her gun and brought the butt down on his right temple. A dull thud. The kid let himself slide down the wall, hands on his face. Stoked by adrenaline, Lucie shot a look at the other rooms. Filthy, a shambles. At first glance, no one.

"Don't make me tell you twice. You see this weapon, shithead? It's a semiautomatic Mann pistol, 1919 model, 6.35-millimeter, in perfect working condition. It's so small and light it goes undetected, but it can make holes in you the size of grapes. I'm alone here. No backup, no nothing. No one to tell me what I can and can't do."

The kid let out a sound between a grunt and a whine, then his voice became clearer.

"What do you want?"

"What's your name?"

He hesitated. Lucie pushed her foot closer to his crotch.

"I said what's your name?"

"David Chouart."

She stepped back, knelt down by Fécamp, and felt his carotid artery. Crowned with a bottle of cheap whiskey. Chouart hadn't gone easy. The tattooed kid looked disheveled, bloodshot eyes, breath like a feral animal.

"You really walloped him. How come?"

The young man rubbed his head with a wince. A lump was already visible.

"I *warned* the little fuck there'd be trouble if he ever showed up here again."

"There are nicer ways to show it. Eva Louts, you know her?"

"Never heard of her."

"Really? Because I just heard her name from down the hall, while you two were shouting at each other."

Chouart gave the unconscious man a hateful look.

"The guy's out of his mind. He comes here and accuses me of murder. I've got nothing to do with that shit."

"Maybe he has good reason? Tell me what's the connection between you two. How did you meet?"

"Nothing to say."

Lucie stood up and nodded toward the researcher's immobile body.

"*He'll* have plenty to say."

She took out her phone.

"In less than five minutes, I'll have every cop in Lyon up your ass. You're better off keeping this between us."

Chouart bared his teeth, like an animal trying to face down an enemy.

"I know that trick. You're going to call them no matter what."

Lucie dug into her pocket, then tossed a plasticized medallion onto his chest.

"I'm here for personal reasons."

Chouart looked at the plastic object, the photo inside, then tossed it at Lucie's feet, an unwholesome smile on his lips.

"Your daughters? What are you, some kind of vigilante mom? Why should I give a shit?"

In an instant, Lucie rushed up to him and jammed the gun against his forehead. She was panting heavily, her face twisted, her finger twitching. Suddenly, the kid's eyes took on a look of terror. He huddled into himself, clenching his teeth.

"All right, all right, stop! I'll talk!"

Lucie waited a few seconds before lessening the pressure, her face pale. Her head was spinning. She'd been on the verge of pulling the trigger. For real. She had never felt like that, not even in the middle of her darkest cases.

"Jeezus, you're fucking nuts!"

"What's your connection to the Cro-Magnon mummy?"

The young man looked broken down. He knew he wasn't dealing with some average cop, but with a walking time bomb.

"I took it."

"A setup? Were you in league with Fécamp?"

"He was supposed to get us into the lab, and our job was to make it look like a robbery."

"Who was the second attacker?"

"This guy I know, some kind of computer whiz. He just did what he was told, he doesn't know anything about it."

Lucie stepped back, not taking her eyes off him. Chouart, docile now, didn't move a hair. She was sure he'd only tell the truth from now on.

"Was it Fécamp who got in touch with you?"

"No. Fécamp was just a middleman. The guy who hired us got in touch with him first, before contacting me. Then one night, the three of us met in a park in Villeurbanne to talk over the deal. The contract was simple. Fécamp got a bundle for bringing me to the mummy when the time came, and I got another bundle for stealing it. Ten thousand apiece. I was supposed to recruit somebody else to help me. It was kid's play. Fécamp had explained everything beforehand: the badge, where the lab was located, the computers containing the files and backups."

He nodded toward the researcher.

"He hates his boss. He creams in his shorts every time he hears that cow complain about the mummy's disappearance. I think he would have done it for free."

"Your employer's name."

"I don't know it."

Lucie took a quick step toward him, threateningly. The man protected his face with both arms. The eagles and snakes of his tattoos stood between him and Lucie.

"I swear! That's all I know! I didn't hear anything more about this business until tonight when this asswipe showed up here, asking if I'd had anything to do with the murder of some student, whatever her name is—fuck me if I've ever heard it before! You can ask him!"

Lucie was sweating heavily; she sponged her forehead with her sleeve. Her nerves were on edge. She needed a trail, a name, some clue to follow. No way was she going to leave here empty-handed. Without hesitating, she leaned over Fécamp and started slapping him, harder and harder.

"Hey, you, wake up!"

After a good minute, the scientist emitted a groan, then struggled to open his eyes. His hand went to his head, his fingers turning slightly red. Blood and alcohol. He stared at Lucie in disbelief, then sat up slightly. He dragged himself to the wall and leaned his back against it, legs stretched out. Lucie didn't leave him time to open his mouth.

"I'll give you ten seconds to tell me who paid you to steal the mummy."

Fécamp squeezed his lips shut, as if to keep from saying a single word. Lucie kicked the bottleneck toward Chouart.

"If he doesn't start talking, cut him."

With haggard eyes, Fécamp looked at the tattooed kid and his black-and-blue temple. The young man picked up the sharp piece of broken glass, without real conviction.

The researcher's eyes swerved back to Lucie.

"You're crazy."

"Three seconds."

Silence. The seconds ticked by. Then the barriers gave way.

"He . . . he contacted me again about two weeks after the theft . . . to make sure the police investigation wouldn't go anywhere. I told him the case was cold, that there were no clues . . . His name is Stéphane Terney."

Lucie felt a huge surge of relief. This kind of revelation was beyond all hopes.

"Why did he want the mummy?"

The researcher shook his head like a guilty child.

"I don't know. I swear I don't know. We met only a couple of times. He was always the one who chose the spot."

"So why would he give you his real name, in that case? Wasn't that pretty risky?"

"He also gave me his phone number. He wanted me to keep an eye out. I was supposed to call him if anybody came around asking about the aurochs fresco, the Cro-Magnon, or left-handers. And tell him exactly what the visitors were after."

"And that's what you did when Eva Louts came to see you. You called him and told him all about her. Her name, and I suppose even where she lived."

"Yes, yes . . . I . . . I can't believe that he . . . was involved in a murder."

"Why not?"

"Because he's a doctor and a respected scientist. Terney's big specialty is problems relating to pregnancy. He wrote a book that made a huge splash in the scientific community three or four years ago."

"What book is that?"

"It's called *The Key and the Lock*. About hidden codes in DNA."

This Terney, from the redhead's description, didn't really seem the delinquent sort. So why the theft? And why recruit a lookout?

"What did you tell him, exactly?"

"That Eva Louts was interested in the drawing, because she'd seen something like it in a prison. Then there was that business about left-handers, too. Basically, I told him what Tassin probably told you."

Lucie thought for a moment. A piece of the mystery seemed to be coming into focus. Without knowing it, the redhead had put Louts in mortal danger by alerting Terney. Worried about the young woman's research, the older scientist might have killed her. But countless questions still remained: What had Eva Louts discovered that could have led to her murder? What was so precious about the Cro-Magnon's genome that it justified such an elaborate theft? What secrets did it contain? Did Terney know about Grégory Carnot's drawings? Had the two men met?

Lucie demanded Terney's phone number, which she committed to memory.

Meanwhile, what to do with *these* two clowns? Lucie was as illegitimate as they were. Impersonating a cop and roughing people up with a loaded gun could get her into serious hot water, jeopardize her ability to raise Juliette. At that moment, she realized just how far she'd gone. Still, she tried to play the part to the end.

"I have your names and addresses. We've got an understanding, the three of us. You know how this works. I'm going to go see this Terney, settle my score, and try to keep both your names out of this shit. I said *try*. I especially suggest you don't make any attempts to warn him. The slightest fuckup, and you can be sure you'll be spending the next several years in jail."

She poked her foot a few times into the researcher's thighs.

"Go on, get out of here! Go back to your lab, analyze your cave bear fangs or whatever it is you do, and make like none of this ever happened."

Fécamp didn't have to be asked twice. Stumbling a bit, he took off without looking back. Lucie bent down and picked up her medallion, unable to keep from looking at the photo of her daughter before she put it back in her pocket.

Then she backed out the door, closing it softly behind her.

She had just one goal in mind now: find Stéphane Terney.

20

With Louts's thesis, the dates they'd established, and the conclusions they could draw, Sharko and Levallois had spent the afternoon trying to retrace the student's itinerary in the month before her death and had laid out their findings for Bellanger's team in a cramped office at number 36.

In the summer of 2009, under the direction of her thesis adviser, Olivier Solers, Eva Louts begins a project expected to last several years. One of her aims is to study hand dominance in major primates, especially man. The first year seems to pass without incident.

Then, around June 2010, Louts's relations with her thesis adviser deteriorate. The student withholds information, becomes protective of her discoveries. Striking off on her own, she decides to push her research further and heads for the most violent city in Mexico, Ciudad Juárez. Do violent populations still contain a greater number of left-handers than the average, as they did tens of thousands of years ago? To her dismay, she discovers this is no longer the case. But instead of giving up, she decides to go to Brazil, for reasons that remain obscure but are important enough to keep her there for a week. On her return to France, she doesn't write anything about Brazil in her notebooks. Instead, she requests authorization to meet with violent criminals, all of them left-handed. On August 13, she meets her first prisoner; and on the 27th, she comes face-to-face with Grégory Carnot. On the 28th, the Alps. Less than a week later, she books another flight to Manaus . . .

Now, as he walked with Levallois down Avenue Montaigne, Sharko felt certain of one thing: something had triggered all this. The trip to Brazil had led to Louts's sudden interest in French killers, which had led to

Carnot. What had clicked in Louts's head? What had she found in Brazil that had then taken her to the mountaintops?

In front of him, Avenue Montaigne glittered in all its excess. Mercedes lined up in front of luxury boutiques: Cartier, Prada, Gucci, Valentino. To the right was the Seine, and in the background the Eiffel Tower. A postcard view for the rich.

The inspector straightened his caramel-colored tie and tugged on the sleeves of his jacket. He glanced at a shop window, which sent back his reflection. His new haircut, the crew cut he'd always worn, made him happy and gave him back his true cop's face. All he needed now was his former build for the old Sharko to be reborn completely from the ashes.

They walked into number 15, a venerable building as white as a palace. The Drouot auction house was the oldest such establishment in the world. A magical, ephemeral museum, where one could acquire anything the human mind or nature had managed to dream up. Usually, the exhibitions of objects, which related to a theme, a period, or a country, lasted for several days. Each year, eight hundred thousand pieces changed hands in three thousand sales. A business even the economic crisis couldn't affect.

Sharko and Levallois asked to speak to the auctioneer, Ferdinand Ferraud. While waiting, they headed toward the auction rooms, taking the opportunity to peek into that evening's exhibit, "The Story of Time." Muffled atmosphere, low lighting, churchlike calm. Couples silently wandered arm in arm among the 450 meticulously numbered artworks, which claimed to trace the human epic from its origins to the conquest of space. Levallois walked to a corner labeled "Meteorites," the center of which was occupied by a fragment weighing one and a half tons. He pondered it with a puzzled eye, just like the other, more elegant visitors who'd come for a final viewing of these objects before possibly acquiring them.

"Honestly, can you imagine having a meteorite in the middle of your living room?"

"Wouldn't get through the door. On the other hand, nothing like it for cracking somebody's skull open."

"You got anyone in particular in mind?"

Hands behind his back, Sharko didn't answer and instead headed toward the minerals. Stalactiform malachite, chalcedony geode, spherules of mesolite . . . In the next room, said a poster, stood skeletons of "wooly rhinoceros," cave bears from the Urals, and especially one, in its entirety, of an adult mammoth. Perfectly staged and lit, with one of its feet resting on a pedestal, the heap of bones was an impressive sight.

"It comes from Russia," said a voice behind him. "They said you wanted to see me."

Sharko turned around to find a man in a snug-fitting dark suit, with a red tie and a giraffe's neck. He had been expecting some decrepit old codger, but the auctioneer was young and seemingly in good shape. The cop looked around and pointed to the others in the room.

"You could have gone up to anyone here. Do I look that much like a cop?"

"The receptionist described you as thin with a crew cut and a jacket that's too large for you."

Sharko showed his ID and introduced Levallois, who had just walked up.

"We're here about a sale that took place last Thursday. It was for mammal skeletons from the . . ."—he took out a flyer he'd gotten at the reception—"from ten thousand B.C. to the present."

"'Noah's Ark.' The show, and the sale, were hugely successful. The Darwin anniversary helped a lot. There's been a resurgence of interest in primitive arts and the return to nature. The fossil market has become so lucrative that it's spawned all kinds of counterfeit traffic, especially from China and Russia."

"We'd like to see the sales records for that day."

The auctioneer glanced at his watch and answered without hesitation.

"Fine. Unfortunately I don't have a lot of time to spare, as this evening's sale is about to begin."

Ferraud asked them to follow. For once they were dealing with someone who wasn't trying to obstruct their inquiry, who seemed perfectly willing to help. Sharko reflected that he must have been used to visits from the Cultural Property Office or Customs. The traffic in art objects was a booming business.

They took a stairway that afforded them a plunging view of the auction room and provided access to a row of offices. Ferraud entered one of them, opened a locked drawer, and took out a folder. He wet his fingertips.

"What exactly are you looking for?"

Levallois, tired of taking a backseat, gave the answer.

"The name of the person or persons who bought chimpanzee fossils, roughly two thousand years old."

The other man riffled through the lists with impressive speed. His eyes suddenly focused into a stare. With a half smile, he looked up at the two policemen.

"We've got exactly one piece from that period—you're in luck."

"Was it bought?"

"Yes."

The two cops exchanged a rapid glance.

"And I remember the buyer. An avid collector. He left us a check for twelve thousand euros. He bought an example of every great ape we had. Four skeletons of excellent quality, with over twenty percent of their original bones."

Sharko knit his brow. The auctioneer explained:

"You should know that these fossils aren't really fossils. That mammoth on auction downstairs, for instance, doesn't even have five percent of its original bones. No one would be interested in it in its actual state—it was too mangled and unaesthetic. The rest of its bone structure is synthetic, made by a company in Russia."

Ferraud circled a name on the sales sheet and handed it to the cops.

"Delivered to his home on Friday morning by our forwarding agents. That really is his address. Is there anything else I can do for you?"

21

Montmartre at night. Shadows fleeing beneath the tired halos of streetlamps. Narrow alleys set with paving stones. An ogive-shaped landmass rising from the crest of Paris, dissected by countless stairways. A labyrinth of intertwining streets, and at the center its Minotaur: Stéphane Terney.

Lucie had parked her car on Rue Lamarck, near a metro stop whose stairs spiraled into the ground. A few small cafés, still open, absorbed the rare passersby. The air was thick and pasty. Atmosphere of late summer, heavy with humidity, as if a storm could break at any moment. In that damp, the neighborhood felt like a fortress, an islet protected by fog, far from the hubbub of the Champs-Élysées or the Bastille.

To get the address of the man who'd masterminded the theft of Cro-Magnon, Lucie had simply called Information. The Paris region had three people by that name, but the street one of them lived on left little room for doubt.

Rue Darwin.

Charles Darwin . . . The father of the theory of evolution and author of *The Origin of Species*, Lucie recalled from her biology classes. Odd coincidence.

Since her return from Lyon, she had kept a low profile. After leaving the apartment of the young hood with the broken bottle, she'd immediately gone to find a copy of Stéphane Terney's book: a fairly specialized tome with lots of charts and graphs. Then, after calling her mother to let her know she'd be home very late, probably not before dawn, she'd gotten back on the highway, without stopping or thinking about anything other than her mission. Foot to the floor, she had only one desire: to stand face-to-face with the man who would surely have to answer for the theft of the mummy, and who could help her understand its puzzling connection to Grégory Carnot.

Walking quickly, she passed by a row of town houses until she stood in front of Terney's: a whitewashed concrete façade, two stories high, with private garage and a solid metal door that made it look like a giant safe. It was now almost eleven p.m. and no light was filtering through the upstairs windows. Much too late to knock without arousing suspicion. All in all, Lucie knew almost nothing about Terney and had to tread lightly: the man behind the stack of diplomas might be highly dangerous.

Weighing her options, Lucie looked around her, then rushed into an alley a few yards away that sliced through the row of houses. The narrow path provided a shortcut to a parallel street and, better still, access to the balconies and gardens behind the buildings. She just had to scale a high cement wall.

After slipping on her wool gloves, Lucie jumped up, gripped the edge, and, after a few attempts, hoisted herself to the top, though not without scraping her forearms and elbows in the process. A moment later, her body fell heavily onto the grass. She gave out a muffled grunt. Nothing broken, but that little exercise showed her, yet again, how out of shape she'd become.

While the fronts of the houses offered only anonymous façades, the backs expressed their owners' peculiarities: hanging terraces, hexagonal verandas, Japanese gardens with lush vegetation. A privileged corner of Paris, safe from covetous eyes.

In Rue Darwin, Lucie had counted the buildings between Terney's house and the alley. After silently crossing through the fourth garden, she gauged that she was at the right place.

Quick analysis of the situation: impossible to get in from ground level because of the covered porch with its double-glazed glass panels. Upstairs, on the other hand, she spied a half-open window. Crouched over, she ran toward the porch, climbed onto the barrel that collected water from the drainpipe, and within seconds found herself on the Plexiglas roof.

Near the window, she drew her weapon from her pocket. Everything was whirring around in her head: her illegal presence, the danger, the problems she'd surely have to face if she broke into the house. But what if someone was injured? She hesitated a few seconds, then, pushed by the same force that had always driven her, she slipped inside.

She pointed her gun at the bed. No one. The room was empty, but the sheets were rumpled. The angles of the room formed opaque cones. Lucie let her eyes adjust to the dark. Two slippers and a bathrobe lay on the floor: Terney could well be somewhere in the house.

Lucie's muscles stiffened; her senses snapped to attention. The minuscule creaks of the floorboards beneath her feet sounded amplified. The man hiding between these walls might have murdered a student; he wouldn't hesitate to eliminate her either.

She pushed open the door with her fingertips and ventured out of the room. Light filtered in from the streetlamps outside. Opposite her, an aluminum guardrail, twisted in a double helix like a strand of DNA, ran along an open hallway that overlooked the living room below. Lucie heard muffled voices, laughter that faded into the humid air outside. She continued, flat against the wall, listening as she silently crept onward. Below, she spotted an answering machine with its message indicator, the number 7 blinking on it.

Seven messages . . . Lucie relaxed a bit. So Stéphane Terney probably *wasn't* home, and might have been away for some time.

She inched forward some more. One gigantic room drew her attention. It was like being in the lair of some macabre collector. In the shadows, skeletons in attack posture. Prehistoric fossils in perfect condition, animals of all types and sizes, which she identified as reconstructions of dinosaurs. Under glass were minerals, shells in stone, body parts. Femurs, ulnae, teeth, flint. The doctor had created his own evolution museum.

A fresco in the back made her stomach tighten. It showed five skeletons. Near them, an inscription on a painted canvas: THE FIVE GREAT APES. She recognized the skeletons of a man and also of a chimpanzee, smaller and squatter and missing the skull and jaws at top.

With a stiff neck, Lucie turned around and noticed that some floorboards had been ripped up. Beneath them was a hiding place, now empty. Someone had obviously been through it.

She left the room. Terney was more than a fanatic: he lived and breathed evolution to the point of residing on Rue Darwin.

An odor suddenly made her freeze. A stench she knew all too well, a mix of rotting flesh and intestinal gas. Her fingers squeezed more tightly around the grip of her Mann. With the toe of her shoe, she pushed open the last door before the stairs and ventured into a cube of darkness. After aiming her gun at the dark corners, she banged her fist on the switch.

The horrible spectacle appeared all at once.

A nude body, no doubt Terney himself, was lying on the floor, on its right side, at the foot of a fallen chair. It had been bound with packing tape, hands in front, feet attached to the chair legs. Wide gashes riddled the torso, arms, and calves: black, frozen smiles that had sliced through the flesh. A piece of tape that had acted as a gag was still half stuck to his cheek. The man had fallen from his chair onto his side, but the index fingers of both hands were stretched straight in front of him, as if he'd been trying to point to something. Lucie turned in the direction indicated. A library containing hundreds of volumes, stacked several yards high. A crypt of paper. Which specific book was the victim trying to point out?

Without approaching, taking care not to disturb anything, Lucie tried to memorize the crime scene, imagine the killer in action. He had unavoidably left something of himself behind, something of his personality in this cold, sinister tomb.

Terney had been mutilated, tortured methodically, without the killer losing his cool. On the floor were cigarette butts, their ends black with burned tobacco. One of them was still embedded in the corpse's shoulder, as if the butt had glued itself to his skin. The partly removed gag suggested that Terney had finally talked. What had his torturer been trying to get out of him?

Lucie nearly felt faint when she heard a muffled noise coming from the back of the room. There was another door.

The noise occurred again. *Boom, boom* . . . Something was hitting a wall. Or rather, someone.

Lucie moved forward, her throat tight. Holding her breath, gun outstretched, she turned the knob and yanked open the door.

A man in black pajamas was sitting on the floor, a fat book open on his knees. Rocking slightly—hence the noise—he turned the pages, imperturbable, concentrated, not even raising his head. He looked barely twenty years old.

Lucie didn't have time to understand or react before dull thuds at the main door froze her in her tracks.

"Police! Open up!"

A deep, aggressive voice. Lucie backed away, unnerved. The seated man still didn't show the slightest reaction, just tirelessly turned his pages. Good Christ, this was incomprehensible! Why didn't he run? Who was he? Lucie had to think fast. If they caught her here, she was done for. Legs flying, she ran back up to the hallway, knocking over a statue placed at the top of the ramp. She gritted her teeth, unable to catch the object before it went crashing down the stairs with a clatter, without breaking.

Metal.

"Stéphane Terney! Open up!"

More thuds, much louder this time. Voices, shouts. Lucie ran toward the bedroom, unable to breathe. The thuds became a full-scale din: the police were using a battering ram. The entry door slammed open just as Lucie landed feetfirst in the garden. Lungs aching, she dashed into the thickets of branches. It was only a matter of seconds. She didn't dare look behind her. The cops must have been discovering the body by now, arresting the sitting man, entering each room in tight formation, rushing to the exits. No doubt in less than a minute they'd light up the back gardens with their powerful search beams. She arrived at the high cement wall, threw herself at it like a stone from a slingshot. Her arms hoisted her up and propelled her into the alley. Her landing was hard, but her knees took the shock. The moment she stood up, her right cheek smacked against the cold partition.

A gun barrel was pressed into her temple.

"Don't move!"

She felt unable to twitch a muscle. A firm fist had yanked her hand behind her back, holding her in an arm lock. She breathed noisily through her nostrils, her mouth twisting. They had trapped her, watching every exit. She was done for, and she immediately thought of little Juliette. She saw prison bars separating their two faces.

Time seemed to expand, then Lucie suddenly felt the tension relax. The man turned her brusquely around; their eyes met.

"F-Franck?"

Sharko's emaciated face floated in the shadows. In the throbbing lights, he looked like a cop from a detective movie. The face of a guy who'd seen it all. He cast a quick glance behind him and hissed, "Goddammit, Henebelle! What the hell are you doing here?"

Lucie was panting, unable to catch her breath.

"He . . . he's dead . . . tortured . . . There . . . there's someone in . . . the room . . . in pajamas . . ."

Sharko lowered his weapon nervously. His eyes darted to the street, then rested on Lucie. In the distance, through the windows of Terney's house, beams of light began sweeping the darkness. The inspector had to think fast.

"Did anyone see you?"

Lucie shook her head, hands on her knees, spitting up a filament of bile.

He gripped her wrist and squeezed hard.

"What are you doing here?"

"Let me . . . go . . . please!"

Sharko didn't even have to fight against his conscience as a cop. The two of them were the same: shattered, wounded inside, and outside the law. He released his grip.

"Go on, get going. Go back up the alley and disappear. You've got less than five seconds. And especially, don't call me, don't leave any trace of our contact, no matter what. I'll call *you*."

He pushed her so hard that she almost fell. Lucie regained her balance and turned around to thank him with a nod, but he was already far away. She took a huge breath of air and began sprinting, like a fugitive, until she finally disappeared into the shadows of Montmartre.

22

Levallois's powerful frame slammed into Sharko at the corner where the alley met Rue Darwin. The young cop with the oilcan jaw was boiling, his muscles made taut by excitement and the smell of the hunt.

"Somebody got away through the rear gardens! Didn't you see anything?"

Sharko turned back toward the cement wall.

"Dead quiet on my end. Who got away? What's going on?"

Levallois peered in every direction, eyes shining. He turned back to Sharko.

"The window of his room was open. The only place he could've got out was back here. I thought I heard you shout."

"Some goddamn cat. You sure you saw somebody?"

"I'm not sure of anything. There's something really weird in there. Come have a look . . ."

Levallois turned, took a few running steps, leapt onto the cement parapet, and his body disappeared into the gardens. Alone, Sharko let out a sigh. That had been a close call. By now, Lucie should be far enough away to be out of danger. Regardless, she owed him a serious explanation.

He hurried toward the house. The officers were dragging a man out in handcuffs. He was bellowing at the top of his lungs, in deep, nasal tones, feet flying in every direction; it took no fewer than three burly cops to restrain him. Bellanger, the group chief, watched the young prisoner through dark eyes.

"What's all this bullshit about?" asked Sharko, slightly out of breath.

"No idea. Terney is dead. This guy isn't talking. We found him turning the pages of a book, sitting quietly, while a corpse lay not three yards away."

"His strange behavior . . . the shouting . . . Mentally handicapped?"

"Very mentally handicapped, I'd say. On the cover of his book is the number 342 in large writing, and the pages are numbered one to three hundred, but they're all blank. The guy has no identification on him, nothing. He's probably the one who came in through the window. He knocked over the metal statue when we tried to get inside. The noise must have frightened him and he hid in a closet next to the crime scene . . ."

Sharko nodded.

"I didn't see anything go by in the gardens. If you ask me, Levallois is chasing a ghost."

Even shut up inside the police car, they could still hear the young man bellowing. In the neighboring houses, lights went on. People stepped outside.

"I'll hand in my resignation if this guy isn't an escapee from a psych ward or something like that," said Bellanger. "But why did he come here?"

They entered the house behind the CSI team. Men in hazmat suits poured into every room.

"I'll meet you at the body," said Sharko. "I want to get a feel for the place first."

While downstairs Levallois gathered information about the victim over the phone, Sharko drifted from room to room, meeting the somber, perturbed, weary faces of his colleagues. Living room, day room, game room, projection room . . . Everything was orderly to a fault, spotless as an operating theater. According to the initial data, Stéphane Terney was a respected obstetrician and immunologist who practiced in the wealthy suburb of Neuilly. He was sixty-five and obviously fastidious. Even the silverware in the drawer was stacked with military rigor. Surely an occupational hazard: working with pipettes and needles all day, bringing babies into the world, must have demanded a rigorous discipline.

The messages on the answering machine were of various types. Two different women—lovers?—were wondering why they hadn't heard from him. Work colleagues were taking the liberty of calling Terney, who was then finishing a three-week vacation, about some administrative matters.

Sharko went up to the large, open fireplace and squatted down. The techs were retrieving the remains of some videocassettes from the ashes—at least half a dozen at first glance, totally incinerated. The tape itself was no more than ash, and the cases lumps of black plastic. No VCR had been found in the house, but the police had discovered the ripped-up floorboards in Terney's fossil room. The place where he had no doubt kept the VHS tapes hidden. The killer must have burned them.

Sharko then made a quick tour of the large room that housed the private collection of fossils and minerals. There must have been a small fortune's worth. The pieces were well cared for, staged with special lighting. The animals seemed to be facing off against one another.

Next he went and joined Bellanger in the library. Barely older than Levallois, Nicolas Bellanger had all the qualities of a team leader: intelligent, athletic, and ambitious. Relations between him and Sharko were neither good nor bad. They worked together, period.

For his part, Jacques Levallois was closely examining the rows of books that the victim had died pointing at. Paul Chénaix, the medical examiner who had autopsied Eva Louts, stood up and pulled off his gloves. Then he wiped his small, round glasses with a cloth.

"Eyes liquefying, excellent abdominal patch, rigor fully resolved. Not entirely green yet. I'd say he bought it between four and eight days ago. The autopsy will give us a tighter window. We can remove the body."

Sharko thought over the information. Between the fatigue and the excess coffee, he felt strange: a slight floating sensation, as if he'd had a few glasses of wine. He nonetheless managed to sort things out in his head:

"Eva Louts was murdered three days ago. Terney was killed before that . . . So clearly he wasn't her killer."

Bellanger looked carefully through the room, spinning slowly around. He was tall and lanky, with eyes black as espresso and tousled brown hair.

"Not to mention that we haven't found the chimpanzee skull in his private collection. The killer first came here, tortured and killed Terney, then took care of Louts, bringing the monkey jaw with him. Say what you will, I can't really see that guy in pajamas committing two murders of this type. From what I hear from the squad room, the fellow's been bumping against things and grunting like an animal. As soon as they gave him back his book, he quieted down. He started turning the blank pages again, without uttering a sound."

Everything in the room caught Sharko's interest. Row upon row of books stretched to the ceiling. The precious woods, bizarre artworks, and high-tech equipment reeked of wealth, as well as a morbid eccentricity.

"You find anything?" he asked Levallois.

"Nothing yet. Did you see how many books there are? How are we supposed to know what he's pointing at?"

The inspector turned back to the corpse. Burned, mutilated, probably with a knife. The ME had turned the body onto its back. Sharko pointed to the wide, deep gash in his left groin.

"Is that what killed him?"

"Yes. The left external iliac artery was severed. That artery is like a river. The victim fell from his chair, his blood poured out, and he died within seconds."

"Curious way of doing away with somebody. Maybe the killer has ties to the medical trade. Or in any case, he knows his way around human anatomy. First he wanted to make him suffer. After he finally got him to spill the beans, probably about where the cassettes were hidden, he eliminated him, then took off as Terney was giving up the ghost. Clean, masterful work. Like with Louts, he took his time."

"There are also nicotine traces on his tongue and gums. The killer must have forced him to smoke those cigarettes so he could burn him."

The ME pulled back a little and pointed to the torso.

"Look at his chest. All together, the cigarette burns form the letters X and Y . . ."

"X and Y—the signs of male gender, right?"

The examiner nodded.

"Exactly. Of the twenty-three pairs of chromosomes we all have, only one pair is different, depending on the sex: XX or XY. All newborns have the X chromosome from the mother, but the father gives them either his X—in which case the child is female—or his Y."

Sharko pondered. The killer had toyed with his victim, but he had also left them a major clue, whether he meant to or not. Somewhat dubiously, the inspector walked over to three paintings hanging side by side on one of the walls. The first showed a bird in flames against a molten sky: the legendary phoenix. The second seemed to depict a human placenta: a fat, transparent, veined bubble. The blood vessels, in scarlet red, were like bizarre serpents and made the whole thing look like a monstrous spider. The third canvas was actually an enlarged photo of a prehistoric human mummy, completely desiccated and lying on a table as if it were about to be autopsied. The inspector wrinkled his nose at the placenta.

"Either I don't know shit about art, or this guy Terney sure had weird taste."

Nicolas Bellanger came up. Both the phoenix and the placenta bore the artist's signature: "Amanda P."

"You know as much as I do. Everything in this house relates to DNA, birth, or biology, even down to the shape of the fixtures. Putting a frame around the photo of some gross mummy, I swear . . . He even lives on Rue Darwin. You can't make this shit up."

"A fanatic to the end, since he ended up with an X and Y on his chest . . . Nice little wink from his murderer."

The ME said good night and took off; he still had work to do. Without a word, the men from the morgue slid the corpse into a black bag. The sound of the zipper echoed to the far corner of the room. Now alone with Sharko, Nicolas Bellanger headed toward the small adjacent closet.

"This is where we found the guy in pajamas. He was shut away in here, with his book. Three hundred meticulously numbered pages, all blank. You ever seen anything like that?"

"Yeah, lots of times. Just visit any psych ward."

Sharko went over to join Levallois. After a moment, he noticed that the books were arranged by subject: science, natural history, geography, then alphabetically within each subject.

"Terney was anal. If he pointed to this area, it's maybe because there's something out of place here. Something that jumps out."

Searching through the books in turn, Sharko came upon a group of provocative titles: *The Right to End Lives That Aren't Worth Living, Euthanasia, Solutions to Aging Populations* . . . Books on eugenics and racial purity by the dozens. On the right, an entire section was devoted to virology and immunology. None of it very uplifting.

Levallois slowly climbed down the ladder, eyes scanning the books within his reach. With his gloved hand, he pulled one from its place on the shelf.

"Bingo! A book about DNA in the middle of the geography section. It's called *The Key and the Lock*. And guess what?"

"Tell me."

"It's written by none other than Terney himself."

Sharko held out his hand and Levallois gave him the book. On the cover was Leonardo's famous drawing of a standing nude man inside a circle and a square. Beneath the title, an alluring copy line: "The Hidden Codes of DNA."

"They call that Vitruvian man," the young lieutenant explained. "Turns out a man with arms and legs outstretched can be inscribed in the perfect geometric figures of a circle and a square. Did you know Leonardo was a lefty?"

"And your point is?"

"Nothing. Just general culture."

Bellanger walked up as Sharko was reading the back cover blurb.

"What's it about?"

"I don't even understand the synopsis. Listen to this: 'Why do the numbers twenty-six and thirteen sound and order the major harmonic of the relations between the billions of codons in the entire human genome and the most frequent codon, among the sixty-four possible types? Why, in the three billion bases forming a simple strand of DNA, does each of these codons possess its mirror image? Why does the entire human genome obey the proportions of the golden mean? Intended for specialists and general readers alike, this book will answer the questions you have long been asking about the implacable work of nature in the construction of life.'"

Bellanger was speechless. Sharko leafed through the first pages.

"It looks pretty complicated, and technical. There are pages and pages of DNA sequences, mathematical formulas everywhere, graphs, and not much text . . . Why would Terney have pointed us toward *this*?"

"It's in the subtitle: the hidden codes of DNA . . . Think of the X and Y on the corpse's chest."

Bellanger looked through the volume for a while with a somber face, then shoved it into a plastic bag.

"I'll get this straight to our biologists in the forensics lab. They can spend all night on it if they have to, but I need to know what kind of shitstorm we've walked into here."

Back at number 36, Sharko approached one of the detention cells. Sitting in a corner, the young man in pajamas was placidly turning his pages one after another. His eyes were bright, shining with an inner glow, as if he

154

were searching for something in those blank pages. He couldn't have been more than twenty, with matted blond hair and long, bony hands, his thumbs slightly curved outward. His lips were murmuring words that Sharko couldn't quite make out.

"Who are you?" asked the cop. "What are you muttering to yourself? What are you looking for?"

The young man didn't raise his head. Jaws clenched, Sharko stood up and headed for a small conference room on the third floor. The faces of the people there were chalky, their features drawn. Empty cups and cigarette butts littered the old table. It was one in the morning and nobody felt like talking anymore. Pascal Robillard was distractedly twisting a rubber band; Jacques Levallois couldn't stop yawning; Nicolas Bellanger gave his final instructions.

"Priority: find out who this guy in pajamas is. We have to make him talk, figure out what he was doing there. So, Pascal . . . you call the mental hospitals and local police stations; we're looking for a runaway. You also look into Terney's background. I want to know who he is, who he worked with, if he had any enemies. Maybe he knew that wacko downstairs, maybe a relation or something. Some younger cousin, a nephew, a kid he's been treating for some reason. Sharko, you look into his professional and private life. Question his colleagues at the clinic in Neuilly and his friends. Judging from the messages on his machine, he was something of a player. Check into that angle, too. The case is getting deeper, and we'll need a hand solving it. So as of tomorrow, most of Manien's team are coming over to work with us full-time, provide some backup and fresh ideas."

Sharko clenched his jaws.

"Aren't they on the Hurault case?"

"The Hurault case? It's gone completely cold. Not the hint of a trail. So the boss put ours at the top of the pile and is allocating us more men."

"Manien's not going to like that."

"Like I care."

Bellanger turned to Levallois.

"Jacques, you get on to the autopsy. It starts in an hour. You prepared to go without sleep tonight?"

The young lieutenant nodded.

"Somebody's gotta do it."

"Fine. I also gave your cell number to the head of the bio lab for the book about DNA, that *Key and Lock* thing. Let's hope he calls you in the middle of the night with good news."

"It *is* the middle of the night."

Bellanger managed a brief smile, looked over his troops, then gave the whiteboard behind him a huge swipe with the eraser.

"Get moving. I've still got a ton of paperwork to catch up on before sunrise. See you later."

Sharko was furious and worried. Sitting at the wheel of his car, he tried to reach Lucie, but no luck. True, it was late, but why the hell wasn't she answering? Had something happened to her in Montmartre before she could get away? Had she had an accident? He screeched to a halt at a red light he almost hadn't noticed. The small woman from the North was again dominating his thoughts and driving him crazy.

As he walked down the hall to his apartment, sore, empty, burdened by dark thoughts, a shadow sitting at his door stood up.

Lucie Henebelle, cell phone in one hand, Terney's book in the other, was waiting for him with undisguised impatience. She looked him straight in the eye.

"Tell me they aren't on to me."

23

Sharko yanked Lucie inside and locked the door behind them. He pulled her by the wrist to the middle of the living room and rushed over to the kitchen window.

"Did anyone see you come here? Did you talk to anyone?"

"No."

"Why didn't you answer my calls?"

Lucie looked around her. The first time she'd been in this apartment was over a year ago. That night, she'd slept on the couch, and he in his room. While the couch was still there, the pictures of his wife and daughter, so numerous back then, had now disappeared. Not a single trace of his past life; no more decorations or trinkets. Why did Lucie have the cold feeling that this apartment had become lifeless, soulless, as if she were visiting it after the owner's decease? She looked at Sharko, who was hanging his service weapon on a coatrack, as he'd always done. How many years had he been repeating the same gesture? Despite his crew cut, the bags under his eyes were even puffier, and his features seemed to be crumbling away like cheap plaster. Fatigue was consuming him like a drug.

Lucie remained standing.

"I wanted to tell you about it face-to-face, not on the phone."

She fell silent a moment, a catch in her throat. Her hands nervously twisted Terney's book.

"I also wanted to thank you for what you did, back there. You put yourself on the line for me. You didn't have to do that."

Sharko went to uncap a beer. At two in the morning, he needed to unwind, and a little alcohol would help. Lucie declined the glass he offered her.

"What's done is done," he answered.

"So tell me, the guy in pajamas—who is he? Is he the one who killed Terney?"

"We don't have a clue for the moment. Given his mental state and his behavior, it's doubtful he could have committed those tortures. Did he see you?"

"No."

"Now your turn: starting from a trip to the Alps, with no information and no nothing, how did you end up at Terney's before fifteen guys from Homicide?"

Lucie sat down on the edge of the sofa and brushed her hair off her forehead. After a day like this and so many miles—walking, driving—her legs could barely support her. Slowly she started telling her story.

"A few weeks before meeting Carnot, Eva Louts had read an article in a science journal and noticed an upside-down drawing. It was a fresco of aurochs, in a prehistoric cave. A unique incident that didn't get much attention in the press, and that Louts herself barely thought about at the time. But ten days ago, when she saw Grégory Carnot's inverted drawing, she immediately rushed to the original cave, so that she could see the aurochs fresco firsthand."

Lucie related her findings in an even voice, leaving out no details. She talked about the family of Neanderthals slaughtered by the Cro-Magnon. About how the bodies were transferred to the genome center in Lyon. About the theft of the mummy. About Arnaud Fécamp and how he'd seemed suspect. She told how she'd trailed him through Lyon, how she'd burst into the apartment on Boulevard de la Duchère, then how she'd sped up to Montmartre hoping to piece it all together. As she talked, Sharko had tensed and his features twisted. He bolted up, furious, and glared at Lucie.

"You could have got yourself killed! What were you thinking?"

"My daughter was killed. Not me. What matters is that I'm here now and we're making progress."

A silence. Lucie finally stood up and went into the kitchen.

"Is the beer in the fridge?"

Sharko nodded. He watched her leave the room, uncap a bottle, and come back. She hadn't lost any of her cop's reflexes, was still just as sharp and alert.

Her voice broke into his thoughts.

"Did you find any trace of the Cro-Magnon and his genome at Terney's?"

"No. No secret lab or any of that stuff. The house was clean. On the other hand, he'd taken a photo of that mummy and hung it in his library, next to paintings of a phoenix and a placenta. As for the genome . . . We didn't find any computer documents at the vic's. Probably swiped."

"Any info about him?"

"It's coming in piece by piece—we'll sift through it tomorrow. What we know now is that he was an obstetrician, specializing in neonatal abnormalities, and the author of the book you're holding in your hands. A polymath."

"Tell me what you've found. How did *you* end up at the victim's house?"

"Go home, Lucie."

"You know me better than that, Franck. You know I'm not leaving."

Sharko let himself fall onto his chair.

"Well, in that case, have a seat."

Her heart in her throat, Lucie sat down opposite him and emptied a third of the bottle with a grimace. She, too, needed to unwind. The inspector squeezed the narrow bottle in his hands.

"Okay, here goes."

Sharko filled her in on the broad strokes of his own investigation. Louts's thesis about hand dominance and its relation to violence. The young woman's studies of athletes and warlike populations, her trips to Mexico and, as yet unexplained, to Manaus. Her request, on her return from Brazil, to meet with violent French criminals, culminating with Grégory Carnot. He stressed that Brazil seemed to mark a turning point in Louts's search and that she'd planned to go back. He also explained how the shard of tooth enamel recovered from Louts's body had led them to Terney, which was where the investigation dead-ended.

Even though she hadn't yet absorbed it all and didn't have all the details, smells, and images that a criminal case can leave in its wake, Lucie let herself be guided by simple deduction:

"Grégory Carnot, a born left-hander, begins making upside-down drawings around the same time he turns violent. We don't know anything about his family history. A child abandoned at birth, adopted, no particular health issues apart from lactose intolerance."

"That's a pretty fair recap."

"Thirty thousand years before this, a Cro-Magnon man, also left-handed, slaughters an entire family, and also draws upside down. Two people notice the similarities and draw connections between them. First, there's Stéphane Terney, a Paris doctor, who seems interested in the Cro-Magnon's genome, and goes so far as to steal the mummy. Then there's Eva Louts, a student in biology, motivated by her thesis and her discoveries about hand dominance and violence, if I've understood right."

"So far so good."

"Both dead, presumably murdered by the same killer. Which must mean they had something in common . . ."

"Eva Louts returns from Brazil and immediately goes to see violent, left-handed criminals. She gathers up information about them, photos . . . then plans to return to Brazil . . . as if . . ."

"As if someone had given her an assignment. Collect the data and bring it back there."

"Exactly."

Lucie shook Terney's book in front of her.

"Left-handers, the Cro-Magnon's genome, DNA, this book and its hidden codes—it all seems connected."

"But we don't know what that connection is."

Lucie took another slug of beer and wiped her lips. She realized she was feeling better. Thoughts were flying, pieces falling into place. Despite everything, they still made a good team.

"Let's think. What could possibly give the same characteristics to two individuals born several millennia apart?"

"DNA? Genes?"

Lucie nodded emphatically.

"It's what's been coming back over and over since the start of this investigation. There always seems to be some link to that damn DNA molecule. And yet, the director of that research lab in Lyon swore to me that violence does not get transmitted genetically. And besides, it'd be ridiculous to talk about family connections between Carnot and some supposed ancestor hundreds or thousands of generations before him."

"Why ridiculous? We weren't born in a vacuum, and those Cro-Magnons have to be *somebody's* ancestors. In any case, I think Terney was on to something. Something that spans the ages, and that the killer didn't want him to reveal."

"The same as Louts . . . Two different paths leading to the same result."

"Death."

Sharko nodded toward the book.

"Were you able to look through that?"

"A little bit. As far as I can tell, it's basically just a book of recipes. You take human chromosomes, unspool their DNA, and put it end to end. That gives you a series of about three billion repetitions of the letters A, G, T, and C, all lined up, which constitute our genetic heritage, the famous human genome. With that, you make a bunch of calculations and look for coincidences, which you interpret as secret messages . . ."

"You seem to know a lot about the subject."

Lucie gave a brief smile, which faded almost immediately.

"I know something about it. A year ago, I took my own DNA to compare it with the burned body in the forest."

Sharko sat back in his chair. Lucie spoke slowly. Her words were heavy as bricks.

"I followed every step that would allow me, from that molecule, to arrive at an identification. I spent days and nights with the lab techs, with face mask and gloves, until the miserable series of A's, T's, C's, and G's from my DNA could be compared with the sample from . . . from . . ."

"From the little victim in the forest."

"Yes. I can describe the process by heart."

Sharko tried to look unmoved, to build an invisible wall around him. But little by little, a poison seeped into his veins. He saw the faces of Lucie's daughters, heard their laughter, felt the sand creak under their small feet. Sounds and smells never fade. That day, on the beach at Les Sables d'Olonne, Sharko had prevented Lucie from accompanying her two girls when they went to get ice cream, because he had something to tell her. It had only taken a minute . . . just one short minute for Clara and Juliette to be kidnapped. The whole thing had been his fault.

Meanwhile, Lucie was thinking to herself. She finally glanced over at the computer.

"I'd like to do some research on Stéphane Terney. He wrote a book, he was well-known, there must be a fair amount about him online."

Sharko took refuge in his beer. The alcohol flowed noisily, heavily in his throat. His mind was pulled in several directions at once. He tipped his chin toward the clock.

"It's almost three in the morning. You're doing just what you did a year ago. You should get some rest."

"You too."

Sharko sighed and took the plunge:

"Are you seeing a shrink? Someone who . . . who can help you get through all this?"

Lucie clenched her jaws, then, involuntarily, leaned toward Sharko and took his hands. She caressed their boniness, wrapped his slender fingers in hers.

"And what about you? Do you see how worn-out you look? What happened to you, Franck? I'm the one who should be in this state. I'm the one who . . ."

He cut her off.

"I have nothing left. No one left."

He stared at the floor with vacant eyes, then stood up suddenly, already regretting his words.

"Anyway, for fuck's sake, I don't have the right to feel sorry for myself in front of you. I'm doing fine, Lucie, whatever it looks like. I've got my little habits and a job that keeps me from thinking about the rest. What more could I want?"

He walked over to his computer, sat in the chair, and turned it on. Lucie came up behind him, bottle in hand.

"Before seeing you again, there were times when I hated you, Franck."

His back was to her. She saw his shoulders tense up. He looked so fragile, as if he were made of porcelain beneath the cop's outer shell. Lucie remembered it all perfectly: a few hours after the twins' disappearance, she had projected all her hatred, all her powerlessness onto Sharko. The people around them, the cops, had advised the inspector to steer clear of her.

"In fact, I don't think a single day goes by without me hating someone. My former captain, my mother, even my daughter, my little Juliette."

She shook her head, nearly in tears.

"You can't understand, right? You must think I'm sick, a terrible mother, or just fucked up."

"I'm not judging you, Lucie."

"The same sentences turn around and around in my head, over and over. Why wasn't it Juliette who left instead of Clara? Why was she the one the police brought down from that room in Carnot's house, and not her sister? Why did he spare her? So many whys that I can't get rid of until I bury Carnot way down deep."

She sighed.

"He's still alive, Franck. Grégory Carnot is still alive through the person who murdered Terney and Eva Louts. This killer doesn't do anything halfway. We might not know what went on in Carnot's head, but there are people out there who do, I'm sure of it. I want to, I *have* to find the killer. Juliette's safety depends on it, and the children she'll have someday. My mother told me you have to resolve conflicts, confront them, and not bury them away. Everything has to end with answers."

She swallowed. Her hands were damp. The little bit of alcohol she'd drunk was already going to her head. Sharko was moved, almost in tears. *Juliette's safety depends on it, and the children she'll have someday.*

"We're in the thick of it, Franck. Violence . . . Just like last year, except that . . . this time, it's being expressed in time rather than space. It's so strange for it to be touching us at this point. As if . . ."

"As if it were pursuing us. It tore us apart, and now it's brought us back together."

Another silence. A heavy sense of unease.

"We're the same, you and I," added Lucie. "We have to follow things through to the end, no matter what the cost."

Sharko turned off his screen. He wasn't sure exactly what he'd been looking for on the computer, other than a way to avoid Lucie's eyes.

"Listen, I'm sorry, but I'm already out of it . . . It's been all over for me for a long time."

"Nothing's over, because you're here, with me, no matter how bad your pain, or your anger."

"You have no idea what my anger is like."

"I can feel it. But don't make me go home without answers. Keep me close to the investigation. Close to you."

Sharko remained expressionless, hand gripping the mouse, unable to make a decision. Very soon, confronted with this silence, this interminable wait, Lucie felt ill at ease, floating, as if a suit of armor that seemed unbreakable, that had withstood so many blows, had suddenly been shattered by a puff of wind. Slowly she turned and headed for the door, stumbling slightly. Her head was spinning and she saw stars. Fatigue, nerves, the miles she'd traveled since yesterday . . .

"I'm sorry for . . . for bothering you," she managed to get out. "I just thought you and I . . ."

Sharko leapt from his chair and slammed his hand against the door. He leaned over to hold her up, and she pressed her face into his shoulder, sobbing as if she'd never stop. She was trembling all over, her strength drained, and feeling faint.

When Sharko tucked her into the sofa, she was already asleep, huddled into herself. With a sigh, he slowly caressed her face, devoured by regrets and remorse.

Then he clenched his jaws and went to shut himself up in his room.

He felt as if he'd slept only an hour or two, vacillating between reality and nightmares. Images, voices, insane ideas hovered at the edge of his senses. Knowing that Lucie was so nearby, so fragile, made him feel ill. As if he were reliving his own past, his suffering, all the anguish coiled inside him.

At 7:30 that morning, as he was staring at the ceiling, stretched out on his bed like a corpse at a wake, he got a call from Pascal Robillard.

The lieutenant had found the identity of the man in pajamas.

His name was Daniel Mullier.

Escapee from a group home in the fourteenth arrondissement.

Autistic.

24

Sharko had gone out quietly, without waking Lucie. Just a quick wash-up in the bathroom, a note scrawled on a piece of paper—that was all. No coffee, no morning radio, no noise. A lingering look at the young woman, a painful urge to crush her against him. He couldn't tell if he wanted to find her there when he got home that evening or never to see her again.

Depressing ride, traffic jams, noise, head full of questions. Not enough sleep, brain already churning. The inspector parked his car in the lot of the Félicité group home. He went to greet Levallois, who was smoking a butt, leaning against the side of his car. His eyes were puffy.

"So how was the autopsy?" the inspector asked.

"Vic tortured for at least two hours, burned with cigarettes in chromosome patterns, then cut for maximum blood loss. He didn't last more than a few seconds. The rest is just forensics that doesn't tell us anything new. I spent a night from hell. Let's hear it for the police!"

The young man seemed to be handling it well enough. Sharko rested a hand on his partner's shoulder and gave it a shake. The two looked up at the tall, Haussmann-style residential facility, separated from the street by a low fence and pleasantly flowering gardens. The fourteenth arrondissement was home to the city's psychiatric institutions, with the renowned Sainte Anne hospital at the head.

"Hear anything about Terney's book?"

"Several biologists were at it all night—they were already familiar with the work. Apart from statistics, math, and various arguments in favor of eugenics, they didn't find anything out of the ordinary so far. But it's a long book and I think it'll take time. They're not sure what they're looking for."

"Did you say eugenics? In the middle of all that mathematical data?"

"The head of the lab said to come see him if we wanted more info. He was in a piss-poor mood."

"If we want more info? Terney's last living action was to point to that book—you bet your ass we want more info!"

The man who welcomed Sharko and Levallois was named Vincent Audebert. He was the director of the center, which housed fourteen high-functioning autistic adults who were incapable of living on their own. Given his mental state, Daniel Mullier had been returned to his environment several hours earlier. One thing for certain, he wasn't the guilty party: according to the director, the fourteen patients had just returned from a week's vacation at a center in Brittany and had only been back for two days—well after Stéphane Terney's murder.

Vincent Audebert nodded toward a window on the ground floor.

"Daniel's room looks out on the courtyard. He'd already tried running away once, but that was two or three years ago."

"What set him off this time?"

"Stéphane Terney had promised to come get him yesterday, to take him to a lecture on DNA. They've known each other for years. Daniel and Terney saw each other two or three times a month. The doctor always kept his promises and Daniel looked forward to these visits. But this time . . ."

He paused for a moment.

"So to show his anger, Daniel started counting the number of grains in a two-pound bag of rice. When he gets like that, he shuts himself up in his room and we let him see his ritual to the end, which normally takes him about four hours. There's no other solution."

"Didn't you notice he was missing last night?"

He rattled a large ring of keys in his pockets and sighed.

"We're not a prison here. There aren't any night rounds or impromptu room searches unless strictly necessary. Daniel got out through his window, climbed the fence, and disappeared into the city. He'd been to Terney's house before; he knew the way."

"Is there any chance Daniel could talk to us or explain what he might have seen or heard? Could he tell us about his relations with Terney?"

"Absolutely no chance. He doesn't speak and he doesn't write anything other than his series of letters, numbers, and calculations. It's his only language. He doesn't understand his own emotions, let alone those of others. That's why it's so difficult to penetrate the bubble that autistics build around themselves. But Terney was able to do it. He'd managed to establish a kind of communication with Daniel, using mathematics."

"What form of autism is Daniel suffering from, exactly?"

"One of the most severe forms. I won't go into details, but in general he shows an utter inability to communicate orally, manifests disturbances in his social development, and suffers from extreme withdrawal. Paradoxically, despite all these debilitating handicaps, he also has what's commonly known as savant syndrome. In addition to a phenomenal memory, he has exceptional abilities in the area of statistics and analyzing numbers and letters. It's beyond anything you can imagine. I'll show you the room we fitted out specially for him—one look will tell you more than all my explanations."

They walked toward the center of the building, which looked like an elementary school. Rows of coat hooks, drawings taped to the walls, empty classrooms with chairs around a circular table. The place gave off an impression of order and cleanliness. The adults must still have been in their rooms, no doubt located in the perpendicular wing. Calm floated over the corridors, like a silky coating of madness.

"How did Terney and Daniel meet?" asked Sharko.

"It was in 2004. The scientist came here. He'd heard about Daniel's ability to analyze huge quantities of letters and numbers. He wanted to meet him because he was thinking of writing a book about DNA, which would involve a lot of statistics. He thought Daniel might be able to assist him by detecting things in the molecule."

"What sorts of things?"

"Mathematical symmetries, immutable laws that the endless succession of A, G, C, and T's always obeyed. Terney was seeking order in chaos."

The director opened the door to a large, circular room, painted white and with very high ceilings. Sharko and Levallois gaped in amazement. All around, hundreds, thousands of volumes, each identical to the others, were arranged side by side over numerous shelves. Even Terney's library seemed tiny compared to this. Numbers were inscribed on the spines, in ascending order: 1, 2, 3, 4 . . .

"Those books are just like the one Daniel had at Terney's," murmured Levallois.

In the middle of the room, Daniel was seated at a desk, an open book in front of him, pen in hand. Opposite him was a jar with dozens of pens, also identical to one another, as well as a lit computer. Daniel didn't give them so much as a glance. He was bent over, absorbed in his task. He was writing, without a pause, with small, quick movements. Looking around, Sharko noticed a piece of red cloth hanging between volumes 341 and 343, to the left. He remembered that Daniel had been found at Terney's with volume 342.

The director indicated the tomes with a sweeping gesture, speaking in a low voice:

"There are exactly five thousand books, each containing three hundred pages. Not one more or less. Terney had them made specially for Daniel. The ones after the scrap of cloth are yet to be filled—in other words, nearly all of them."

Levallois's eyes widened.

"To be filled? You mean . . . by Daniel? But . . . what's he writing down?"

The director took down the volume marked 1 and opened it.

"He's jotting down the complete genome of modern man . . . The totality of the three billion A's, C's, T's, and G's that compose the DNA of our forty-six chromosomes laid end to end. The great encyclopedia of life. The most powerful manual in the world, which contains, in encrypted form, the construction of our internal workings, the journeys of our ancestors, a set of instructions that the little Champollions present in our organisms have been reading for hundreds of thousands of years, so that they can create the proteins that enable us to live."

Levallois leafed through the pages, unnerved, almost in a trance. Thousands upon thousands of letters, written in a tiny hand one after the other—AAGTTTACC . . .—on every page of every volume on every shelf.

"You're holding the very beginning of the sequence of chromosome one," explained the director. "It's been six years since Daniel started, ten hours a day, during which time he's written something like fifty million letters."

Sharko looked at the infinite succession of paper, the improbable quantity of work still to be done.

"Good lord . . ."

"You could say that. It's an endless task. At this rate, astoundingly fast though he is, even if he worked 365 days a year it would still take him more than a hundred years to finish. We already know he's going to spend the rest of his life doing this—jotting, jotting, jotting . . ."

The two cops looked at each other.

"But why?" asked Sharko.

"Why? Because he has no other way to express himself, no way to channel the flood of energy burning up his brain."

With a sigh, he nodded toward the computer.

"Daniel posted two different genomes of modern man onscreen, which he got from the Genoscope site. I'll spare you the details, but look how he works: he visualizes the contents of the first genome at the top of the screen, memorizes it, and copies it onto these pages before pressing the NEXT button and moving on. The genome stretches across millions of successive screens!"

"Why is he displaying two genomes onscreen, if he's only copying one?"

The director pointed to the underlined letters in the book. There was at least one per page.

"He's not merely recopying the genome. He's also underlining certain letters, each time there's a discrepancy between his reference genome and the other one onscreen."

"Are you saying there's that little genetic difference between two genomes—between two distinct individuals?"

"Exactly. You share more than 99.9 percent of your DNA with an aborigine in the Australian outback, a black, a Chinese, and a Mongol. Genetically speaking, you're closer to those people than two chimpanzees chosen at random in the jungle. That's why we talk about the human genome and not *genomes*, and that there aren't as many genomes on the Internet as there are humans. In fact, there are only two available, because at the time two projects had been launched simultaneously. The genomes for all humanity are roughly the same, apart from a few small 'errors' that account for, oh, let's say, differences in eye color. Among the three billion A, T, C, and G bases in the DNA of each of our cells, only three or four million of them are in different places; those are the only differences between one human and the next. Your own genome, Inspector, is practically identical to Daniel's, or to mine, apart from those few underlined letters."

Sharko was astounded. But he also felt enormous pity for this man, who had his whole life ahead of him and who'd spend it copying what a supercomputer could handle in a mere few seconds.

"What's Terney's book about, exactly? Why did he bring Daniel into it?"

"At first, the book was supposed to deal only with statistics. Stéphane Terney enjoyed using those A, T, C, and G's to make a number of calculations, depending on their placement, their repetition, and the number of them in the DNA chain. For instance, he'd divide the total number of ATA sequences by the number of CCC—we call series of three letters 'codons'—and come up with remarkable numbers, like thirteen, or seven, whereas we were expecting to find completely random numbers with lots of decimal places. Daniel helped him. Terney even talks about the golden section, about remarkable mathematical series . . . In short, he said that all the magic of nature was expressed in DNA through hidden codes."

"Hence the drawing of Vitruvian man on the cover. The perfection of humanity, hidden in DNA."

"Precisely. Personally, I'm rather skeptical of these 'revelations.' When you go looking for something in such a mass of numbers and letters, you're bound to find it . . ."

He made a face.

"This book should have been no more than a vulgar *Da Vinci Code* of DNA, but I think it was actually just a pretext. Terney really used it to broadcast his ideas about eugenics. To make a case for euthanasia, the systematic abortion of fetuses with abnormalities, the elimination of aging populations, which he considered a virus on the planet. Terney is—or rather, was—for the purity and youth of humanity. As he saw it, certain 'races,' certain genetic conditions upset the perfect mathematical equilibrium that he'd managed to find in the human genome, with Daniel's help. The 'intruders,' as he called them, weren't worthy of figuring in the genetic legacy we'd bequeath to our descendants. He used Daniel against people like . . . well, like Daniel. I found his approach reprehensible."

Sharko thought of the weaker members of a school of fish. Terney had tried to pass the same message, but from a genetic viewpoint.

"And yet, you let him continue to see Daniel," he said.

"At first I tried to put a stop to their relations. But Daniel was so unhappy, and his seizures got worse. Terney, by communicating through numbers and letters, brought him something important. I think that, deep down, he really loved him. DNA was the key to the lock that kept Daniel prisoner, and Terney gave him that key. So I turned a blind eye, but believe me, I was no fan of Terney's. Now that he's gone, I have to admit I'm a bit sad, because I don't know what will become of Daniel . . ."

Sharko looked at the young autistic, who got up, set down his pen in a corner, and took a new one from the can. He looked over the shelves and shelves of blank books, most of which would never be filled. In that illogical spiral, he suddenly had an intuition.

"Has Daniel read *The Key and the Lock*?"

"It's his bedtime reading, so to speak. He looks through it almost every evening, tirelessly . . ."

Sharko and Levallois exchanged a brief glance, as the director continued:

"But 'read' isn't exactly the right word, as I'm sure you've realized. Naturally, he doesn't understand the eugenicist sentiments, nor the words themselves. It's hard to explain briefly how his mind works, but . . . he scans through every book he gets his hands on as a series of letters, so to speak. To oversimplify, let's say that connections light up in his head, that groupings immediately take on color before his eyes when he's reading a text. At a glance he could let you know that a given page contains fifty instances of the letter e, without being able to tell you what that page is about."

Sharko quietly squeezed his fists.

"I'd very much like to see that copy."

The director nodded.

"It's carefully put away in his room, always in the same place. I'll be right back."

He disappeared down the hall.

"It's terrifying," murmured Levallois. "We do nothing but complain, and this kid who's barely twenty is going to spend the rest of his life here, in this room."

"Mental illness is a slow poison."

Sharko moved closer to Daniel. The young man's shoulders hunched a bit tighter when he felt the presence behind him, like a cat on the defensive, but he didn't stop writing. His right thumb and index finger were deformed, bony. He held the pen the way you hold a screwdriver handle. The inspector would have liked to reassure the young man, rest a hand on his shoulder, give him a little human warmth, but he didn't.

Audebert returned. Sharko took the copy of *The Key and the Lock* and leafed through it attentively. Entire pages contained only DNA sequences, from which Terney derived his theses. There were no marginal notes by Daniel, but Sharko saw that certain pages were dog-eared, more worn than the others. For instance, page 57. At the top was written: "Consider, for instance, the following DNA sequence." Below it, several hundred A's, T's, C's, and G's succeeded one another to form a series. What amazed the inspector was not that senseless group of letters, but rather the fact that every one of them, without exception, had been underlined by Daniel, just as in volume one of the encyclopedia of life. He showed the page to Vincent Audebert.

"Can you tell me why he did that?"

Audebert squinted.

"I'd never paid attention . . . But . . . He underlines whatever differs from the reference genome. With the computer, he can do research into the genome . . . Perhaps he looked up that sequence on the Genoscope Web site and couldn't find it? If that was the case, he might well have underlined all of it."

Sharko turned more pages. And found it again. Pages 141, 158, 198, 206, 235, then 301 . . . Always prefaced by: "Consider, for instance, the following DNA sequence," and always underlined. Daniel had been diligent.

Levallois moved toward volume two, opened it, leafed through a few pages, and shrugged . . .

"I don't get it. You say there's just an occasional difference between individuals. One discrepancy every thousand or two thousand letters. How could Daniel have underlined so many successive differences?"

"Stéphane Terney might have written completely random sequences, just as examples. Or else . . ."

The director appeared disturbed. He thought for a few moments, then suddenly snapped his fingers.

". . . or else I have another possible explanation."

He took back the book and looked through it carefully.

"Because of Daniel and Stéphane Terney, I had to do a lot of studying up on DNA, to keep up with them. I know which parts of the molecule correspond to such rapid, grouped, and extensive changes in the sequences. They're called microsatellites."

He nodded toward the encyclopedia of life.

"One day, Daniel will write pages on which hundreds, even thousands of successive letters will be underlined, just like here, before everything becomes normal again. Those will be microsats. Your forensic technicians use them every day in DNA analysis, because they're like fingerprints. They're unique to each individual, and they're always located in the same place in the genome."

Sharko and Levallois again looked at each other, amazed.

"So these microsatellites could serve as genetic fingerprints," said the inspector.

The director nodded vigorously.

"Exactly. Gentlemen, I believe seven different genetic fingerprints have been hidden in this book, in the midst of other, harmless data. Seven barcodes of seven individuals who might exist on this planet."

25

The two cops had rushed into the forensic lab on Quai de l'Horloge. The place was divided into different departments, such as Toxicology, Ballistics, and Document Analysis. A concentration of technology, a labyrinth of machines each more costly than the last, which analyzed blood, cigarette butts, explosives, hair follicles, you name it. Confessions extracted through science.

Jean-Paul Lemoine, the head of the molecular biology lab, was waiting for them in a narrow office. Age about forty, with short blond, almost gray, hair and heavy eyebrows to match. His job, and that of his team, was to operate huge machines, such as thermal cyclers and sequencers, which copied, cut up, and analyzed bits of DNA.

He offered the two men a seat, looking a bit embarrassed.

"Microsatellites . . . Your man is right. They were buried in the mass of information that book contains. We'd probably have found them eventually, but lord knows after how many days, or weeks."

He looked at the open book in front of him.

"In any case, it was clever of him to hide genetic codes in a published book. When it came out, Terney sent unsolicited copies to universities and prominent scientists. A kind of propaganda for eugenics behind a smokescreen of mathematical data."

He slid the book toward Sharko.

"What else can I tell you? The exact procedure we use to establish a genetic profile?"

"Not really, no. We came here to see if we could start a search for the seven genetic fingerprints in the national database."

That had been Sharko's idea. The French national DNA database, or FNAEG, stored genetic information on everyone who'd been convicted of a sex crime since 1998, and since 2007 they'd been able to add almost every offender that the police had ever brought in for questioning. A match between DNA in the database and DNA found on a crime scene could pinpoint a suspect.

Lemoine looked skeptical.

"Uh . . . I'd have to enter the letters of the sequences into the computer by hand—normally it's all automated. We usually get a saliva sample to analyze, or clothing with sperm on it; we put the sample in the machine and the individual's barcode comes up. But here, we don't have any samples, just . . . paper. Look at these pages, you saw as well as I did: a genetic fingerprint can run up to a thousand letters. It would take hours to enter all that, and that's assuming there isn't a single mistake. It would take a huge amount of concentration, and we'd have to do it seven times over. I was already up all night working on this, and I've kind of had it."

He shrugged sheepishly. He obviously had only one wish right now, and that was to go home.

"You know, Inspector, the FNAEG contains less than a million and a half genetic profiles of defendants, not even two percent of the French population. That's *French*, Inspector, not worldwide. And besides, there's no guarantee the genetic fingerprints in this book are even real. They could be . . ."

"People have been killed over this," Sharko interrupted. "These fingerprints are real, I'd stake my life on it. Terney put them in his book and established a friendship with an idiot savant so that one day, if anything happened to him, people would find out. Even if Daniel Mullier hadn't been present at the crime scene, it's obvious we would have found him eventually, one way or another. He was like . . . like a key, meant to open this particular lock. Please—just do it."

After a moment's reflection, the scientist set down his empty cup and acquiesced with a faint groan.

"All right. I'll try. I'll need someone to read it to me as I type."

He picked up the book and handed it to Sharko, who passed it to Levallois.

"You're on. I didn't sleep last night and my eyes are burning."

Levallois grunted. "Do I look like I got much sleep?"

With a sigh, the lieutenant sat down next to Lemoine.

"Most of all, there can be no mistakes," the scientist warned him. "I'll tell you where to start." He circled a specific letter. "Okay, begin reading from here. Slowly but steadily."

"AATAATAATAATGTCGTC . . ."

Levallois began reading while Lemoine typed. After about twenty minutes, he breathed a sigh of relief—"Finished!"—and the biologist hit Enter. They waited a few seconds. The first genetic fingerprint was instantly compared with the millions of others stored on secure servers.

A phrase appeared onscreen: "No matches found." Disappointment showed on their faces.

"First fingerprint unknown. It looks like your theory doesn't pan out, Inspector. Shall we quit?"

"Keep going."

They started up again. Second fingerprint: no match. Coffee, a cigarette for Levallois, a lot of pacing for Sharko. Third fingerprint: no match. Fourth fingerprint . . . purring of the processors, hum of the fan. Lemoine's eyes widened.

"I don't believe it. We've got one!"

Sharko leaped from his chair and rushed across the room. Lemoine read aloud what the screen had brought up. First and last name, date of birth.

"Grégory Carnot. Born January 1987."

Sharko felt as if he'd taken a bullet in the gut. Levallois stared at the screen as if he couldn't believe his eyes.

"Good Christ, what does that mean?"

"Do you know him?" asked the scientist.

The young lieutenant nodded.

"The girl who was murdered, at the start of this investigation—she went to see him in prison. At least, I think she did."

He looked Sharko in the eye.

"Am I wrong, Franck? Eva Louts did go to see Carnot, didn't she? He was on that list of prisoners, wasn't he?"

Sharko anxiously placed his hand on the other's shoulder.

"Go stretch your legs a bit, I'll take over from here."

"Your eyes look like raisins. You can't make a single mistake. Sure you can do this?"

"What do you think I am, brain-dead?"

Levallois got up from his seat. The inspector sat down, eyes glued to Carnot's genetic profile. Why had Terney hidden the killer's identity in his book? What was the relation between the two men? He shook his head and concentrated on the letters as if on a crossword puzzle.

"Shall we?" said the biologist.

"Let's get started."

Sharko began reciting the rows of letters, meticulously following them with his index finger. Inwardly, he struggled not to slip into distraction. Lemoine typed in silence. The hands of the clock slowly advanced.

Fifth profile: unknown. Levallois returned with three cups of coffee from the vending machine. Unfortunately, the sixth didn't yield any results either. The men took a breather. Sharko yawned and rubbed his eyes; Lemoine cracked his knuckles, at wits' end.

"Come on, one more, before our brains give out."

On the seventh and last profile, the result sent back by the FNAEG exploded in their faces.

Results found.

But it gave no name or photo. Lemoine clicked on the link for more details.

"The record was sealed by the police. It's a trace that's been in the system for only three days, unidentified. Which means . . ."

Sharko sighed, rubbing both hands over his face.

". . . that it's from DNA gathered at a crime scene, but that its owner hasn't been arrested yet," he completed. "It also means that the perpetrator has probably committed his first serious crime, since he wasn't in the database before. I think I know the answer, but can you tell me what sort of crime we're dealing with here?"

The biologist answered in a blank voice.

"Homicide."

26

*L*ucie is floating just above the ground. Her body glides forward without her feet touching the floor, as if she's being carried by a divine breath, cold and silent. She tries to turn her head, but a kind of neck brace with huge blinkers holds it firm. Her anxious gaze finally latches on to a small square of light piercing the uniform darkness. A storm rumbles loudly, the earth trembles, and the next second a torrent of heavy objects rains down from the skies. Vases . . . Thousands of identical vases come smashing around her in a din like the end of the world. Oddly, none of the projectiles hits her, as if she were protected by a shield. The invisible breath grows stronger and Lucie's form slices through the deluge and rises higher off the ground, until it enters the blinding light. She squeezes her eyes shut in pain, until the brightness softens and her vision slowly returns. Now she's floating above hundreds of autopsy tables, aligned horizontally and vertically. The corpses laid out on them are also all identical. Small, naked, unrecognizable. And charred . . . Their faces are a portrait of agony. As for their bodies . . . an arid land . . .

At the exact center of all those dead, Lucie notices that one of the children seems to be in a different position: instead of lying alongside its body, its hands are folded over its volcanic chest, with something in them. Lucie shifts her weightless form toward it, gives a slight jerk that enables her to move fluidly and uniformly through the air. She comes closer, while a smell of burning wafts up like a solar flare. Suddenly the child's eyelids snap open, revealing two black pits of horror. Lucie screams without any sound escaping her mouth. She tries to turn back, but her body continues to glide through the air, inexorably bringing her closer to the abyss of those eyes. She finally sees what the child is holding: a vase, exactly the same as the ones raining down outside. The black eye, the left one, is now as huge as a tornado. Lucie feels incapable of fighting it and lets herself be sucked in. The *child holds out the vase to her, which she grasps just as the eye swallows her . . . And she falls, screaming . . .*

Lucie started awake in a sweat, a shout on the edge of her lips. At the borderline of consciousness, she opened her eyes. The walls, the ceiling, the minimal decoration . . . For a few seconds, she wondered where she was; then her thoughts gelled. L'Haÿ-les-Roses, Sharko, their late-night conversation . . . followed by a black hole.

Rumpled clothes . . . disheveled hair . . . socks on the floor . . . She sat up, still shaken. Not a week went by without all those dead children coming to haunt her. Always the same scenario, every time, leading her irrevocably to an endless free fall into that same eye. She knew the dream was trying to tell her something. The vases probably had something to do with the flaw in Clara's iris; the improbable rain indicated that she had to open her eyes, pay attention to those vases. But why?

"Franck? Are you here?"

No answer. She glanced at her watch. Good lord, almost nine o'clock. She lunged for her cell phone. Messages. Her mother was worried at not hearing from her. She immediately called to reassure her, tell her everything was fine.

On the phone, she had a hard time finding the right words to explain why she wouldn't be coming straight home without rousing her mother's incomprehension, and her anger. In answer to her improvised explanation, harsh words flew from the other end of the line: How could Lucie let herself sink back into the nightmare that had shattered her life? Carnot, that human waste, was dead, dead and buried—why couldn't she just let him lie? Why did she have to keep chasing ghosts? Where had she spent the night? And so on and so forth. Five minutes of letting her vent.

Without losing her temper, Lucie asked how Juliette was. Had her mother brought her to school that morning? Was the little girl getting along well with her new classmates?

Marie answered with a few curt yeses, then hung up.

Lucie thought to herself that, deep down, her mother was right. She had never been capable of establishing a stable, complete relationship with her daughters. To give them the love of a *real* mother. Her job as a cop had been both cause and excuse. She needed to miss her girls to really feel her love for them; she wanted to see the absolute worst around her, track down the vilest scum, so that she could come home from work at the end of her tether and realize how lucky she was to have a real family to cherish.

But since the tragedy, Lucie had had to confront another, less tolerable truth: she had never loved Clara as much as she did now. And when, in her eyes, Juliette became Clara, she gave her all her affection. But when Juliette remained Juliette . . . Sometimes Lucie was filled with love for her, and at other times . . .

She preferred not to go too far down that path. With a sigh, she walked into the kitchen. There was a note for her on the table: "Make yourself some coffee. There are still some things of yours in the bedroom closet." Lucie headed toward the bedroom. The magnificent model railway had been completely dismantled, the rails stuffed haphazardly into plastic trash bags. Not a single decoration or trace of color, bed neatly made, sheets smoothed out, like the room of a dying person. Even the little O-gauge OVA Hornby locomotive with its black car for wood and coal, the one thing that never left Sharko's possession, was nowhere in sight. A wave of sadness came over her.

She found her clothes from the previous summer in the back of the closet. They had been scrupulously packaged in cling film, with two tiny mothballs. Sharko was throwing out the trains that had been so dear to him, but he'd kept the clothes of a woman he expected never to see again . . . Maybe he still cared about her after all. Maybe there was still a thin, fragile thread connecting the two of them.

She took the packet of clothing and was surprised to discover, behind a stack of Sharko's sweaters, a box of cartridges and a revolver. It was a Smith & Wesson .357 Magnum. Lucie picked it up. Most cops kept a second weapon at home, normally to use for target practice or because they were collectors. Out of curiosity, she opened the cylinder and shivered when she discovered a single bullet inside. A bullet in the first chamber, that would come roaring from the barrel if one pulled the trigger. Could this have been out of neglect? Given the state Sharko was in, could he have committed such an oversight? She chose not to wonder about the use he might—or intended to—put the gun to, and instead set it back in its place.

From the package, she took a pair of black jeans, clean underwear, and a short-sleeved tan sweatshirt. Now the bathroom. A piece of paper on the wall documented the cop's rapid weight loss. He was down to nearly 150 pounds. Lucie's heart sank. She washed and dressed as quickly as possible in the deathly silence, facing the overly large mirror in which she couldn't keep herself from imagining Sharko pondering his solitude, every morning, every evening, every night. The ordeal of a driven man, who was trying to live out his sentence to the very end. And if one day it all broke down, the gun would be there to help out. Unable to stand such a thought, she ran out of the bedroom.

After having a cup of coffee and washing a few dishes, she noticed an envelope next to the computer. She didn't recall seeing it the night before. Had Sharko put it there in the night? Had he left it for her on purpose?

She opened it. It contained photos of the Terney murder scene: shots of the library, the museum with its fossils, the three strange paintings hung side by side—Lucie winced at the placenta and the Cro-Magnon mummy—and of course the body itself, photographed from every angle. She made a face. The older man had been tortured to the depths of his flesh. His eyes were staring into nothingness, as if seeking a final answer to the question every victim must ask himself before dying: why?

After turning on the computer, she opened a browser and typed "Stéphane Terney" into the search box. It yielded a long list of responses, including a lengthy Wikipedia article and several interviews with the scientist. Lucie clicked on the links and was surprised by their wealth of detail. She thought to herself that the Internet could be pretty handy.

And she started reading.

Stéphane Terney was born on March 8, 1945, in Bordeaux. The insert photo showed him at around age fifty. Dark suit, stringent features, thin, straight lips without the hint of a smile.

In his youth, Terney is mainly interested in athletics, like his father, who in his day had been the French champion of the 400-meter dash. By dint of intense training, at the age of fourteen young Stéphane competes in the Aquitaine regional championship for the 10K run, racking up competition after competition, but never quite making it into the top three. He soon begins neglecting his studies and, at age sixteen, finds himself enlisted in the army, Fifty-seventh Infantry Regiment, which boasts an excellent team of long-distance runners. Terney impresses his superior officers as a runner, but, with the Algerian War raging across the Mediterranean, they also have him train as a medical orderly. When his training is over, to his dismay, they send him to the city of Oran in the northwest. The dual infiltrations into the city by the Algerian FLN and the paramilitary OAS are provoking outbreaks of violence. Kidnappings, assassinations, and horror reign over both the Muslim and European populations. Terney cares for the wounded as best he can.

On July 5, 1962, civilians armed with guns and knives attack buildings where Europeans live, breaking down apartment doors, opening fire in restaurants, kidnapping, shooting bystanders, or slitting their throats indiscriminately. People are hanged from meat hooks and mutilated, their eyes gouged out: the atrocity seems to know no bounds. Because of the peace accords, the French soldiers hesitate to intervene. When Terney ventures into the streets, it's as if he's entered another world. Two images mark him to his very soul. The first is a man sitting against a wall, still alive, holding his entrails in his hands with an odd smile. And the second . . .

Lucie's hands fluttered as she sat there, feeling uneasy. So many sordid details . . . In his interviews, Terney had shared some extremely private and painful memories, exposing them for all to see. Was it a way of cleansing himself? A need for recognition?

Taking a deep breath, she read on.

Terney continues patrolling with the troops. Suddenly, he hears wailing from inside one of the houses. At first the orderly thinks it's a cat, then realizes it must be an infant. He pushes open the door. His combat boots skid on thick, black blood. Opposite him, on the ground, he discovers a dead woman, naked and mutilated. A baby is howling between her legs, lying in a milky puddle on the tile floor. The infant is still attached to its mother by its umbilical cord. With a scream, Terney rushes forward and cuts the lifeline with a pair of scissors. The slimy, blood-covered infant falls abruptly silent and dies within seconds. Soldiers find Terney petrified in a corner, the dead child crushed to his chest.

One week later, he is back in France, discharged from the military on the grounds of psychological fragility.

At the age of nineteen, Terney no longer sees the world in the same way. Suddenly, it becomes excruciatingly clear to him how precious human life is and he feels the irrepressible need to accomplish "something important for his fellow citizens." It's then that he takes up the study of medicine in earnest. Had this been his true calling all along? Whatever the case, Terney proves to be a brilliant student in Paris, specializing in obstetric gynecology. He wants to treat pregnancies and bring babies into the world.

From that point on, the mechanism of creation, from fertilization to birth, and all the processes of the female reproductive system fascinate him. Soon, as a complement to his primary studies, he becomes a specialist in the immune system, especially in the behavior of defense mechanisms that ensure the survival of the embryo and the fetus. Why does the immune system, which attacks all foreign bodies and even rejects transplants, allow an organism, half of whose genetic material is from an outside entity (the father), to develop in the maternal womb? What secrets of evolution allow for in vivo birth, actually inside the human being?

Terney becomes a fanatic about the great questions of life and builds a dual career: one as an obstetric gynecologist, the other as a researcher. By the time he's thirty, he is already publishing heavily in the scientific journals. In 1982, at the age of thirty-seven, he becomes one of the world's leading experts in preeclampsia, a gestational hypertension that can affect women during pregnancy. A mysterious, unexplained condition that affects 5 percent of women and generally results in the baby being born weak and underweight.

Lucie yawned and stretched. Various links took her to related entries on immunology, preeclampsia, obstetrics . . . Much more informative than a police report. She got up and poured herself another cup of coffee. A glance out the kitchen window. She could see the ash trees in Parc de la Roseraie, where Sharko liked to take walks. Did he still spend an hour or two there every week, sitting on his favorite wooden bench? Did he still go every Wednesday to visit his family's gravesite? She wondered—and found she really wanted to know if he did. In the distance, wrapped in gray fog, she could make out the minuscule Eiffel Tower and the infinite sea of buildings.

Lucie wandered back into the living room. Terney seemed to be a brilliant individual who had found his life's purpose in the chaos of the Algerian War. But what profound scars had the violence left in him? What did he feel whenever he brought a baby into the world? Was it like treating an inner wound? Redressing the world's injustices?

She sat down once more and resumed reading, cup in hand.

It is while specializing in DNA and deepening his knowledge of preeclampsia that Terney begins developing his first theories about eugenics. He is often on the road at the time, meeting colleagues in immunology and shrewdly advancing his ideas, citing as his examples such social disorders and health hazards as tuberculosis, syphilis, and alcoholism; birth defects resulting from increasingly late pregnancies; and the overall weakening of humanity's gene pool. Social welfare programs for the poor, the sick, and the underprivileged become his primary target. He is openly hostile to Christian charity. In his obstetrics practice, where his excellence helps make up for his arrogance, he doesn't hesitate to recommend abortion to his patients when the pregnancy shows even the slightest risk of abnormality. *For the good of all.*

Terney continues to speak in public, hammering away with his examples. In lectures before substantial audiences, he asks his listeners to raise their hands if they have a friend or family member who has been affected by cancer. He tries the same thing with diabetes, and then with sterility. More hands go up. Terney then asks everyone who has raised a hand at least once to do so again. Nearly every hand in the room goes up. Then he hits them with a shocking statement: "Our population is too old and its genetic resources are being depleted. For the first time in history, the health of the current generation—our children—is worse than the generation that preceded it."

Lucie stopped reading again, struck by that last paragraph. She too would have raised her hand: one of her former colleagues at work was diabetic, and her uncle had died of throat cancer at the age of fifty-two. She also thought about Alzheimer's and allergies, increasingly common ailments that hadn't existed fifty years ago.

Disturbed, she went back to the article.

Terney's personal life: In 1980, at the age of thirty-three, he falls in love and marries. Six years later, he gets divorced. His wife, Gaëlle Lecoupet, a prominent attorney, does not accompany him to the provinces when he accepts the directorship of the Obstetrics Department in Colombe Hospital, a major maternity hospital about a hundred miles from the capital.

Suddenly, Lucie's throat tightened.

The city where Terney had practiced medicine, from 1986 to 1990, hit her like a thunderbolt.

Reims.

Where Grégory Carnot was born, in January 1987.

Dumbstruck, Lucie put a hand to her face. It was just too much of a coincidence. Reims . . . Could Terney have worked in the same hospital where Carnot was born? She snatched up her cell phone and called the public records office in Reims. After being shunted from one administrative office to another, she got the name of Grégory Carnot's birthplace.

Colombe Hospital.

Lucie hung up.

She realized that she was sitting in a corner of the room, forehead against the wall like a little girl in detention.

One certainty now drummed on her mind: strange as it seemed, Stéphane Terney must have brought Grégory Carnot into the world in 1987. And twenty-three years later, a criminal investigation was bringing the two men together again. This could not be mere chance. It couldn't.

And yet, as much as she puzzled over it, Lucie still couldn't figure it out. Had Terney been keeping tabs on Carnot all those years? Might he even have arranged to become his mother's obstetrician? And if so, why?

Lucie skimmed the rest of the article.

After Reims, Terney more or less fades from public view. He returns to Paris in 1990, marries and divorces several more times, burning through relationships like cigarettes without ever having a child of his own. He practices in a clinic in Neuilly, continues his research into preeclampsia, delves further into immunology, and leaves obstetrics on the back burner. In 2006, he writes his book *The Key and the Lock*, sending thousands of free copies to schools and targeted individuals, thus reviving for a moment his reputation and eugenicist positions. Then he fades back into anonymity and resumes a perfectly normal practice.

Lucie turned off the computer and looked at the keys to her car, which were on the living room table. She now had the name of a maternity hospital and a birth date. Even if Grégory Carnot's mother had given birth under seal of anonymity and put him up for adoption, there must have been files, people with whom Terney worked at the time, who might be able to tell her something about the obstetrician, his relationship with Carnot's mother, the infant, or even the birth itself. Perhaps that cursed child, or his parents, had left a trace in people's memories? Perhaps the biological mother had left her identity buried in a file?

She had to try, do everything she could to understand what might possibly connect Terney to her daughter's killer. She could be in Reims in less than two hours.

Before heading out, Lucie stopped to think. She knew she would run into roadblocks in a place as administratively cautious as a hospital. Merely claiming to be a cop wouldn't work anymore. She needed a fake police ID. Not a perfect one, just something she could flash at people— who generally didn't know what they really looked like anyway.

She had an ID photo in her wallet, and Sharko had an excellent color printer.

Lucie went back online. There was no shortage of sites for making fake ID's, "for entertainment purposes only." Driver's licenses, diplomas, birth and marriage certificates . . . Fifteen minutes later, the printer spat out the false document on a sheet of white card stock. She had decided to stick with the name Amélie Courtois: better to stay anonymous. Lucie carefully cut out the card, rumpled it slightly to make it look older, glued on the identity photo from her library card, and slipped it behind one of the small, slightly opaque squares of plastic inside her wallet.

That should see her through the first 10 percent of it. Nerve and experience would handle the other 90.

Fake ID or no, she had become a cop again, working a parallel space where no one would think to look, not even Sharko. Because no one knew Grégory Carnot as well as she did, it would take them a while to find the link between him and the clinic where Stéphane Terney had practiced more than twenty years ago.

She picked up the Terney crime scene photos and her jacket and went out, slamming the door behind her.

She didn't notice the man sitting at the wheel of his car, parked in front of the building.

27

The official Peugeot 407 with Levallois at the wheel had just veered onto Highway A6a, heading toward Fontainebleau. The late-morning traffic was moving easily—a relative notion on the roads around Paris—and the cops didn't have to turn on the siren to open a passage.

Before that, Sharko had stopped by number 36 to pass along his discoveries and fob off the day's assignment—questioning Terney's friends and coworkers—onto a colleague.

At present, the two cops were speeding toward La Chapelle-la-Reine, a small town just south of the Fontainebleau forest. They had an appointment with the captain of the local gendarmerie, Claude Lignac, who had briefly held the bag on a rather sordid case: a double murder in the woods, committed by a killer whose DNA figured in the book Terney had written in 2006. Given the unusual and particularly grisly nature of the crime, the gendarme had been forced to hand over the investigation to the Major Case squad in Versailles.

Obviously, apart from the officers at 36, no one knew that the genetic code of the man who had committed this double homicide six days ago figured in the pages of a scientific textbook that had come out four years earlier. In order to prevent leaks, especially to the press, the cops were keeping that information strictly confidential. Officially, they were looking into the murder because it might be related to an ongoing case about which, for the moment, they couldn't give out any details.

Sharko switched the radio station, landing on "Zombie" by The Cranberries. Levallois smiled at him.

"You've been sprucing yourself up a bit these past few days. New suit, new haircut . . . and you don't look quite as sad. You got a girl?"

"Why is everybody asking me that, for Christ's sake?"

"They say you've had something of a dry patch since your wife died. So I just figured . . ."

"How about you keep your figuring to yourself."

Levallois shrugged.

"We're partners. Partners tell each other things. With you, it's like talking to the lamppost. Nobody really knows what you were up to at Violent Crimes. And why don't we ever talk about anything but the case? Why don't you ever ask about . . . about *my* life, for instance?"

"Because it's better that way. The job seeps into your life enough as it is; don't let your life get into the job. Leave your wife and kids, if you've got any, at the door to number thirty-six. You're better off."

"I don't have any kids yet but . . ." he hesitated, "but my wife is pregnant. We're having a little girl."

"Good for you."

A cold, toneless reply. Levallois shook his head and concentrated on the road, the investigation. The case was sucking him in more and more each day, and each day he got home a bit later. He caught himself feeling a growing excitement the deeper he sank into the shadows. Would he, too, end up like Sharko? Sticking with the cut-and-dried, he aired aloud his thoughts about the case:

"Terney wrote his book in 2006. He already had Carnot's genetic code, and also the killer's from Chapelle-la-Reine, when they weren't even in the database. Our genetic fingerprints aren't readily accessible, so he has to have met those two at some point and taken samples of their blood, hair, or saliva. And he had to have access to the kind of machines they've got at CSI, in order to extract their DNA profiles."

Sharko nodded.

"There are seven genetic profiles in the book. Two of them are already in FNAEG, and we know they're violent killers. That means there are potentially six psychos somewhere out there. The bodies in Fontainebleau show that one of them is now active. As for the others, they're ticking time bombs, and at this rate it won't be long before they go off, too."

"Maybe they already have . . . Maybe the other anonymous cases have already killed but didn't leave their DNA at the crime scene. Or maybe it was in another country? What do we really know about it?"

A reflective silence followed these words. Who were these shadow warriors? What unleashed this violence in them and pushed them to commit such heinous crimes? Sharko rested his forehead on the passenger-side window and stifled a yawn. Even in circumstances like these, sleep returned like an acid and gnawed at him from inside.

While Sharko dozed, jerking awake every time his head lolled forward, the car exited the highway, arriving at La Chapelle-la-Reine barely ten minutes later. Population three thousand, fields on all sides, the forest edge barely a mile away. The police station looked like any other administrative building: monotonous and depressing. A concrete block sporting the tricolored flag and the word "Gendarmerie." On the parking lot sat two shabby blue police cars.

Levallois parked at an angle, wrenching Sharko from his torpor.

"Honestly, I don't get it," the younger man said. "What the hell are we doing out here? Major Case is in charge of the investigation and they've got all the files. Why don't we just go straight there and save time?"

"The guy we're here to meet, Claude Lignac, must be pretty bitter about having this one taken away. I'll bet you he's better informed than anybody else around here. And besides, he won't ask too many questions. I like it when people don't ask too many questions."

"The boss wanted us to go see Major Case. We're circumventing correct procedure here, and I'm not really comfortable with that."

"Major Case would have given us a few scraps of information at most. Despite what you think, rivalry between state and local police isn't just an urban myth. You have to know how to let go of procedure and trust your instincts."

They got out of the car and walked into the building. A young man, wearing the regulation navy blue sweater with epaulettes indicating the rank of sergeant, saluted and ushered them into the office of Captain Claude Lignac. The captain, about thirty-five years old, had small round glasses, a fine, elegant mustache, and particularly jovial features: he looked like the stereotypical English inspector. After introductions and some routine questions about why Homicide was interested, he picked up his car keys and a file.

"You'd like to see the crime scene right away, I presume?"

"If you could take us there, we'd appreciate it. We'll talk at the scene. Have you been keeping up with Major Case's findings?"

The local policeman shrugged.

"Of course. Those guys from Versailles might have kicked us off the case, but this is my turf, and what goes on here is my business."

He walked ahead of them to the door. Sharko winked at his colleague. Claude Lignac got into his car and headed off, with Levallois following behind. In barely five minutes, the forest swallowed them up. Leaving the local highway, the gendarme took a crazily twisting shortcut, drove for another five minutes, and finally parked at the edge of a hiking path. Slamming of doors, soles crunching the earth. Sharko pulled his jacket closed; the temperature had dropped noticeably, as if in testament to the magnitude of the tragedy the trees had witnessed. Around them, a few bird cheeps and crackings of old wood were lost in the vast space.

Claude Lignac motioned for them to follow. In single file, they walked over the slightly damp earth, amid the undergrowth, the beeches, and the chestnut trees. The captain veered off into a slightly denser area and pointed to a carpet of vegetation, made of lichen and rotten leaves.

"This is where a rider found them. Carole Bonnier and Eric Morel, two kids who lived in Malesherbes, about twelve miles from here. According to their parents, they'd come to spend a few days in the woods, camping and rock climbing."

Sharko squatted down. Traces of dried blood still stained the leaves and the base of a tree. Thick, strong spatters that attested to the frenzied nature of the crime. Lignac took some photos from his pocket and handed them to Levallois.

"I got these from Major Case. Look what the bastard did to them."

The sudden bitterness of those words surprised Sharko. Levallois's face darkened while Lignac continued filling them in:

"They're pretty sure he first hit them in the face and stomach, almost hard enough to knock them out. The autopsy revealed subcutaneous hematomas and a number of broken blood vessels, which shows how violent the blows were."

"Did he use a weapon of some kind, maybe a stick?"

"No, he went at it barehanded at first. Only afterward did he use one of the rock axes he'd taken from their backpack, to finish the job, so to speak. We'd never seen anything like it around here."

Lips pressed tight, Levallois handed the photos to the inspector.

Sharko looked at them carefully, one after the other. Wide views of the crime scene, close-ups of the victims' wounds, faces, and mutilated limbs. A slaughter.

"They got the full treatment," said the policeman in disgust. "The ME up in Paris counted forty-seven axe wounds for him, and . . . and fifty-four for her. He hit them wherever he could, with remarkable strength and determination. Apparently the impact of the metal on their bones was hard enough to cause fractures."

Sharko handed back the photos and stared for a while at the stained earth. Two different monsters, Carnot and this one, had acted one year apart, but with almost exactly the same, extremely violent m.o. Two savages that Terney had already listed in his book in 2006.

Two out of seven . . . Seven profiles that, in all likelihood, would belong to the same race of killers. Hence Sharko's odd question:

"Do you know if the killer was left-handed?"

A question that, as Sharko expected, took the other man by surprise.

"Left-handed? Uh . . . You'd have to ask Major Case, but as I recall they didn't say in the autopsy report. The weapon used in the crime had symmetrical double edges, so there's no way of knowing from the wounds. Why do you ask?"

"Because your killer probably *is* left-handed. He'll also be tall and stocky, age between twenty and thirty. Are those footprints in the ground his?"

"Yes, he wears a size eleven. But how did you . . . ?"

"Powerful build, no doubt taller than six feet. Were you able to reconstruct the exact circumstances of the crime?"

Sharko carefully scanned the surrounding area, especially the tree trunks. He was looking for carvings in the wood. Could it be that, like Carnot and the Cro-Magnon, the killer had made an upside-down drawing? But despite his sharp eye, he didn't spot anything of note.

"More or less," said the gendarme. "Time of death is estimated at about eight a.m., six days ago. We arrived fifteen minutes after the rider called, around nine-thirty. There was a pot on the lit gas burner, all the water had evaporated. We think the victims were making breakfast. They were in sports clothes, shorts and T-shirts. The tent was still up and the quilts folded down. There were a couple of ATVs chained to a tree."

The captain stepped forward and brushed a few leaves aside with his toe.

"The victims were lying right here, near the tent. They hadn't had time to run, or hadn't tried to. The killer almost certainly came up by the path we've just taken—it's fairly popular with hikers, cyclists, and riders. Then he left the path, cut through the ferns, and approached the campsite. Major Case isn't sure whether he tried to chat them up first or just attacked head-on."

Sharko thought to himself that this cop had the right instincts: he was keeping close tabs on the investigation. A way for him to show he still ruled his little roost, and especially to get a break from the daily routine.

"Any witnesses?"

"None. It was a bit too early for hikers, and anyway they would have kept to the path. The circumstances of the murder were reported in all the local papers, I made sure of that—I've got a few connections. We put out a call for eyewitnesses."

"Good. Did you get any results?"

"No, no one came forward. The killer was lucky."

"They often are. Until they get caught."

Sharko stepped over some branches and returned to the path. He called back:

"You couldn't see the tent from this path, is that right?"

The gendarme adjusted his small round glasses.

"Correct. Those kids must have known they weren't supposed to camp in the woods, so they chose a hidden spot. How did the killer find them if he was just passing by? Probably from the sound of their voices. And if the water was boiling, he might have spotted the steam in the cool morning air. At that point, it would have been easy to track them."

The man was detail-oriented. Sharko rubbed his chin, again squinting at the surroundings. The vegetation was dense, and you couldn't see more than ten yards. Levallois rubbed his hands together as if he were cold.

"Any ideas about the killer's profile?" he asked.

Lignac nodded, eager to relay the details and show off his skills.

"Physically, we know the bastard wears a size eleven and that he had hiking boots. The presence of a Y chromosome in the DNA confirms he's male—and a hefty one, at that, given how deep the shoeprints go. Like you said, easily six feet. He didn't steal or disturb anything. The victims weren't sexually assaulted, the bodies weren't moved postmortem. Everything was left as is, with no attempt to conceal the crime. As if it were all in a murderous frenzy . . ."

The same as with Carnot, thought Sharko.

"Major Case has got molds of the shoeprints, fingerprints, DNA up the wazoo, on the bodies, the weapon, and in the backpack where he got the ax. The whole thing happened like lightning, nobody saw a thing. According to the ME, some of the stab wounds were sloppy, careless. He came along, killed them haphazardly, driven by what looks like a mad rage. The couple was just unlucky enough to be in his path."

Sharko and Levallois exchanged a glance. As with Carnot, this tended to disprove the hypothesis of a killer stalking his victims, studying their habits and movements. The two kids had just been in the wrong place at the wrong time.

"You figure he's a local?"

The policeman pushed a bit deeper into the ferns and stopped near a tree.

"We're all pretty sure of it. There's something important and rather peculiar I haven't told you yet. Come over here . . ."

The cops approached. Lignac pointed to the ground.

"Here, at the base of this tree, we discovered about a dozen burned matches, with a matchbox advertising a drink popular with kids, 'Vitamin X.' Major Case thinks the killer just sat here after the crime striking matches, one by one, staring at the bodies. Most of the matches were broken, which suggests he was under severe mental strain, like a pressure cooker. Clearly he needed to sit a while, calm his nerves; maybe he didn't feel well enough to go straight home. Maybe he was suffering a breakdown. In any case, as I said, he wasn't the careful type. He didn't make any effort to cover his tracks."

He headed toward the crime scene with a sigh: never again would he walk in these woods without thinking of the massacre.

"This box of matches is a real gift from heaven—it was almost certainly his, since the kids had a lighter. It gave Major Case a precious bit of information, because the only way you could get it was as part of a promo about a month ago, when they handed them out at a club in Fontaine-

194

bleau, the Blue River. I'm certain the killer is hiding in the city and that he went to that club."

"Why Fontainebleau itself and not some other town in the area?"

Lignac shook his head.

"It was a special event—you had to be a resident to get in."

Sharko and Levallois shot each other a glance. Information like this was more than they'd hoped for.

"And . . . does Major Case have anything in particular on this club? Any potential suspects?"

"For now, their investigation hasn't led anywhere. The promo drew a lot of people, practically every kid in town. Head count more than five thousand—the place was packed. The only reliable information they've got is the killer's DNA. They might try testing all the young adults who were there that night and wear size eleven shoes, but it would take a long time and cost a bundle."

"Especially if the killer only went to the club that once . . ."

Sharko began pacing back and forth, hand on his chin. The police were tracking a ghost, a monster who had no apparent motive, who might now be holed up at home and wouldn't come out again until driven by another murderous impulse.

As he gazed once more at the scene, an idea suddenly flashed through his mind. It was totally improbable and would likely take him all afternoon, but it was worth a try. Eva Louts, with her thesis and her research, just might be handing him his killer on a platter.

He tried to conceal his excitement:

"All right, then. I think we've seen all there is to see."

Back at the parking lot, he thanked Claude Lignac and let him walk away. Then he held out his empty hand to Levallois.

"The keys. I'm driving this time."

He took the wheel. Levallois didn't hide his skepticism.

"DNA everywhere, that bit about the matchbox—don't you find it all a bit much? It's as if the killer wanted to get caught."

"That might be the case. He might want to lead us to him because he himself doesn't understand his actions. He knows he's dangerous and could do it again."

"So then why doesn't he just turn himself in?"

"Nobody wants to rot in jail. The killer's leaving himself a chance, and also absolving himself of guilt: this way, he can tell himself that if he kills again, it'll be our fault because we couldn't stop him in time."

Sharko turned onto the local highway, heading toward Fontainebleau. The young lieutenant frowned.

"Can I know what you're up to? Are we going to that club to redo what Major Case already did? We've got other fish to fry."

"Not even close. The two of us are going on a treasure hunt. We've got a huge advantage over Major Case: we know that Grégory Carnot and our anonymous killer have Terney's book in common. Both of them blew a fuse, both are young, strong, and I'd bet my eyeteeth they're both left-handers."

"How do you know that?"

"It's the same muck we've been paddling around in since day one. Louts went to interview killers in prison, until she hit upon Carnot. She was killed because of her research on lefties. You need any more reasons? We'll divide the labor. Your job is to rent a car for the afternoon and go see all the doctors in Fontainebleau."

The young lieutenant's eyes widened.

"What's that, a joke?"

"Do I look like I'm joking? You're looking for a patient who's male, young, solidly built, who has balance problems, and who sometimes sees the world upside down. Maybe he wouldn't have put it quite that way, maybe he just complained about vision problems, or violent headaches. In short, something that could be related to hallucinations or mental disturbance."

"But this is crazy! Why?"

"Grégory Carnot, the last name on the list of violent offenders, had all those symptoms. He sometimes saw the world upside down. It never lasted very long, but it was intense enough for him to lose his balance. And it was also linked to his outbursts of violence."

Levallois knit his brow.

"Why didn't you say anything about this at the briefings?"

"Because it wasn't important."

"Not important? Are you nuts?"

"Don't take it the wrong way."

Levallois kept silent for a moment, frustrated.

"Fine, whatever. And what are you going to do in Fontainebleau while I go chasing after every quack in town? Have a beer?"

"How uncharitable you are! I'm going back into the killer's childhood, hoping he lives and has always lived in Fontainebleau. I'm looking for left-handers, like Eva Louts, except *I'll* be making the rounds of nursery schools."

28

Lucie felt a pang as she pulled into the parking lot of Colombe Hospital, in the Reims medical center. Maternity hospitals all look the same. Despite the apparent austerity of those long concrete vessels with their rows of identical windows, they breathed life; people went in as husband and wife and came out as dad and mom, prouder, happier, more responsible. A fruit of nature was created from the blend of their chromosomes, and the incredible alchemy of birth transformed them forever.

Lucie thought of her own experience. Nine years already . . . Most of her memories of that time had faded but certainly not anything connected with the birth of the twins. Lucie recalled her mother's panic when her water had broken in the dead of night. The race to the hospital, the beep of the monitors in the minutes just before she gave birth. She could see her mother's face hovering near, their hands seeking each other, in agony, while the doctors and nurses busied themselves around her swollen belly . . . Clara had come out first. Lucie could still hear her shrill little scream as her lungs first inflated. She remembered having sobbed out every tear in her body when the midwife placed the two identical, gluey infants, with their greenish skin, on either side of her chest. A nurse had immediately come over with two tiny name bracelets. She had asked Lucie which one was Clara. The young woman had tipped her head toward the child on the left, the first one out of her womb.

And today, she was dead, killed by a monster born in this very hospital. Her sister Juliette had almost suffered the same fate.

That bastard had first seen daylight twenty-three years before.

Lucie slammed the car door shut, her head buzzing with questions. Why was she standing here, alone and far from home, in front of such a symbolic place, when on practically the same date the previous year she'd been walking into a morgue? Had an invisible evil transformed Carnot into a child-killer? Was he born with some sort of predisposition for murder?

Squeezing the envelope with the Terney crime scene photos, Lucie headed for reception and flashed her fake police ID, just long enough for the receptionist to register the tricolor motif.

"Lieutenant Courtois, Paris Homicide. I'd like to speak to the head of your obstetrics department."

This kind of introduction, a firm, authoritative voice making a specific request, sliced through hesitations and refusals. All people had to hear was the word "homicide" and they obediently picked up their phones. The receptionist spoke into hers for a few moments, then hung up with an anxious smile.

"Dr. Blotowski is expecting you in Obstetric Gynecology. His office is on the third floor, last door on the left. You'll see his name on it."

Lucie thanked her and took the stairs, slowly. In nine years, she had never again set foot in a maternity ward.

After walking down an endless corridor of half-open doors, she entered the office of the chief physician, a man of about thirty-five or forty. He had a shaved head and was wearing a small, neatly trimmed goatee of a handsome light gray that set off his blue eyes. He offered Lucie a chair, briefly introduced himself, and asked what he could do for her.

Lucie, as Amélie Courtois, had set the envelope with the photos on her knees. She rested her slightly trembling hands on her thighs and spoke in a moderately assured voice.

"First, I want to know if you knew Stéphane Terney. He was the head of the obstetrics department before you, from 1986 to 1990."

"I started here six years ago, after Dr. Philippe, who was Terney's successor. I know him only by reputation. Despite his controversial opinions and his rather rigid way of thinking, he contributed a lot to this hospital. His work on preeclampsia is highly regarded and serves as the basis for work being done even today throughout France. Is he involved in your investigation?"

"To some extent, yes. He's been murdered."

The doctor sat back in his chair, mouth agape.

"Oh, my! How did it happen?"

"I'll spare you the details. I came here because on January 4, 1987, a child named Grégory Carnot was born in this hospital under seal of anonymity. I know he was transferred to a public nursery in Reims, where he was adopted at the age of three months. My investigation requires that I remove the anonymity surrounding his birth, and the first thing I need to know is the name of his biological mother. I have to talk with her about the birth and her relations with Dr. Terney. Find out how well they knew each other. And also talk to her about her son."

The doctor looked uncomfortable. He began fiddling with a letter opener that he'd taken from a pocket of his white coat.

"Sealed births are highly protected under French law. Normally speaking, only the child himself, once he reaches maturity, can authorize lifting the seal. He is then given access to a confidential file left by his mother, in which she has provided her identity and whatever information she wished to impart, such as her family history, information about the father, or her reasons for putting the child up for adoption. Those files might just as easily be empty, if the mother doesn't wish to be found—which, frankly, is often the case. Still, I hope you can understand that I can't just hand over a sealed file without a court order."

Lucie held the doctor's gaze, nodding at each of his statements.

"We've filed the request, and I can assure you you'll have your court order in a couple of days. But you know how slowly the wheels of justice can turn, Doctor, and as cops in the field, we can't always wait. Lives are at stake, and people are suffering. You know what that's like."

"I'd like to help you, but . . ."

The photos Lucie placed on the desk cut him off midsentence.

"You wanted to know what happened to Terney. Here's your answer."

The man looked at the photos in horror.

"How could anyone do such a thing?"

"Sick people exist everywhere. His killer tortured him for hours, with cigarette burns and knives. As for Grégory Carnot, the poor infant born under seal, he ripped open his own throat in a prison cell last week, with his bare hands. And do you know why he went to prison?"

"No."

"He killed an eight-year-old girl, stabbing her sixteen times, then burned her body beyond recognition. That little girl was my child."

The obstetrician lowered his eyes and slowly put the photos back down. Lucie had bombarded him with sordid details, and for the first time he appeared disarmed. He threw a sidelong glance at the photo of his own son, next to his computer.

"I . . . I'm so terribly sorry."

"Don't be. Just help me. The only person who was liable to request that sealed file died on the floor of a jail cell. The sickest kind of killer is lurking in our streets. We're after him, Doctor, we're after him, and we can't afford to wait for some lousy paperwork. So I'm asking you once again to show me that file."

Blotowski hesitated for a few more seconds, then picked up the phone.

"I'm coming down to the archives," he said in a dry voice.

He hung up, put the letter opener back in his breast pocket, and stood up.

"Come with me. Everything's stored in the basement."

With a sigh of relief, Lucie picked up her photos and followed him out. Thanks to a special key that Blotowski inserted in the control panel, the elevator let them out in the basement, where they followed a narrow, neon-lit corridor. Fat pipes ran along the black walls. The ventilation system huffed noisily, as if in a ship's boiler room.

Before them spread a veritable labyrinth. People rushed in all directions; lab coats brushed against each other in the dim light.

They turned a corner, then another. With a different key, Blotowski opened a metal door, which led to the Maternity archives. Like a fish in water, the doctor went straight to the correct row, near the back of the storage area. Large adhesive labels applied to the shelves indicated years and months.

"Here we are, January 1987. So let's see . . . letter C."

He ran a finger over the layers of document binders until it stopped at one of them.

"Brachet to Debien. Okay . . . We should be able to find what we need in here. Admissions records, gynecological exams, birth certificate, and notes on the delivery."

He took down the binder that contained a number of files, turned several heavy divider sheets, then came to the name he was looking for.

"Here we are. Grégory Arthur Tanael Carnot. Born January 4, 1987."

He opened the metal rings and pulled out a fat plastic pouch. Lucie stared at those three given names written on the white label: Grégory Arthur Tanael . . . Why those three, specifically? Had he been named after his father and grandfather? Despite the anonymity, his mother might have used those names to preserve small traces of Carnot's past, his ancestry. Even if she had then abandoned him, for reasons Lucie wanted to know.

Inside the pouch was the sealed folder. The doctor put it aside and picked up the medical files. The neon lights lit the old paper in cold, bluish tones.

The obstetrician read aloud, with evident reluctance.

"So . . . Mother was admitted to Obstetrics on December 29, 1986. It was indeed Dr. Terney who took charge of her care as soon as she arrived in the hospital. In fact, from what I can tell, he was also her gynecologist and had been seeing her since the fifth month of pregnancy. Moreover . . ."

He fished through the transparent pouch.

"Now that's odd . . . I can't find the records of her gynecological exams—the sonograms and checkups. They should have been here with the rest."

"Are you sure?"

He leafed through the papers again to make sure he hadn't missed anything.

"No. Nothing here. It could be an oversight. Maybe somebody consulted the files and forgot to put them back. Unfortunately, it's not uncommon for old papers like these to get lost in the administrative maze."

"Right, it's not uncommon. Let's leave it at that."

Lucie felt more and more that she was on the right track. Something strange and mysterious was hidden in Stéphane Terney's past. She nodded at the pouch the doctor was holding.

"You've got the woman's admission forms, so you must have her name right there without having to open the sealed file."

He turned the document toward Lucie. In the spaces for the person's name, it said simply "Mme. X."

"It's like that throughout. Preservation of anonymity at the mother's request."

Lucie's jaws tightened. Fortunately there was still the sealed file. A number of questions flew to her lips.

"Why was she admitted to Obstetrics a whole week before giving birth? Did she have particular problems?"

Blotowski leafed through the pages. Everything was written down: intravenous drips, medicines administered, blood tests, heart rate, even the name of the nurse assigned to her room. In that regard, there was complete transparency; Stéphane Terney had been aboveboard.

"From what I read here, Terney diagnosed the patient with preeclampsia. She had to remain under observation. Hence the hospital."

Preeclampsia . . . Stéphane Terney's specialty.

"What exactly *is* preeclampsia?"

"It's the translation of a vascular insufficiency in the fetoplacental unit. A placenta that is very poor in blood vessels, if you like, which generally causes the infant to be born underweight. It can cause numerous problems for the mother, especially arterial hypertension and proteinuria—in other words too much protein being eliminated in the urine. Most of the time, in the first trimester of pregnancy, the future mother complains of severe headaches and a buzzing in her ears. There are a lot of theories, but not much more: we know how to prevent it today, but we still don't know what causes it. Dr. Terney did a lot of work in this domain, especially on the genes responsible for preeclampsia and placental vascularization deficiency. Is that a bit clearer?"

"Yes, a bit."

The obstetrician turned the pages.

"Very well. So . . . Mother's medical history, not much to report. Other than that she was lactose intolerant."

"Like her son."

"That makes sense. It's hereditary."

The rustle of pages made a particular sound here—somehow amplified, crystalline.

"The birth took place at two thirty-four a.m., in room three. Terney, a midwife, an anesthesiologist, and the nurse treating the patient were present in the delivery room. The doctor noted that Mme. X began having convulsions, her heart rate rapidly increased. Oh, oh my . . ."

"What?"

He raised his eyes to Lucie.

"It says here that Grégory Carnot's mother died on the delivery table of a catastrophic hemorrhage. To put it plainly, she bled to death."

Lucie was unable to hide her disappointment: could this be where her trail ended, in the depths of these archives?

"And the baby?"

"Grégory Arthur Tanael Carnot . . . delivered by C-section. Nine pounds fifteen ounces and . . . twenty-one and three-quarter inches? That's . . . highly unusual. Most babies whose mothers suffer from preeclampsia are born small and frail, precisely because of the lack of blood vessels in the placenta. Still, this kind of situation does occur."

"Often?"

"No, on the contrary. But we still don't know entirely how preeclampsia works, especially with regard to the interactions between mother and fetus. Genetic predisposition can also play a part. It's very complicated."

Already different from the others at birth, thought Lucie. He kills his mother, and doesn't fit the preeclampsia statistics . . .

The physician's index finger ran down the sheet.

"Apparently, no particular problems with the baby at delivery. The remarks here are standard for most births."

The doctor pulled out the neonatal file, giving it a quick once-over.

"Growth, checkups . . . everything's normal. That said, Dr. Terney did order an unusually high number of blood tests for the infant, from what I can tell."

"Does it say why?"

He shook his head.

"Nothing here. The infant remained in Neonatal for nine days before being sent to the nursery. That's typical as well."

Back into the transparent pouch, from which he took out copies of the birth and death certificates. It made Lucie feel odd to see the two documents side by side. Mother and son, one dying as the other is born.

"Birth certificate drawn up right after delivery. Mother's and father's names left blank, which is common for children born under seal. Just so you know, when the child is adopted, the public records office, which keeps its own copy of the birth record, fills in the blanks with the names of the adoptive parents. But here in the archives, we always keep the original, the one the head physician establishes at delivery."

He looked at the next sheet.

"Death certificate, filled out by Terney as chief physician: 'Death due to preeclampsia and massive internal hemorrhage.' Date, time, persons present. It all seems in order."

"That's it? A woman dies in the hospital and there's no autopsy, no inquest?"

"Not if the family didn't request one. Which seems to be the case here, since I'm not finding any other papers. You know, when there's a death like this, there's always a debriefing with the chief physician, a medical inquest—and sometimes an autopsy—but only if the cause of death is unexplained. We also look through the prior records to try to understand what happened. Please believe that *any* death in the hospital, and especially during childbirth, is taken extremely seriously."

Lucie crossed her arms, chilled by these revelations. She had the sense that something essential was missing. The human rapport between Terney and his patient, the reasons why the child was abandoned . . .

The more she thought about it, the more unsettled she felt. She knew the answers were just out of reach, without her being able to grasp them. As her eyes wandered over the folder, she suddenly fixed upon Carnot's three given names, written on the large label in front.

"Grégory Arthur Tanael Carnot. My god . . ."

A long silence, during which Lucie froze completely. The doctor noticed her consternation.

"What's wrong?"

Lucie could barely recover her voice. Her entire body was on fire.

"That . . . that name. Who gave it to him?"

"I assume it was the mother—she must have told them the names she wanted to give the child before the delivery. After the birth, the names would have been entered on the certificate by the obstetrician or the midwife. If she hadn't given any names, those spaces would have remained empty, and the public records officer would have chosen three first names, the third of which would have acted as the child's family name. 'Carnot' isn't a first name, so it must have been the mother who provided it . . . Why do you ask?"

Lucie snatched up the file and pointed her finger at each first letter of the names of her daughter's killer.

"His initials form G A T C. The bases of the DNA molecule."

The doctor frowned.

"That's true. But how could you have noticed that?"

"Let's just say . . . I've been dealing with that molecule quite a bit lately."

Blotowski, raising an eyebrow, took the small, sealed brown envelope from the pouch.

"Curious coincidence, in any case."

"It's no coincidence. And it wasn't the mother who chose those names. It was Terney."

Blotowski didn't answer, absorbed in his thoughts. What this woman was telling him was hard to swallow. Lucie nodded at the sealed envelope in his hand.

"Now will you open it?"

The specialist undid the seal with his letter opener. Lucie thought to herself that this secrecy business was nominal at best: any staff member with the right key could come in here and pop the seals to discover the mother's name.

Blotowski opened the envelope and showed it to Lucie.

"Empty. The mother preferred to keep her identity secret. I'm sorry."

Lucie remained frozen. She couldn't just go away on such a note of failure. Grégory Carnot was born here. People named in these files had taken care of him, fed him, washed him from the time of his first wail. They had to know things about that child. Just as the doctor was putting the clear plastic pouch back into the binder, she stopped his arm.

"Wait a minute."

She snatched up the admitting papers, glanced over them rapidly, then stabbed her finger at the name of the nurse who was present at the birth. The woman must have looked after the mother for the entire time she was in Obstetrics. It was reasonable to think the two women would have talked, shared confidences. The nurse might well know something about the relations between Terney and Carnot's mother.

"Pierrette Solène. Does she still work here?"

"I've never heard of her."

The physician put the binder away and smiled.

"Just so your visit isn't a total loss, I'll check the personnel files and give you her address—you never know, maybe she still lives there. Would that do? And afterward, perhaps you might let me take you for a cup of coffee, Miss Courtois?"

29

It was well past one o'clock when Lucie knocked on the door of Pierrette Solène's home in the suburbs. Apart from the coffee she'd had at the maternity hospital with Blotowski, who had begun flirting with her openly, she hadn't eaten since leaving Paris. After this visit, she would absolutely have to find a place for lunch. She had to recharge her batteries if she didn't want to fall asleep at the wheel and wind up in a ditch. She'd covered more miles in the past two days than she usually did in a year.

The nurse lived in one of those small, low-cost cinderblock bungalows with chalk-white façades on the outskirts of town. According to the records, she would have been sixty-eight years old now, and had left Colombe Hospital eight years earlier for a retirement that she no doubt well deserved.

Pierrette Solène opened her door a crack, blocking the space with her body. She was dressed simply in a long flowered dress and black pumps from another age. Wrinkles furrowed her forehead and cheeks like grid lines, tracing complex geometric patterns. She was wearing large glasses with brown frames, the lenses slightly enlarging her pupils, the stems attached to a cord.

"Sorry, whatever it is you're selling, I'm not interested."

"I'm not selling anything. I'm with the police."

Lucie showed her card a bit longer this time. Suspicious, Pierrette Solène examined it closely, eyes slightly squinting. Lucie did her best to reassure her:

"Nothing to be afraid of, you're not in trouble. My investigation has led me to Colombe Hospital. According to the personnel records, you worked there for over thirty years. I'm trying to reconstruct something in the past, and I'd like to ask you a few questions about one episode in particular."

208

Pierrette Solène glanced toward the sidewalk and Lucie's 206 parked at the edge of the street.

"Where's your partner? On television, the police always work in pairs. Why are you here on your own?"

Lucie gave her a polite smile.

"My partner is off questioning other parties at the hospital. You shouldn't believe everything you see on TV. Being a cop in real life is a different thing altogether."

After hesitating a moment longer, the sexagenarian invited the other woman in. Five minutes later, Lucie found herself on a sofa topped with a thick wool coverlet, a cup of black, sweet coffee in her hands. A European shorthair slinked affectionately between her calves. Pierrette's face lit up when Lucie asked about Stéphane Terney.

"I worked under him for the four years he practiced at Colombe. He was a good doctor, a dedicated man. He always took on too much."

"How do you mean?"

"He had a finger in everything: obstetrics, gynecology, immunology. Anything having to do with procreation fascinated him. He never punched a clock but spent all his time at Colombe. At work, he kept his staff on a tight leash. He didn't like people taking vacations. All he cared about was work, work, work."

"Did he often handle deliveries himself?"

"Yes. Despite his gruff exterior, he loved bringing babies into the world. In any case, he came into the operating rooms at least once a day, to cut the umbilical cords and talk to the mothers he'd treated as a gynecologist. It didn't matter what time it was. I'd never seen a department head like him. He pushed us pretty hard, but overall we liked him."

Lucie thought of her online research. Terney the medical orderly discovering the baby lying on the ground, still attached to its mother by the umbilical cord. Algeria and its traumas had never really left him. Bringing her coffee to her lips, Pierrette gave Lucie a sad look, as if the reason for the visit had suddenly dawned on her.

"Has something happened to Dr. Terney?"

Lucie gave her the terrible news and let her absorb the shock. Behind her thick lenses, Pierrette stared at the floor with empty eyes. Memories of the hospital must have been flooding in, good and bad, which would now take on a whole new significance because of this death, and would be shut away in a precious box. Lucie seized the opportunity:

"Tell me about the night of January 4, 1987, when Dr. Terney helped deliver a baby boy that he named Grégory Carnot. You were on call that night, in room three of the maternity ward. The mother died on the delivery table, from massive internal bleeding caused by preeclampsia. Do you remember?"

The nurse's face seemed to close in on itself and freeze. Then her upper lip began trembling, and the old woman passed her hand over her mouth in astonishment. She set down her cup, which clinked against the porcelain saucer. Lucie squeezed her fists together: twenty years later, Pierrette Solène still bore the scars from that night. The former nurse abruptly stood up and said, "That's all too far in the past. I'm sorry, but I don't remember."

Lucie stood up as well and stood only inches from her.

"There's no way you've forgotten. What are you afraid of?"

Pierrette hesitated for a few moments.

"Can you promise I won't be in any trouble?"

"I guarantee it."

A pause. The nurse thought it over. Lucie knew she must have been carrying a heavy secret, one that Terney might have forced her to keep all these years. Now that he was dead and she'd left the hospital, the locks might finally loosen.

"You spent time with Carnot's mother during her hospital stay. You brought her her meals, cared for her before the delivery. Do you remember her name? It's very important."

"Of course I remember. It was Amanda Potier."

Lucie felt a great wave of relief at finally being able to put a name to that blank face, to that woman who had perished in childbirth in horrible pain. She didn't ask for a paper and pencil to write it down, not wanting to alarm the other woman and interrupt the flow. It all had to remain informal, spontaneous. But she was memorizing every word.

The nurse continued:

"She was very young, twenty or twenty-one at most. A beautiful woman, with long black hair and dark eyes."

"Why did she want to give birth anonymously?"

"She decided she didn't want the child, and it was too late to abort . . . Her louse of a boyfriend had abandoned her a few weeks earlier. She felt incapable of raising a child all alone, at her age."

Lucie clenched her fists, reminded, despite herself, of her own story. But she had to put that aside for now.

"Tell me what you remember, whatever comes to mind. Take your time."

Pierrette kept her eyes closed for a long while, then opened them again.

"Amanda Potier was an artist, a painter, but she was just getting started and couldn't make a living off it. She had a small apartment on the outskirts of Reims, just a few miles from here. She and Dr. Terney knew each other even before her admission; he'd bought a few of her paintings at a show to give her support, encouragement. She seemed to be very fond of him. He even commissioned some paintings from her, having to do with DNA and birth, which he wanted to decorate his house with. She told me privately that he had weird tastes, but he was paying her well."

Lucie recalled the painting she'd briefly seen hanging in Terney's library and in the crime scene photos. That vile placenta, and the signature "Amanda P." in the corner.

"Amanda told me he sometimes took her to lunch, where they mainly talked about art. Then one day their conversation turned toward her pregnancy. The doctor convinced her to leave her regular ob-gyn and see him instead. He followed her care for the last four months of her pregnancy."

Lucie tried to think even as she was listening. It sounded as if Terney had been eager to get close to Amanda, and to her baby. Had Terney intentionally made contact with the expectant mother? Was he keeping an eye on her, even as she took him for a friend? Had he bought her paintings merely to gain her confidence? Lucie asked the question that leapt into her mind.

"Do you know why the doctor came to Reims in 1986? Why this hospital? Terney had an excellent job in Paris; he directed huge research projects and traveled widely. Why would he cloister himself away in the provinces?"

Pierrette shrugged shyly.

"I think he just seized an opportunity. Dr. Grayet, his predecessor, was three years away from retirement. He resigned when Dr. Terney applied for the job."

Lucie's heart jumped.

"Resigned? Three years before retirement? Had he been planning that?"

The nurse shook her head with lips pressed tight.

"Grayet had never said a word about it, and we would never have believed it. But that's how it was . . . He wanted to enjoy life a bit more, I think. He left the hospital quietly, without any big fanfare."

"What was the doctor's name—his first name, I mean?"

"Robert. But you won't be able to question him. He died from Alzheimer's five years ago. I went to his funeral. It was sad that he ended up like that."

Lucie stored away the main information. Could Terney have forced his predecessor to leave so he could take his place, and thereby get to know Amanda Potier and become her doctor? She felt almost lightheaded. It seemed completely unreal. And yet the dates matched perfectly. Terney left Paris in 1986 and moved to Reims precisely when Amanda was expecting. He took charge of her prenatal care, overseeing her delivery in early January 1987. According to her research, Terney had divorced a few weeks before leaving Paris. Had something precipitated the breakup? Had his first wife found out something related to Amanda Potier or Robert Grayet?

Lucie put these questions aside for the moment and continued:

"Didn't Amanda Potier have any family? Didn't anyone visit her in the hospital?"

"Yes, of course. Her parents lived in Villejuif and were very supportive. Her mother was a beautiful woman, still young, who looked a lot like her. A prospective grandmother at little more than forty . . ."

The nurse ran her finger around the rim of her cup. These memories were obviously painful, but Lucie didn't let up.

"During her hospitalization, how did the doctor behave toward her?"

"He was there constantly, staying very close to his patient. Day and night. He even pitched in with our nursing duties. I remember the tests he had her take, the blood samples. Amanda was extremely tired, and her belly was enormous. I remember she ate constantly. Fruits, biscuits, whatever she could get her hands on."

"Were she and the doctor close?"

The woman clenched her jaws.

"Not close enough for him to shed a tear over her death, in any case."

Lucie pondered this, increasingly disturbed. She was certain now that Grégory Carnot had never been normal. Something about him had fascinated the doctor. Something that might even have pushed Terney to get a divorce, change cities, and arrange his life around the child.

"Tell me about the delivery."

Pierrette Solène swallowed hard.

"The night of January 4, Amanda's readouts started going crazy. Her blood pressure shot up, her heart was racing. She was still a week before term, but we had to get the baby out no matter what. The doctor immediately called in the anesthesiologist and a midwife and had her brought to the delivery room."

Her voice was now trembling.

"From that point on, everything happened very fast, and went from bad to worse. The patient went into convulsions and she started hemorrhaging. We couldn't stabilize her. The doctor performed a cesarean. It was . . . horrible. She soon lost several pints of blood. It was as if her body was emptying itself of energy. We couldn't understand what was happening."

Lucie felt her hair stand on end.

"Amanda Potier wasn't even conscious for the birth of her son. In my thirty years on the job, I had only seen three mothers die in childbirth. Each time it was a deeply traumatic, inhuman experience that I wouldn't wish on anyone."

Lucie imagined the atmosphere in that delivery room. Blood everywhere, the flat line of the electroencephalogram, the sunken faces. And the horrendous feeling of failure.

"And what about the baby?"

Pierrette made a grimace of disgust.

"*He* was in great shape, while his mother was bleeding out. A nice fat baby, much higher than normal weight, in fact. Extremely rare for a case of preeclampsia."

She spoke with great bitterness, tinged with revulsion.

"Did you ever find out what happened with the infant?" asked Lucie.

"No. He was sent to Neonatal, and that wasn't my ward. I never knew what became of him, and to tell the truth, I didn't really want to know. His mother had died before my eyes, while he seemed just fine. And with what you're telling me today, it makes me feel even worse . . ."

Pierrette ran her hands over her face. She seemed to hesitate, sighed, then finally said:

"That night, I saw something, Miss. Something I've never told anyone. Something that seemed to contradict the doctor's diagnosis of preeclampsia."

Lucie leaned forward. She felt as if she were at the edge of the abyss, as did the nurse, who continued slowly:

"It had to do with the vascularization of the placenta."

The placenta . . . Lucie thought once again of the painting in Terney's library. The nurse struggled to let out the words that had probably never emerged from her lips.

"You know, preeclampsia causes the placenta to be very, very poor in blood vessels. This is always the case, even if the child is of normal size. When this child was removed by cesarean, the doctor quickly suctioned out the placenta that had remained in the womb. The midwife and anesthesiologist didn't see anything, since one was busy with the baby and the other trying to stabilize the patient. But *I* saw it."

A pause. Lucie was all focus.

"What exactly did you see?"

"That placenta. It was like . . . like a spider's cocoon, it had so many blood vessels on the surface. To be perfectly honest, in all my career I'd never seen such a well-irrigated placenta. That might be why the baby was so big and round—he had everything he needed to develop normally."

Lucie bolted out of her chair, nerves on fire.

"Hold on a second . . ."

She ran to her car and came back with the envelope containing the crime scene photos. She pulled out the one showing the placenta painting and handed it to the nurse.

"Is this what Amanda Potier's placenta looked like?"

Pierrette nodded.

"Precisely. It was as vascularized as that. But . . . where did this come from?"

"From the doctor's house. He asked Amanda to paint it for him. Which means the doctor knew about the ultra-irrigated placenta."

The nurse handed the photo back to Lucie.

"The whole thing is so strange. Could he have known from the ultrasounds?"

"I think so, yes."

There was a pause, both of them trying to understand. Lucie also pointed to the painting of the phoenix, just in case, but the nurse had no idea what it could mean.

Pierrette continued her tale:

"You might not believe me, but when . . . when the doctor saw his patient's placenta after the delivery, I saw his eyes shine. As if in . . . fascination. It was very quick, not even a second, but that was the feeling I got."

She rubbed her forearms.

"Look, I'm telling you the truth, I've got goose bumps. When he saw I'd noticed, he gave me the coldest look I've ever received in my life. As he suctioned, he stared at me without saying a word. And I understood that I had to keep quiet about this . . . And then a minute later, the mother was dead."

Tonelessly, Pierrette continued her story to the end.

"There was a debriefing several hours after the delivery, with the head of the hospital, Dr. Terney, the anesthesiologist, and the midwife. They drew up a report. Officially, Amanda Potier died of preeclampsia. Terney had all the figures, the test results, the proofs of proteinuria, high blood pressure, even the statistics of how many preeclampsia cases resulted in normal-weight births. The hospital was off the hook. Her parents never wanted to bring suit."

"And what about you—you never mentioned the placenta?"

Pierrette shook her head, like a child trying to deny her guilt.

"What would that have changed? It was my word against the doctor's. The placenta had been destroyed. And besides, the mother was dead and there hadn't been any medical malpractice. She had bled out without our being able to stop it. I didn't want to complicate matters or jeopardize my career."

She sighed, looking deflated.

"You want to know what I think, twenty-three years later? The illness that killed Amanda Potier looked like preeclampsia, and it could be diagnosed that way because of certain symptoms, but that's not what it was. And with what you've told me today, I'm convinced that the doctor knew it all along. That horrible painting proves it."

She got up from her armchair, using her hands as support.

"And now, please excuse me, but I don't think there's any more I can tell you. It's all in the past. It's too late to revive those old ghosts. The doctor is dead, may his soul rest in peace . . ."

"It's never too late. On the contrary, it's in the past that all the answers are hidden."

Lucie stood up from the sofa in turn. Her trip hadn't been in vain, even if many questions remained unanswered. In any case, she was certain of one thing: slowly but surely, the obstetrician had woven a canvas that led to the birth of a monster.

Even if she was moving forward in a complete haze, Lucie knew that her search for the truth was growing sharper all the time. Amanda Potier, Stéphane Terney, and Robert Grayet, his predecessor at Colombe, were dead, taking their secrets with them. For Lucie, there was only one remaining solution: she had to go see Stéphane Terney's first ex-wife, the one he'd divorced just before his sudden move to Reims.

One of the traces of the past that just might contain a particle of the truth.

30

Sharko had a clear, and slightly unorthodox, idea in mind: as Eva Louts had done on a larger scale, he was going to make a list of left-handed former pupils in Fontainebleau.

First, he stopped in at City Hall to get the addresses of the local nursery schools: seven in all. Then, taking a deep breath, he headed off to the first address, the Lampain School, located in the east of the city. Lost in his thoughts, he drove through the different neighborhoods without paying much attention to his surroundings. He was thinking of his tortuous investigation and of those horrible murders, but mostly he was thinking of Lucie Henebelle. Had she looked at the photos he'd left for her near the computer? Was she still in his apartment or had she gone home? He couldn't keep from calling her, just to find out.

She answered on the third ring. From the roar in his earpiece, Sharko realized she, too, was in a car. The letdown was immediate.

"It's Franck . . . You're driving. Maybe I should call you back later."

"It's fine—I've put you on speaker."

She said nothing further. Why wasn't she talking? Why didn't she ask him how things were progressing?

"Are you on the way to Lille?"

Lucie hesitated, unprepared for his call. Should she tell him the truth and risk having him prevent her from seeing this to the end? Instead, she chose to go on the attack so she could dig a bit deeper, undisturbed.

"Yes. I saw your note on the kitchen table, especially the part about my clothes in the bedroom. Don't worry, they're gone—I've cleaned every trace of me out of your apartment. Sorry about leaving the door unlocked, by the way, but I didn't have a key."

Sharko thought quickly, with a feeling of doubt. Something was off.

Could she so easily have given up, just because of a simple note on a table? She, the Lucie Henebelle he knew? He tried sounding her out:

"How come you left so late?"

"You should have woken me up this morning. It took me a while to remember where I was. What happened last night? I don't remember a thing."

"You were falling over from exhaustion. So I put you to bed on the couch, like . . . like last year. It's kind of strange, when you think about it, how things repeat themselves. I wouldn't have thought."

The spaces between their words seemed endless. Sharko felt embarrassed and awkward. He couldn't help asking:

"I did a bit of work last night and I left the computer on. Were you able to find out anything about Stéphane Terney?"

"What was the point? I got your message loud and clear: you're the investigator, you're the one with the resources. I'm nothing in all this."

Sharko's eyes welled up—and yet, even as his heart bled, he felt a bit relieved.

The GPS signaled that he had reached his destination.

"Well, I'll let you go. I'll call you sometime, if I ever get to the bottom of this case. Good-bye, Lucie."

"Wait, one last thing: the guy in pajamas . . ."

"He's got nothing to do with it. He's autistic. He and Terney used to spend time together, that's all. Wrong place at the wrong time."

He hung up sharply, gritting his teeth, without even giving her time to respond. He sat in his car for five minutes, trying to buck up his spirits.

Pushing his disappointment aside, he walked toward the school, a pretty little flower-decked building, with a large recess yard surrounded by a green fence. It radiated youth, innocence, the beginning of life. The front door was locked. Sharko felt feverish. Whenever he got too close to a school, the memory of his daughter Eloise assailed him. He again imagined her among the other children, playing with wooden blocks or running around with her friends.

With a sigh, he rang the intercom and introduced himself. The principal, Justine Brevard, received him in her office. A stout, genial-looking woman of around fifty, who must have inspired the children's trust. Obviously, she had heard about the double murder in the forest, like everyone else in town.

"It's horrible, what happened to those young people. But how can I help you?"

Sharko cleared his throat.

"Well, it's like this . . . We've been able to establish a fairly precise profile of the killer. We think he's between twenty and thirty years old, that he's tall, has a stocky build, lives in this city, and especially that he's left-handed. If I'm not mistaken, teachers normally compile aptitude reports on the pupils in their class, is that right?"

"That's correct. We note down coordination, verbal ability, class participation, and a number of other factors."

"Including hand dominance? Left- or right-handed?"

A spark flashed in the administrator's eyes.

"I see where you're heading with this. You think your killer attended our school when he was younger, is that it? And that our records might help you identify him?"

"Your school or some other in the city, yes. I'm simply looking for something that must be relatively uncommon in a class of twenty-odd children: boys who are bigger and stronger than the others, and who are also left-handed—that's the most important criterion. I'm interested in the mideighties through early nineties. Would you still have those records?"

She stood up.

"Fortunately, we do. Come with me . . ."

They headed toward a room filled with file cabinets, arranged by year. The director started with the drawer marked 1985 and pulled out various envelopes containing the children's administrative records. The files were even more detailed than he'd hoped. And in each was an identity photo of the child in question.

"We fill out these forms every trimester," Justine Brevard explained, "to evaluate the child's progress and his or her aptitude in class. See, here's a space for hand dominance. And room for comments about things like health problems, food restrictions, or allergies."

She wet her index finger and quickly leafed through the records. She pulled one out.

"I have a left-handed girl."

"You can put that one back. According to the DNA, we know our killer is a male."

She searched through some more until she got to the end.

"That's it for 1985. Nothing here, apart from that left-handed girl."

"That's fine—the fewer there are, the better."

"Let's try the next ones."

Sharko helped. Together, they gathered all the records for left-handed boys. Each time, there might be one, two, in rare cases three boys in a grade, which yielded about twenty records for the ten years in question.

Among those records, Sharko looked carefully at the faces, the body type, the height, using the class and identity photos. He came across blond and brown-haired boys, curly-haired boys, boys with glasses, shy or self-confident, of different sizes, planted in the midst of their classmates. Some, frail or small, didn't correspond to the image the inspector had of the killer, but could they be eliminated even so? Wasn't it possible that they could have sprouted up later in childhood? So many years between then and now. Facing this reality, the cop understood that the task would be harder than he'd thought. And besides, when he got down to it, he couldn't know for sure. The killer might well have lived in Fontainebleau for only a few years and grown up somewhere else. He wasn't at all sure his hunch would pan out. Nevertheless, he asked for a photocopy of all the records he had in hand, thanked the director, and left the establishment feeling a bit down.

The one positive point: it had only taken about a half hour.

Sitting in his car, Sharko tried to refine his selection, to favor certain profiles among all those left-handers. He chose the biggest, strongest boys. He refined it further: some of the children would now be thirty, which might be a bit old for going to dance clubs. Given this, he made another pile. But even then, he was still holding nine records. Kids of four or five, all smiling, but otherwise no different from one another. It was impossible to put one profile ahead of another. No demonic looks, no black flames in the eyes. Only innocence shone from these faces.

Discouraged though he was, he pushed on, telling himself that, at worst, Major Case in Versailles could take DNA samples of all these individuals, to compare with the traces left at the crime scene. In certain sensitive cases, they sometimes took mass samples after they'd narrowed it down to a rough grouping. It was expensive, but the truth was worth it.

He visited more schools. Despite outward differences, they all took similar care in storing records, a testament to the national education system. The hours passed; Sharko amassed his photocopied sheets, eliminated as many as he could, put them aside, without any really jumping out at him. He had hoped that a connection would occur in his head, an intuition that would immediately guide him to the right file. But nothing, absolutely nothing . . . These kids were too young, still had their childish faces: puppy fat and happy looks. How could he make out a killer from that? As Levallois had pointed out, our genetic fingerprints aren't displayed on our foreheads.

He stopped in a café for some strong coffee, just as a pick-me-up. After calling his partner, who hadn't made any progress either, he downed a sandwich and dozed off in the front seat of his car. Half an hour later, he woke up and got back on the road, pasty-mouthed.

The Victoire School, second-to-last of the seven. *Maybe a symbolic name*, Sharko thought to himself with a sigh. Intercom, director, introductions, explanation, archives. A circuit he was starting to know by heart, and that was wearing on his nerves.

Once more, the years passed by, the records piled up. Sharko was awestruck by such an even distribution of left-handers in nature: each time, the proportions remained roughly the same. Zero, one, or two lefties per class of twenty: it was so precise, as if nature itself had put these classes together. He remembered what the primatologist had said, the data in Louts's thesis, which predicted that in a few hundred or thousand years, there wouldn't be any more left-handers at all. Certain classes in the nursery schools already attested to that disappearance.

Once again, names, faces, physiognomies paraded by his eyes. As he was mechanically sifting through the records, putting the occasional ones for left-handed boys aside, he felt his heart turn over in his chest.

With trembling fingers, he picked up the record he'd just set aside.

It was from 1992. The boy, born in 1988, would be twenty-two today.

His name was Félix Lambert. Left-handed. Light brown hair, blue eyes, lightly tanned skin, and fairly big, even though some in the class photo were bigger. At first glance, nothing extraordinary. Sharko had already come across physiques like this in earlier records.

And if his gaze hadn't fallen on the space for additional comments, he would simply have put this record with the others, among the potentials.

But in the comments area, someone had written in capital letters: "No milk products. Lactose intolerant."

Sharko stared at the child's gaze, his toothy smile. He ran his finger over that angelic face.

The cop was almost certain he had, before him, the identity of the man who had killed the hiking couple. The same identity that Stéphane Terney had hidden in the pages of his book, mixed in among long, harmless sequences.

The inspector didn't bother continuing his search and told Levallois to stop his own right away. He thanked the director and ran out of the school building. Five minutes later, he was peeling through the city phone directory, at a corner post office that was about to close its doors. He found two Lamberts in Fontainebleau: Félix and Bernard. Same telephone number. Probably father and son . . .

He picked up his young partner in front of the car rental and sped off with the address before his eyes.

At the end of the road, a killer was waiting.

31

According to Information, Gaëlle Lecoupet, Stéphane Terney's first wife, lived in Gouvieux, a quiet town located near Chantilly. Lucie had lost a lot of time in traffic jams trying to leave Greater Reims, so it was getting on to the end of the afternoon when she skirted Chantilly, famous for its château, its racetrack, and its golf courses. After a few more miles, she parked in the graveled driveway of a large private house set back from the road, just behind a huge Audi and a Mercedes convertible.

A man with graying hair stopped trimming the rose bushes and came up to her. After Lucie showed him her fake ID and said she wanted to talk to Mme. Lecoupet about a case involving her first husband, he pointed Lucie toward the residence without a word. His lack of commentary suggested that neither he nor his wife had been notified of Terney's death, nor had the cops from number 36 yet delved this far into the past in their search for his killer.

The mistress of the house was standing in a large covered porch that was filled with climbing plants and about a dozen cats of various breeds and colors. The animals prowled around her legs, purring, while she poured milk and kibbles into a parade of saucers.

"Darling, it's the police for you," said the gray-haired man. "About Stéphane."

Gaëlle Lecoupet stopped dead and turned a surprised face to Lucie. She was a tall, slim woman, beautiful without makeup, wearing an old T-shirt and a pair of jeans that didn't quite match the status of the environs. Longish, well-cut gray hair fell onto her delicate shoulders. She set the cat food on a table, wiped her fingers on a towel, and came up to Lucie. Before shaking her hand, she shot her companion a look, asking him to leave them in private. The man, though clearly concerned, went back outside to his gardening. Gaëlle Lecoupet closed a glass door, shutting off the porch, then turned to Lucie:

"Is my ex-husband in some kind of trouble?"

The cop announced his violent death, without softening the truth. She wanted to plunge the other woman into the nauseating atmosphere of the investigation, shock her into cooperating.

Success. Gaëlle Lecoupet let herself fall into a chair in the living room, agitated, and brought a hand to her face.

"My god! Murdered . . . It feels so strange to hear something like that."

Lucie remained standing, sizing her up. Without mincing words, she began questioning.

"Were the two of you still in touch?"

Gaëlle Lecoupet shook her head sadly and took a moment before answering.

"We hadn't seen each other since the divorce. Not a phone call, letter, nothing. Since then, I've only heard of him indirectly, through articles in the scientific press."

"We believe his murder is related to his past, especially around the year 1986, when he was practicing in Reims. Can you tell me why he suddenly moved there, when he had such a good situation in Paris?"

This time, the sexagenarian answered without a pause.

"Practicing medicine in the provinces was a good opportunity for him. Leaving Paris allowed him to be a full-time obstetrician, which was what he loved more than anything. He always preferred direct contact with his patients, the expectant mothers, the babies. In Paris, there was always some conference to attend, an article to write, or an interview to grant. He wanted to leave all that behind and go back to practicing medicine."

It was the kind of neat, ready-made answer that never satisfied Lucie. Gaëlle Lecoupet must have spoken those words many times before, whenever she'd had to justify what happened. She hadn't given any thought before answering. The ex-cop told herself she'd have to dig deeper, delve further into the couple's private life. So she asked some basic questions, nothing very challenging, simply to put her subject at ease and revive the past. She didn't learn much of anything new. Stéphane Terney was brilliant, ambitious, involved . . . He liked being talked about, gave a lot of interviews. Seemingly an ideal husband in some ways, completely devoted to medical science and biology, but whose job mattered more than his family. He didn't want children, "for fear of seeing them grow up in a world headed for collapse."

After listening to these banalities, Lucie opted for the direct approach.

"Now I'm going to ask you a slightly more personal question: was your divorce because of his departure for Reims?"

Lecoupet frowned.

"As you say, that's rather personal. I don't really see how that can help you in your investigation, Miss . . . ?"

"Lieutenant Amélie Courtois. Your ex-husband got himself killed, and we're trying to explore every trail, to understand the motives of his killer, who very definitely knew him. Any information we can gather, including on Terney's past, is highly important. So please answer my question."

The woman hesitated, then finally gave in.

"I had no desire to leave everything behind and start from scratch. I'd worked hard to establish my law practice, and I was starting to build a solid clientele, to become known in a profession where the competition was stiff. So I decided not to follow him there. I liked it in Paris, I had every reason to stay. It's as simple as that."

"Does the name Robert Grayet mean anything to you?"

"No, not really."

"And yet it should. He was the department head your ex-husband replaced in Reims. I imagine Terney must have mentioned him. Since his departure for the provinces was the cause of your divorce, right?"

"It's just that . . . it's all so far in the past. I really don't remember. My husband met a lot of people. It's possible I did hear the name, but I couldn't possibly tell you under what circumstances."

Lucie felt the blood rush to her temples, but she did her best to keep calm. She was convinced this woman was hiding the truth and that, despite everything, she was protecting a man she had once loved very deeply.

"Listen to me, Mme. Lecoupet. Your husband was tortured with cigarette burns and mutilated by a cold-blooded monster. I'm here because I'm certain his murder is related to what happened all those years ago, in the maternity hospital in Reims. I'll lay my cards on the table: a few weeks after he took over the post at Colombe, your ex-husband began treating a patient named Amanda Potier. She died in the delivery room on January 4, 1987, before his eyes."

Lucie let a few seconds pass, gauging the other's reaction. Clearly, she hadn't been aware. The ex-cop continued in a firm, assured tone:

"I don't believe the two of you separated over career conflicts or geographical distance. I'm certain your husband went to that hospital specifically so he could treat that patient and deliver her child, whatever the cost. Robert Grayet's resignation was certainly the result of a payoff. That money obviously came from somewhere. So now, I'd appreciate it if you'd can the stock phrases and tell me what really happened. Why was your ex-husband so set on going to Reims?"

The woman put a hand to her face with a long sigh. Then she stood up.

"I have to go to the attic for a moment. Please wait here."

Once alone, Lucie began pacing back and forth. She felt full of energy and, in a way, proud to be making such progress, alone, far from the beaten path. It proved she was still alive, capable of more than just answering phones in a dead-end call center.

Gaëlle Lecoupet reappeared with a small, transparent, slightly dusty bag in her hands. It contained an old videotape, black and without a label, which she put in the DVD/VHS player. She picked up a remote and walked over to the window looking out on the garden. She gave the double curtains a sharp tug and locked the entrance door.

"I don't want Léon to see these images . . . He doesn't even know this tape exists."

She came back toward Lucie and invited her to sit down. Her jaws were tight, her fingers gripping the remote.

"You're quite right. I didn't divorce Stéphane because of my practice or my clients. It had to do with . . . with what he was hiding from me."

There was a silence. Lucie tried to restart the conversation with the first thought that occurred.

"Would it have anything to do with his interest in eugenics?"

"No, no, nothing like that. I knew about Stéphane's beliefs before I married him. Besides, at the time I shared some of his ideas."

Gaëlle Lecoupet caught the look of surprise flashing across Lucie's face and explained further:

"You mustn't take eugenicists for monsters or Nazis. There's nothing

226

evil in pointing out that the welfare system, alcohol, drugs, and an aging population are counter to what nature intended, or that they prevent society from developing properly. It's just another way of making us face up to our responsibilities and confront the ecological holocaust we're bringing about."

She looked tenderly at her cats—some of which, rescued from the streets, were in sad shape—then turned back to Lucie.

"About two years before our divorce, Stéphane began having secret meetings. He claimed he was going to his bridge club, but by chance I found out he was lying. I thought he was having an affair, so I began to follow him—and I discovered that it wasn't a woman he was seeing, but two men. Two individuals he met several times a month in the stands of the Vincennes Racecourse, near where we were living. My husband wasn't a gambler, so what was he doing there with two strangers?"

"Do you know who they were?"

"I never found out. Stéphane never left a single trace in writing, no names, nothing. They were most likely scientists like him, or anthropologists."

"Specialists in other civilizations? What makes you say that?"

"When you see this tape, you'll understand."

"And, can you describe these men, what they looked like?"

She shook her head.

"No, it was too far away, too hazy. I always kept my distance, so I never saw them very clearly. Roughly, I'd say that one was dark-haired, average height, normal build, probably my husband's age, or thereabouts. And the other . . . I'm not sure. Maybe blond. I'm not sure what else to tell you about them. In twenty-five years, people change so much, and memories can fade so quickly. On the other hand, I can tell you about Stéphane, about how different he seemed whenever he came back from the racetrack. About how he started acting mysteriously, spending more and more time locked away in his study."

"You never asked him about those meetings, what he was up to?"

"No. I wanted to know what it was about. The meetings took place over the course of a year. Stéphane grew increasingly paranoid and forbade anyone from entering his study, even when he was there. And when he left it, he locked the door behind him. I didn't know where he kept the keys, since he took such care in hiding things. He never left anything to chance."

Her eyes grew darker and her pupils dilated. The doors of the past opened wide.

"But it often happens that when one doesn't want things to be seen, they become all the more visible. I knew Stéphane was hiding something in his study, something that mattered greatly to him, and I wanted to know what it was. One time when he was out for the day, I called a locksmith. He easily opened the study door, but in the back of the room was a tall metal cabinet, also locked shut, that Stéphane had bought a few months earlier."

"When he began meeting those men . . ."

"Yes, right around then. I had to know what was inside. So I asked the locksmith to do the same thing on one of the drawers. However, that lock was a lot harder to open, and the stupid locksmith, for all his supposed 'expertise,' ended up breaking it. The drawer came open, of course, but I knew Stéphane would immediately realize I'd been through his things. And there was no way to repair the damage. I felt terrible."

Sadly, she nodded to the VCR.

"In the drawer was a videotape. Surely one of the ones the men at the racetrack had given him."

"Are you saying there was more than one tape?"

"In the other drawers, yes, I'm certain of it. Unfortunately I was never able to watch them. This tape is a copy I quickly had made, that same day, which I hid before he got home. The original tape had a label on it with the words 'Phoenix number one,' which also suggests there were other cassettes."

At the mention of that odd name, Lucie suddenly recalled the painting of the firebird in Terney's library, to the left of the placenta. The phoenix . . . She knew she was putting her finger on something huge and unsuspected, but she couldn't yet grasp its essence.

Gaëlle Lecoupet's deep voice snapped her out of her thoughts.

"Now, if you'll allow me, we're going to watch this. I hope you have a strong stomach."

Excited by these new discoveries and the connections already forming in her head, Lucie gazed back at her.

"I'm a cop—we're born that way."

The woman pressed PLAY.

32

Facing the two viewers, a black screen. Then a time stamp at bottom: "6/9/1966," and various shades of gray. Leaves, trees. The violence of the jungle. The images parade by in black-and-white. A film of middling quality, probably shot with amateur equipment. Palms, vines, and ferns press in around the person holding the camera. Under his feet, on a slope, grasses creak. In front, a gap opens in the wall of vegetation, revealing huts farther below. Judging from the weak light, it must be evening, or perhaps daybreak. Unless the jungle is so dense that it keeps any light from filtering through.

The camera penetrates downward, advancing over black, humid ground: a square about 150 feet on each side, on which the vegetation tries to encroach. One can hear footsteps, the rustling of trees on either side. The lens focuses on the remains of a fire. Amid the ashes are small, charred bones, stones arranged in a circle, animal skulls.

Lucie briefly rubbed her chin, not taking her eyes off the screen.

"It looks like an abandoned native village."

"It is indeed a native village, but 'abandoned' isn't entirely accurate. You'll see in a minute."

What could she mean? The ex-cop felt her palms grow moist as the film progressed. Onscreen, cries perforate the silence, and the image freezes on the leafy canopy. Not an inch of sky at this point, only foliage, stretching endlessly. About three or four yards overhead, a colony of small monkeys scatters into the branches. The piercing screams are now constant. The camera zooms in to one of the primates, with a dark body and light-colored head. The animal spits in fury and disappears up a vine. Despite the vastness of the place, there reigns an atmosphere of enclosure and oppressiveness. A living prison with chlorophyll bars.

The cameraman finally loses interest in the inquisitive monkeys and moves farther forward, toward a hut. The image jostles to the rhythm of his slow, heavy footfalls. At a glance, the roofs seem to be made of woven palm fronds, and the walls of bamboo stalks tied together with vines. Archaic dwellings, each able to house four or five persons, and straight out of another age. At the entrance, one can suddenly make out a cloud of mosquitoes and flies, giving the impression of a sandstorm.

Lucie recoiled a bit on her sofa, feeling ill at ease. Her eyes prepared to meet horror at any moment.

The person holding the camera enters the hut slowly, like an intruder watching for the slightest movement. All light disappears, black spots flutter about. The sound track is heavy with buzzing. Unconsciously, Lucie scratched her neck.

Masses of insects. She feared the worst.

The beam of a lamp, probably attached under the lens, rips through the darkness.

And the horror appears.

In back, in the ray of light, six bodies, twisted like caterpillars one next to the other. Apparently an entire family of natives, completely naked. A mix of bloated faces, of desiccated eyes teeming with flies and larvae. Blood is leaking from their nostrils, their mouths, their anuses, as if they have exploded internally. Their bellies are swollen, probably with intestinal gas. The cameraman spares no detail, offering endless angles and close-ups. All the corpses have the black hair, callused feet, and leathery skin of ancestral tribes. But they are unrecognizable, consumed by anguish and death.

Lucie felt as if she'd forgotten to breathe. She could easily imagine the stench in that hut, the havoc the heat and humidity wreaked on the putrefying bodies. The frenzy of the fat, green flies said it all.

Suddenly, one of the bodies quivers. The dying figure opens large, dark, sick eyes toward the camera. Lucie jumped and couldn't keep from crying out. A hand reaches out, begging for help; slim, black fingers clutch the air before the arm falls heavily onto the ground like a dead trunk.

Alive . . . Some of them were still alive.

Lucie threw a quick glance at her neighbor, who was twisting a handkerchief in her hands. She remembered the violence of her nightmare: the charred infant suddenly opening its eyes, just like here. In a daze, she turned back to the film. The horror continued. The cameraman nudges the bodies lightly with the toe of his boot, checking to see if they are alive or dead. An inhuman action. Lucie didn't regain her breath until he had backed out of the slaughterhouse. Above, the monkeys are still there, oppressive, this time frozen on their branches. It is as if a heavy lid is covering the entire jungle. The respite is short-lived. The other huts contain the same spectacle: massacred families, mixed in with last survivors that the unseen cameraman has filmed and left to die like animals.

The film ends with a wide view of the decimated village: about a dozen huts, their inhabitants dead or dying, abandoned to the jungle shadows.

Blackness.

33

"Tell me about lactose intolerance. Who does it affect, in what proportions, and why?"

While driving, Sharko had called his friend Paul Chénaix, the medical examiner. He wanted information about the causes and frequency of this trait, to make sure he wasn't heading down the wrong path. He put the phone on speaker for Levallois's benefit.

The specialist answered after a moment's pause.

"This goes back to my old studies of medicine and biology, but it was unusual enough for me to remember. At the time, it really threw me. It has to do with natural selection and evolution—you know much about that?"

Sharko and Levallois shot each other a quick glance.

"Do we ever. My partner and I have been in it waist-deep. Go ahead."

"Fine. So the first thing to know is that lactose is a compound specific to mammals' milk. The individual difference between tolerating lactose or not is purely genetic. Lactose intolerance occurs in humans after the infant has been weaned from his mother, in other words from the moment they try to make him drink cow's milk."

"Nothing unusual so far."

"Hang on, this is where it gets weird. Lactose tolerance—and I did say 'tolerance'—is relatively recent in the evolutionary scale. It goes back only about five thousand years and only exists in human populations that domesticated cows in order to consume their milk. In humans, we find the gene that allows us to tolerate lactose in the same geographical regions where cows also have the gene that encourages high levels of milk production."

"So . . . nature acted both on cows and people, modifying their DNA by creating genes that hadn't existed before . . ."

As he said this, Sharko was thinking of Louts's thesis: violence in a population that inscribes the left-handed trait in their DNA. Culture influencing genetics.

"Right you are. Milk gene for the cows, milk tolerance gene for people. If I recall correctly, it's called coevolution, kind of like an arms race between cow and man: natural selection made it so man, originally a hunter-gatherer who lived exclusively on meat and fruits, could now drink the milk of the cows he domesticated. Because of this, it also made the cows better milk producers. And the more they produced, the more people drank . . . Hence the 'arms race' part. It's pretty amazing, don't you think?"

"So if I've understood you right, it means that people who are lactose intolerant today don't have this protective gene, because their ancestors didn't raise cows?"

"That's it in a nutshell. Intolerant individuals must have descended from ancestors who lived far from areas where milk cows were domesticated. The farther away the cows were, the less these people tolerated milk or developed the gene. When I was a student, the statistics were something like five percent lactose intolerants in Europe and something like ninety-nine percent in China, for example. The fact is, a good seventy percent of the world's population is still intolerant. Does that pretty much answer it?"

"That's terrific. Thanks, Paul."

The inspector hung up. Levallois pursued his own train of thought:

"So tell me if I've got this right: Grégory Carnot and Félix Lambert have in common not only their extreme violence and young age, but also deeper genetic factors. Some are obvious, like their size, build, and the fact that they're left-handed, and some more subtle, like being lactose intolerant."

"You've got it. I'm not sure what we're dealing with here, but clearly there's something to do with medicine and genetics behind all this."

The car turned off under the foliage. The army of trees closed in around the Peugeot and the sky disappeared. Rows of black trunks rose on either side, revealing only the occasional façades of handsome homes. In the fading light, the inspector navigated by GPS. A bit farther on, he turned onto a narrow road, drove a few more yards, and saw the Lambert house, set back near the tree line at the end of a large, wooded lawn: a superb two-story, nineteenth-century mansion, built from large blocks of white stone with a slate roof. Ivy devoured the façade, forming a second wall of vegetation. Two cars, a sports coupe and a classic Peugeot 207, stood in the driveway.

"They're here," the inspector whispered. "Lambert junior and senior. Not exactly destitute, are they?"

"Now's when we should be calling for backup."

"I'd like to get a look around the place first."

The inspector parked farther along, on the side of the road, and came back on foot to about ten yards from the entrance. Entry was protected by a locked gate, and the entire property—which spread over several acres—seemed to be encircled by a brick wall a good ten feet high.

"No way we can buzz the intercom," the inspector said in a low voice. "We'll have to use the element of surprise so that Lambert doesn't ambush us or make a run for it."

"So how are we going to get in, then?"

"You're kind of slow on the uptake, aren't you? Follow me."

"What? Wait, shouldn't we call in first? This isn't . . ."

Sharko began skirting the wall, heading into the dense woods.

". . . correct procedure," the young lieutenant muttered between his teeth.

After a brief hesitation, he ran after his partner, who was already disappearing into the vegetation. The trees crowded in around him, ferns attacked his ankles, branches twisted against the wall, as if nature were trying somehow to reassert its rights. After moving forward for several minutes, Sharko stood back a bit to get a better view, and managed to make out the top of the house's western façade.

"Looks like a windowless gable. The perfect spot to get onto the property without being seen."

Levallois stamped his foot.

"You're out of your mind! Shit, this guy massacred two kids. We don't know what sort of monster we'll come face-to-face with in there. And besides, we . . ."

Sharko walked up to him and looked him in the eye, cutting his diatribe short.

"You can either come with me or stay here feeling sorry for yourself. But in either case, shut your trap, got it?"

The inspector scanned the trees and found a branch low enough to hoist himself up, while keeping the soles of his feet flat against the wall. He wasn't cut out for this kind of acrobatics anymore, and he made his way up like a disjointed puppet. But it didn't matter how he went up or how much pain his tired limbs felt: all that counted were results. His jacket covered with greenish smears, his loafers half ruined, he landed in the thick grass with a heavy grunt, then ran to the wall of the house.

Levallois followed several yards behind. He flattened himself against the house next to Sharko, weapon in hand.

Sharko caught his breath. Not a movement around them, save for a few birds in the branches and the trembling leaves. The atmosphere was too calm, too quiet. It didn't bode well. Sharko rolled quickly onto the next wall, his partner right behind. Ivy brushed over their shoulders. Moving cautiously, he threw a quick glance into the first window he came to. A huge room, very high ceiling, enormous chandelier. No doubt the living room. Sharko heard a noise. He shut his eyes and listened. Bass notes droned through the walls.

"The TV," whispered Levallois. "Sounds like the volume's turned up full blast."

Hunched over, Sig Sauer in his fist, the inspector continued forward and headed toward another window, which looked into the kitchen. Levallois covered their backs, casting quick glances in every direction. He saw the inspector blanch and freeze in his tracks.

"What is it?"

Sharko was looking through the window. His eyes were squinting toward the tile floor.

Their hearts were racing.

"Shit! I don't believe it . . ."

Inside the house, trails of blood stretched from a chair and into another room. Someone had dragged a badly wounded body; given the shape of the trails, probably by the feet. Breaking out in a sudden sweat, Sharko rushed to the next window.

A dining room. A body lay on the floor, eyes staring at the ceiling. His face was black, covered in dried blood, as were his shredded clothes, no doubt the work of a large knife. The man's head was bald, with just a few gray hairs. He must have been about fifty.

"Looks like Lambert's father."

The two cops flattened against the wall, breathing hard. The situation had just changed. Levallois was white as a sheet.

"We've got to get out of here. We've got to call for backup."

His voice was broken by his anxious breathing. Sharko leaned toward his ear.

"They'll take ages to get here. There's a killer hiding in that house. We're going in. Can you do it?"

Levallois pressed into the ivy, head against the wall. He stared at the sky with round eyes. Then he nodded, lips pressed shut. Silently, Sharko crept toward the door. He pushed down the handle with his elbow. Locked. Then, without a second thought, he took off his jacket and rolled it around his hand and wrist.

"Get ready. We're going in. You cover the left, I'll take the right."

Standing at the window, he gave the glass a sharp rap with the butt of his gun, shattering it with a loud crash. As fast as he could, he cleared away the shards of glass with his protected arm and yanked on the latch inside. Less than ten seconds later, two armed silhouettes tumbled into the dining room. The sounds from the television made the walls shake: evidently a music channel. The house seemed to be holding its breath. The rooms, too large and lifeless, made them feel dizzy. Muscles taut, Levallois vanished briskly into the next room, then reappeared a few seconds later, shaking his head.

Suddenly the two partners froze, holding their breath. They heard the sound of footsteps just above their heads. A heavy movement, regular as a pendulum, that lasted no more than five seconds. Cautiously, they crossed the entrance foyer and moved toward the staircase, Sharko in front. Their feet were suddenly in water, which was oozing slowly from upstairs. Along the oblique walls and on the carpet was a string of bloody handprints.

"Left hands . . . Jesus, what happened here?"

As quietly as he could, the inspector climbed the stairs, keeping his gun aimed at the wall in front of him. His heart sent the blood pounding into his temples. In his alert muscles he could almost feel every vein pulsing, hear his body preparing to meet danger. A vile odor assailed him, a mix of shit, piss, and blood. Entire sections of carpet had been ripped up, and the wood of the steps was saturated with water. It was like advancing into a nightmare.

Upstairs, the cops turned right and went past the bathroom.

The faucet in the sink was turned on full, water flooding everywhere. Dirty clothes floated in the bathtub.

They kept moving. Every door was wide open except the one in back, its handle covered in blood. The bloody handprints led up to it, with no ambiguity. The monster was huddled in his lair.

Waiting.

Panting, Sharko took up position right next to the door, slightly crouched. Holding his breath, he tried to push down the handle with the butt of his gun, but it was locked.

The cop raised his gun against his cheek and breathed out. He could feel Levallois's warm breath on the nape of his neck.

"This is the police! Open up and let's talk."

Silence. The cops then made out little mewing sounds, like whimpers. They couldn't tell if they were made by a man or a woman. A victim that Lambert had kept alive?

They gave each other a horrified look. Sharko tried to reason one last time.

"We can help you. You just have to unlock the door and give yourself up quietly. Is there someone in there with you?"

No response.

Sharko waited a moment longer, nerves on full alert. The maniac was probably armed, but no doubt with a knife or he would already have fired. At that point, total silence had fallen over the house. The cop couldn't stand waiting any longer and decided to go in.

"You wait here. I wouldn't want to take a pregnant woman's husband from her."

"Go fuck yourself. I'm going in with you."

Sharko nodded. Without a sound, the two cops positioned themselves in front of the door. Levallois aimed his barrel at the lock and fired. An instant later, the inspector gave the door a mighty kick and rushed into the room, his Sig Sauer in front of him.

Immediately he pointed it at the colossus who was standing in a corner, huddled over, fists crushed into his chest. He was alone. His eyes were an intense, feverish yellow, lined by purplish shadows.

He had ripped the skin from his cheeks and was glaring directly at Sharko. Solidly planted on his spread legs, the inspector didn't flinch. Levallois aimed his gun as well.

"Don't you dare move!"

Félix Lambert was unarmed. He closed his eyes, biting his fingers until they bled while his face contorted in pain. His gums were raw, his lips dry as parchment. Madness scorched his features. He was baleful, unreal. Shaking violently, he suddenly snapped open his eyes and bolted for the window. Sharko barely had time to cry out as the murderer flew headfirst through the glass.

His body slammed against the ground thirty feet below, without so much as a whimper.

34

Gaëlle Lecoupet pressed Stop and ejected the tape with trembling hands.

"I hadn't seen it in years. It's still just as horrible . . ."

Lucie had a hard time coming back to reality. Had she seen that right? The film's documentary aspect horrified her as much as its content: the veracity of the images and garbled sound track seemed to deny the possibility of trickery or staging. It had actually happened, somewhere in the world, forty years earlier. Something violent had struck those natives in the heart of the jungle, and someone aware of the massacre had come to record it with his movie camera. Someone sadistic enough to film the survivors without lifting a finger to help.

The men at the racetrack . . . the authors of Phoenix no. 1.

Perhaps even the killer or killers Lucie was after.

She heaved a sigh. Since the beginning, this investigation had dredged up only shadows and mysteries, confronted her with her own past, forced her to dig into her deepest reserves of strength to keep going.

Getting hold of herself, Lucie turned to the other woman.

"That village was completely wiped out. It was like, I don't know . . . some kind of virus, in the middle of nowhere."

"Yes, probably so. A virus, as you say, or some kind of infection."

"What do you know about this film?"

Gaëlle Lecoupet pursed her lips and changed the subject.

"You can imagine what happened when Stéphane came home, the day I'd gone into his study. Discovering I'd searched through his cabinet. And me, demanding some sort of explanation about that vile film and those mysterious men that he'd been meeting for months. That day, it all burst apart between us. Stéphane disappeared for several days, taking all his secrets with him, his papers and tapes, without a word of explanation.

When he returned from wherever he'd been, it was only to announce that he was moving to Reims and that he wanted a divorce."

She gave a long sigh, clearly still upset even a quarter of a century later.

"It was as simple and sudden as that. He sacrificed our marriage for . . . for something that obsessed him. I never knew why he buried himself so suddenly in that hospital in Reims. I had imagined, as I told you earlier, that he wanted to get back to his roots. And maybe even get away from all that filth, those strange men who could film such abominations. Now all I have left of him is this old tape."

Lucie asked again:

"And . . . were you able to get anything from those images? Did you ever try to understand what it was about?"

"Yes, at first. I lent the tape to an anthropologist. He'd never seen anything like it. Given the state of the bodies and the little information he had, he couldn't tell me what tribe it was. Only the monkeys gave him a reliable indication."

She rewound the tape and froze the image on one of the primates in close-up.

"Those are white-headed capuchins, which you only find in the Amazon rain forest, near the border of Venezuela and Brazil."

Lucie suddenly felt as if an abyss had opened at her feet and that, all at once, the plain truth blazed before her eyes. The Amazon . . . where Eva Louts had traveled right after Mexico. And where she was planning to return. Could there still be any doubt? Lucie was convinced the student had left Manaus and headed into the jungle, that she had gone in search of that village and that tribe. It explained the withdrawal of cash, the weeklong trip: an expedition.

Gaëlle Lecoupet pursued her story:

"After that, I stopped searching. It hurt too much. Our sudden breakup and divorce had been painful enough. I wanted to leave all of it behind me and start over. The first thing I did was to put that horrible tape at the bottom of a trunk. I felt profound denial toward what I'd seen, I didn't want to believe it. Deep down, I didn't really want to understand what it was about."

She shook her head, eyes lowered. This woman, who had all the trappings of happiness, was still bleeding inside, beneath her elegant exterior.

"I don't know why I never got rid of it. Maybe I thought someday I'd try to learn the whole truth. But I never did. What good would it have done? It's all in the past. I'm happy with Léon, and that's what matters."

She placed the black plastic cassette in Lucie's hands.

"You've come all this way. You'll discover the truth, you'll get to the bottom of it. Keep this cursed tape, do what you like with it, but take it away from here, get it out of this house. I never want to see or hear of it again."

Lucie nodded, without losing her cop's instincts.

"Before I go, would you mind burning it onto a DVD for me?"

"Yes, of course."

Finally, the two women said good-bye. Getting in her car, the ex-cop nodded politely to Léon, put the cassette and the DVD on the passenger seat, and started up, her head buzzing.

A few miles from Highway A1, Lucie pondered which direction to take. Lille or Paris? Left or right? Her family or the investigation? See Sharko again or forget him completely? Lucie thought of him and sensed she could falter at any moment. All the feelings she thought buried forever were slowly rising to the surface.

Paris to the right, Lille to the left . . . the two extremes of a deep wound.

She made up her mind at the last minute, veering right.

Once more she'd have to go back in time, plunge more deeply into the shadows. One of her daughters had been murdered beneath the sunshine of Les Sables d'Olonne more than a year ago, without her really understanding why.

And today, she knew that it was in the terrifying depths of a jungle, thousands of miles away from home, that the answers might be waiting.

35

The sun had already started sinking through the foliage when police cars screamed up to the isolated property of the Lamberts. CSI van, crime scene photographer, squad cars for the officers. That Thursday evening, in the still summerlike temperatures, the men were on edge: they'd already started the week with horrors enough, and the situation didn't seem to be getting any better now that there were two new corpses to deal with.

Sharko was sitting against a tree in front of the house, head resting in his hands. The shadows were falling over his face, pressing against him as if to swallow him whole. In silence, he watched the different teams bustle about, the morbid ballet common to all crime scenes.

After the CSI team had finished its meticulous labors, Félix Lambert's body had been covered in a sheet, then sent off to Forensics, along with his father's. From the first indications provided by the degree of rigor mortis, Bernard Lambert had been dead at least forty-eight hours. Two days that the father had spent splayed out on the floor of the dining room, soaking in his own blood, with the TV on full blast and water pouring from the sink in the upstairs bathroom.

What had gone through Félix Lambert's head? What demons had pushed him to commit such horrors?

With a sigh, Sharko stood up. He felt drained, worn down to the bone by too long a day and too twisted a case. Dragging his feet, he joined Levallois and Bellanger, who were arguing bitterly at the entrance door. The tension between them was palpable. The more time went on, the more the men felt the pressure. Marriages would burst asunder, and bars would see policemen with frayed nerves drowning their sorrows.

The team leader finished with Levallois and took the inspector aside, near a fat blue hydrangea bush.

"Feeling better?" he asked.

"A little tired, is all. I'll be fine. I slugged down a thermos of coffee the guys brought; it picked me up a bit. To tell the truth, I haven't eaten much these past few days."

"Nor slept, for that matter. You need to get some rest."

Sharko nodded toward the area cordoned off with police tape—the spot where Félix Lambert's body had lain a few moments before.

"Rest time will come later. Were you able to notify the family?"

"Not yet. We know Lambert's older sister lives in Paris."

"What about the mother?"

"Not a trace for the moment. We're just getting started, and there's so much to do . . ."

He sighed, looking worn down. Sharko had been in his shoes once upon a time. Leading a squad in the criminal police was nothing but a thicket of hassles, a position in which you got shat on from above and below.

"What do you make of this mess?"

Sharko raised his eyes to the smashed upstairs window.

"I met the son's eyes before he jumped. I saw something in them I'd never seen in the eyes of any human being before: pure, unadulterated suffering. He was ripping the skin off his own cheeks, and he had pissed on himself, like an animal. Something was tearing him up inside and driving him insane, making him completely disconnected from reality. An evil that drove him to commit unspeakable acts, like the massacres of those hikers and his own father. I don't know what it's about, but I'm convinced what we're looking for is hidden inside him, in his body. Something genetic. And Stéphane Terney knew what it was."

Silence surrounded them. Nicolas Bellanger rubbed his chin, staring into space.

"In that case, let's see what the autopsy has to say."

"When's it being done?"

His boss didn't answer immediately. His mind must have felt like a battlefield after a major encounter.

"Uhh . . . Chénaix is starting at eight tonight. First the father and then the son. Some evening."

The young chief cleared his throat; he seemed preoccupied, ill at ease. Sharko noticed his discomfort and asked what the matter was.

"It's about Terney's book," said Bellanger. "The genetic fingerprints naturally drew our attention to Grégory Carnot, the last prisoner on Eva Louts's list. So Robillard called Vivonne Penitentiary, and guess what he discovered . . ."

Sharko felt himself grow pale. So they'd found out. While he kept silent, Bellanger continued.

"He discovered that you hadn't just called on the phone. You actually went there to question the prisoner on your day off. You know what Robillard's like, he dug a bit deeper and found out someone else had been there, too, the very same day. And not just anyone: the mother of the two girls Carnot kidnapped, named . . ."—he took out a sheet of paper—". . . Lucie Henebelle. You know her?"

Sharko's blood froze, but he didn't flinch.

"No. I went there to talk with one of the prison shrinks about a prisoner on the list, that's all."

"And you didn't say a word. The part that bothers me is that you've known for a while that Carnot was found dead in his cell. So why didn't you say anything about it? Why didn't you tell anybody about this business of the upside-down drawing, the violent outbursts, or the lactose intolerance?"

"Those were just details. I didn't think they had anything to do with our case. Louts went to see him and asked the usual questions, just like she did in the other prisons."

"Just details? It was those details that led you here! You lied to us, you kept it all to yourself, selfishly, to the detriment of our investigation and to the colleagues working with you. You made this personal."

"That's not true. I'm trying to catch a murderer and understand what's going on, just like the rest of us."

Bellanger shook his head energetically.

"You've gone off the rails way too many times. You break into a private home without informing your colleagues or any authorization. Those are procedural infractions that could shoot our entire investigation to hell. And not only do you enter the premises illegally, now we've got two bodies on our hands. We're going to have to explain that."

"I . . ."

"I'm not finished. Because of you, Levallois is facing the full barrage and'll probably end up with an official reprimand on his record. I'm in for a shitload of hassles. Major Case is already overworked; they'll be here any minute to figure out what the fuck we're doing in this mess to begin with. What got into you to try and go around them?"

He paced back and forth.

"And to top it all off, Manien's now got involved."

Sharko saw red. Just hearing that creep's name made him want to puke.

"What did he tell you?"

"He trotted out your actions at the Frédéric Hurault crime scene. Your negligence, your complete disregard . . . He claims you intentionally contaminated his crime scene, just for spite."

"Manien's an asshole. He's trying to use the situation to fuck me over."

"It's too late."

He looked Sharko squarely in the eyes.

"You do understand that I can't just let this slide, right?"

The inspector clenched his jaws and started walking toward the house.

"We can deal with that later. For now, we've got work to do."

He felt pressure on his shoulder, forcing him to turn around.

"You don't seem to get it," Bellanger said in a loud voice.

Sharko shook himself free.

"I get it perfectly. But I'm asking you, let me stay on the case for a few more days. I'm getting a feel for this one, I can sense we're getting close. Let me attend the autopsy and follow any new trails it opens. I need to see this one through to the end. Afterward, I promise, I'll do whatever you want."

The young chief shook his head.

"If this had just been between us, I could probably have delayed things a bit, but . . ."

"It's Manien, is that it?"

Bellanger nodded.

"He knows everything, the shit that happened here and about Vivonne. He's already got the people he needs behind him at thirty-six, and at this point I don't have a choice."

The inspector's fists tightened as he caught sight of Marc Leblond, Manien's right-hand man, talking on his phone in the distance while looking straight at him.

"His spies blabbed . . ."

"No doubt. I'm forced to take disciplinary action, the way we would with anyone else in this situation, to protect myself and the team. I don't want everyone else to have to pay for your mistakes, especially not Levallois."

Sharko looked sadly over at the kid who was pacing nervously some distance away, arms folded and eyes downcast. He must have been worried for his future in the department, fearful that his ambitions could come tumbling down in a heartbeat.

"No, especially not him. He's a good cop."

"I know . . . But it's not over for you. There'll be a ruling on your case. They'll certainly weigh in your years of service, the crimes you've solved. We all know how much you've done for the force over the years."

Sharko shrugged with a nervous cackle.

"I spent the last five years shuttling between my office and a psychiatric hospital, where they were treating me for fucking schizophrenia. Every Monday and every Friday, week in and week out, I sat with a shrink who tried to figure out what had gone tilt in my head. If I'm still here today, it's because I had the backing of a good man who's no longer on the force. There's no one left to support me. I'm screwed, period, amen."

Bellanger held out his open hand. With a sigh, the inspector took his police ID and service weapon and slapped them into the other man's palm. It tore his heart out. He looked at his chief without managing to hide his sadness.

"This job was all I had left. Make no mistake, you've buried a man today."

With those words, he walked away from the property without a backward glance.

36

For a moment, Sharko couldn't believe his eyes.

She was there, really there, in his kitchen.

Lucie Henebelle.

The cop stood frozen for an instant at the door of his apartment. The sofa, the living room table, the television, and the rest of the furniture had all been moved around. A large green plant had pride of place on a pedestal table in the corner, and there was a pleasant smell of lemon in the air. Sharko walked slowly toward the kitchen, his mind reeling. Lucie gave him a quick smile.

"You like it? I figured it might do you good to change things around a bit. And besides, I needed to keep myself busy while waiting for you to get home. Nerves, the whole thing . . . I . . . I bought the plant at a place near here. I know you like them green and fairly large."

She set the table as if she were spring-loaded. Her ease at finding the dishes and silverware made it seem as if she'd always lived there.

"I also figured you might be hungry."

She opened the fridge and pulled out a large serving dish particolored with different foods, along with two bottles of beer.

"I wasn't sure exactly when you'd be back, so I got Japanese takeout. It'll be a change from all those noodles you've got stacked in your pantry. It looks like the Salvation Army in there. Okay, well, let's eat and then we can get down to work."

Sharko looked at her with a tenderness he was unable to hide. He wanted to take a firmer tone, but he didn't have the strength.

"Get down to work? But . . . Lucie? What are you doing here? I thought you went back home."

He went over to the window and glanced down at the street. Lucie caught the worry in his eyes.

"Strange as it seems," she said, "I like being here. Come on, come sit."

The cop remained frozen, back to the window, arms hanging limply and his head crowded with conflicting emotions. Finally, he undid his jacket and removed his empty holster, which he hung on the coatrack. The detail didn't pass by Lucie unnoticed.

"What happened to your gun?"

He looked at her, lips pressed tight.

"They . . . they suspended you?"

She understood immediately and ran up to hug him.

"Oh, I don't believe it . . . and it's all my fault."

With a sigh, Sharko caressed her back. He felt so at peace, holding her like this.

"It's not your fault. I've fucked up too many times lately."

"Yeah, but they know about Vivonne, don't they?"

Sharko closed his eyes.

"They don't know anything about Louts's trip to Montmaison, or about Terney's theft of the Cro-Magnon."

"So what's got you so worried?"

Sharko took a step back and massaged his temples.

"My former boss, Bertrand Manien, has been on my back since the beginning of the investigation and he's doing everything he can to make my life a living hell. Our meeting in Vivonne must have made him curious. He's like a tapeworm; he'll keep digging and find out about the two of us, last year. He'll realize I wasn't just interested in Carnot's past as a murderer. He'll find out about our relationship, and about the twins."

Lucie's heart was pounding.

"I understand—it's very private and it's none of their business. But would it really be so bad if they knew, when you get down to it?"

The cop pulled up a chair, collapsed into it, and uncapped his beer. His jacket and shirt were wrinkled from the long day.

"We . . . they found two more bodies today."

Lucie's eyes widened.

"Two more bodies? Tell me everything."

The inspector took a deep breath to let out the tension of the last several hours, while Lucie unwrapped the sushi and little containers of soy sauce.

"So many things have happened . . . Basically, it all revolves around Terney's book *The Key and the Lock*. Hidden in the pages are seven genetic fingerprints. It was Daniel, the young autistic at the crime scene, who set us on the right track. Two of those fingerprints are already in the national database. The first belongs to . . . to Clara's killer."

He expected to read more surprise in Lucie's eyes, but she remained calm, merely taking a swallow of beer in turn.

"And the second one?"

Sharko outlined the series of events that had led him to Félix Lambert. The conversation with the local gendarme, Claude Lignac; the visits to the nursery schools; the part about lactose intolerance. Lucie noticed that he was unburdening himself freely, without putting up any barriers, without holding anything back. She felt that the deeper they delved into this blackness, the more she was gradually rediscovering the man she had met the year before. Only his outer shell was dented; inside, he was still the same. He told her of his hunch, talked of the suffering he'd seen in young Lambert's eyes, of the horrible sense that some evil was gnawing at him from within. The same impression that Grégory Carnot's psychiatrist had had, before Carnot committed suicide. While he hadn't seen any upside-down drawings at Lambert's, Sharko was convinced the two men had suffered from the same mysterious illness.

After listening carefully, Lucie went to get the small brown envelope containing the photos of Stéphane Terney's crime scene, the videocassette, and the DVD. She took out the photo of the paintings in the doctor's library and handed it to Sharko.

"My turn now. I've also made some progress on my end."

With his chopsticks, the inspector lifted a piece of sushi to his mouth, with a hint of a smile. It was the first time Lucie had seen him do that.

"Why am I not surprised?" he asked. "You're incredible."

"Mostly, I'm a mother prepared to do anything to get at the truth."

He looked at the photo while Lucie swallowed a piece of sushi.

"What's with these hideous paintings again?"

"You were wondering how Terney got Carnot's genetic fingerprint? He arranged it so that he was the one who delivered him, twenty-three years ago. And he took a huge number of blood tests, from which he was able to establish a DNA profile. It's as simple as that."

In turn, she began relating her discoveries since that morning. Reims, Carnot's birthplace and the city where Terney had practiced medicine. Her visit to Colombe Hospital, Carnot's full name, and her conversation with the former nurse. The hypervascular placenta, the gleam in the gynecologist's eye at the moment of birth . . . And finally, her detour to see the doctor's first wife, who had told her of his odd behavior and given her the videotape.

Sharko handled the black plastic case with a dark look in his eyes.

"We found melted videocassettes in Terney's fireplace. They'd been hidden under the floorboards. The killer had come looking for them, which is why Terney was tortured. Unfortunately we weren't able to get anything from them."

"Those were probably the originals. This is a copy."

"What's on it?"

"Possibly the key to this whole case. His wife told me the original had a label on it, with the words 'Phoenix number one.'"

Sharko ran his finger over the photo.

"Phoenix . . . The bird that's reborn from its ashes."

"Exactly. I did some research. The phoenix has the gift of longevity and never dies. He symbolizes the cycles of death and rebirth. Legend has it that, since he didn't have a female, when he saw his time of death approaching, he ensured his posterity by setting fire to his own nest. He then perished in the flames and a new phoenix was born from the ashes. It's awful, but I couldn't help thinking of Amanda Potier and Grégory Carnot. She dies, but the child is born from her womb, after destroying the nest . . ."

"If each of these paintings has a particular meaning," said Sharko, "we still need to figure out what the photo of the Cro-Magnon is doing there. There's obviously a reason for it . . . Those three paintings are like Terney showing off his secrets, figuring no one will be able to understand them."

Lucie picked up the DVD.

"Come see this."

She went into the living room and slid the disc into the computer.

"Before we start, I should tell you this takes place in the Amazon."

"The Amazon . . . Eva Louts's trip. Don't tell me you've figured out what she was doing in Brazil?"

"Not entirely, but I'm getting there. The film lasts ten minutes. Brace yourself."

Sharko sank into the unwholesome universe of the film. He, too, jumped when the two eyes suddenly snapped open, oozing with fever and disease. So many stabs of the knife added to the shadows, again and again.

When the documentary was over, the inspector got up with a sigh and went back to sit in the kitchen, where he picked up the VHS tape in silence. He turned it over in his hands without looking at it, his eyes seemingly caught in the void. Lucie came up to him.

"What are you thinking about?"

He was shaken.

"We can't be certain of anything, Lucie. Apart from the Amazon, there's nothing that ties Eva to those natives. Do you realize that film goes back more than forty years? There's no clear connection."

In a troubled silence, he gobbled down sushi after sushi, not even tasting them. Lucie could see how upset he was. She moved into his field of vision.

"Of course we can be certain! It's too much of a coincidence for them *not* to be connected. We've got all we need to go on, except for one essential detail: the name of that tribe."

"And what if we knew it? Where would that get us?"

"It would help us understand why Louts wanted to go back there, with all those names and photos from her prison visits. And a bunch of other things as well."

Sharko noticed a frightening gleam in her ice-blue eyes. He felt she was capable of leaving everything behind and heading into that cursed jungle. He tried to regain control of their conversation; the terrain was much too slippery and dangerous.

"Let's forget about the tape for the moment and take it all from scratch, piece by piece."

He grabbed a sheet of paper and a pencil, energized by Lucie's revelations and almost forgetting that he'd been suspended barely an hour before. The investigation still had him in its clutches, gnawing at him without his being able to resist.

"Let's put everything in order. So what do we have to work with, exactly? We need a central knot, a hub that the whole investigation turns around."

"Terney, of course."

"Right, Terney. Let's focus on him . . . Let's try to retrace his steps to get a clearer picture, and find the correspondences between your findings and mine. There are certainly things that will intersect and help shed light on all this. You're the one who looked into his past, so you go first."

Lucie paced back and forth, charged like a battery. Sharko took notes as she started talking.

"I get the sense that 1984 is the beginning of the whole story. It was the year Terney met the men at the racetrack. One or both of those individuals is the man who shot the film. Without a doubt, they're the ones we need to find today, probably about the same age as Terney, since they were already adults in 1966. One of them, or maybe both, is *our* man."

"Easy, okay? Let's not jump to conclusions too quickly. Keep going."

"Fine. So the men meet a number of times. Terney becomes more reserved, more secretive and mysterious. Then the men give him several videotapes."

"Why do they give him the tapes?"

"Maybe to show him what they've discovered? Make him aware of a . . . I don't know, some sort of research? Or some monstrous project they want him to be a part of? 'Phoenix number one' sounds like an introduction. The birth of something."

"How did the three men meet in the first place?"

Lucie answered without hesitation.

"Terney was a well-known scientist. The other two must have found *him*."

"That sounds plausible. What next?"

"In 1986, Terney gets divorced and leaves for Reims. Right afterward, he enters into contact with Amanda Potier and becomes her gynecologist. In January '87, he delivers Grégory Carnot, while the mother dies in childbirth. Highly vascularized placenta, which contradicts the diagnosis of preeclampsia. Terney collects samples of the baby's blood. The blood has his DNA. Is the DNA hiding something? Phoenix?"

"Hold on, just a second . . . There, okay."

"Nineteen-ninety, Terney returns to Paris. Neuilly clinic. I don't know a lot about that."

"They're looking into it at number thirty-six. Interviewing his colleagues and friends. Unfortunately we won't have access to the info."

"We can do without it for now. Let's move on."

Sharko nodded.

"Okay, my turn now. Two thousand six, publication of *The Key and the Lock*, with the help of a young autistic—who by the way is never acknowledged in his book. Terney hides seven genetic fingerprints in it. Carnot, Lambert, and five others who, if they follow the pattern, must also have the same morphological and genetic characteristics."

He fell silent for a few seconds, then added:

"Most likely seven left-handers, big, strong, and young. Lactose intolerant. Prey to bouts of sudden, extreme violence when they reach adulthood. Even if Terney didn't deliver every one of them, he probably met them when they were small. In your view, how can seven individuals present such similar characteristics?"

"Genetic manipulation? Seven mothers who unwittingly received special treatments during their pregnancy? Amanda Potier and Terney were close. He treated her as a patient. She was depressed and alone. He could have given her whatever he wanted. What's to say he didn't do the same with the other mothers? He or some other doctor? Maybe people he'd met through his lectures on preeclampsia. Why not other eugenicists? Those guys might have gotten together like a little sect."

Sharko nodded energetically.

"Apart from the sect business, it holds up."

"Yes. When we look at the bottom line of our two investigations, it does hold up. Terney might not have delivered every one of those babies, but he was in contact with the mothers. He, or those two other fanatics working with him."

Sharko segued immediately.

"Anything else?"

"Yes, something important. Beginning of 2010, theft of the Cro-Magnon and its genome in Lyon."

The inspector picked up the photo of the three paintings. He concentrated on the one showing the close-up of the prehistoric man lying on a table.

"Right. What was really behind that theft? We haven't quite figured that out yet."

"We haven't had time. Maybe now's the moment, since we're on a roll."

She took out the photos she'd gotten from the genome center in Lyon and laid them on the table.

"Here's a crime scene from thirty thousand years ago. Cro-Magnon, left-handed, age pinpointed between twenty and thirty, slaughters three Neanderthals with a harpoon. Terney stole the Cro-Magnon, then photographed it and mounted the photo in a frame."

Sharko looked carefully at the photos, one by one.

"I wonder where that mummy is now."

"Doesn't this crime scene remind you of something?" asked Lucie.

"It's exactly what happened at the Lamberts' the other day."

"Or what happened with Carnot and Clara a year ago."

Sharko paused a moment, thinking, then finally said:

"The same inexplicable fury. An explosion of pure violence."

Lucie nodded.

"And we can assume Terney *didn't* deliver the Cro-Magnon."

They exchanged brief smiles. Lucie continued:

"Let's look at the seven profiles in the book. For reasons we don't know yet, Terney, in the 1980s, studied a group of children with certain genetic traits in common, including lactose intolerance. Children who are predisposed to violence and begin murdering people when they reach adulthood. At the time, Terney is interested in their blood and DNA. He seems to be looking for something in particular."

Sharko popped a piece of salmon sushi into his mouth.

"The mythical violence gene?"

"We already talked about that—it doesn't exist."

"We know that now. But couldn't he have believed in it in the eighties? And regardless, aren't we dealing with some kind of hidden impulse, an outburst of violence that seems to come out of nowhere? It makes you wonder."

Lucie stared at him for a few seconds before answering.

"To tell you the truth, I have no idea. But . . . let me play this out. So, imagine that the discovery of the cave and that prehistoric massacre comes to Terney's attention. He makes an immediate connection: what if what he was looking for in those seven children—or what he'd noticed, or what he'd artificially induced by giving the pregnant women some kind of medicine—had been *naturally* present in that Cro-Magnon man? So with the help of those guys at the racecourse, or maybe acting alone, he gets in touch with a biologist at the genome center in Lyon, waits until they decode the genome, then steals the data at just the right moment, without leaving a trace."

Lucie raised her finger, eyes alight.

"Imagine how important this genome is for Terney. Now he's got not only the genetic profile of the seven children, but also the entire, decoded DNA molecule of an ancestor going back more than thirty thousand years. An ancestor who butchered an entire family, and who falls into precisely the same category that Terney seems to be studying."

"Another of his 'children,' so to speak."

"Exactly. This is a major discovery for him, monstrous as it is. Perhaps *the* great discovery of his life."

"Where are you going with this?"

She looked at the photo of Cro-Magnon in its frame.

"The gynecologist was an extremely cautious man, meticulous, and more than a little paranoid. He always protected his discoveries but left hidden clues, as if he couldn't resist having his little joke on the world: the genetic codes in his book, the phoenix and placenta paintings, and those tapes he kept locked away in his study."

"And that he stashed under the floorboards in his house."

"Right. So don't you think he would have preserved the information about the Cro-Magnon genome somewhere? Wouldn't he have protected it like all the rest?"

"That's why his killer took all his computer equipment."

Lucie shook her head.

"No, no. Terney wouldn't have been satisfied with a simple computer backup. It was too obvious, and too easy to steal. All the virus protection in the world can't keep that stuff safe, and hardware can fail—he was too smart for that. And too extravagant as well."

"You're thinking of that third picture, is that it? The Cro-Magnon photo?"

"Of course. But . . . how do we figure it out? I know there's a logic to it somewhere."

After a moment's reflection, Sharko bounded from his chair and snapped his fingers.

"Good lord, that's it! The key and the lock!"

Lucie frowned.

"What about the key and the lock?"

"I think I've figured it out. Are you ready for a quick trip to Paris?"

Sharko had easily popped the seals on the door to Terney's house. Lucie waited in the street, hidden from sight, watching to make sure no one should catch them unaware. Quickly, he crept upstairs, heading for the library. With his gloved hands, he unhooked the frame with the photo of Cro-Magnon, rolled the picture up, and squeezed it in his hand. Two minutes later, he was back outside.

And heading for the fourteenth arrondissement.

Daniel Mullier was now wearing a tracksuit, but otherwise he had barely moved since the last time. The same box of pens, same lit computer, same Volume 342. Sharko had warned Lucie to prepare for a shock when she saw that strange room, where a man's life came down to several miles of paper. At the threshold, she looked quietly around, while Vincent Audebert, the director, approached Daniel alone. Sharko remained silently in the background.

Audebert entered the autistic's visual field, said a few words to gain his attention, then slid the photo of Cro-Magnon and some blank sheets of paper in front of him. At that point, Daniel interrupted his incomprehensible task. With a slightly awkward movement, he picked up the photo and stared at it fixedly. Slowly, as if the whole thing were following an irrefutable logic, he took a blank sheet of paper without looking away, changed his pen for a red one, and spontaneously began jotting down series of letters.

Audebert discreetly backed away, rubbing his chin with one hand.

"I can't get over it—it worked. The photo is a trigger. Stéphane Terney used Daniel like . . ."

"A living memory," Sharko completed. "An anonymous autistic, lost inside a rest home. The key to open the lock."

He and Lucie watched the young man work in silence. The red ballpoint flew over the paper. Daniel was hunched over, concentrated, writing at breakneck speed. After half an hour, the young autistic pushed the sheets and the photo to one side and seamlessly returned to his earlier task.

The director of the home picked up the sheets and handed them to Sharko.

"A DNA sequence," he whispered, "written from that mummy's photo. Does this mean you have the genetic code that belonged to an actual Cro-Magnon?"

"Seems like it," answered Sharko. "Does this sequence mean anything to you?"

"How could it? It's just a succession of letters, and this time it doesn't even look like a genetic fingerprint. I'm not well versed enough to know what it means. You'll have to ask a geneticist."

Lucie also looked carefully at the papers.

"This might be the famous hidden DNA code. The key to this whole business."

The two ex-detectives thanked the director, who accompanied them to the exit.

"Good-bye, Daniel," murmured Lucie, who had stayed behind with the young autistic for a few seconds. But Daniel didn't hear, encased in his bubble. Lucie finally left the room, closing the door softly behind her.

Once they were in the parking lot, Sharko stared at the sequences with a worried face.

"We're getting too carried away, Lucie. We've got the data, but . . . what do we do with it? We can't access the case files anymore."

"Why, because you've been suspended? So what? Listen . . . I know it's serious, I didn't mean it like that, but . . . it shouldn't keep us from moving forward. We can keep going without them. We've got this DNA sequence, the tape from the Amazon, and we can get all of it to the right experts first thing tomorrow morning. A geneticist for the sequence and an anthropologist for the tape."

"And what if we did, Lucie . . . ?"

"Don't be defeatist, we've got work to do. Félix Lambert and his father are dead, but they had family. We should question his mother about her pregnancy, her time in prenatal care. We try to find out if she was given any medicines, something unusual while she was expecting. If we find a connection with Terney, that'll already be a huge step. Maybe we can even track down those guys from the racecourse. We'll keep moving forward the best we can."

Lucie looked at the three mysterious sheets of paper.

"I need to know what Phoenix was about. I'll go as far as I have to, with or without you."

"Would you go all the way into the jungle and risk your life? Just for some answers?"

"Not just for some answers. So I can finish grieving for my daughter."

The inspector heaved a long sigh.

"Let's go home. You can polish off the sushi and recharge your batteries. You're going to need it."

Lucie gratified him with a wide smile.

"So we're on? You're coming with me?"

"I wouldn't be smiling if I were you, Lucie. There's nothing funny about what we're likely to do or find. People have been killed over this."

He looked at his watch.

"Let's head to the apartment and grab a bit of rest. At ten o'clock, we hit the road again."

"Ten o'clock? Where are we going?"

"To get some answers at the forensic institute."

37

The section of Paris that looked out onto Quai de la Rapée was dozing peacefully. Small yellowish lights floated in the cabins of the barges. Orange reflections danced on the water, disappeared, formed again elsewhere, in perpetual motion. Despite the apparent calm, a screech of iron and rubber regularly disturbed the tranquility of the place: the few riders of the elevated metro line were being carried toward their homes or heading out to meet Paris by night.

Ten thirty p.m. Jacques Levallois, Nicolas Bellanger, and another officer had just come out of the forensic building. Hidden in the Peugeot several yards away, Sharko and Lucie could clearly make out the red tips of their cigarettes floating in the dark like fireflies.

"They're with a cop from Major Case," murmured Sharko. "They were the ones investigating the murders in Fontainebleau and we pulled the rug out from under them. I'll bet the shit hit the fan over *that*."

Under the caress of the streetlamps, the three men talked, yawned, paced back and forth, clearly agitated. After five minutes, they got into their respective cars and drove off. The two ex-cops scrunched down when the headlights swept over them. They gave each other a complicit look, like two misbehaving kids trying not to get caught.

"Look what you make me do," whispered the old cop. "With you, I feel like a teenager again."

Lucie was nervously fingering her cell phone. She had called Lille an hour before, but Juliette was already sleeping. Her mother had all but hung up on her, furious at her long absence.

They waited a bit longer, then got out and walked into the night. Sharko had a shoulder bag in which he'd stashed the three sheets with Daniel's markings. The institute stood before them, a kind of great whale that gobbled up every corpse within a ten-mile radius. The main door opened like a huge maw ready to swallow you whole, to suck you into a belly filled with stiffs of every variety: accidents, suicides, murders. Lucie suddenly stopped walking. Her fists jammed into her sides, and she froze at the building's austere entrance. Sharko went back toward her.

"Are you sure you're okay? You've barely said a word since before. If it's still too hard to go into a morgue, just say so."

Lucie took a deep breath. It was now or never: she had to chase the old images out of her head and work past her suffering. She resumed walking.

"Let's go."

"Stick close. And don't say a word."

They went through the entrance and immediately the temperature dropped. The thick redbrick walls let nothing filter through, especially not hope. Sharko felt relieved when he recognized the same night watchman he'd often seen in the past: he wouldn't have to use that stupid fake police ID Lucie had made for him.

"Evening," he said in a flat voice. "The double autopsy—what room's it in?"

The man gave Lucie a quick glance, then jerked his head without asking questions.

"Number two."

"Thanks."

Side by side, the two ex-detectives entered the shadowy tunnels with their parsimonious lighting. The building was vast, the walk endless. Just then Lucie caught sight of a small square of yellow ahead, the lighted window in the security door, and without warning she was transported one year back. She was in the Carnot house, with the SWAT team. She saw Grégory Carnot flattened to the ground by the cops, while she ran up the stairs, breathless . . .

Suddenly a voice broke through, close to her ear.

"Hey! Hey, Lucie! Are you with us?"

She realized she was leaning against the wall, her forehead in her hands.

"I . . . I'm sorry. Something . . . weird just happened. I saw myself in Carnot's house, running upstairs to find Juliette."

Sharko looked at her silently, encouraging her to continue.

"The strange thing is that I have no memory of actually entering the house."

Her eyes grew troubled.

"The men entered Carnot's. I got there a bit later, with the second team. They told me to stay downstairs, they kept me from going in. Then one of the officers came back to the entrance, holding Juliette . . ."

Lucie raised her hands to her head, eyes half closed.

"It's so strange. It's . . . it's like there are two different realities."

Sharko gently took hold of her wrist.

"Come on, I'll bring you back to the car."

She resisted.

"No, I'm fine. Let me come with you. Please."

After a moment, Sharko let go of her wrist. Reluctantly he walked ahead of her, entering the room first.

Paul Chénaix was standing between two empty dissection tables, rinsing the floor with a water jet. Another ME whom the inspector had seen before was sticking labels on tubes and specimen jars. Indifferent, he greeted them with a nod and a tired "Hey." After at least three hours of autopsies, the two men must have been exhausted.

Chénaix interrupted his rinsing and looked at his watch in surprise.

"Franck? Your boss said you weren't coming this evening." He shot a glance at Lucie. "There are more romantic places to bring a date. Are you all right, Miss? You don't look like you're feeling too well."

Lucie walked forward unsteadily and held out her hand.

"I'm feeling fine. I'm . . ."

"A friend and colleague from Lille," Sharko interrupted.

"Colleague from Lille?"

A thin smile above the man's perfectly trimmed goatee.

"My first wife came from Lille. I know the city well."

Sharko quickly changed the subject without giving Lucie time to answer.

"Give me the broad strokes of the Lambert autopsies."

"Why don't you ask your coworkers? They were just here."

Sharko thought quickly. Apparently Bellanger hadn't let on that he'd been taken off the case.

"And they're probably on the way home now to see their wives and kids," said the inspector. "It'll only take you a few minutes, if you stick to what's relevant. I need to work on the file tonight. It's important."

Chénaix set down his pressure sprayer and called to the other ME.

"I have to go to the morgue for a minute. I'll be back."

In his bloodstained scrubs, he headed toward a draining board.

"I'll bring this with me."

He picked up a jar filled with a translucent, yellowish liquid. Sharko screwed up his eyes: the container held something that looked like a human brain.

Dr. Chénaix walked in front of them in the hallway. As they headed downstairs, he murmured in Sharko's ear, "Can I talk in front of her?"

Sharko put a friendly hand on his shoulder.

"There's something you have to do for me, Paul. Don't breathe a word of our visit to anyone. Because of a screwup with the paperwork, I'm no longer on the case—I didn't want to say it in front of your colleague back there."

Paul Chénaix frowned.

"You're putting me in an awkward position. This information's sensitive, and . . ."

"I know. But if anyone really does ask you about it, just tell them I lied to you. I'll take the heat."

A brief pause.

"All right."

Chénaix didn't ask any more questions; they both knew it was better that way. They arrived at the basement. The medical examiner pressed a switch. Crackling neons, dull lighting. No windows. Hundreds of metal drawers, aligned vertically and horizontally, as if in a macabre library. In a corner were bags full of clothes and shoes that no one knew what to do with; soon they'd be heading for the incinerator. Lucie, lagging slightly behind the two men, folded her arms and rubbed her shoulders. She felt cold.

Chénaix set the jar on a table against a wall, went over to a drawer, and pulled it out, revealing a corpse with slightly bluish skin. It seemed flaccid, more latex than dermis, and the veins were practically bulging through the surface. Every incision, from neck to pubis, had been carefully stitched up: if the family were to claim the body, it had to be presentable. Sharko moved as close as he could, practically pressed into the slide rail. The odor of rotting flesh was strong but still bearable. Chénaix pointed to certain parts of the corpse's anatomy and explained:

"The father was struck numerous times with a poker. The same weapon was used to perforate his vital organs. Several ribs were broken; the killer showed incredible strength. It was brutal and violent, and it all happened in just a few seconds. For the precise details, the exact location of the wounds and all that, it'll be in the report I give your chief tomorrow. If you want to read it, you'll have to work it out with him. Sorry, but no copies can leave this building . . ."

Sharko spent a few more seconds looking at the lacerated body, then nodded.

"I'll be fine without it. Now the son. He's the one I'm interested in."

Chénaix left the drawer as it was and opened the one next to it. Félix Lambert's face was horribly disfigured but his skin was lighter colored, like pale wax. His powerful body filled the space like a block of ice.

"They look alike," Sharko noted. "Same nose, same facial shape."

"Father and son by blood, no doubt about it."

Trembling slightly, Lucie had come farther forward. This really was one of the worst places in the entire world. All one found here were dead souls and shattered bodies. There was no aura, no warmth that might have suggested a human presence. She would have liked Sharko to hold her close, comfort her, warm her, but the inspector's eyes were dark, impenetrable, and entirely preoccupied with the investigation. Noticing her presence, the examiner stepped back a bit to leave her room.

"Cause of death is rupture of the cervical vertebrae. Here again, death was instantaneous, no question."

"I can confirm that, I had a front-row seat. He threw himself out the window in front of me."

"But even when the cause is as certain as it is here, protocol still demands we do a complete workup, A to Z. And sometimes we happen on a little pearl, like this time."

"What do you mean?"

He pointed his finger toward the corpse's brain. The scalp had been set back in place, but they could still make out the red, regular line left by the Stryker saw.

"In here is where it all happened. When I opened up, I saw that the brain presented with an incredible amount of deterioration around the frontal and prefrontal lobes. It was literally spongy, full of little holes. I'd never seen anything like it."

He went to get the jar. The whitish mass floated in the liquid.

"Here, look at this . . ."

The two cops could plainly see the damage. The upper portion of the brain looked as if it had been chewed at by hundreds of tiny mice. The sponginess was remarkable.

"What *is* that?" asked Lucie, horrified.

"It seems to be an infection that gradually deteriorated the brain tissue, until it finally reached this stage. I cut some sections and examined the other part of the brain, the left hemisphere, to get a better sense of what was going on. I think the initial damage goes back months, perhaps even years, starting gradually and eventually getting to this point. Creutzfeldt-Jakob, the famous 'mad cow' disease, produces exactly the same spongiform degeneration. But in this case, I can't find a trace of any known pathogen. The rest of the organism is completely intact."

Silence enveloped them. Lucie stared at the two corpses with pursed lips. She thought about Grégory Carnot, who had died by ripping out his own throat. Had *his* brain wasted away like this?

"Do you think Félix Lambert could have killed those two hikers and his father because of this . . . thing?"

"It seems clear to me the two are related. The areas of the brain we consider the seat of emotions were strongly degraded. Almost as if they were invaded. And as I said, over a period of at least several months."

Lucie blew on her hands. Like it or not, this discovery raised questions about Grégory Carnot's responsibility for his actions. This disease, with its particular form of degeneration, might have forced him to do what he did, independent of his will or his consciousness. The questions burst forth in her head. How had Félix Lambert contracted this "thing"? Was this what Terney had been so fixated on? And if so, how did it relate to the placenta and reproduction, or the fact that the gynecologist had been interested in Carnot even before his birth? Could certain kinds of medicine or prenatal treatments provoke such horrors in a child? And what did any of it have to do with the jungle?

The ME continued his explanations:

"The emotional centers, when they work right, release serotonin, a neurotransmitter that inhibits aggressive behavior. If something prevents the release of serotonin, the individual reverts to primitive forms of behavior that once allowed him to meet his fundamental needs in order to . . ."

". . . to survive," Sharko completed.

The examiner nodded.

"It's funny you should mention that and that we talked about lactose intolerance this afternoon—it all has to do with evolution, and it reminded me of something I learned when I was in med school."

"Such as?"

"Oh, nothing, really. It's too silly. I didn't even mention it to your colleagues and I . . ."

"No, we'd like to hear."

He hesitated a few moments, then said:

"Well, to tell you the truth, when I saw this brain today, I wondered how the man could still have been alive, how he could have fed himself or slept. He was living with a fifth of his brain completely shot to hell, which in itself would have knocked any neurologist back on his socks. Then I recalled the case of this guy Phineas Gage, a railway man in the 1800s, in America somewhere—they loved trotting out this story in neurology. What happened was, there was an explosion, and an iron bar went through the top of his skull, through his brain, and out his eye. Much of the left frontal lobe was destroyed, but Gage somehow managed to survive. But the thing was, from this honest, upstanding fellow, he suddenly became vulgar, aggressive, and hot-tempered, though he still retained all his wits and functions."

Chénaix leaned on the table.

"What's remarkable about Félix Lambert's brain is that, at first glance, the spongiform areas seem to have developed only in the neocortex and the limbic system. The reptilian brain, which roughly corresponds to the brainstem located near the back of the neck, was completely unaffected. Gage's iron bar hadn't touched that area either."

"Reptilian brain, limbic system—what's all that mean in real-people language?"

"What we call triune brain theory is pretty commonly accepted these days. It's based on the fact that, over the millennia, the evolution of the brain occurred in three phases. In other words, three successive brain structures were superimposed, so to speak, like layers of sediment, to form our big, high-performance brain of today. It would also explain why our skulls are bigger than the first primates'. The first brain, then, the oldest one, is this reptile brain, which is shared by most living species. It's well protected, buried way down beneath the skull, and it's the brain structure that's most resistant to trauma, for example. It's the one that ensures our survival and responds to primary needs: eating, sleeping, and reproducing. It's also responsible for certain primitive behaviors, such as hate, fear, and violence. The second brain, the limbic, mainly regulates memory and emotions. And the third, the neocortex, is the most recent; it's located at the outer layers and deals with intellectual faculties, like language, art, and culture. It's where thought and consciousness reside."

Sharko looked closely at the diseased brain, flabbergasted. Concepts related to evolution had come back yet again, even here in the morgue, inside the most fascinating organ of the human system. Could this be just chance, a strange quirk of circumstance?

"So . . . what you're saying is that this illness eats away at part of the brain, but it leaves our survival faculties intact? And because of this, it unleashes primitive, violent instincts, which normally the other two parts of the brain keep under control?"

"Theoretically speaking, yes. From a pathological and anatomical standpoint, it's a lot more complicated than that. We know the three brains are interconnected, and that even a tiny lesion in the wrong place, even in the limbic system or the neocortex, can kill you or make you insane. Félix Lambert, sadly for him, might have been lucky to live so long. As for the fact that the affliction—or infection, if you prefer—didn't touch the reptilian brain, you shouldn't see that as some kind of indication that the disease is intelligent. I think it was only a matter of time. In any case, given how rapidly the illness was progressing, the man had no chance."

Lucie and Sharko looked at each other in silence, aware that they were closing in on something monstrous. Eva Louts and Stéphane Terney had been brutally murdered to prevent anyone from retracing this to its source.

What was this disease? Had it been injected, transmitted genetically, released into the air?

"You didn't find anything similar in the father's brain?" asked Sharko.

"Not a trace. Perfectly healthy specimen. Well, except for the obvious."

"And could the disease have caused visual disturbances? Like a tendency to draw upside down?"

"Sure. It looks like certain areas around the optic chiasma were also affected. The individual would first have experienced problems with his vision, loss of balance . . . warning signs, before the pain and violence kicked in. If Lambert and Carnot ended up committing suicide, it's because they couldn't stand the excruciating pain in their heads. It must have felt like Hiroshima in there."

Firmly, the ME shoved the two drawers closed. The bodies disappeared, swallowed by the cold shadows. When the metal door slammed, Lucie started and leaned against Sharko. Paul Chénaix finally removed his latex gloves, tossed them in the wastebasket, and rubbed his hands together, before taking a pipe and pouch of tobacco from his pocket.

"The two halves of the brain are going off for a thorough workup, with the various samples. The case has raised a lot of questions, and I hope the lab guys will be able to tell us what we're dealing with pretty quickly."

He headed toward the light switch to turn it off, but Sharko intercepted him, a DVD in hand.

"Enjoy your smoke, take your time. But afterward, I'll need to get your thoughts for just another minute, on a movie. Your medical opinion."

"A movie? What kind of movie?"

Sharko shot a final glance at the brain slowly rotating in the fluid, barely lit by the neon lights in the hallway. He thought to himself that five other individuals, somewhere in these streets or in the country, alone or in families, were harboring the same time bomb in their skulls, which had probably already begun counting down. Monsters capable of killing their children, their parents, or anyone else they happened to meet.

Time was of the essence.

He felt a shiver run up his spine, and answered:

"The kind that will keep you awake at night."

38

L ocated one floor up, Chénaix's office looked like your typical doctor's examining room. A skeleton mounted on metal wire hung in a corner, while two bookshelves buckled under specialized tomes and articles about pathology, forensic anthropology, and general medicine. Old posters showing the human body papered the walls. The only thing missing was the examination table. For a human touch, the ME had hung photos of his family here and there: a wife and two daughters under the age of ten. It was his reminder that life consisted of more than just death.

Giving off a smell of stale tobacco smoke mixed with the more rancid odor of corpses, the ME sat at his computer and slid the DVD into the drive. Lucie and Sharko had sat down facing him, in silence. No one felt like talking. They were still haunted by the image of that ravaged brain, which had driven its owner to commit the most heinous acts imaginable. Lucie was also thinking about the implications of these findings: the possibility that Grégory Carnot had been merely an unfortunate guinea pig, and that the people truly responsible for her daughter's death were still at large. They, too, would have to answer for their crimes.

The doctor watched the ten-minute film attentively. Like any normal human being, he recoiled at the scene in the hut; but overall, his face registered no particular disgust or emotion, and the two cops were unable to gauge what he was feeling. Death in all its forms was his trade; he had learned how to tame it, and he looked upon it the way a mason looks at a half-built wall.

It was only after the viewing that he showed a clear interest.

"This is an exceptional document. Do you know where it comes from?"

Sharko shook his head.

"No, it's just a copy. We know it was shot in the Amazon."

"The Amazon . . . Your tribe was decimated by an epidemic of measles."

Lucie knit her brow. She had been expecting something a hundred times worse, on a par with the horrors she had discovered up until then. Some hideous plague, like Ebola or cholera. Or even—why not?—the same thing that had affected Lambert. For her, the measles was just one of those illnesses you got as a kid, like rubella or the mumps . . .

"Only measles? Are you sure?"

"Don't say 'only measles.' It's a very aggressive virus that used to ravage populations and, when it's fatal, it can cause incredible pain and suffering. As for whether I'm sure . . . I'd say about ninety-five percent, yes. The symptoms are textbook. There's the obvious presence of Koplik spots, even though the eruptions on the skin aren't that pronounced, plus weepy eyes, which are very dark because they're probably red. But one characteristic of the illness is that in the most severe cases it results in internal hemorrhaging, which causes the patient to ooze blood through the nose, mouth, and anus. Like here. And given the incredible virulence of the disease, I can guarantee that this population had never experienced it before this. Their immune system was totally unprepared for the virus—it simply didn't recognize it."

He gave Sharko a somber look that, in conjunction with his dark eyes, seemed baleful.

"Remember what I said about cows and milk drinkers. It's the same thing here, and it's still the same principle. Viruses like measles, smallpox, mumps, or diphtheria first incubated in domestic animals. Then they mutated and acquired the ability to infect humans. This ability proved to be very advantageous for them, so it was favored by natural selection. High population densities in both the Old and New Worlds sustained them and helped them spread, and at the same time humans developed immune defenses so that they wouldn't be wiped out completely. Viruses and humans cohabitated in another arms race. I'd even be tempted to say they nourished each other, and they went through the centuries hand in hand."

"So the virus that decimated that village came from a 'civilized' individual, if I can use the word?"

"No doubt about it. Today, man is the only possible carrier of measles. The virus was in this fellow, in his organism, as it might be in yours at this very moment. Except you don't know it, because your immune system and the vaccines you got as a kid have made it harmless."

Chénaix slid the DVD out of the computer and handed it back to the inspector.

"To my knowledge, no one has ever filmed an epidemic of measles as violent and deadly as this. In the early sixties, it was impossible to find societies, even primitive ones, in which the adults were so lacking in antibodies that it could cause such a holocaust. So there's only one conclusion: before the time this film was made, this civilization had never met a modern man, since the measles, even from thousands of years earlier, had never reached it. It's probable that the person who shot this documentary was the first outsider that tribe had ever seen, going back centuries. This was an extremely isolated community."

Finally, the medical examiner stood up, prompting the two detectives to do the same. He turned off his screen.

"For now, that's all I can tell you about it."

"That's a lot. Tell me, do you know Jean-Paul Lemoine, the molecular biologist at the crime lab?"

"Pretty well, yes—he and his team handle most of the biological analyses we send out. And they'll be the ones studying Lambert's brain. How come?"

Sharko opened his shoulder bag and handed over the three sheets of data that Daniel had written.

"Can you ask him to give this a once-over as soon as possible?"

"A DNA sequence? What's it from?"

"That's the big question."

The doctor heaved a sigh.

"You *are* aware you're taking advantage, at least?"

Sharko held out his hand with a smile.

"Thanks again. And don't forget . . ."

"I know—you were never here."

39

O nce back outside, the detectives took a deep breath, as if resurfacing after an underwater plunge. Never had the sound of a car zipping by been so reassuring. Everything, even the air itself, seemed to weigh on their shoulders. Sharko walked to the edge of the Seine and, hands in his pockets, watched the amber-colored glints winking at him. Around them, Paris nestled into its heavy blanket of lights. Deep down, he loved this city as much as he hated it.

Lucie came up quietly beside him and asked, "What are you thinking about?"

"A ton of things. But especially all this business about evolution and survival. About those genes that will do anything to propagate, even if it means killing their host."

"Like praying mantises?"

"Praying mantises, bumblebees, salmon. Even parasites and viruses follow that logic; they colonize us to preserve their existence, and are very smart about it. You know, I was thinking about the notion of an arms race. It reminds me of a passage in *Through the Looking-Glass*. Did you ever read Lewis Carroll?"

"Never did. I'm afraid my tastes in literature tended to be a bit darker."

Lucie moved closer. Their shoulders were almost touching. Sharko stared at the horizon with dilated pupils. His voice was gentle, limpid, belying the violence that pressed down on them harder with each passing minute.

"At a certain point, Alice and the Red Queen are in this race, and Alice suddenly realizes that no matter how fast they run, the scenery never changes. And the Queen says, 'It takes all the running you can do, to keep in the same place.'"

He let the silence drift for a moment, then looked Lucie deep in the eyes.

"We're like any other species, any other organism. We do whatever we have to to survive. You and I, the antelope in the savannah, the fish in the sea, the poor man, the rich man, black, white . . . we all keep running to survive, and we have been since day one. Whatever tragedies knock us down, we always get up again, and we run harder and harder. If we can't manage it, if our brain doesn't come up with the defenses to keep us going, the arms race is over and we die, eliminated by natural selection. It's as simple as that."

His voice vibrated with such emotion that Lucie felt tears welling in her eyes. Without second-guessing herself this time, she finally squeezed against him.

"We've been through the same suffering, Franck, and we've both kept running, each on our own. But today we're running together. That's the most important thing."

She moved slightly away. Sharko gathered on his fingertip the tear she couldn't help shedding and looked carefully at that little diamond of water and salt. He took a deep breath, then blurted out simply:

"I know what Eva was looking for in Brazil, Lucie . . . I understood the moment I saw that film."

Lucie stared at him in surprise.

"But why didn't you . . . ?"

"Because I'm afraid! I'm afraid of what's waiting for us at the end of this road, do you understand?"

He turned away from her and walked as close as he could to the edge of the embankment, as if he were about to jump in. He stared at the opposite side for a long time, in silence. Then, with a painful breath, he said:

"And yet . . . out there is where your spirit is pushing you. So that you'll finally know."

He pulled out his cell phone and punched in a number. At the other end, someone picked up. Sharko cleared his throat before talking:

"Clémentine Jaspar? Inspector Franck Sharko here. I know it's late, but you said I could call at any time, and I need to talk to you."

40

Sharko hadn't said a word in the car. Lucie watched him drive, saw the muscles in his neck and jaws tense beneath the skin. She knew what he was thinking about: the answers he expected to get from the primatologist. The words that would send the two of them off on the trail of Eva Louts, so very far from here. To a place that Sharko dreaded.

Clémentine Jaspar lived only a few miles from the primate research center, in a house on the outskirts of Meudon-la-Forêt. While the house itself didn't look like much, the tree-lined property around it stretched for thousands of square yards. All around, small lamps spent the solar energy collected during the day, forming pleasant blue-tinted oases amid the trees. Clémentine Jaspar had apparently wanted to create an environment for herself that reminded her of a distant land.

Wearing an ample, brightly colored tunic, the primatologist greeted them on a large, dimly lit deck with teakwood furniture. As she sat down, Lucie was surprised to see a chimpanzee open the picture window and come up to her.

"Good lord!"

With her large, agile hands, Shery picked up a glass full of iced tea and noisily sucked down the liquid through a straw. Jaspar shot an embarrassed look at Sharko, who watched the scene in childlike amazement.

"I thought I'd closed the door, but . . . Listen, I'm counting on you not to tell anyone about Shery being here, in this house. I know it's against the rules, but ever since what happened, I don't feel comfortable leaving her alone in the center."

"Nothing to worry about. We're also counting on you not to mention *our* presence here. Let's call this an unofficial visit. The official investigation is headed off in one direction, but the two of us are convinced the answers lie elsewhere."

The scientist nodded with a knowing look. After emptying her glass in record time, Shery slowly loped toward the garden, near a solar lamp, and settled in, sitting like a meditating Buddha. She stared at the guests with a well of wisdom in her eyes.

"It's going to rain tomorrow," observed Jaspar. "Shery always does that the night before it rains. She's the best barometer there is."

"My daughter would love her," Lucie confided, amused.

"Shery adores children. Come over sometime with your daughter and they can spend the day together, just the two of them."

"Really?"

"Absolutely."

Jaspar offered her guests some iced tea. Lucie watched her move around, picked up on the complicit glances she and the chimpanzee exchanged. She thought to herself that no one on this planet was meant to live alone; people always had to attach themselves to something, whether a friend, a dog, a monkey, or toy trains . . . She sipped her drink in silence, thinking of her little daughter, who must have been asking for her. Lucie tried to remember if she'd spoken to her even once on the phone since the day she'd left their apartment in Lille. She hated herself so much for that.

The temperature outside was still mild; the late summer breeze soothed their heavy eyelids. The primatologist asked how the investigation was coming along and Sharko hastened to answer.

"The vise is closing. But we're going to need some more of your help, or your expertise. And I didn't want to ask over the phone."

He leaned forward a bit, his hands flat on the table in front of him.

"Here it is: we now know that Eva Louts was tracking down violence throughout the world and throughout history. She went to one of the most dangerous cities on the planet to look through criminal records and met with left-handed killers who had committed especially gruesome murders. She studied all those extreme cases with a single goal: to verify the correlation between hand dominance and violence."

Jaspar nodded, intrigued. Sharko continued, surprised at how fluently he could speak of evolutionary biology, something he'd known nothing about only a few days before.

"You told me at the botanical gardens that, these days, there was no more advantage for violent individuals, or individuals who had come from

274

violent backgrounds, to be left-handed, given the modern development of our weapons."

"That was the explanation Eva had advanced, yes."

"And you also said it was a great disappointment for her when she realized this in Mexico."

"I suppose it was. Like any researcher, she must have wanted to confirm her findings by observing a high proportion of left-handers with her own eyes. To see the living proof of her theory, so that she could then reveal it to the world. Unfortunately, the Mexican criminals were no more left-handed than you or I."

"But Eva never gave up. She struck out in Mexico, so she went looking somewhere else. In the virgin lands of the Amazon . . ."

He allowed a silence to sink in. The two women stared at him intently. Sharko turned toward Lucie:

"The minute I saw that film, I knew what she'd gone to find in the jungle was violence in its purest state. A violence cut off from any civilization, any human influence. An ancestral violence that had been perpetuated in the heart of a primitive tribe. Would she finally find her left-handers this time?"

Lucie raised a hand to her mouth, as if the obviousness of it had suddenly struck her in the face. Jaspar drank her tea thoughtfully, then nodded with conviction. Her eyes were shining.

"What you're saying makes sense, even though I don't care much for the term 'primitive tribe,' since they're just as evolved as we are. The aboriginal tribes have not been contaminated by the modern world, with its factories, wars, and technology. Any ethnologist will tell you: studying these tribes is like a time machine, because the genomes evolved differently—they're closer to the first *Homo sapiens* than they are to us. They've probably preserved prehistoric genes and haven't acquired others."

Lucie and Sharko looked at each other: the elements fell together logically in their minds. The investigation rested on three pillars: first, the Cro-Magnon; second, Carnot and Lambert. And between them, as an obvious link, the lost tribes, the true connection between prehistory and the modern world.

Unhesitatingly, the inspector took out the DVD and put it on the table.

"This is precisely what we're looking for: an Amazon tribe that was discovered in the 1960s. Some of the population was wiped out by an epidemic of measles. This is a tribe that almost certainly fights, or fought, its neighbors by hand or with knives to survive and conquer territory. A tribe that, in the past and maybe still today, was reputed to be the most violent, the most bloodthirsty in the Amazon, or even in the world. They're the ones Eva Louts went to find in Latin America, looking for her left-handers."

He handed Jaspar the DVD and described its sordid content, before concluding:

"Louts knew about the existence of this community, she knew where to find them. So there has to be a record of this population somewhere. Can you help us find their name, as fast as possible?"

The scientist got up to fetch a sheet of paper and wrote down the information the inspector had given her.

"This isn't really my field and I wouldn't know where to begin, but I have a friend who's an anthropologist. I'll call him first thing in the morning and get this disc to him. I'll let you know as soon as I've found out anything."

"Perfect."

The two ex-detectives finished their drinks, talking briefly about the case and about what Eva Louts might have become in a world without crime.

But that world wasn't exactly around the corner.

As they left the garden, Lucie took a long look at the great ape, who was staring at the stars as if looking for traces of her kin. Lucie thought to herself that humans were unique, in that we possessed positive characteristics that no other creature, not even that chimpanzee, could boast; but also in that we were capable of behaviors such as genocide, torture, and the extermination of other species. Could the good we were capable of make up for all that evil?

Before they got to the car, she laid her hand on Sharko's shoulder.

"Thank you for everything you're doing."

He turned to face her and gave her a smile that faded all too quickly.

"I didn't want to come here. I didn't want to let you in on what I'd discovered. Now the Pandora's box is open. I know that your body and your mind are going to drive you to go there, no matter what. But if you have to go, then I want to go with you. I'll come with you to Brazil. I'll come with you to the ends of the earth."

She hugged him.

He closed his eyes when she kissed him on the lips.

Their shadows stretched along the trees. The shadows of two doomed lovers.

41

They had run to keep up with the landscape.

Because they both wanted to survive. And live.

Live through the death that had separated them.

Closely entwined in the bed, Lucie and Franck savored every second after their lovemaking, because soon time would speed up again. Like Alice through the looking-glass, they would have to get up and start running, run without catching their breath or looking back. Run, perhaps, so that they never had to stop.

And so they enjoyed the tender motions, lost themselves in each other's gaze, smiled at each other constantly, as if trying to reclaim everything they had lost.

Finally, the first words came from Lucie's mouth. Her breath was warm, her naked body burning.

"I want us to stay together this time, no matter what happens. I never want us to be apart."

Sharko had kept his eyes glued to the numbers on the alarm clock. It was 3:06. He finally turned the appliance around so that he'd never again have to see the cursed numbers that haunted him every night. No more 3:10 a.m.

"I want that, too. It's what I've wanted more than anything in the world, but how could I have believed it possible?"

"You've never stopped believing. That's why you kept my clothes in your closet, with two little mothballs."

Lucie rested her ear on Sharko's chest, at the level of his fractured heart.

"You know, when I followed that biologist in Lyon, and I found myself facing that kid with a broken bottle, I . . . I nearly killed him because he'd snickered at my daughters' picture. I shoved the barrel of a gun into his temple and I was this close to squeezing the trigger. This close to abandoning Juliette just so I could put a bullet in his brain."

Sharko didn't move and let her speak.

"I think I projected on him all the violence I was never able to take out on Carnot. The poor kid was like a catalyst, a lightning rod. That violence was buried in me, in that miserable reptilian brain the ME told us about. We all have it in us, because we were all hunters like Cro-Magnon. That episode made me understand that . . . that deep down I still harbored the remains of . . . of something ancestral, probably animal, maybe even more than other mothers."

"Lucie . . ."

"I gave birth to my daughters, I raised them the best I could. But I never loved them as I should have, as human beings are supposed to. I should have been with them all the time. We're not here just to wage war, or hate one another, or hunt down killers. We're also here to love . . . And now I want to love Juliette. I want to take my child in my arms and think about the future, not the past."

Sharko gritted his teeth. He had to dominate the emotions that were threatening to drown him. Lucie saw the little bones rolling in his temples. He tried to speak, but his lips remained paralyzed. Lucie felt his unease and asked:

"Is it what I just said that's bothering you? Am I frightening you?"

A long silence. Sharko finally shook his head.

"I'd like to talk to you about something, but I can't. Please don't ask me any more than that. Just tell me if you can live with someone who harbors secrets. Someone who'd like to put everything he's lived through behind him, who'd finally like to see a little ray of sunlight. I need to know. It's important for me to know, for the future."

"We all have our secrets. I have no problem with that. Franck, I want to tell you, about our sudden breakup last year . . . I wasn't in a right frame of mind. My daughters had disappeared and . . . I'm so sorry for driving you away like that."

"Shhh . . ."

He kissed her on the lips. Then he rolled over on his side and turned out the light.

When he turned the radio-alarm back the right way, the digital display read 3:19.

He closed his eyes but, even though he felt good, calm, he couldn't fall asleep.

He could already feel the fetid breath of the jungle pressing down on him.

42

Lucie woke to a smell of warm milk and croissants. She stretched languorously, put something on, and walked out into the kitchen, where Sharko was waiting for her. He had on a nice white shirt under his suit and he smelled good. Lucie kissed him on the lips before sitting down to the breakfast he'd prepared for her.

"It's been a long time since I've had croissants," she admitted.

"It's been a long time since I've gone out to get any . . ."

She loved rediscovering these simple, shared habits, things she'd almost forgotten. She dipped the pastry into the milk, to which she'd added a bit of cocoa. She tried to check her cell phone, but the battery was flat dead. She noticed that Sharko, who was standing opposite her, was nervously fiddling with his own cell. His breakfast had just been some coffee and dry biscuits.

"What's the matter?"

"I reached out to a colleague in Narc to get the addresses of Lambert's family."

"And?"

"And I have the address of his sister. She lives in the fourth arrondissement. I called and got the grandfather. They're all a wreck and he didn't want to talk to me. He said he didn't understand why we were persecuting them, the cops had already been by yesterday, and the Lamberts needed to be left in peace. Then he hung up."

Lucie took a healthy bite of her croissant.

"Okay. Let me just finish breakfast, hop in the shower, and off we go."

About a dozen persons with drawn faces were gathered in a large apartment on the fifth floor of a Haussmann-style building, located near Île de la Cité. An upscale home, and no doubt an outsized rent. Lucie and Sharko had remained at the entrance, facing a man of about sixty-five or seventy, well-trimmed gray mustache, black suit, and hard face. Behind him, the family was in mourning, under the shock of recent events, struggling to understand the carnage that had taken place in Fontainebleau. Puffy, red-rimmed eyes turned toward them.

The man with the mustache, who had already spoken to Sharko on the phone, immediately went on the attack.

"Leave us the hell alone! I don't care if you're with the police, can't you see you're not welcome here?"

He was about to slam the door, but Lucie stepped forward.

"Listen, sir. We understand what a painful time this is, but we'll only be a moment. We believe your grandson was not entirely responsible for what he did, and we need to talk to you."

Lucie had weighed her words carefully. She imagined herself in the man's place, the reaction she'd have had if someone had come to tell her Clara's killer wasn't responsible. She probably would have gutted him then and there. But then, this was a different situation: his son's killer was his own grandson.

"Not completely responsible? What are you talking about?"

The voice had come not from the grandfather but from behind him. A young woman appeared in the doorway. She must have been about twenty and seemed very weak. Lucie noted her round, swollen belly: she was pregnant and clearly due to deliver soon.

"Pay no attention, Coralie," said the older man. "The lady and gentleman were just leaving."

"I want to know what they have to say. Can you give us a few minutes, Grandpa?"

Grinding his jaws, the man freed the way. The young woman had to lean against the door, stumbling slightly. Her grandfather held her up and glared at the cops.

"Her child is due in less than two weeks, for God's sake! And you want to interrogate her? Fine, but I'm staying within earshot. And don't you dare get her more upset with your questions."

The young woman wore a gold chain with a crucifix over her dark clothes. She wiped her nose with a handkerchief and spoke in a weak, almost imperceptible voice.

"Félix is . . . Félix was my brother."

Lucie put a hand on her shoulder and led her into a larger area, near the stairwell, where several chairs were scattered about. Sharko and the grandfather remained behind. The man with the mustache leaned against the railing and heaved a long sigh. Sharko realized he would soon be a great-grandfather, though he was barely seventy. Had it not been for the tragedy, he would have left a large, beautiful family behind him.

Coralie Lambert let herself drop slowly into a chair. Unconsciously, she fingered the pendant on her chain.

"How . . . how can you say Félix wasn't responsible for what he did? He killed my father and two strangers in cold blood."

Sharko kept to the background. He sensed that Coralie Lambert would speak more freely to another woman, who could better understand her suffering. Lucie, for her part, was aware that she must not talk about the autopsy or their findings; she had gone over this with Sharko before arriving. Saying too much risked ruining the whole thing. The old man, who was watching over his granddaughter like a hawk, would be quite capable of calling the police to complain, and she and Sharko would immediately be blown. She had to remain neutral, invisible.

"It's just a theory for the moment," said Lucie, trying not to commit herself. "Your brother seemed perfectly normal. No previous history of violence. To suddenly commit acts of such cruelty, for no reason, can sometimes have long-standing psychiatric or neurological causes."

"We've never had anything like that in our . . ."

Sharko cut off the grandfather, who was moving to intervene.

"Let my colleague do her job and please stay out of it."

The man glared at him. Lucie continued:

"We have to explore every trail. To your knowledge, did your brother show any particular signs of health problems?"

Lucie was feeling her way forward. She knew nothing of Félix Lambert's life but hoped this would provoke a reaction from the sister.

"No. I always got along well with Félix, we grew up together until we were eighteen. I'm a year older than he is, and I can assure you we had a wonderful childhood, very happy."

Her words were intercut by brief sobs.

"Félix was always . . . very even-tempered. What happened—I just

don't understand it. He was finishing up his architecture studies. He . . .
he had so many plans for the future."

"Did you see each other often?"

"Oh, maybe once a month. It's true that I hadn't seen him as much
lately. He . . . said he wasn't feeling so well, he complained about being
tired, getting headaches."

Lucie recalled the state of his brain, like a sponge. How could it have
been otherwise?

"Was he living with your parents?"

"The house belonged to my . . . father. He's . . . he was a businessman
and wasn't home much. He'd just come back from China, where he'd been
for almost a year."

"What about your mother?"

Coralie Lambert suddenly caressed her belly, with small, precise, unconscious movements. The belly, the crucifix . . . the crucifix, the belly . . .
Lucie knew that the future baby and God would help her get through this.
Coralie would talk to them when she felt low, and one would listen more
than the other.

After a long silence, she looked over at her grandfather, at a loss. Despite Sharko's exhortations, the man couldn't help coming to her aid.

"Her mother, my daughter, died in childbirth."

Lucie stood up and approached the man, a feverish look in her eye.

"When she gave birth to your grandson Félix, is that right?"

The old man nodded, lips pinched. Lucie gave Sharko a deadly serious
look, then said slowly and clearly:

"It is very important that you tell us everything you know about that
birth."

"Why?" the man answered harshly. "What does that have to do with
anything? My daughter died twenty-two years ago and . . ."

"Please. We can't afford to leave any stone unturned. The roots of your
grandson's actions might stretch back to his birth."

"What do you want me to say? There's nothing to tell. It's too personal,
and . . . Do you have any idea what we're going through right now?"

He held out his hand to his granddaughter.

"Come, Coralie, let's go in now."

Coralie didn't move. Everything was so shaken up in her head that she couldn't think straight.

"My father used to talk about my mother a lot . . ." she finally murmured. "He loved her very much."

Lucie turned toward her.

"Please, go on."

"He wanted her to stay alive in our minds. He wanted us to . . . to understand her death . . . From what he told me, the doctors concluded it was severe preeclampsia, which caused massive internal bleeding. My mother . . . my mother bled to death in the delivery room, and the doctors couldn't do anything to stop it."

Lucie could barely swallow. Amanda Potier had died in exactly the same way.

"Does the name Stéphane Terney mean anything to you?"

"No."

"Are you sure? He was an obstetrician."

"Absolutely certain. I've never heard that name."

"What about you?" Lucie asked the grandfather.

The man shook his head. Lucie turned back to Coralie.

"Where did your mother give birth?"

"In a clinic in Sydney."

"Sydney . . . Australia?"

"Yes. My brother and I were both born there. My father worked there for three years, and my mother went with him. After the tragedy, Poppa came back to live in France, in the family house in Fontainebleau."

Lucie straightened up, nervously putting her hand in front of her mouth.

"And . . . did your father tell you about any problems your mother might have had during her pregnancy? Was she seeing a doctor?"

The expectant mother shook her head.

"My father always said my mother never took so much as an aspirin. She had a remarkably strong constitution, Grandpa could tell you. She didn't believe in medicines or in anything that had been synthesized or manipulated by science. She wanted to give birth the natural way, in water, and she refused to be treated during her pregnancy. It was how she chose to live her life. For both pregnancies, she didn't know if she was carrying a girl or a boy. All the advances of science were of no interest to her. She believed in the magic of procreation, of birth, and she knew it would all turn out well because she was devout and put her faith in God . . ."

Her eyes drifted off into space for a long time. Lucie had no further questions to ask; her theories had crumbled. If Terney had ever gotten to know Félix Lambert, it was after his birth, perhaps during a regular exam, a routine blood test, or any number of other ways. But certainly not beforehand.

Coralie finally reacted when she felt a little kick in her womb. She tried to stand, and her grandfather rushed forward to help her.

"Don't you see how you need rest? Let's go in now."

"Just one last thing," Sharko interrupted. "Does anyone in your family have Amerindian roots or come from South America? Perhaps Venezuela, Brazil, or the Amazon?"

The grandfather gave the cop a scathing look.

"Do we look like Indians to you? We've been pure-blooded French for generations and generations! I promise you, you haven't heard the last of this."

Lucie quickly jotted down her cell phone number on a card and slipped it into the man's breast pocket.

"We can't wait."

Without answering, the two Lamberts disappeared into the apartment. The door slowly closed behind them.

"People are born and they die," Lucie said sadly, "and God's got nothing to do with it. God's got a big strip of packing tape over his mouth and his hands tied behind his back."

Sharko chose not to answer. Lucie's nerves were on edge. He pulled out his cell phone, which had started vibrating.

"Terney didn't manipulate the birth of Félix Lambert, the way he did with Carnot. He didn't create this particular monster."

"Apparently, the monster created himself. And Terney might simply have been content to find out and add him to the list."

Sharko showed Lucie the display screen.

"It's Clémentine Jaspar."

286

The inspector moved away down the hall, answered, and returned a few minutes later. Lucie gave him a questioning look, and Sharko nodded.

"Yes . . . Her anthropologist friend came through."

Lucie closed her eyes in relief. Sharko continued:

"He wants to meet us in Vémars, some backwater a few miles from De Gaulle Airport, at around eleven. Let's get going."

43

It was raining when the two ex-cops pulled up at a house located near a grain silo slightly outside of town. Beneath a gray sky with diffuse clouds, before a horizon of dull green and yellow fields, the dwelling looked like a sleeping, wounded animal. The garden had gone to seed, the paint was peeling from the walls in fat tongues, and some of the windows had been smashed.

An abandoned property. Sharko and Lucie shot each other a surprised glance.

The inspector parked the car at the end of a dirt road, behind an old Renault hatchback in a long-discontinued model. A man got out and came toward them. They shook hands.

The anthropologist Yves Lenoir, about fifty years old, seemed a plain-spoken sort of fellow. Dressed unfashionably in brown suede trousers, red wool sweater, and a checked shirt, with a white beard and salt-and-pepper hair, he immediately inspired trust. His deep green eyes shone under the thick line of his light-colored eyebrows, osmotically reflecting all the jungles whose populations he had surely studied. Leaning on a cane—he had a pronounced limp in his left leg—he walked toward the carriage gate, which turned out to be unlocked and opened with a simple push.

"Clémentine told me how important this case was to you. I wanted to meet here, where Napoléon Chimaux used to live. In fact, this was originally his father's house."

"Who's Napoléon Chimaux?"

"An anthropologist. I'm certain he's the one who shot the film Clémentine lent me. He's also the one who discovered the tribe on the DVD."

Lucie's fists tightened. She had one immediate question:

"Is he still alive?"

"Yes, last I heard."

They entered the house through a large glass door on the side, off of what must have been the living room. A few ghosts of furniture still lay around, armchairs with cracked plastic covers, layered with dust. Dampness had warped much of the woodwork. Not a single trinket or picture to be found; the drawers and doors were wide open, the cabinets completely empty. The light had dimmed, as if night had decided to fall earlier here than elsewhere.

"Everyone in the village must have been in here at some point or other. Out of curiosity. You know how people are."

"I can see that they made off with everything," said Sharko.

"Oh, well, that . . ."

Yves Lenoir walked up to a ruined table, blew off some of the dust, and set down his cane and a brown shoulder bag, from which he pulled the DVD.

"If possible, I'd like to keep a copy of this precious film and show it to various anthropological societies, especially in Brazil and Venezuela."

Sharko now understood what the man was after. He was offering them a guided tour of Napoléon Chimaux's world, but in return he had a few requests of his own. The inspector decided to play along.

"Sure. You can have an exclusive on it when the time comes." He saw a thrill flash through Lenoir's eyes. "But for now, I'll have to ask you not to breathe a word of this until we've finished our investigation."

The anthropologist nodded and put the DVD in the inspector's outstretched hand.

"Of course. Forgive me for pressing the point, but . . . I'd love to know how you came by this extraordinary document. Where did it come from? Who gave it to you?"

Sharko reined in his impatience and briefly sketched out the broad strokes of the investigation, while Lucie looked around the room. Lenoir had never heard of Stéphane Terney, or Eva Louts, or Phoenix.

"Now we'd like to ask *you* a few questions," Lucie interrupted, walking up to the two men. "We'd like to know everything you can tell us about Napoléon Chimaux and that tribe."

Their voices echoed, while outside the rain drummed more and more insistently against the roof. Lenoir gazed at the sky for a few seconds.

"The tribe you're asking about is called the Ururu. An Amazonian tribe that remains largely unknown, still to this day."

He took a book from his bag, along with a map that he unfolded. The book was thick and heavily thumbed through, its cover worn and faded. The author was Napoléon Chimaux.

"Napoléon Chimaux," murmured Lenoir.

He had pronounced the name as if it were distasteful. He handed Sharko a color photocopy of the man's portrait.

"This is one of the few recent photos anyone has seen of him. It was taken secretly, with a telephoto lens, about a year ago in the jungle. Chimaux is the French anthropologist who discovered the Ururu in 1964, in one of the most remote and unexplored areas of the Amazon. He was only twenty-three at the time, which was during the darkest period of the Brazilian dictatorship. He was following in his father's footsteps. Arthur Chimaux was one of the greatest explorers of the last century, but also one of the most unscrupulous. When Arthur came back between expeditions, it was here, to Vémars. Despite all the marvels he'd seen, I think he appreciated the simplicity of a place like this."

Sharko gazed at the picture. Napoléon Chimaux seemed unaware of the photographer. He was next to a waterway, makeup on his face and dressed in khaki like a soldier. Despite being nearly seventy years old, he looked a good ten years younger, with dark brown hair and a face as smooth and polished as steel. Sharko couldn't say exactly what it was about the photo that gave him the creeps.

Lenoir spoke with a certain amount of compassion and respect in his voice.

"Arthur Chimaux knew the Amazon very well. He was highly influential in political circles in northern Brazil and got a lot of support from people like the heads of mining concerns or prominent opponents of natives' rights. He died tragically in 1963 in Venezuela, a year before his son discovered the Ururu. He'd left him a huge amount of money."

Lenoir picked up the book and handed it to the inspector.

"*Discovering the Savage Ururu.* It was the only book Chimaux wrote about them. He talks about his incredible expedition, all the times he barely escaped death, the horror of his first encounter with the people he calls 'the last living group from the Stone Age.' He passes the population off as a living relic of prehistoric culture, capable of phenomenal violence.

He says, and I quote: 'Before me is an incredible picture of what life must have been like for a good portion of our prehistory.'"

Lenoir apparently knew the work by heart. Sharko leafed through the pages and stopped at a black-and-white photo of a native. A colossus with bellicose eyes and fleshy lips, completely naked, staring at the camera as if he were about to devour it.

Lenoir commented on the photo: "The Ururu have light skin and hazel eyes. Chimaux called them the 'White Indians.' In 1965, he brought back skeleton fragments that suggested 'Caucasoid' features."

"Meaning that the Ururu originally came from Europe?"

"Like all the Indians native to America. They descended from the first hunters of the Paleolithic Age, who crossed the Bering Strait at least twenty-five thousand years ago. That said, they're most likely the only tribe to have remained morphologically and culturally similar to the Cro-Magnon."

The inspector handed the book to Lucie. In silence, they exchanged a troubled glance, through which snaked the same incomprehensible path: Cro-Magnon, the Ururu, Carnot, and Lambert . . .

The chain of time.

Leaning on his cane, Lenoir began walking through the house toward the stairway, still pursuing his explanations:

"Chimaux isn't very kind to the Ururu in his book. He describes them as bloodthirsty, a horde of killers who constantly start tribal wars. Most of them are young, strong, and aggressive. They practice barbaric rites, culminating in a horrific death. Chimaux lays a lot of stress on his description of their extreme violence, the archaic and direct way they kill, which they learn at a very early age. If you look at the photos, you'll see that their tools and weapons are made of wood and stone. In 1965, the year his book came out, they hadn't yet discovered metal."

Sharko, who had continued to leaf through the book, pointed at a photo of four Ururu men armed with axes.

"Come over here, Lucie. Look how they're holding their axes."

Lucie went closer and, even before looking at the photo, knew the answer.

"Four men, three of them left-handed . . . Does Chimaux talk about that peculiarity?"

The anthropologist peered at the photo as if seeing it for the first time.

"Left-handed? Goodness, you're right. No, he never mentions it. It's strange there are so many of them."

They went upstairs. The creaking steps reinforced the sense of violating someone's privacy. Lenoir had switched on a flashlight. On the walls, kids had left a bunch of messages along the lines of "Marc + Jacqueline" in a heart. Lucie felt profoundly uneasy in this silent, lifeless, pernicious house. They entered a small bedroom, its window looking out on the fields. A mattress lay on the floor next to its dilapidated box spring.

"This is where Napoléon Chimaux grew up with his mother."

They could still make out the wallpaper of a child's room, its regularly repeating pattern of boats and palm trees. Foretastes of travel.

"In his book, Chimaux establishes a strict parallel between the structure of Ururu society and that of numerous primates. As with certain baboon troops, the villages split once they exceed a certain size. According to Chimaux, the 'savages' are like those monkeys: Amazonian primates whose complete lack of morality turns murder and bloody rituals into tribal ideals."

Standing in the middle of the room, Lucie looked through the book in turn, stopping at each photo. The Indians had terrifying faces, and some of them wore makeup. Lucie couldn't help thinking of the movies about cannibals she'd seen when she was younger, and she shuddered involuntarily.

"Where is he?" she asked. "Where is Chimaux today?"

"I'm getting to that, just let me finish. In 1964 and '65, Napoléon traveled the world, talking about his discovery and writing his book. He went to universities and research institutes with his photos and bone fragments. A number of scientists were interested in his findings."

"Scientists? Why?"

"Because the 'market value' of a tribal group rises depending on how remote or isolated they are. For scientists, biologists, and geneticists, blood from someone in those tribes is worth more than gold. The blood from another age has unique genetic properties, you understand?"

"I understand all too well."

"But in neither his book nor his lectures did Napoléon *ever* divulge where in the Amazon the Ururu lived, so that no one could 'steal' his population from him. Only he and his expedition crew—outlaws and gold diggers, whom he jealously protected—were able to retrace that path . . . In 1966, Chimaux suddenly disappeared from civilization. According to the locals, he only came back to this house now and then, and only for a few days at a time."

"Nineteen sixty-six was the date of the film," Lucie pointed out.

Yves Lenoir nodded, a somber look on his face.

"We know that for all these years he's been living in the largest of the Ururu villages, where apparently he reigns as supreme master over the entire population. You know, the passage of time has done away with virgin territories. Today, there isn't a square mile of this planet that hasn't been charted. Satellite photos, airplanes, increasingly lavish and well-financed expeditions. We now know geographically where the Ururu live; it's around the upper part of the Rio Negro. You can even get there relatively easily. But the Ururu are one of sixty Indian communities that have no contact with the outside world. For years, explorers were afraid to go there, because Chimaux's book had described them as being so vicious. But the spirit of adventure proved too strong, and there were more and more expeditions. Still, those who ventured into those regions to find the Ururu were driven out by force, with a clear warning from Chimaux never to come back."

Each of his words was like a poisoned dart. The people and the area he described sounded like hell on earth. Still, Lucie was convinced that Louts had managed to get to Chimaux, and that she'd intended to go back again.

In the narrow confines of the room, Lenoir struck his cane against a wall, knocking loose a bit of plaster.

"We anthropologists couldn't figure out how Chimaux had managed to become so integrated into this population, how he'd been able to climb to the top of their hierarchy and impose his rule on them. Seeing your film, I now know the answer, and that's why this document is crucial. There's no question that Chimaux went back in 1966 with the measles virus in his bag."

There was a silence disturbed only by the rain and wind. Sharko took a moment to absorb Chimaux's madness and cruelty.

"Do you mean that . . . that he brought it on purpose, like in a vial, specifically to wipe out some of the Ururu?"

"Precisely. Primitive peoples have their beliefs, their gods, and their magic. Carrying such a weapon of mass destruction, the anthropologist made himself look like a god or a demon, who could annihilate dozens without laying a hand on them. From then on, the Ururu must have worshiped him as strongly as they feared him."

"That's monstrous," murmured Lucie.

"And that's exactly why this film has to be shown to the anthropological societies. People need to know so that they can take the necessary action. Today, no foundation or NGO knows how to integrate the Ururu into the Amazon Indian populations. They're all afraid to go near."

"It's certainly monstrous, but it doesn't explain the title 'Phoenix number one,' which was written on the tape," noted Sharko. "It's not just about measles. Phoenix suggests something bigger, something even more monstrous. That contamination was only the beginning of *something* . . ."

Lucie took up the thread, on the same wavelength as her partner.

"It must have been Napoléon Chimaux who was here in France, in Vincennes, in 1984 and 1985, along with another man. The two were in contact with a gynecologist. They gave him several tapes of the same nature. Does that ring any bells?"

The anthropologist thought for a few moments.

"Chimaux did come out of the jungle from time to time. He was seen in Brazil, Venezuela, Colombia, and here as well. He kept up relations with people in France, we know that for a fact. In 1967, he was detained in Venezuela with a shipment of test tubes—from France, in fact—which he was planning to use to take blood samples from the Ururu. He had no authorization from any kind of scientific regulatory commission, no documents. He claimed he wanted to take the blood samples to help 'his' Indians, to study the different strains of malaria infecting the area. It raised a stink at the time, but Chimaux wiggled out of it, no doubt by having greased a few well-chosen palms, and also thanks to the pull his father's name still carried in the region."

Lucie paced the room, hand on her chin. Napoléon Chimaux's break with the civilized world in 1966, the film from the same year, the test tubes in 1967 . . . At the time, Stéphane Terney couldn't have been involved: he had returned from Algeria only a few years earlier to begin a career as an obscure ob-gyn. What sinister plot was Chimaux hatching in the Amazon rain forest? Who else had been involved? Who had supplied the measles virus? And who was supposed to analyze the Ururu blood samples?

It had to be the second man at the racetrack.

Three men knew the secret of Phoenix.

Terney the obstetrician. Chimaux the anthropologist. And the unknown scientist.

"Do we know where those test tubes came from, which French laboratory?" Lucie asked, her nerves straining.

"Not to my knowledge. A plane had left France with the crate, but Chimaux never gave any further information. He must have been working with a lab, that's certain. But he knew how to protect his sources."

Lucie leaned on the windowsill. Behind her, the rain clattered against the panes like small children's hands. She sighed:

"He got caught that time, but you can bet he continued smuggling. What was he coming back to this house for? To do what?"

"We don't know that either. But after they tried to kill him, he disappeared into the jungle for good, and he hasn't been seen since."

"Wait, tried to kill him? *Who* tried to kill him?"

"It made the news. It was in . . . 2004, if I remember right. I followed the story closely, since I'd been so interested in Chimaux's career. Napoléon was stabbed here"—he pointed to his left groin—"but he was with a woman that night, who surprised the killer just as he was about to strike. It saved his life. His iliac artery was barely scratched. The killer fled, and Chimaux was lucky to have survived."

Lucie and Sharko gave each other a knowing glance. The would-be assassin's method left no doubt: the man who had eliminated Terney by severing his iliac artery had attempted to kill Chimaux six years earlier.

"What did the police investigation turn up?" asked Lucie.

"Not much. Chimaux claimed it was an attempted robbery. That said, the minute he'd recovered, he disappeared into the jungle and among his 'savages' forever."

Sharko tried to hand back the book, but the other man refused.

"You can hold on to it, along with the photo. Give it all back when you give me the DVD."

He shrugged his shoulders, vexed.

"It's all such a waste. Today, it's clear that the Ururu have been increasingly contaminated by civilization—even if it hasn't entirely wiped them out, it's encroaching more and more. They're no longer pure, and they know the outside world exists. They've discovered metal, technology, they've seen airplanes in the sky. By keeping them for himself, Chimaux deprived the world of a paramount discovery, the chance to know the real history of his people, and what prehistory might have been like . . ."

They went back down to the living room in silence, feeling drained. This house had sheltered a perfectly normal child who had grown into a monster. What horrors had he committed in the heart of the Ururu tribe? What other horrors were contained on those Phoenix tapes? How many pints of blood, how many samples had traveled through the jungle and on to France? And for what reason?

As Yves Lenoir was about to head outside, Lucie stopped him.

"Just a moment. We'd like to go there, just as Eva Louts did. Tell us how to go about it."

His eyes widened.

"Go to the Ururu territory? The two of you?"

"The two of us," Sharko repeated, in a voice that brooked no objections.

After a hesitation, the anthropologist returned to the middle of the room.

"It's no small feat. You do realize that, don't you?"

"We know."

He took a map of northern Brazil from his bag and unfolded it on the table. Sharko and Lucie squeezed in next to him.

"Getting to Brazil is no problem. You don't need a visa, just a passport. I'd strongly recommend you get vaccinated for yellow fever and take anti-malarials. If your student went to meet the Ururu, she traveled about five hundred miles north of the capital, toward the Venezuelan border. She almost certainly got a plane from Manaus to São Gabriel da Cachoeira, the last town before the pure jungle. There are two or three flights a week from Charles de Gaulle; they're popular with tourists trekking up Pico da Neblina, the highest mountain in Brazil."

"You seem to know a lot about it."

"Practically every anthropologist in the world has been there; it's where you find the largest Indian reservations. Some have even tried their luck getting to the Ururu, obviously without success. Rather than buying your tickets alone, do it through a tour operator. This way your flights will be taken care of all the way to São Gabriel, and more to the point, they'll take care of getting you the necessary documents from FUNAI, the National Indian Foundation. There are police and soldiers who patrol the river and they don't go easy; you're better off having your papers in order if you want to cross through the Indian territories along the Rio Negro. At that point, leave the tour and get your own guide. The locals there are used to foreigners; you won't have any trouble finding one."

He marked the exact spot on his detailed map. A veritable no-man's-land.

"From here, you should count on a day's journey by boat, then another on foot to reach the Ururu territories. The guides will bring you there if you pay them well. I won't say people ask often, but often enough. In any case, to my knowledge, the results are always the same: Chimaux and the Ururu drive away anyone who comes near their villages, and sometimes it gets ugly."

Lucie looked closely at the map. Flat green areas stretching forever, mountains, vast rivers slicing through the vegetation. So very far from Juliette.

"We'll give it a shot all the same."

"I would gladly come with you if it weren't for this leg of mine. I know the jungle pretty well—it's not your typical forest. It's a world in motion, made of illusions and traps, where death might await at any given step. Keep that in mind."

"It's our daily bread."

They shook hands and wished one another good luck, then separated beneath the rain and drove off. Before turning the ignition, Sharko looked at the photo of Napoléon Chimaux.

"They try to kill him in 2004 . . . right around the time Stéphane Terney starts writing his book *The Key and the Lock* and hides those genetic codes. He obviously got scared and tried to protect himself. Our killer must have terrified him."

"After the attempt on his life, Chimaux claimed it was a thief, to protect himself as well. He must have known who tried to kill him. But if he'd talked . . ."

". . . He would have screwed himself, because of Phoenix. And I suspect it explains Louts's role in all this. Since Chimaux was trapped in the jungle, he might have used her as a kind of . . . scout, or courier. He sent her back to get him something."

"The names, faces, and characteristics of left-handed murderers?"

"Yes, quite possibly. Extremely violent left-handed murderers, between the ages of twenty and thirty."

Sharko turned on the engine.

"There's one last thing I need to check."

In the animal housing facility of the primate research center, Sharko and Lucie followed Clémentine Jaspar in silence. The latter walked up to Shery and showed her the recent photo of Napoléon Chimaux. Using Ameslan gestures, she asked: "You know man?"

As any human would have, Shery took the photo in her large hands, looked at it, and shook her head. She'd never seen him before.

Lucie looked at Sharko with a sigh.

"We've got Terney, we've got Chimaux. We're still missing the third man. The scientist . . ."

". . . Who casually eliminates anyone who gets in his way. A vicious, single-minded animal, willing to do anything to survive."

"And given where things stand, I unfortunately see only one place where we can go to learn his identity."

"To the monster himself: Napoléon Chimaux."

44

The departure for Manaus was scheduled for the morning after next, Sunday at 10:30, which left Lucie time to get ready for the trip and especially time to spend with Juliette. Before leaving Paris three hours earlier, she had borrowed Sharko's cell phone—hers needed to charge—to tell her mother she'd be getting home around 4:30.

It was now 4:45. Although she was very late for the end of the school day, she parked on Boulevard Vauban and ran up to the building. The gates were locked, parents and children having already deserted the place for the weekend. In front of her, the playground was dismally empty. But it didn't matter. Lucie liked this school; she could have spent hours there, alone, basking in her own childhood memories. She gazed at the stretch of blacktop with delighted eyes.

Then she rushed home to her apartment. For the first time in many months, she was happy to return to that familiar structure with its brick walls, to see the faces of the students who lived in the neighborhood. Was it because of Sharko, their night of lovemaking, their shared confidences? Because she felt she was still able to love, and could tell herself everything *wasn't* over? When she opened the door, she saw Marie Henebelle sitting on the couch, watching TV. Toys, dolls, and notebooks from summer vacation were still there, on the floor, scattered about in duplicate. There was a wonderful smell of childhood, laughter, a joyful presence.

Lucie greeted Klark, who slobbered all over her face, then rushed over and kissed her mother on the cheeks.

"Hi, Mom."

"Hi, Lucie . . ."

They gave each other slightly strained smiles.

"I'll be right back, I'm just going to say hi to you-know-who," said Lucie.

Marie noticed she was holding a present. One of those create-your-own-fashion kits. In high spirits, Lucie headed toward her daughter's room. Her heart was pounding. She opened the door and saw Juliette greet her with a lovely smile.

Lucie beamed at her daughter, then noticed the cell phone she had bought, lying in a corner. She picked it up and checked the liquid crystal screen. None of her messages had been listened to.

"Didn't you get all those messages I left you?"

"Gramma didn't show me how it worked. I don't think she likes it."

"Gramma can be a bit old-fashioned," Lucie told her daughter with a wink.

She didn't hear her mother come into the room behind her.

Marie stood there stiffly, a desolate look on her face.

"I'm sorry to interrupt, but a policeman from Paris came by this morning. Don't you think you owe me a few explanations?"

Lucie stood up, frowning, then looked at her daughter with a smile.

"I'll be back in just a minute, my lamb."

She went out, closing the door behind her. The two women walked back to the living room.

"What do you mean, a policeman was here?" she said in a whisper. "Who?"

"His name is Bertrand Manien. He came up from Paris. He asked me a lot of questions about Franck Sharko and you. And what happened last year."

Lucie recognized the name: Sharko had told her about him.

"Manien is Sharko's former boss. Why did he come here?"

"I don't know, he didn't say. He just asked questions."

"And you answered them, just like that? Our relationship and . . . what happened afterward?"

"What was I supposed to do? He was a detective, and not a very nice one. The odd thing is that he wanted to know all about Clara and Juliette, and how they got along with Sharko."

Lucie started unpacking her travel bag, deep in thought. Manien had driven all the way from Paris; he'd come here, to her home. He'd been alone . . . so he was investigating unofficially. What was he looking for? Why was he so interested in the twins? What was Sharko concealing from her?

She went to pour herself a Coke from the refrigerator, suddenly feeling less warmly toward the chief inspector: she and he would be having a long talk about this on the plane. For now, she made sure Juliette wasn't within earshot, collapsed into an armchair, and began telling her mother the broad strokes of her last few days. She described how deep the investigation had sunk in its claws, compelling her to see it all the way to the end—which unfortunately meant having to leave again the day after tomorrow.

"So," Marie said sarcastically, "what hellhole are you visiting this time?"

"The Amazon."

Her mother stood up, hands to her face.

"You're out of your mind. Completely out of your mind."

Lucie tried to reassure her the best she could.

"I won't be alone. Franck is coming with me, and we'll be going with a tour group, with a guide and everything. People go there all the time, you know? Besides, I . . . I must have the e-ticket in my in-box already. Franck is very organized. I'll be safe with him. We're just going to land in Manaus, go meet with an anthropologist, and come back. Nothing more."

"Nothing more? Do you hear what you're saying?"

Lucie clenched her jaws.

"Yes, I hear it just fine. You can scream and yell all you want, but nothing is going to stop me from going there."

She lowered her eyes.

"I'm sorry, Mom, but . . . I'm going to have to ask you to take care of Juliette a few more days."

Marie sighed through trembling fingers. Tears streamed down her face, and the words, the secret words she had kept buried in herself for so long, tumbled out as if by themselves:

"Take care of Juliette? Don't you know it's *you* I've been taking care of for the past year? That it's you and you alone I've been trying to protect from . . . from your head?"

Lucie stared at her in astonishment.

"What are you saying?"

Marie paused for a long moment, trying to get hold of herself.

"I'm saying that everything is exploding in your head, and I don't know if it's a good or bad thing. So yes, maybe you should go there, to the other end of the world, to find your own answers. Maybe that's your path to recovery after all."

"Recovery from what, for God's sake?"

Without answering, Marie went to fetch her handbag and her shoes, which she set down by the door. She wiped her nose with a handkerchief.

"Do what you have to. I'm going to gather up a few things that have been lying around here too long and go spend some time at home. I'll come back before you leave to say good-bye and look after . . . your dog."

In the hallway, Marie choked back a sob. She went into her room, pulled out her small wheeled suitcase, and threw in some jumbled clothes from the closet.

Lucie gave a long sigh at the closed door of Juliette's room. That damned cell phone was ringing again. It was probably voice mail pinging over and over, until someone finally decided to check the messages.

She opened the door wide.

She walked past the bed and picked up the phone. She erased all her messages without listening to them. Then she put away the fashion kit that was lying on the floor next to a still-wrapped school bag and a pile of un-touched objects: a pearl necklace kit; a scooter bought for Christmas, still in its box; a dress encased in plastic, still with its price tag.

There was no child anywhere in the room.

Nor anywhere else in the apartment.

45

Saturday evening

Sharko pushed his old leather suitcase into a corner of the bedroom and reassured himself that everything was finally ready for their adventure in the Amazon. He'd been surprised how easy it was to find a tour operator through a "last-minute bookings" site. Thank you, economic crisis. Officially, he and Lucie were going on a trek—medium difficulty—up Pico da Neblina, called the "Cloud Trek." The person on the phone had barely asked what kind of shape they were in (fortunately) and had given him a list of equipment to bring along. Sharko had paid for the ten-day expedition, including fees, food, miscellaneous costs, and insurance for two. Money spent for nothing, but no matter.

Despite the short notice, he'd tried to think of everything. Medicines, bug repellent, antiseptics, toiletry kit, knee socks for hiking, thick pants, new backpack, miner's lamp, mosquito netting . . . On the bedside table lay his passport and a printout of his e-ticket. Lucie had received hers, in an e-mail that also contained the same list of items to pack.

He had added that he was thinking of her.

She had answered that she was too.

They were to meet at the airport at 8:30 the next morning, two hours before takeoff. The tour operator would be responsible for getting the group to São Gabriel, lodging them for the night in a hotel, then guiding them down the Rio Negro toward the tallest peaks in Brazil. Except that at that point, Lucie and Sharko would split away from the group and get their own guide to lead them to the Ururu.

Just a stroll through a giant natural park, he sighed to himself.

Finally, he headed off to bed, knowing sleep wouldn't come easily. So many shadows surrounding him. He was dying to call Lucie, hear her voice, tell her how much he missed her. He was dying to take care of her, shelter her from the storm raging in her head.

Two cursed lovers, he thought. He had finally driven his imaginary Eugenie out of his own head, and now Lucie was picking up where he'd left off, as if this particular evil simply bounced from one person to another, without ever fading away. Sharko knew all too well the vile outlines of that hidden curse. After his daughter Eloise had died, miserable little Eugenie had begun visiting him unannounced, appearing to him off and on for more than three years, resisting every attempt to dislodge her. At first, they had probably tried to tell Lucie that her little Juliette didn't exist—or no longer existed—that she was the product of Lucie's imagination, but it had done no good: her mind blocked it out, created its own reality, and rejected anything that threatened it, setting up a wall of tantrums, denials, and refusals. And so her loved ones—her mother—had probably decided to play along, both hoping for and dreading the moment when Lucie would finally be able to confront reality.

For the reality was that Clara and Juliette were both dead, victims of Carnot's madness.

Since the beginning, Sharko had known exactly what had happened that night in late August 2009, seven days after the discovery of Clara's body in the forest. The investigation was about to break open. Thanks to cross-checks, witness statements, and composite sketches, they were on the point of arresting Grégory Carnot. Despite the hellish suffering she was going through, Lucie had followed the case, stayed with the teams. The night of the arrest, she had run upstairs with the other police, toward the small light coming from the bedroom. She had found the incinerated body on the floor—Juliette's body—and had collapsed, to wake up two days later in a hospital. Her mind had shattered. Partial amnesia due to severe psychological shock, among other ills . . . In Lucie's head, Juliette had progressively returned in the days following the tragedy.

Juliette had become a hallucination. A little ghost that only Lucie saw at certain moments, when her mind tried to remember. In the little girl's room, near the school, walking beside her.

Alone in his large bed, huddled under the blankets, Sharko felt terribly cold. Lucie, this investigation, his own demons . . . The night before, he had read Napoléon Chimaux's book, discovering for himself the violence of the Ururu, their barbarous, inhuman rituals, but also the ambition and cruelty of the book's young author. As he had written, "The chief organized a raid to capture the women of a distant tribe. They went to the place and asked the natives to teach them how to pray, using gestures and grunts. When the men knelt down and bowed their heads, they decapitated them with axes made of sharpened stone, grabbed their women, and fled."

What were they like today? How, in forty years, had this tribe evolved in the presence of the French explorer? Internet searches hadn't turned up anything; the Ururu, like their white chief, remained a mystery, unapproachable, prey to legends and questions. He told himself once again that seeking them out might be pure folly.

But everything had already been taken from Lucie and from him.

They had nothing left to lose.

In the haziness of his thoughts, at the borderline of sleep, the inspector couldn't help thinking of Francis Ford Coppola's film *Apocalypse Now*: the viscous plunge into the bowels of human madness, showing itself more nakedly as the heroes venture deeper into the jungle. He imagined Chimaux as a kind of Colonel Kurtz, covered in blood and guts, howling to the sky and subjugating a horde of savages. He could clearly hear the word repeated at the end of the film, in that haunted, sepulchral voice: *the horror . . . the horror . . .*

After a while, sounds and images blended together in his head. He was unable to tell whether he was dreaming or awake. But he started up in a fright when he heard the dull knocks at the door of his apartment. In a daze, he glanced at the alarm clock. It was exactly six in the morning. Not 6:01, not 5:59. Sharko felt his throat constrict. Six a.m. on the dot had a particular meaning, known to any police officer.

He got up, threw on a pair of pants and a T-shirt. He hid his passport and e-ticket as best he could, shoved his suitcase in the closet, and slowly walked to the door.

When he opened, not a word. Two dark silhouettes flattened him against the wall. With precise, brutal movements, they wrenched his hands behind his back and cuffed him. They waved a duly executed arrest warrant in front of his face.

Then they led him out into the rising dawn.

46

Charles de Gaulle Airport, Terminal 2F

Thousands of electrons gravitating around atoms of steel. Gallons of stress, billions of interconnected neurons, a compacted view of the world via huge electronic boards: Bangkok, Los Angeles, Beijing, Moscow . . .

Lucie nervously glanced at her watch next to the check-in counters. She was surrounded by adventurers of all stripes, mostly young, some of them couples, or singles out for a thrill. Twenty-two people—including her and Sharko—en route for a ten-day expedition in the heart of the jungle, watched over by Maxime, their guide. Some were already trying to chat him up, get on his good side, but Lucie's mind was elsewhere.

She had taken her place in line because the plane was due to depart in less than an hour and a quarter and Maxime had insisted. What the hell was Sharko doing? He wasn't answering his phone and hadn't sent any word. Was he having trouble with his phone? Caught in traffic? Lucie reassured herself he'd have to show up. So when it was her turn, she went ahead and put her suitcase on the scale. The attendant checked her ticket and passport, slapped a label on the brand-new duffel bag, and pushed a button. Her belongings disappeared behind strips of rubber, heading for the cargo hold.

Lucie moved apart from the group, excited and nervous, keeping to herself. A little later they heard an announcement: passengers for Manaus were kindly requested to proceed to the departure gate. Lucie crushed her coffee cup in her hand and, after a long hesitation, went up to a bank machine. She withdrew the maximum allowed on her credit card, twenty-five hundred euros. It would put her account seriously in the red, but too bad. She nervously passed through the security check, constantly turning around, scanning the crowd, craning her neck. She was still expecting a sign, a voice calling out her name. Once past the security scanner, she stood indecisively for a few more minutes, then followed the last stragglers to the departure lounge, where the stewards were already boarding passengers: her group of adventurers, simple tourists of all ages, Brazilians heading back home . . . Once more, Lucie considered dropping the whole thing and going back.

Swept forward by the flow of bodies, she moved closer to the airline personnel. She waited for the last possible instant before finally holding out her boarding pass.

There were two announcements: passenger Franck Sharko was asked to proceed immediately to Gate 43 for final boarding call. Lucie found herself still hoping and tried to make one last call before cell phones had to be switched off.

Then they closed the airplane doors.

Twenty minutes later, the Airbus A330 took off from the Paris airport. A guy of about twenty-five who looked like Tintin took advantage of the empty seat to sit next to Lucie. A clingy single man who started in about treks and camping gear. Lucie politely dismissed him.

Her forehead glued to the window, she thought to herself that she could never, ever catch a break in this miserable life.

Like Eva Louts, she was heading off to meet the savages with a huge question hanging on her lips: what could have happened to Franck Sharko to make him miss one of the most important rendezvous of his life?

47

The "interrogation rooms" at number 36 are not at all as we imagine them. No one-way mirror, no sophisticated equipment, no lie detectors. Just an absurd little garret office, in which the ceiling looks like it's about to come down on your head and the cabinets stuffed with case files press in as if to choke you.

Sharko was alone, perched on a basic wooden chair, cuffs on his wrists, facing a wall with a calendar and a small desk lamp. Manien and Leblond had let him stew for a few hours, locked in there like a caged lion. It was Sunday. The hallways were empty, and Manien had chosen an office on the administrative floor, below Homicide, ensuring that no one would bother them. No water, no coffee, no phone. Those bastards didn't respect any of the protocols. They wanted him nervous, tense, and especially they wanted him to wonder. An old cop's tactic, which forced the suspect to ask himself a thousand questions and start doubting himself.

The inspector had had enough. It was almost noon. Six hours, handcuffed, ass on this rock-hard chair, in a stifling office that stank of acrimony. He thought of Lucie and his insides twisted up. She must have tried calling his cell over and over, worried and impatient. And she had finally left for Manaus, he was sure of it.

She had ventured into the shadows on her own, without an explanation.

That idea alone drove him insane.

The two shitheads came back into the room, cigarettes dangling from their lips. They walked back and forth, slowly, without saying a word, just to show they were working his case. This time, Manien had a thick file under his arm. He put a CD on the desk and asked bluntly:

"Did you ever talk with Frédéric Hurault at Salpêtrière?"

"Talking with somebody doesn't make you a murderer."

"Just answer the question."

"It happened now and again."

Manien left the room again, whispering to his colleague. They were going to toy with him, take advantage of their allotted twenty-four hours to make him sweat. Many people trapped in these offices confessed to crimes they hadn't committed. The trick was to deprive an addict of his heroin, an alcoholic of his bottle, a mother of her child. They threatened, intimidated, pushed you to the limit. Every human being has a psychological breaking point that can be reached through intimidation and humiliation.

Alone once more, Sharko stared at the CD on the desk. What was on it? Why were they asking about Salpêtrière Hospital? Why had the DA authorized his arrest? A good hour later, the two men returned with more questions, then left yet again.

Then another salvo. This time, Manien sat down opposite Sharko, across the desk, while Leblond stood near the closed door with folded arms. The moron was fiddling with a rubber band.

Manien turned on a digital recorder and tipped his chin toward the CD.

"We've got proof you killed Frédéric Hurault."

Sharko didn't flinch. Any cop or shrink could tell you: to survive an interrogation, you had to deny and keep denying, weighing your words carefully. And never ask, What proof?

"I didn't kill him."

Manien opened his thick folder, making sure Sharko couldn't see what it contained. The inspector nodded toward the manila cover.

"What's in there, a ream of white paper?"

Manien took out a photo and slid it toward the inspector.

"It's white enough, but it's not paper. Have a look."

Sharko hesitated. He could refuse to cooperate, stand his ground, but he did as told. Since the moment he'd been taken into custody, Manien had been sparring with him. They both knew how it worked; they both knew that at the end of twenty-four hours, there'd be only one winner.

When he saw what was in the photo, he was overcome by violent anxiety, and his face contorted. He felt like screaming. He couldn't repress a shudder.

"I see this one got a rise out of you," said his interrogator.

Sharko clenched his fists behind his back.

"It's a picture of two little girls drowned in a bathtub, for fuck's sake!"

Manien blew out a cloud of smoke, as if to make himself look devilish.

"Do you remember the first time we talked about Frédéric Hurault, in my office? It was last Monday."

"I know it was last Monday."

"Why didn't you mention that his daughters were twins?"

Sharko remembered all too clearly the apocalyptic sight from that long-ago Sunday morning in 2001. Small bodies, absolutely identical, their heads shoved under the water. He tried to remain calm, even though it felt like his nerves could shatter at any moment. Manien had found his weak spot, the bad kneecap he'd keep pressing on until it tore the ligaments. Sharko told himself that from this point on, he'd have to hold out. Just hold out.

"Why should I? Was it important? Do you really think *that'll* help you track down his killer? I can't believe you're still hitting a brick wall on this case."

Manien turned the photo around and put it right in front of Sharko, giving the knife a further twist.

"Look at them. Pretty little blond twins, barely ten years old. Their father shoved their heads into a bathtub full of water, both of them at the same time. Just imagine the scene . . . Doesn't it remind you of anything?"

Sharko felt the storm rumbling in his head, but he kept silent. Words and phrases echoed. *We've got proof you killed Frédéric Hurault.*

Manien strung out his conclusions:

"Let's go back a year. August 2009. You flirt with a colleague from Lille, Lucie Henebelle, pretty little thing, nice-looking piece of ass. My compliments."

"Go fuck yourself."

"She's the mother of two eight-year-olds. Twin girls. And they get themselves kidnapped right on the beach while you're sitting there having a cozy little chat with the lady."

He intercut his sentences with long silences, watching for the slightest inflection on his suspect's face.

"They find the first body five days later in the woods, burned beyond recognition . . . Even her mother doesn't know her. And the second, found seven days after that, has suffered the same fate in the perp's house. So eight years after Hurault, here you are again, faced with the murder of twins. Except this time, it's personal. It's as personal as it can get. Crazy how fate can keep dishing it out."

Sharko had removed himself mentally. His body remained made of stone, but inside he was boiling. How had Manien got hold of all those details? How far had he gone in violating his privacy?

"So from that point on, it's all downhill for you. No more cushy desk in Nanterre. You come back to Homicide, in my squad. You're a real wreck. You can't get over what happened, so you scrape shit from the street, because that's all you've got left. Henebelle would just as soon slit your throat as look at you. As far as she's concerned, you took away her children. And there's no way you can give them back . . ."

Sharko didn't answer. What could he say? What could he do? He contented himself with giving Manien a disgusted stare. Manien blew another cloud of smoke at him. His face was gray, emotionless.

"Sometimes, to give somebody something, you have to take from somebody else. That's what you did—you took a life. A life that deserved to rot in hell. A life that looked a lot like Grégory Carnot's. Eye for an eye, and all that."

Sharko sighed, then stood up. He walked around a bit, cracked his neck joints. He stopped in front of the silent reptile and looked him in the eyes.

"Since we're probably going to be here for some time, couldn't you remove these cuffs?"

"Go ahead," Manien ordered his subordinate. "He knows the rules."

Leblond undid the cuffs. Sharko forced himself to smile.

"Thanks, that's very kind of you. And while you're at it, would you mind fetching me a cup of coffee and some water?"

"Don't push it," were Leblond's only words before he finally left the room. Manien had also stood up. He walked to the barred window and, hands behind his back, stared out at the rooftops before resuming.

"You know, this business with the eyelash and the DNA on Hurault's clothes really had me going. A cop like you, if you committed a murder, you wouldn't leave a hair at a crime scene like that. You'd have put on a mask or a ski cap, taken all sorts of precautions."

"So you know all you need to know. You must be looking for somebody else."

"Unless you did it on purpose."

He turned around suddenly, staring deep into Sharko's eyes.

"You killed someone, but you're a cop, so something way down inside you, something unconscious, told you you'd have to pay your debt. Leaving proof of your presence there was like . . . like a way of absolving yourself of the crime. You could tell yourself that if we didn't catch you, then it wasn't really your fault. But you didn't want to make it too easy. That's why you contaminated the scene the day we found the body. Given where the crime took place, you knew thirty-six would catch the case, and you wanted to stir things up a bit. Complicate our job by leaving that ambiguity about the DNA. Did you leave it there when you committed the crime, or when we found the body?"

"It's an interesting theory, but I'm not that masochistic. Why would I want to spend the rest of my life in prison?"

Manien smiled. He went over to the desk drawer and pulled out Sharko's Smith & Wesson, bagged and unloaded, which he waved in front of him.

"Hence the gun, with just one bullet in the chamber."

Sharko felt like ramming his head into the other man's nose. Manien kept at it:

"You bought it last March in a gun shop in the sixth, according to your bank statement. You do Hurault, and if the law catches up with you, you off yourself. Because deep down, you want to die; it's just that you don't have the balls to do it on your own. You'd have to be cornered like a wild beast. There'd have to be no other way out."

"You're crazy."

"Except, Henebelle has now come back into your life. And that's changed everything, because now you don't want to die anymore. Now you've got just one thing on your mind: to figure a way out of this mess."

Sharko shrugged.

"For the Smith and Wesson, I was planning on joining a firing range. You can check it out. The bullet in the chamber came from a box of cartridges that you must also have found in my closet. So I didn't take it out—so what? People forget things sometimes, don't they? Your explanation's a real corker, but it'll never stand up in court. You've got nothing against me, no material proof, no witnesses. You've hit a dead end, and that's why you're making such a hash of this. You play at intimidation, even if it means screwing up procedures and your career along with them. It's so delicate going after a cop from thirty-six . . ."

Sharko sat back down on his chair.

"It's either you or me—the DA must have told you that, right?"

"None of your business what the DA said."

"If you're still empty-handed tomorrow morning at six, I'll be in a position to fuck you both."

Manien's jaws clenched.

"Yeah, you'll be in a position."

The squad leader ripped the cups from Leblond, who had just returned, and slammed them on the desk. Half the water spilled on the inspector's knees. Manien snatched up his folder and headed straight for the door.

"Except you'll never be in that position. Because the proof we've got is on that CD right there in front of you. And to show we're not panicking and we're confident of our case, we won't come back to see you until late tonight, for the kill. So until then, you can just stew in your own lousy juice."

48

anaus, or perpetual sweat. A city of crushing humidity and equatorial heat. The mercury never dropped, not even at night. The moment she passed through the sliding doors, Lucie wasn't just perspiring, she was dripping. The jungle breathed, the waters of Rio Negro saturated the air and went for the lungs. The Amazon rain forest, though invisible, announced the local color.

After changing currency, Lucie and the group guided by Maxime rode in a minibus to the small local Eduardinho Airport. One and a half miles of road. Concrete high-rises in the distance, multilane highways, industry. Advertising billboards in Portuguese between the palm trees and the mangroves.

Maxime gave them bottles of water and snacks, with big helpings of tourist information that Lucie couldn't have cared less about. Manaus, former rubber capital . . . Colonial mansions built with French materials, etc., etc. Her cell phone had automatically switched over to the Brazilian network Claro and she tried desperately to reach Sharko. It must have been around 10:00 p.m. in France. Still no message, no news.

Only one airline, Rico Linhas Aéreas, flew into São Gabriel da Cachoeira. At 6:32 p.m., the group took off on board a small-model Embraer EMB. The landscape was breathtaking, its opulence arrogantly expressed. Lucie saw before her the formation of the Amazon River, resulting from the confluence of the black waters of Rio Negro and the yellow waters of the Solimões. At certain points, its breadth reached nearly twenty-five miles. A few scattered villages marked the last vestiges of civilization. Slowly, the sun set over the emerald horizon, slit by liquid clefts, dark mires, secret swamps. Brown wounds opened, as mountains broke through the vegetation. Lucie imagined the mysterious life teeming below, those millions of species of plants and animals that struggled to survive, reproduce, perpetuate their genes in the tropical swelter. The Ururu were one of those species. Predators of the shadows that had come down through the centuries, carrying with them a prehistoric violence.

She drifted off, then started awake when the landing gear hit ground two hours later. A burst of applause as the engines shut off. The airport boasted all of two runways, with barbed wire around them, and a large un-painted building. No rolling walkways here; they pulled out your bags on the tarmac. It smelled like hot asphalt and especially like river water, that peculiar blend of silt and deadwood. Passport control, customs. Oppressive military police presence. Harsh, inquisitive looks. Remnants, according to Maxime, of the dark years when the mining companies hunted down and massacred the natives for the gold, lead, and tungsten to be found in the up-per Rio Negro. Today, these police were men of the jungle, who traveled the river in canoes and looked for poachers in the forest: traffickers in precious woods, medicinal plants, and animals. Not to mention drugs. The borders with Colombia and Venezuela were just a hundred miles away, and the FARC not much farther. For the first time, Lucie was happy to be with the group. She didn't know a word of Portuguese—it wasn't the sort of language they taught in northern France—and she wanted to avoid complications.

The group was mobbed the moment they exited the airport. People of-fered to take their picture with a sloth in their arms, a boa around their neck, a baby caiman on their knees. Some held out pamphlets in English: boat tour up the Rio Negro, visit to Indian reservations, excursion in the jungle. Merchants and guides squeezed around them by the dozens . . .

At that point, it occurred to Lucie how she might speed up the process. In the tumult, she moved away from the tourists, pulled out a photo of Eva Louts that she'd had blown up, and let herself be submerged in the flood of locals.

"Who knows?" she asked in English. "Who knows?"

The photo circulated from hand to hand, was crumpled, sometimes disappeared, until a man of about forty, with a long black beard and a dark, gaunt face, approached her. *A mix of white and Indian*, Lucie thought. The man answered in English, "I know her."

Behind her, Maxime called his charges, as best he could, to gather on the parking lot near a minibus. Lucie looked squarely at the other man and drew him aside.

315

"I want to go where she went. Is that possible?"

"Everything is possible. Why the Ururu?"

So he knew about the Ururu; he really had brought Louts there. His voice was somber. The man's shirt was half open and soaked with sweat; his black chest hairs jutted out. He's got the face of a crook, thought Lucie, but she didn't have much choice.

"To meet Napoléon Chimaux, like she did. How much?"

The guide pretended to think about it. Lucie watched him carefully. He was tall, strongly built, and had scars everywhere. His hands were as fat as rock crabs.

"Four thousand reais. That includes the crew, the boat, equipment, and food. I take care of everything. I'll bring you there."

He had spoken in French—with a pronounced Latin American accent but perfectly understandable. Lucie didn't try to bargain. The price corresponded to the amount of cash Eva Louts had withdrawn.

"Fine."

They shook hands.

"Are you staying at the King Lodge?" he asked.

"Yes."

The man handed back the photo.

"Tomorrow morning, five o'clock sharp. That way, we'll get to the end of the river before nightfall and sleep there before setting out on foot the next day. Full payment up front. Don't forget your authorization papers and some cash for the trip downriver."

"Tell me what happened with Eva Louts. What was she looking for out there?"

"Tomorrow. By the way, my name is Pedro Possuelo."

He disappeared into the crowd, as discreetly as he'd come. A shadow among shadows . . .

The trip from São Gabriel was a trek in itself. They took another minibus with mismatched doors and a grinding engine. Lucie couldn't make out much of the town, even under a full moon, but she could sense its poverty. Half-crumbled concrete walls, tin roofs, dusty sidewalks under hanging lightbulbs. These people didn't even have a road by which to leave the area; the jungle enclosed and strangled them.

Maxime, whose face was beginning to betray his exhaustion, still kept up his explanations, playing his role to the hilt: after the occupation by the Carmelites and until the beginning of the twentieth century, the waterfalls along the river had turned São Gabriel into a garrison town. The large freighters from Manaus couldn't advance any farther into the jungle because of the rapids. The Indians came from the other side, in light canoes, to buy and sell commodities, making the spot into a trading post for goods and services. The current population—fewer than twenty thousand—was composed mainly of natives who had left the forest: growers, merchants, and artisans who maintained ties with their birth regions. São Gabriel wasn't just a town in the forest, housing the headquarters of NGOs such as FUNAI and IBAMA or the National Health Foundation. It was also a town *of* the forest.

The travelers arrived at the King Lodge, a small hotel at the edge of the jungle, managed by whites. Bright colors, giant fans, palm trees in the lobby. Maxime gathered his troops and retrieved the FUNAI authorizations from one of his colleagues, who had arrived earlier. He handed out the documents to each traveler and explained the next day's program: departure at ten o'clock in a motorboat to reach a campsite sixty miles upriver, night in a hammock in the middle of the jungle with a dinner of typical local fare.

After giving final instructions, he said goodnight and left everyone to their own devices.

Exhausted, Lucie went to her room on the ground floor and turned on the fan. She checked her cell phone: no network connection; they had reached the end of the civilized world. With a sigh, she went to take a good, long shower. She needed to rid herself of that obscene dampness, refresh her spirit and regenerate her body.

She slipped on a pair of shorts, a T-shirt, and flip-flops, and went down to the hotel lobby; it had a phone booth that she'd already noticed when she arrived. A man was reading the paper on a bench, some young people were having a drink at the bar. She tried one more time to call Sharko: it must have been nearly 3 a.m. in France. Voice mail. Feeling hopeless, she left the phone number of the hotel and hung up.

When she went to bed, she was surprised not to find any mosquito netting, then recalled what Maxime had said: the acidic waters of Rio

Negro kept insects away. Still, she spotted a large moth against the glass. She opened the window to let it out and stared at the night. Infinite blackness in a pure sky, a handful of fireflies, crackling, squawks, screeches. Lucie thought of the monkeys on the videotape, the white-headed capuchins. Perhaps they were out there, right nearby; maybe they were watching her. Around her, the trees shook, the branches vibrated, and Lucie half expected to see dozens of mysterious animals leap from them.

Just before shutting the window, she glimpsed a spot of light in the dark. Something circular and gleaming.

The full moon seemed to be reflecting on . . .

Binocular lenses.

Lucie suddenly couldn't breathe. Could she be mistaken? Was her imagination playing tricks on her in her exhaustion? No . . . A dark shape was looking in her direction, at the edge of the jungle, about thirty yards away.

Lucie could feel her heart pounding. She tried to control her emotions and closed the window without locking it. She drew the curtains, turned off the light, and quickly returned to the window, casting a furtive glance outside. She stared into the void. No doubt about it, someone was near the tree line, moving but not coming closer.

The shadow was waiting.

Waiting for Lucie to fall asleep.

Gripped by panic, Lucie looked around the room. Moonlight filtered through the curtains and onto the sides of furnishings. She made out a bedside lamp, a vase with tropical flowers . . . She yanked with all her might on a coathook screwed into the wall and finally managed to pull it out. She was now holding a piece of wood about fifteen inches long, with metal hooks. Quickly, she arranged the quilt and pillows beneath the sheets to make them look like a body.

Then she hid in the bathroom, between the window and the bed.

Who knew she was here? Who was watching her? Locals? Indians? The military? Had the photo of Louts she'd circulated at the airport fallen into the wrong hands? This was a small town, and news must travel fast.

Lucie thought of the murders of Louts and Terney, the attempted murder of Chimaux. Time seemed to stretch into infinity. The fan thrummed, stirring the thick, unwholesome air. Lucie could hear herself panting like a cornered animal. She was crazy not to go down to Reception for help.

But she needed to know.

Suddenly, a sound at the window: the handle turning. Then a body moving heavily on the carpet. Lucie held her breath, heard the slight hiss of a lid being removed. She knew the intruder was very close, just on the other side of the wall. He surely had his back turned. She got a good grip on her weapon, raised it over her head, and burst into the room.

She struck just as the shadow near the bed was turning toward her. The wood struck his skull, and the hooks dug into his face. The metal sliced through his cheeks like butter. Lucie just had time to notice the tanned face, combat fatigues, and green beret: a soldier. The man grunted and, half dazed, threw his fist straight in front of him. Lucie was hit in the temple and knocked backward. The wall shook, a vase broke with a crash. She had barely regained her wits as the silhouette leapt through the window. She moved to jump after him, but a fat black shadow crossed her field of vision and froze her in her tracks.

A spider.

The creature was just on the edge of her bed, almost balancing over the void. It seemed to be staring at her, exploring the texture of the sheets with its long legs. It was all black, with a red hourglass on its upper abdomen.

Lucie scuttled back on her hands and knees, almost crying out. Then she spun around and flew into the hotel corridor, while her two young neighbors stepped outside to see what all the noise was about.

Overcome by emotion, she collapsed in their arms.

49

Manien's husky smoker's voice. "The recording on this CD here comes from the psych ward of Salpêtrière Hospital. It's dated March 14, 2007, and it was given to us by Dr. Faivre, Frédéric Hurault's psychiatrist. Do you know Dr. Faivre?"

Sharko squinted. In the narrow confines of the office, the bright light of the bulb was hurting his eyes. Shadows clung to the file cabinets and shelving, plunging them into a tenacious darkness. Manien had been grilling him for more than twenty minutes already. In the course of the day, he had brought him sandwiches, coffee, and water but had denied him a phone call.

Leblond wasn't in the room, but he hadn't gone far. Now and again, they could hear his soles creaking in the hall.

"I've heard of Dr. Faivre," Sharko replied.

"Nice guy, with an excellent memory. I asked him a few questions, and from what he told me, you saw each other from time to time, you and Hurault, since you were being treated in the next department over. Does that ring any bells?"

"Vaguely. So what?"

Manien picked up the CD.

"Did you know the psych ward has surveillance cams?"

"Like everywhere, I imagine."

"They especially have them in the lobbies and in front of the hospital, where the patients sometimes go to have a smoke and a chat. It's where you used to have your coffee while waiting for your appointment . . . They keep it all archived, for security reasons and in case of problems down the road. They keep the recordings for more than five years. Five years, can you imagine? I suppose that's not too surprising, when you're dealing with loonies . . ."

Sharko felt he was on a slippery slope. If his interrogators had put wires on him, they would have seen that, despite his outer calm, his tension level had just spiked, and his body begun to sweat abnormally. The last day and night had been pure hell. This time he didn't answer at all. Manien sensed he was gaining traction and pushed on.

"I'm sure you can guess that we found several instances of you and Hurault talking together. I've spent the last two days looking through these tapes. Hours and hours of watching retards stumble around in pajamas."

"And?"

"And? And so I asked myself, what can a child-killer, who's been judged irresponsible for his actions and who got off with just nine years in psych, what can he possibly have to say to the cop who put him away?"

"No doubt stuff along the lines of, 'How's your schizophrenia coming along? Still hearing voices?' The usual chitchat when two loonies get together. How am I supposed to remember?"

Manien twiddled the CD between his fingers. A ray of light danced on the surface, like the sinister eye of a lighthouse.

"The video on this CD has no sound, but we can clearly see both your lips. We were able to reconstruct one of your conversations with the help of a lip-reader."

Manien got off on the intrigued look that flashed across Sharko's face. He stood up abruptly, a smug twinkle in his eye.

"That's right, *Chief Inspector*, you're screwed. We found a recording."

Silence. Manien twisted the knife a little more.

"That day, Hurault told you he'd pulled it over on everybody—cops, judge, and jury. He confessed he was fully aware of what he was doing when he killed his two girls. And that's why, three years later, you stabbed him in the gut several times over with a screwdriver. You made him pay."

Stunned, Sharko leaned forward to pick up his cup of water. His fingers were trembling and his eyes stung. His entire organism was about to give in. Of course, he could demand to see what was on the CD, but wouldn't that be playing their game and digging himself in even deeper? His words and his reactions had been recorded; now it would all work against him . . .

He tried to read Manien, hesitated a long time. His eyes fell on the calendar behind the other man.

He choked back the words that were about to come out of his mouth.

He leaned back in his chair and made a quick mental calculation.

Then he slapped his two open hands to his face.

"You're bluffing. Jesus fucking Christ, this whole interrogation is just hot air!"

For a second, Manien looked shaken. Sharko was exultant. He took a moment to calm his nerves, then asked:

"What was the date of that recording again?"

"March 14, 2007. But . . ."

Manien turned around to look at the calendar behind him, not understanding. When he turned back toward Sharko, the inspector was standing, fists planted on the desk.

"That's three years ago. If I've figured correctly, it was a Wednesday. And I *never* had any sessions at the hospital on a Wednesday. They were always on Monday, sometimes on Friday when I had to go twice a week. But never Wednesday. You know how I know? Because my wife and daughter died on a Wednesday, and it's the day I go visit their graves. I was going to the hospital to get rid of the little girl in my head who reminded me of my daughter, and to do that on a Wednesday would have been unthinkable. The illness wouldn't have allowed it, don't you see?"

Sharko snickered.

"You tried to beat me down with details, dates, places, to make me think you had something. But you overdid it and got yourself caught in your own trap. You don't have any video of me and Hurault. You were just . . . supposing."

Sharko took three steps backward. He could barely stand.

"It's three o'clock in the morning. I've been rotting in this stinking office for twenty-one hours. The battle is over. I think we can call it quits now, don't you?"

Manien gave the ceiling a spiteful glare. He picked up the CD and flung it in the trash. Then he shut off the digital recorder with a sigh, before giving a coarse laugh.

"Goddammit . . . Son of a bitch . . ."

He stood up and slapped his hand noisily on the calendar.

"You can't convict somebody because he starts parking his car underground. Right, Sharko?"

"No, you can't."

"There's one last thing I'd like to know. Just between us, how did you manage to get Hurault into the Vincennes woods without leaving any traces? Not a phone call, not a meeting, no witnesses, nothing. I mean, shit, how did you *do* it?"

Sharko shrugged his shoulders.

"Why should there be any traces when I didn't kill him?"

As he was about to leave, Manien called to him one last time.

"Go in peace. I'm dropping the case, Sharko. The file will go cold and get stacked up with the others."

"Am I supposed to say thank you?"

"Don't forget what I said the other day: nobody knows about this. The DA acted in secret, as did I. He doesn't want any waves."

"Meaning what, exactly?"

"Meaning that if you try to fuck me with what happened here, be prepared for all this shit to explode in your face. And frankly, Sharko, between you and me, you did the right thing offing that bastard."

Sharko went back inside the room, picked up his holstered weapon, and held his hand out to Manien, who held out his own with a smile. Sharko grabbed it, yanked the police captain toward him, and jammed his head smack into the other man's nose.

The cracking sound, like the shock, was huge.

50

Once back home, Sharko rushed over to his cell phone and listened to his messages. There were six of them. Lucie, at Charles de Gaulle. Lucie, in Manaus. Lucie, in São Gabriel. Each more panicky, desperate, and distant than the last. At the sixth, he switched out of voice mail and immediately dialed the number of the hotel she had last called from, the King Lodge. Operators, interminable wait. Five minutes later, they were finally connected. Sharko felt his heart contract. Her voice was so faint, so far away.

"I had some problems, Lucie. Problems with Manien. They wouldn't let me call because I was in custody."

"In custody? But . . ."

"Manien's been trying to screw me over since the beginning, I'll explain everything. Please forgive me. I'm taking the first flight out. I want to be with you. I want to be near you—we should be looking for the answers together. Please, Lucie, tell me you'll wait until I get there."

In the hotel lobby, Lucie stood alone against the phone booth. She had put a bandage on her left temple. Everything was still a big jumble in her head.

"They tried to kill me, Franck."

"*What?*"

"Someone snuck into my room and put a black widow in my bed. If I'd been asleep, I wouldn't have stood a chance."

Sharko's fingers gripped the phone. He paced back and forth, feeling like he wanted to bang his head against the wall.

"You have to go to the police! You have to . . ."

"The police? The guy was a cop, or a soldier. I don't know anything about this town, this world. I think if I talk to someone, it'll only make things worse. We're in the middle of nowhere here. I told the hotel staff I'd left my window open, which you're never supposed to do. And that I'd panicked and banged my head when I saw the spider. Nobody suspects a thing."

Lucie noticed the receptionist staring at her. She turned away and lowered her voice.

"That goddamn murdering scientist knows why I'm here, I'm sure of it. I circulated Louts's photo at the airport, that's how he must have found out. All I know is they tried to make my death look like an accident."

Sharko had already gone to his computer and entered a search for a flight to Manaus.

"The first flight is two days from now—*shit!*"

A silence.

"Two days? That's too long, Franck."

"No, no, listen to me: you stay quietly at the hotel and surround yourself with people until I get there. Change rooms, try not to spend time alone, eat at the hotel restaurant, and especially don't go into town."

Lucie gave a sad little smile.

"Two days is too long. If . . . if I stay here, where I am, I'm done for. The killer won't give up. He's going to keep at it. I don't have a weapon or any way to defend myself. I don't know what my enemies look like. Listen, I've already found a guide. I leave at five in the morning for the jungle. Finding Chimaux is my only hope."

Sharko put his hand to his head.

"Please, wait for me."

"Franck, I . . ."

"I love you."

Lucie felt tears welling up.

"I love you too. I . . . I'll call again soon."

And she hung up.

Sharko rammed his fist into the wall. He was here, thousands of miles away from her. And there was nothing he could do. In his rage and his powerlessness, he went to open a beer, which he downed in several gulps. Then a second one. The liquid ran down his chin.

Then he started in on whiskey. Not in moderation.

Lurching across the room, he saw his Smith & Wesson on the table. He picked it up and threw it at the television.

An hour later, he collapsed, dead drunk.

Sharko struggled to get up off the couch when he heard the knocking at his door. He squinted at his watch through bleary eyes: five in the afternoon.

Almost twelve hours of heavy alcoholic sleep.

Coated tongue, breath like a sewer. Disoriented, he dragged himself upright and shuffled to the door. When he opened, Nicolas Bellanger was standing there, a dark look on his face. He came straight to the point:

"What are you playing at with Chénaix and Lemoine?"

Sharko didn't answer. Bellanger walked in without being invited, noticed the empty bottles on the coffee table, the gun on the floor, the smashed TV.

"Shit, Franck, did you think you could keep at it on the sly and no one'd be the wiser? You're still investigating this case on your own, aren't you?"

Sharko rubbed his temples, eyes half closed.

"What is it you want?"

"I'm trying to understand why you were so anxious to get a decoded DNA sequence. I'm trying to find out what you've learned, and how and where. Who wrote that sequence?"

Limply, Sharko headed into the kitchen and glanced at his phone. No messages from Lucie. She must now have been somewhere in the middle of the river. He chucked two effervescent aspirin tablets into a glass of water and threw the window open wide. The fresh air felt good. He turned back to his chief.

"First tell me what *you've* found out."

Bellanger nodded his chin toward the inspector's chest.

"Go get dressed, swallow a tube of toothpaste, and fix yourself up. We're running over to the lab. Did you tell anybody about this sequence? Who knows about it?"

There was urgency and gravity in his words.

"What do you think?"

"Good. We're locking down everything. Nobody is to know about this, nothing can leak out. This lousy case is threatening to become an affair of state."

The inspector downed his aspirin with a grimace.

"Why's that?"

Bellanger took a deep breath.

"The three sheets of paper you handed in—those letters are the genetic code of an absolute monster."

The young chief looked Sharko straight in the eyes and added:

"A prehistoric virus."

51

The river was dark and acidic, like a foretaste of hell. Inky waters leaching tannin from plant debris, logjammed streams from wooded isles, tangles of vines, knotted roots. Rio Negro widened and narrowed, strangled by the walls of the forest. The rising dawn could barely filter through the leafy canopy, where colonies of monkeys shrieked, attracted by the rumbling of the motor. The *Maria Nazare*, a small riverboat, looked like a steamboat in miniature, with a maximum capacity of six people. Lucie was one of four on board—herself and three crewmen. There was her guide, Pedro Possuelo, as well as Candido and Silverio, two young Baniwa Indian brothers who, according to Pedro, lived in São Gabriel with the twelve members of their family. Three men armed with rifles, machetes, and knives, sitting among coils of rope, jerry cans of gasoline, pots, and scattered food supplies. Individuals whom she knew only by their first names. She wasn't entirely reassured, but her guide seemed honest enough: he had come to pick her up at the hotel, chatted with the staff, and told them she'd be with him from now on. People knew the man, and knew she was with him.

At regular intervals along the banks, imposing signs appeared, announcing the presence of Indian territories: ATENÇÃO! AREA RESTRITA. PROHIBIDO ULTRAPASSAR ... Customs notes punctuating the waterway. Pedro came and leaned his elbows on the stern next to Lucie. He was eating small crackers made from cassava—everything here was made from cassava—and offered her one, which she accepted. It was good, chewy, slightly salty. It put something in her stomach.

"I picked up Eva Louts at the airport exit, the same as I did with you," said Pedro. "I told her I could bring her out there, to the edge of the Ururu territory."

"How did it go, 'out there'?"

After swallowing another mouthful, Pedro plunged his hands into a basin and ran clear water over his face. The air was thick, saturated with humidity, marking the transition between the rainy and dry seasons. Ahead of them, the sun was just rising: a fat, severed fruit the color of blood.

"The first time I tried to go to the Ururu territory must be about fifteen years ago. This millionaire anthropologist, kind of an eccentric, wanted to try his luck."

He showed a wide scar on his left collarbone, as well as tiny buckshot under his skin, around his thighs.

"Buckshot from a rifle . . . I've kept it as a souvenir of my years battling poachers. I was young and fearless then. The man paid me a fortune to go there. Exploring conditions were a lot harder than they are today. The boats weren't as good, no GPS, and the Ururu were buried way back in the jungle. Today they've come closer to the riverbanks. A few hours after we got out of the boat, Chimaux and his savages came this close to killing us—he just had to snap his fingers—like that . . . But he realized he had more to gain by letting us live than by slaughtering us. These days he uses guides like me as messengers."

Nervously tapping the tips of her tall hiking boots on the metal stern, Lucie watched the black, peaceful flanks of the river. She imagined the gray faces watching her, armed with bows and blowguns. She imagined giant serpents rising from the waves. Too many horror movies and other idiocies from the West, giving her a false image of this lost world.

"Messengers? How so?"

"These days, we'll bring anybody who wants to go up to the edge of the Ururu territory, no questions asked. I don't care what you plan to do over there. As long as I get paid enough to keep the wheel turning, you understand?"

"Perfectly."

"Those foreigners . . . Chimaux likes to terrify them. He hides in the jungle, prowls around them, sometimes wearing this hideous makeup. Sometimes he attacks them, just as a warning, to show whose territory it is. He's completely crazy."

Lucie's fingers clutched the ship's rail. Pedro spoke in a natural tone, as if death and horror were his daily bread.

"He spins a wheel of fortune to decide what fate they'll suffer. Every adventurer knows how it works, knows the rules, the dangers, but they all want to try their luck, because that's what exploring is about. Everyone wants to learn the secret of the Ururu. Chimaux's book had the opposite effect of what he'd intended. Instead of scaring people off, it just made them more curious. There's no shortage of people on this earth who want to see horror close up."

Pedro nodded at the inaccessible riverbanks.

"The Indians are dangerous. Not that long ago, it wasn't warning signs you saw posted along the river, but heads on spikes. The natives are out there, all around us. Most of them despise us. Whenever whites have come, they've brought only wars, hardship, and disease. These natives have been massacred, enslaved; they've seen their women raped. Years have gone by, but the old wounds remain. Today, the nice Westerners think they'll win them over with hats or iPods, but they're still the invader."

Lucie realized how fragile the world was, with its sensitive borders, constantly moving like the boundaries of vegetation. Pedro stared deep into her eyes.

"You're like that girl—you don't look like the kind I usually bring out here. You know there's no life insurance with me, right, and that you might leave a few feathers behind too?"

"Yes . . . Yes, I do."

Lucie let the silence and the emerald light envelop her. She was afraid, not of dying, but of leaving the world without saying good-bye to those she loved. Despite everything, she felt it was in this luxuriant blend of life and decay that her fate awaited her.

The engine backfired, startling her out of her reverie. A dead log floated downriver, rolling slowly on itself like a wounded crocodile.

"Was Louts able to make contact with Chimaux and the Ururu?"

He nodded.

"Something happened in the jungle, with her. I don't know how she did it, but she got through. Chimaux took her with him for three days. I've never known him to allow anybody onto his lands. My crew and I waited for her at our camp, outside the territory, keeping our rifles handy."

He spat in the river.

"She didn't say anything on the return trip. She knew how to keep a secret. But she did let me know she was coming back and that she'd be in touch when she did. Then she left for France and we never saw her again."

Pedro Possuelo turned around at a signal from one of his men. He headed to the prow, with Lucie following. A blast of the foghorn. The Brazilian pointed toward a large hut at the edge of a distant pontoon dock, which nearly blocked the river.

"We're coming to the FUNAI outpost. They control all access upstream. Don't forget, officially, you're touring along the Indian reservations." He shoved a camera into her hands. "Photojournalist. Okay?"

"Okay . . ."

He held out his hand.

"Two hundred."

Lucie gave him the cash that would spare them too many questions, searches, delays. The engine changed gears; fat white billows of smoke curled from every side of the boat. Gradually, black, human shadows appeared in the haze. Machine guns slung across the shoulder, fatigues, combat boots: soldiers. They walked slowly on the dock, while one had remained in the hut, a huge satellite phone to his ear. The sides of the *Maria Nazare* slowly butted against the fat mooring buoys. Pedro jumped onto the pontoon dock and shook hands: these men knew each other. A few words exchanged in Portuguese, checking papers, money passing from one hand to the other, a few questioning looks toward Lucie. Then smiles, pats on the shoulder: they were through. Pedro hopped back onto the boat, called for them to leave.

Gas to the motor, starting off . . .

At that moment, the man from inside the hut came out and stood in the middle of the dock, hands flat between his belt and his stomach. Through the wisps of fog, he fixed Lucie with a cold smile. Two thick, reddish scars, still fresh, striped his face.

Lucie swallowed hard. The man with the black widow.

As the boat gathered speed, she saw him bring his index finger to his throat and make a slow, horizontal movement, while moving his lips.

Lucie didn't need to understand Portuguese.

You're dead . . .

His thick shadow finally dissolved in the fog. Pale, Lucie looked at Pedro distrustfully as he sat cross-legged on the deck, scaling fish with his knife. The soldier had let them pass. Why? Should she be wary of her own guides? What was waiting for them at the end of the trail?

"Who was that man in the hut?" she asked.

Pedro answered without looking up, busy with his fish.

"Alvaro Andrades. Here they call him the Lord of the River. I saw what he did; I think I got what he said to you. 'When you come back, you're dead.' What's going on with him? I don't want any trouble."

"You won't have any. Are he and Chimaux in touch?"

Pedro got up, bringing his fish and his basin.

"Andrades controls the river. Word around here is that he's looking for Chimaux. He searches all the boats heading the other way, toward São Gabriel, top to bottom. He'll search us too on the way back. That's why what he did worries me. What's he got against you?"

"I have no idea, I've never met him."

He headed down to the lower passageway, leaving Lucie alone with her thoughts. So Chimaux was trapped in the jungle. After the failed attempt on his life, the killer had bought the military, no doubt putting a stiff price on the anthropologist's head.

From then on, time seemed endless. Jungle gave way to more jungle, ever more compact and oppressive. The beauty of the bone-white foothills of Pico da Neblina yielded to endless rows of trees, flat as shingles. A lost, desolate horizon.

Eleven hours later, the engine slowed. Meanwhile, they'd had a meal of fish cooked in spicy broth, some porridge, and home-brewed beer. Before them, the river was like a Russian doll: ever narrower confluences, nested one inside the other, right to the end. Occasionally something shone on the banks—mica, fool's gold—or else caimans disappeared beneath the waves. Lucie found Pedro more and more surprising by the minute. How was he still able to navigate in this labyrinth of swamps choked with rotting tree trunks? The guide didn't mind boasting: he was the only one who dared come this way, which saved them precious time. Vegetation had invaded everything: water, earth, and sky. Roots drank, dug deep, crept forward. Vines hung in the water like endless stalactites; twisted branches scraped the black surface. A universe without frontiers, hostile to any form of human existence.

Pedro turned the boat about thirty degrees until he was only a few yards from shore.

"This is where we drop anchor," said the guide. "We won't get any farther in the boat. In three hours, it'll be nightfall. We'll sleep here and tomorrow we start walking."

There were cracking sounds, birds the color of fire took wing, and Lucie's attention was drawn by small monkeys with white faces. The capuchins from the video, watching them . . . Pedro was looking toward the jungle. His eyes narrowed. He picked up his rifle and checked to see that it was loaded. With a shiver, Lucie followed his gaze.

"What is it? Did you see something?"

The guide motioned discreetly toward some large banana leaves, which trembled on the right, then on the left, before regaining their chilling quiet.

"I don't think we'll have to wait 'til tomorrow or walk very far. They're already here."

52

A virus . . . The word echoed over and over in Sharko's brain like a tape loop.

A virus from another age, as old as humanity, that had probably infected the Cro-Magnon in the cave and made him drunk with violence. What could it be related to? Had it also contaminated Grégory Carnot and Félix Lambert? Where did it come from? How had it spread?

The inspector and the Homicide squad leader arrived at their destination. On the way, they had spoken only a few words, each one sunk in his private torment. Sharko was thinking of Lucie. By then, she must have been at the edge of the unknown, powerless and fragile. How would she make it back out? What if something happened to her? If she were wounded or . . . how would he even hear about it?

In a locker room adjacent to the lab, the two men put on sterile coveralls.

"Are you sure it's not dangerous to go in there?" Sharko finally said. "That virus, I mean . . . It can't infect us, can it?"

"It isn't airborne and it can't spread by touch, if that's what you're worried about. And besides, it's a controlled environment."

Sharko slipped on a pair of overshoes.

"What about the investigation? What's happening? Anything new?"

"You ready? Let's go in."

After passing through an airlock, the two men entered the molecular biology lab. The room was filled with every variety of microscope, from electron to scanning tunneling, enormous machines set on antivibration platforms, hundreds of pipettes, stacks of petri dishes. At nearly 4 p.m., things were agitated in that universe of the infinitely small. People were running back and forth, conferring animatedly.

"Their orders are not to tell anyone about what they've found here,"

Bellanger whispered. "With what's going on under their microscopes, they're all on edge and aware that they might be making the discovery of the century."

Jean-Paul Lemoine rushed up to them in a state of high excitement. He firmly shook Sharko's hand.

"Give him the details," said Bellanger, "so that he can grasp the full import of this."

"Everything? Even the part about Félix Lambert? I thought you said . . ."

"Everything."

The head of the laboratory rubbed his chin, probably wondering where to begin. He pulled Sharko over to a quieter area in the back of the room.

"Hmmm . . . It's not easy to explain. First thing, do you know what a retrovirus is?"

"Tell me."

"AIDS is a good example. Basically, a retrovirus is a little wise guy with some scissors and paste, and using these he integrates his genome—his own sequence of A, T, C, and G's—into the DNA of the cells he's contaminated, and hides there. As such, he becomes invisible to the body's immune system, which then becomes powerless to fight it. Thanks to the cell mechanism, the virus's hidden genome is read and analyzed by our little internal engineer, who goes over every letter of the DNA. This little engineer, who doesn't realize he's got an intruder on his hands, does what he'd normally do with any sequence he reads: he makes a protein, which will serve to build human tissues. Except that in reality, this protein is a new virus let loose inside the organism, which will go infect another cell and start the process over again, and so on ad infinitum. This propagation occurs to the detriment of the other cells, like the decrease in lymphocytes in HIV, and therefore of the body's immune defenses. Broadly speaking, that's how a retrovirus works. Oh, one last thing: a retrovirus is called 'endogenous' if it's transmitted from generation to generation. It hides in the embryo and can stay dormant for twenty or even thirty years."

An embryo . . . Sharko recalled the tragic deliveries of Lambert's mother and Amanda Potier, the fatal hemorrhages. Could this be related to that? Bellanger brought them hot coffee. The biologist took a small sip, then continued:

"So, as I was saying. Until not so long ago, we thought that ninety-eight percent of the DNA molecule had no particular use. We called that part—and still call it—'junk DNA.' All of our genetic heritage, the thirty thousand genes that make up our blue eyes, dark hair, or stocky build are distributed over only two percent of useful DNA. The rest is just . . . filler, waste."

"Two percent? So in a way, you could . . . burn almost the entire encyclopedia of life without causing any genetic damage?"

"That's what we believed for a long time."

Sharko imagined Daniel's vast library reduced to a single shelf.

"But the fact is, nature never creates anything useless. And we finally realized, when we decoded the genome, that an earthworm had almost as many genes as we do. And yet we're infinitely more complex. Which must mean that the so-called junk DNA contains a number of secrets. Today we know that certain portions of that junk DNA participate in the organism's functioning, interact with the genes we've identified. They're the keys to a whole multitude of locks, if you will, which could never be opened without them. Most of all, we've recently understood that more than eight percent of junk DNA was composed of genetic fossils. The fossils of thousands of retroviruses from past generations, which we call HERVs, for human endogenous retroviruses."

Sharko sighed, a hand on his forehead.

"I had a miserable night last night—can you put that a bit more plainly?"

The biologist gave him a pinched smile.

"More plainly? All right, let's see. There are thousands of 'aliens' in our genome, Inspector. They live among us, hidden in a dark corner of our DNA. A kind of ancient AIDS, prehistoric monstrosities, mummified microscopic serial killers, which infected our ancestors millions of years ago, then were transmitted from generation to generation and now lie dormant in the DNA of every person on this planet."

This time Sharko got a clearer picture, and the horrible thought of it made him shiver. He imagined the DNA molecule as a kind of net dredging up everything that lay around, storing it all away without ever purging itself, just getting fatter and fatter.

"What keeps all those fossilized retroviruses from waking up? How come they aren't infecting us now?"

"It's more complicated than that. Every time, the process is the same: the infectious agent inserts itself into the cell's DNA, including the reproductive cells, then is transmitted through procreation like any other genetic heritage. Over time, the HERV undergoes several mutations—its A, T, C, and G's change—and it gradually loses its ability to be harmful. Like all those volcanoes that became extinct over geological time."

"And why does the retrovirus mutate?"

"Because of evolution. If it's harmful to humans, if it contains more drawbacks than advantages, the evolution of the human race will do everything it can to eradicate it. So over thousands of years, the virus progressively finds itself unable to do what it was designed to do, in other words manufacture a complete viral envelope that lets it forge its destructive path from cell to cell. But that doesn't mean it's dead. Certain mutated retroviruses were *tamed* by evolution and now play a very advantageous role in certain physiological processes. For example, a mutated retrovirus from the HERV-W family participates actively in the formation of the placenta. Stéphane Terney was among those who claimed that if this particular retrovirus hadn't invaded living species a long time ago, mammals would never have existed. Females—including human females—would have given birth outside the body, most likely in eggs. The mutated retrovirus thus played a major part in the evolution of these species of animals."

Sharko tried to pay attention. Certain words, like "placenta," "virus," "Terney," kept ringing little warning bells in his mind.

"So Terney was knowledgeable about retroviruses?" he asked.

"As an immunologist and with regard to what I just explained, yes. I'll give you one more example of evolution taming a foreign body in humans: sickle-cell anemia. It's a hereditary illness fairly common among African populations, which hasn't been eliminated by evolution because it confers a greater resistance to malaria. The advantage gained from it—the antimalarial protection—is deemed to be greater than its disadvantages."

Lemoine set down two sets of three printed sheets in front of the inspector. The one on the left was in Daniel's handwriting. Each sheet contained an infinite series of A, T, G, C.

"Let's cut to the chase. On the left you've got the mysterious retroviral sequence you gave us, and I hope you can tell us where you got it."

"How do you know it's a retrovirus?"

"All retroviruses have the same signature, the same starter initiating the sequence. When you see a pistol, you can identify the make, right? Same for me with DNA."

He pressed his finger onto one of the sheets on the right.

"These pages show the sequence of one of thousands of fossilized retroviruses found in the junk DNA of all of us—yours and mine. We know this retrovirus belongs to the HERV-W family. We find it somewhere in the first third of chromosome two. Until today, we had no idea what its function might have been in past millennia. All we knew was that this sequence had appeared only in the hominid branch, because we don't find it in the genome of any other animal, vegetable, or fungus."

"A virus specific to humans . . ."

"So it seems. We know nothing about it. Its function, its virulence, its destructive power at the time. But the case you're working on is about to mark a turning point in genetics and molecular biology. I'd even say a turning point in human evolution."

Sharko was stunned by such grandiose claims. He looked at the twin sets of papers, put the two top pages side by side. The sequence on the right was practically identical to the one on the left, apart from the occasional extraneous letter that the biologist had highlighted in Day-Glo blue. The difference occurred roughly once every hundred letters.

"Some of these anomalies, we're not sure which, rendered this retrovirus inert," Lemoine explained. "It's now just a piece of debris in our DNA and has no influence on our organism."

He moved the two sets of papers apart and put a third between them.

"Now take a look at this middle sequence."

Sharko squinted. The new sequence was again nearly identical to the others. But there were far fewer highlighted letters, at most about twenty per page. A sequence very close to that of Cro-Magnon but not entirely identical either. Sharko looked at Lemoine with a concerned face.

"This is the virus that infected Félix Lambert, isn't it? It's what you found in his brain."

The biologist nodded.

"Precisely. On the left is the sequence you brought us. In the middle, the one we found in Lambert's brain cells. And on the right, the harmless sequence we all share today. Moving from left to right, you see an increase in the number of anomalies. Now come have a look through this electron microscope."

Sharko put his eye to the lens. He saw a large, black ball in the center, surrounded by twisted filaments like barbed wire, with two longer strands that made it look like a jellyfish, a Portuguese man-of-war. It was ugly, monstrous, and seemed to be gliding calmly in a sea of oil. Sharko's hair stood on end. The microscopic world was glacial and frightening.

"Meet GATACA," said Lemoine. "It's the name we've provisionally given the pathogen present in Lambert's cell tissue. This is an ancestral virus, slightly mutated, since it shows a few anomalies, as you saw on those pages. Its genome contains exactly eight hundred thousand twelve ATGC bases—it's barely smaller than AIDS. Naturally, we still don't know how it works or replicates itself. Looking at what we found in Félix Lambert's organism, we think GATACA slowly and quietly invades the cells of the human body—and more specifically, the brain cells—over a period of years, like HIV. Then it moves into attack mode when its host reaches adulthood, somewhere around twenty. It's too early to tell if it's the secretion of hormones that triggers it, or the biological clock, or cell aging. All we know is that, from that point on, it begins a highly accelerated cycle: it multiplies at a prodigious rate in the brain's nerve cells, especially the surface areas, and disrupts everything in the host, a little like MS or Alzheimer's. We know what happens then. The individual has problems with balance, he becomes aggressive and commits violent acts . . ."

Sharko empied his coffee with a grimace. His throat felt dry.

"Is it contagious?"

"Not by breathing or through contact, but perhaps sexually. We just don't know. Another thing we don't know is if it works differently in men and women. We don't know how or when GATACA got into Félix Lambert's system. Nor do we know who created GATACA. According to Terney's book, Grégory Carnot was carrying the virus, and at least five others are in the same boat. But why them in particular? We'll need weeks, even months to understand all this and figure out how to stop it. Can you imagine the damage it could cause, especially if it *is* transmitted through sexual contact? The number of people infected could grow exponentially."

He picked up the pages Sharko had given him.

"What you've discovered here is fundamental. This sequence you gave us seems to be the original, pure, unmutated form. It might be even more violent and harmful, and it might spread more easily. Today we know how to manufacture and grow viruses. Given what we already know of the damage GATACA can cause, can you imagine the monstrosities that could be unleashed by someone holding the recipe—the genetic sequence—for such a prehistoric virus?"

"You mean administering it to people without their knowledge? Contamination?"

"Sure. As well as being spread through sexual activity or handed down genetically."

"From parents to children . . ."

"Future generations, which would gradually all become infected, and quickly. People dying at the age of twenty or thirty, intoxicated with violence. Tell us what you know. We'll be liaising with the Ministry of Health to set up emergency research teams. We have to move fast. The more time passes, the more we risk losing control of this virus altogether."

"Tell us," Bellanger repeated. "We've given you everything we've got. Now it's your turn to pony up."

Sharko thought for a moment, still shaken by these horrible revelations. He had to play it very carefully. Bellanger, Lemoine, and the other cops knew nothing about Lucie's investigation. The theft of Cro-Magnon, the tapes, Phoenix, the Amazon tribe, the research into Terney's past, the mothers dying in childbirth—how much could he tell without putting Lucie in danger? On the other hand, did he have the right to keep these revelations to himself? Lives were at stake—and God only knew how many.

He looked searchingly at the three sets of pages lying next to one another. To the left, Cro-Magnon, with the virus in its pure form. In the middle, Lambert, with the virus still active but mutated. On the right, the rest of humanity, with the inactive virus.

Three different forms of the virus, because evolution had mutated it over time. So then, three different epochs. But how was that possible, since Lambert hadn't been more than twenty-five years old?

The chain of time, he suddenly thought. The chain of time with its three links: Cro-Magnon, humans of today, and between them, the Ururu.

As if hit with a blinding light, he suddenly understood.

He slapped his forehead with a groan.

"Félix Lambert and Grégory Carnot didn't catch the virus," he murmured. "Nor were they injected. No. This filth was already inside them from the moment they were born. They got it from their parents, who in turn . . ."

He stopped short and looked his boss in the eye.

"Just give me a few more hours to check something out. And after that, I promise I'll explain everything."

"Sharko, I . . ."

Without leaving Bellanger time to answer, he turned to the biologist.

"This sequence comes from a Cro-Magnon man, thirty thousand years old. Call the genome center in Lyon, and you'll get all the answers you need."

With those words, he backed away, then stopped to ask one last question:

"Tell me something: could the presence of this mutated virus make its hosts left-handed?"

The biologist thought for a moment and seemed to make a connection.

"Lambert was left-handed, as was Carnot. So you think that . . . ?" A pause. "Yes, yes, it's possible. Recent research suggests that there's a gene linked to hand dominance, located on chromosome two, in fact, and right next to those fossilized retroviruses. In genetics, it's common for the expression of certain DNA sequences—the retrovirus, in this case—to influence the 'behavior' of neighboring genes. This explains the emergence of certain cancers, for instance, such as leukemia or lymphoma. But to understand that, I'd have to tell you about chromosomal translocation, and . . ."

No longer listening, Sharko backed away a few more steps and took off at a run.

53

Pedro knew how to read the jungle. He interpreted variations, decoded shapes, sensed dangers: insects, snakes, spiders, which sometimes dropped at their feet like writhing clusters. With precise movements, he sliced through tangles with his machete, forging unlikely paths. He, Lucie, and the two Indians had plunged into the green vise, rifles in hand, packs on their backs. All around them, the jungle expanded, contracted, devoured. Endless stalks of bamboo stood together like prison bars, branches of rubber and teak trees stretched their formless webs. Docking the boat along the marsh had been impossible; they'd had to walk up to their knees in the stagnant water for a good ten yards. Lucie was soaked. Her forehead, back, and neck were dripping. Every breath seemed to burn her lungs like ammonia. With a knife, Pedro had cut a small hole in his new shoes so that the water could escape more easily and help avoid blisters. He chopped with his machete at the base of a bamboo stalk. Water poured from the hollow cylinder; he put his flask against it and filled it without a word. His eyes were moving constantly, running down the dark perspectives. Farther on, he bent toward the thick vines wrapped around the black tree trunks.

"Look here—they've been broken off."

He moved a bit farther forward, showing other breaks. A narrow, unsuspected pathway had recently been opened.

"We call this the Indian path: a thin trail through the jungle . . . No doubt about it, the Ururu are here."

Anxious, Lucie looked all around her, but she couldn't see more than a few yards. Even the blue of the sky had disappeared, giving way to endless rolls of greenery. Here everything was outsized, including the ants. Pedro poured a little cool water over his curly hair, then looked at his waterproof GPS.

"We won't go too far from the boat. In two hours it'll be dark. Let's walk a little farther, just straight ahead. They'll be here before nightfall, I can feel it . . ."

They continued forward, alert. The branches and leaves trembled with every step. Lucie couldn't help comparing the jungle to a human brain: a vast, interconnected network sending signals back and forth, adding to and subtracting from each other, in cooperation or competition. Symbiosis, osmosis, but also predation and parasitism. Each fundamental element constituted a small knot, which formed a larger knot. Death led to rot, rot spawned the bacteria that enriched the earth, the earth created leaves, leaves bred species, species formed an ecosystem—a fragile entity of awe-inspiring richness, in constant equilibrium between life and death, degradation and majesty.

Finally, they reached a kind of clearing, where from below came the rumble of a mountain stream. Everything, even the tree bark, oozed dampness. In the Amazon rain forest, the staggering level of humidity—nearly 100 percent—was the worst adversary. It made it difficult to light fires, rotted the skin off your feet, and fostered diseases. Standing back, Lucie was catching her breath. Her entire body was in pain. Far from Rio Negro, the mosquitoes came fast and furious. Suddenly, she thought she saw a silhouette in the dense trees behind her.

It moved quickly, easily.

Branches began to wave, vines vibrated, on all sides of them. Silence, movement . . . silence, movement . . . As if figures were suddenly gathering around them, dancing to a slow rhythm. Lucie remembered the horrifying faces in Chimaux's book.

They were there, encircling her.

At Pedro's orders, the two Indians set their weapons down at their feet, then raised their hands in a sign of peace. Around them, the shadows came into focus. Eyes, noses pierced with bones, faces appeared among the bamboo, before disappearing again, like floating masks. Then there were cries, shrill chants, bursts of sound that made the monkeys scatter deep into the canopy. Pedro explained under his breath that they must absolutely not move, just wait until Napoléon Chimaux deigned to show himself. Lucie did her best to stand straight, look self-assured, but she was trembling all over. Her life, her future—none of it was hers to decide anymore.

How long did the intimidation last? She couldn't be sure. Here, time dissolved, reference points fell to pieces. Finally, the palm leaves parted and the anthropologist appeared, seemingly alone, apart from the fact that everything around him was vibrating, like a steamroller just waiting to advance. He was tall, powerful; he stood firmly, dressed in khaki fatigues. His head was bald and his large, dark eyes were bloodshot. His forehead and cheeks bore ochre markings in broken lines, like furious zigzags. Hands on his hips, he sniffed the air as would a predator stalking its prey. Lucie recalled the images from the Phoenix tape: the boot nudging the corpses in the huts . . . She wanted to grab a rifle and jam the barrel between his eyes, until he told her the whole truth. But if she so much as twitched, she'd be dead: a good thirty hatchets and lances must have been aimed straight at her, ready to slice her skull clean in two.

Chimaux's deep voice dripped like slow poison.

"Give me one good reason not to kill you where you stand."

The man ignored the guides, spoke directly to Lucie. She raised one hand in a sign of peace, and dipped the other hand, slowly, cautiously, in the front pocket of her shirt. She held out a photo.

"Here's my reason. Eva Louts."

She had answered in a dry, no-nonsense tone. She wanted to appear strong, fearless, because she had reached the end. The end of her search, the end of the world. Everything had to end now. Chimaux gave an evil smile.

"Come closer, closer . . . so that I can see the picture better."

Without hesitating, Lucie walked forward, away from her guides. They were now less than three yards apart. Chimaux held out his arm, a sign for her to stop. Then he squinted at the photo.

"It looks like her. Eva Louts . . . But what else, young lady? Have you no more to tell me? Arouse my curiosity."

"Arouse your curiosity? Try this on for size: you're waiting for Eva Louts, but she's not coming back, ever. She's been murdered."

Chimaux raised one eyebrow slightly, but otherwise showed little reaction.

"Is that so?" he grimaced.

Lucie pushed further.

"Mutilated in a chimpanzee's cage. Stéphane Terney is also dead, with his iliac artery slit. Does that remind you of anything? I know about the

344

mothers who died in childbirth, the brains that turn to sponge and drive people to murder. I saw the first Phoenix tape. When Eva Louts came here, you accepted her because she was able to surprise you. She knew the Ururu were left-handed and violent. She'd found a link that no one who came before her had suspected. So you decided to let her into your world. You forged a trusting relationship with her, and you sent her back to France with a mission: bring you back the names of extremely violent left-handed prisoners. You're looking for those cursed children who are starting to slaughter for no reason, is that it? Why? Is it because they're the final fruit of Phoenix, and the killer is preventing you from coming out of the jungle to see their faces? I've come here to find answers. Finish with me what you started with her."

Chimaux tilted his head to one side, then the other, his eyes open wide, as if he were trying to read deep within Lucie. He looked like a strange animal suddenly confronted with its own reflection. His face and forearms were a maze of scars. His chest swelled under his military shirt, and he gave out a long, raucous cry. Instantly, dozens of naked silhouettes surged from the trees, hatchets in hand, and ran screaming toward Lucie. Paralyzed, she didn't have time to react. A hideous creature, twice as heavy as she, grabbed her. Another opened the palm of his enormous hand and blew a white powder into her face. Lucie felt a burning in her nostrils and windpipe. A second later, her legs gave way. Hands kept her from falling. Damp skins pressed against her. She smelled plant odors, mud, and sweat. Everything started spinning; trees and faces seemed to twist out of shape, melt away like wax. She saw herself lifting away from the ground, unable to move. And then, as the black flies poured into her skull, she felt Chimaux's warm breath against her neck.

"You wanted to know what Phoenix looks like? We're expecting a birth tonight. You'll be in the front row. And afterward . . . I'll drink your soul."

They carried Lucie into the jungle.

The palm leaves closed behind them, like a theater curtain. A few cracking branches. Then silence.

54

A virus, handed down from the father or mother to the child. A monster cleverly hidden in the DNA, interacting with the hand-dominance gene, just waiting for the right moment to awaken, proliferate in the brain of the host organism, and destroy it. Sharko didn't know much about viruses or their strategy, but the ten days he'd spent on this case had led him to a crazy hypothesis. A hypothesis he absolutely had to test.

It was a tired-looking man with a gaunt face who answered the door, on the fourth floor of the Haussmann-style building where Sharko had already come with Lucie to question the sister of Félix Lambert. The inspector introduced himself without showing his fake ID. His firm voice and impassive expression did the job.

"Police, Homicide division. I'd like to speak to Coralie Lambert. We've already met."

"Masson. Her name is Coralie Masson. We've been married for over a year."

The man, Patrick Masson, was not even thirty years old. He invited Sharko into the huge apartment without asking questions. The young woman was lying on a sofa, a pillow under her neck and hands on her stomach. She was watching television. She tried to sit up at the cop's entrance, but Sharko walked forward quickly, palm outstretched.

"No, please, don't get up. I won't be long."

The inspector asked Patrick to leave them alone for a few moments.

"I'll be outside having a smoke," the young man said to his wife. He waved his iPhone, latest model. "If you need me, just call."

Sharko pulled up a chair so he could sit facing Coralie and looked at her swollen belly. He rubbed his hands together: he had to play it close to the vest. And especially, nothing about his discoveries in the laboratory.

"It's almost time for the birth," he said calmly, with a half smile.

Limply, Coralie aimed the remote and turned off the TV. She had pearlescent skin and dark rings under her eyes. She was so young.

"I don't think you came here to talk about my baby."

Sharko cleared his throat.

"You're right. The question I came to ask might seem strange, Mme. Masson, but are you lactose intolerant like your brother?"

The young woman finally sat up with a small grimace and made herself comfortable amid the cushions. Her ankles were swollen, surely an effect of a pregnancy whose impending conclusion promised to be difficult. In a dish on the floor lay some apple cores, empty biscuit packages, and an open jar of strawberry preserves.

"Yes, I am, but why do you ask?"

"Because, as I said last time, our investigation has led us into medical territory, and it's not just about Félix. It's bigger than that. That's all I can say for now, but I promise I'll tell you more as soon as I can. Were your father and mother intolerant?"

"My father could drink milk with no problem, but my mother was intolerant as well."

"Did you know that in Europe, lactose intolerance is mainly found in immigrant populations and their descendants?"

"I didn't. But what exactly are you trying to say?"

"That at a certain point, there was probably some foreign blood in your family lineage. Blood that brought this intolerance and . . . uh . . . unfortunate side effects. And I believe it was relatively recent."

Coralie looked outraged. She ran her tongue over her dry lips and knit her brow. She stood up with difficulty, went to open a drawer, and came back with a photo album, which she handed to Sharko.

"We are not immigrants, Inspector. We have been pure-blooded Frenchmen for many generations. Some members of my family drew up a family tree, with roots stretching back to the 1700s. You'll find it in there, at the beginning."

Sharko opened the album. Large sheets of paper had been glued and folded inside, showing an extensive family chart.

"I'm not disputing the truth of your lineage," said Sharko. "What I mean is, well, a child can just as easily be born from an extramarital affair, without it appearing on the family tree. A cheated-on husband, perhaps."

Coralie kept silent, her lips pressed shut. Very quickly, Sharko spotted the branch for Coralie and Félix Lambert. Their mother, Jeanne Lambert, an only child who had died on the delivery table ... Their grandparents ... Dates, names, places of birth, all very French. According to the tree, Jeanne Lambert was born in Paris in 1968. The date immediately sent up a flare in the cop's mind. The "Phoenix no. 1" tape, shot in 1966 ... The smuggling of test tubes between the Amazon and France, in 1967 ...

Like an implacable machine, everything fell together logically in the cop's brain. His theory seemed to check out. He looked Coralie in the eye.

"You are lactose-intolerant. Your mother Jeanne was, too, but not your father. So the intolerance comes from the maternal side." He pointed his finger at two boxes: Geneviève and Georges Noland. "Here's my question: were your grandmother or grandfather on the maternal side also lactose intolerant?"

Coralie thought for a few seconds.

"My grandfather drank coffee with milk a few days ago, exactly where you're sitting now. He divorced my grandmother a long time ago, but she drank milk too. They ... they aren't intolerant." She paused a moment. "So that means ..."

Sharko could barely remain seated. He had, before his eyes, the genetic break in Félix Lambert's lineage. He ran a hand over his lips, realizing the breadth of his discoveries and all the horror they implied.

"Do you have any pictures of your mother and her parents?"

Coralie took the album and leafed through it, before giving it back to the inspector.

"Here, that's my mom and my grandmother. And here, Mom and Grandpa. You won't see any of the three together—my grandparents had already separated well before that. In these photos, Mom must be about fifteen. She was so beautiful ... She was nineteen when she had me, and twenty when Félix was born."

Sharko looked carefully at the color photos. Jeanne was a black-haired teenager, with dark eyes, certain features that clearly took after her mother, like her nose, the way she smiled. Coralie said aloud what was running through Sharko's mind.

"My mother doesn't look like my grandfather, that's what you're thinking, isn't it? It's ... inconceivable!"

Sharko pressed his lips shut. The child wasn't Georges Noland's, he was now certain of it. A certainty took shape in his mind, relating to the Ururu, the smuggled blood, the business about viruses and evolution: as crazy as it seemed, Coralie and Félix's grandmother had received, probably without her knowledge, the semen of an Amazon Indian who was lactose intolerant, massive, and violent. Spermatozoa carrying a virus. The horror had taken place between 1967 and 1968. A horror intended to be spread from one generation to the next.

His mind reeling, the cop shut the album and slowly handed it back to Coralie, forcing her to stretch out her arm. He noted which hand she used to take it.

Her left.

His heart sank. In a halting voice, he said, "Tell me your child is a girl."

Coralie looked at him strangely, then shook her head.

"No, it's going to be a boy."

Sharko tried to keep calm, but inside he was falling apart.

"Are . . . are you being seen by a doctor?"

"Yes, but I . . ."

"What do the sonograms say? Is everything normal?"

Coralie seemed at a loss before this policeman who asked such direct, personal, and seemingly pointless questions.

"Of course everything's normal! The baby is nice and big, in perfect health." She smiled. "He . . . he's always moving! I've never had such an appetite, I can't stop eating, he's such a little piglet. There's only that minor problem with my placenta, but it's not ser—"

"Hypervascularity?"

"How did you know that? What does it mean?"

Sharko's last doubts dissipated. Coralie was carrying GATACA within her. After obliterating his mother, Coralie's baby would grow up and transmit the retrovirus to his own child in turn, before his brain began eating itself and set him off on a violent rampage. A cursed cycle, destined to repeat as long as children were born in this family. Feeling devastated, Sharko squatted down in front of the young woman, searching for the right words.

"Is your maternal grandmother still alive?"

"Of course. But what's going on? Please, tell me!"

Sharko had trouble grasping the subtleties of the virus: the mothers seemed to die giving birth to boys, but were they spared when they had girls? Why? How? So many questions crowding to his lips.

"I'm aware of certain facts that I can't divulge at the moment, since we don't yet have proof. I can only tell you that something happened between your maternal grandparents. Something genetic, related to your mother's pregnancies. That's where the flaw started, if I can call it that, which was passed down to your brother Félix . . ."

He fell silent a moment, not wanting to tell her that she, too, was affected, and that a monster shaped like a man-of-war was nesting in her DNA and in that of her baby.

"I need to question your grandparents. I need to know what happened during your grandmother's pregnancy, and which doctors might have treated her."

"Did you say a flaw? What flaw? We've never heard anything about a flaw. My grandfather would certainly have said something about it to the family. He's a geneticist, that's his specialty. He's the one who cared for my grandmother during her pregnancy. Repairing genetic flaws is his job, and there's no one better at it."

Sharko felt as if he'd been punched in the face.

"Did you say . . . a geneticist?"

"A great geneticist. I don't know a lot about it, but I know he discovered some important genes, a long time ago. He became quite famous for it. For years, he's been the head of a major lab that specializes in helping couples who are having trouble conceiving, hormonal insufficiencies, that kind of thing. He helps them become pregnant. What do you want with him? What's going on?"

Sharko stood up, not sure if his legs would hold. It all seemed so clear now. Inseminations . . .

He also understood the attempt on Lucie's life in São Gabriel. Georges Noland had been present when Lucie questioned Coralie. Sharko remembered asking if anyone in their family had Amerindian origins, and Noland had cut him short. At that moment, the geneticist must have realized how far they'd gotten, and imagined one of them would end up going to Brazil. Lucie had even given him her card with her phone number.

Without realizing it, she had delivered herself to the monster, who must have used his army contacts in the Amazon to try to get rid of her quietly by making it look like an accident.

The inspector stared at the young woman in horror, unable for a moment to gauge the breadth of his discovery and, especially, the measure of Georges Noland's perversity. The man had injected a virus into the body of his own wife, thus placing a curse on every succeeding generation. He had killed Louts and tortured Terney. In the shelter of his laboratory, he had inseminated who knew how many women with hormonal problems, embedding a deadly virus in their own DNA. How could any human being do such things?

With a trembling hand, he took out a pad and pen from his pocket.

"I'd like to talk to him. Could you please tell me his address?"

A long silence. Coralie sighed. She caressed her belly to regain her calm.

"At this hour, he must still be in the lab. My grandfather never stops working. The company is called Genomics and it's based in Villejuif, near the cancer institute."

Sharko wrote down the information, teeth clenched. Behind him, the husband reappeared, a lighter in his hand. The inspector pocketed the notepad, then gently shook the young woman's hand.

"Please take good care of yourself."

He left her in a state of great confusion, pulled her husband into the hallway, and spoke to him in an urgent voice.

"Has Coralie ever told you about her mother? Her death from massive internal bleeding when Félix was born?"

"Yes, of course."

"Then listen carefully: you are going to take her to the hospital immediately, because it's very likely that what happened with her mother will happen to her as well. Tell the doctors every detail you have about Jeanne Lambert's death, and tell them that if they don't do something, the same thing will be triggered when Coralie gives birth to her baby. Something that will cause her to die of a massive hemorrhage. The whole thing is genetic."

The man was on the verge of collapse. Sharko laid a hand on his shoulder.

"There might still be a chance to save her, but you have to go now. And, whatever you do, do not let her talk to her grandfather. I'm heading to Villejuif. This whole thing is his doing."

He ran down the stairs three at a time. Once in his car, he drew his Smith & Wesson from its holster, loaded it, and sped away from the curb.

55

Lucie was floating outside of time. She was finding it hard to raise her lids over her bloodshot eyes. A large fire was burning before her, its flames dancing so high they set the shadows ablaze. She was sitting on the ground, cross-legged, unable to stand, as if her limbs were no longer hers. Behind her, around her, a sound rumbled, voices from men's throats beat time in unison, bare feet pounded the ground in a slow drumming rhythm. Hands and arms waved in the dark, describing incomprehensible figures. Lucie felt herself wavering and her eyes rolled in their sockets, assaulted by sharp flashes. Where was she? She couldn't marshal her thoughts. Everything blended in her head, as if a tunnel had opened into the void where her memories flowed. Faces . . . her father, her mother, Sharko. They spun around, mixed together, stretched out, swallowed by a throat of ink. In the deep recesses of her skull, she heard the laughter of little girls, saw the white sand spurt before her eyes in slow motion. At first hazy, the faces of Clara and Juliette slowly came into focus. Lucie put out her hand to touch them, but they evaporated in the night. Smiles, then tears. Lucie faltered, her head fell back, while the tears bathed her face. She felt her body falling, then a caress on the back of her neck. Seeds and mushroom powder fell on the incandescent coal set between her legs. There was a backwash of burning smoke that enveloped her face. Lucie swooned, then came to in a trance. The smoke, the smell of plants and roots enveloped her, toyed with her senses.

Suddenly the crowd parted and a roar went up, accompanied by brandished hatchets. Four men carried a woman who was lying on a carpet of leaves and branches. She was completely naked and covered in painted figures. They set her down near the fire. Designs snaked around her swollen belly.

Chimaux sat next to Lucie and breathed in a brownish powder.

"These plants we're inhaling have unimaginable powers, especially the power to heal ailing bodies and minds. Breathe them in, breathe deeply, and let yourself be carried away . . ."

He shut his eyes for a few seconds. When he opened them again, they were burning like braziers.

Sharko screeched to a halt in front of a NO PARKING *sign and burst from his car, the Smith & Wesson shoved in his belt. He ran past the huge Gustave-Roussy cancer institute toward a tall glass-and-steel building, with stream-lined contours and wide automatic doors, above which red and black letters spelled out the word "GENOMICS." He walked up quickly to the reception desk, flashed his fake police ID, and asked to see Georges Noland immediately. The receptionist reached for the phone to call her boss, but Sharko intercepted her.*

"No. Take me to him."

"He's working in a 'clean room' on Sub One. It's where we store our tissue samples. I don't have access and . . ."

Sharko pointed to the elevator.

"Can you get there on that?"

"Only with a badge—there's no other way to get down."

"In that case, call him, but don't say it's the police. Tell him his granddaughter is here to see him."

She made the call.

"He'll be here momentarily."

Sharko went to the elevator and waited. When the doors opened, he flew inside and slammed Noland against the back wall, jamming the gun into his stomach.

"We're going back down, you and I."

The elevator door opened onto a hallway. In front of them, protected by thick glass partitions, stretched a large room on the cutting edge of technology. Men and women in surgical masks and sterile coveralls were working at monitors, pressing buttons that controlled huge cryogenic pressure equipment. Sharko forced Noland into the first office they came to, locking the door behind them. He pushed the geneticist against the wall and cracked the butt of his gun on the man's head. The other bent in two, hands on his forehead. The cop pressed the barrel into his cheek.

"I'll give you ten seconds to call Brazil and cancel the contract on Lucie Henebelle."

Georges Noland shook his head.

"I don't know what you're . . ."

Sharko yanked him onto his side and stuck the barrel into his mouth, practically down his throat.

"Five, four, three . . ."

Noland gagged and started nodding rapidly. He spat several times. The cop shoved him violently toward the phone, his entire body tense and trembling. Noland dialed the number; they waited . . . Then words in Portuguese. Sharko didn't understand the language, but he could make out that they were talking numbers, money. Finally, Noland hung up and let himself fall heavily into a desk chair on wheels.

"They went down the river at dawn. Alvaro Andrades, the officer who guards the river, will let them pass freely when they head back."

Sharko felt a surge of relief. Lucie was still alive, somewhere. He walked up to Noland and grabbed him by the collar of his lab coat, before propelling him and his chair into a corner.

"I'm going to kill you. I swear I'll do it. But first, tell me about the retrovirus that looks like a man-of-war, the genetic profiles, about those mothers who die in childbirth. Tell me about your relations with Chimaux and Terney. I want all of it. Now."

Napoléon Chimaux nodded toward the expectant mother, whom other women, young and old, came to caress on the brow, in a long procession. At his side, Lucie was wavering, her head lolling forward, then backward. His words echoed, deep and deformed:

"All magic, all mystery, the entire secret of the Ururu is there before you. The most fantastic model of evolution that an anthropologist could ever hope to encounter. Look how serene that pregnant woman is. And yet, she knows she is about to die. In such moments, they are all in perfect communion. Do *you* see any special violence in this population?"

Thick veins bulged on his neck.

"The Ururu know exactly what sex the child will be. The mother eats more if it's a boy, her belly becomes enormous, and she grows very fatigued in the final months of pregnancy. The male fetus sucks up all her energy. He wants to come into the world, to survive at any cost. The placenta becomes hypervascular to bring him more oxygen and nourishment. The child will be big, strong, and perfectly healthy . . ."

Chant succeeded chant, the rhythm of pounding feet accelerated, faces spun around her. Lucie let the perspiration drip into her burning eyes. Apart from hazy silhouettes, she couldn't make anything out. She remembered vaguely . . . the boat, the jungle . . . She saw herself lying on leaves, Chimaux's face up close to hers. She heard herself talking, weeping, telling him things . . . What had he done to her? When had this happened?

Suddenly, a man burst from the crowd armed with a sharpened stone, its cutting edge fine as a scalpel. He knelt before the pregnant woman.

In silence, Noland mopped the blood dripping down his temples. Then his thin, evil lips suddenly curled.

"Science has always demanded sacrifices. But you couldn't possibly understand such a concept."

"I've already run across lunatics like you, the 'enlightened' ones who think the rules don't apply to them. Don't you worry about what I do or don't understand. I want the whole truth."

The geneticist's dark eyes stared directly into the cop's, who read only disdain in them.

"I'll give you your truth. I'll shove it right in your face. But how certain are you that you want to hear it?"

"I'm ready to hear anything you have to say. Start at the beginning. The sixties . . ."

A silence. Two pairs of eyes ready to devour each other. Noland finally capitulated.

"Right after he came across the Ururu, Chimaux approached my laboratory about analyzing some blood samples from the tribe. At first it was just to gauge the state of their health. There wasn't any malevolent intent; it was routine whenever a new population was discovered. This was 1965, around the time when he'd just written his book and was doing his lecture tour. I alone had the privilege of working with him, because he valued my work on genetics and shared my ideas."

"What sort of ideas?"

"That we must oppose increases in life expectancy. The rise in the elderly

population goes completely against nature's wishes. The 'gerontocracy' is only . . . creating problems, triggering new diseases, and polluting our planet. Old age, delayed procreation, all those medicines that prolong our existence are violations of natural selection . . . We are a virus on this planet. We reproduce and forget to die."

"Look who's talking—you're not exactly a teenager yourself. Neither were Chimaux and Terney. The pot's calling the kettle black, don't you think?"

"The difference is, we know it. A virus can't eliminate itself. We're trying to find the antidote."

He spoke with disgust, emphasizing every word.

"When Chimaux realized old age didn't exist in Ururu males, just as in prehistoric times, that their society kept itself in check through deaths and fatal childbirths, he asked my scientific opinion. Did the Ururu perform their rituals because of culture, a collective memory perpetuated down through the generations, or did they perform them because genetics gave them no choice? We got to know each other, respect each other. He took me where no one else had ever been, so that I might see his great white Indians with my own eyes."

Sitting cross-legged, Napoléon Chimaux calmly rested his hands on his knees. The flames were reflected in his dilated pupils. Lucie was barely able to listen to him. Rapid, devastating thoughts flew from her mind, to the rhythm of the tall flames flickering in front of her: she saw scoops of ice cream fallen onto the seawall . . . a car speeding down the highway . . . a charred body on an autopsy table . . . Lucie jerked her face away, as if slapped. She was rambling, trying to focus on Chimaux's voice among the moans and screams inside her skull. She wanted so badly to understand.

"This man you see opposite you is the father, and he is going to remove the infant before killing the mother."

The young native, made-up from head to foot, had knelt next to his wife. He spoke to her in a soft voice, stroking her cheek. And Chimaux's voice, constant, heady, at once so distant and so near.

"The husband has reproduced. His genes have now ensured their future, because the baby will be born big and strong and will make a good hunter. The man is barely eighteen years old. Soon he will find other partners, women from the tribe. He will spread his seed again . . . Then, in a few years, at another ceremony, he will take his own life. The old women will have handed down to him the art of killing oneself properly, without needless suffering, and in accordance with their traditions. Imagine my stupefaction when I discovered the workings of the Ururu, so many years ago. They eliminated the women when they gave birth to males but let them live when they had girls. They killed men in their twenties, who had done everything nature expected of them: fight when necessary and ensure their own posterity and the continued existence of the tribe. Why did such a peculiar, such a cruel culture exist in just this one tribe? What was the role of natural selection in all this? What role had evolution played?"

He drank a dark liquid that made him grimace, then spat to the side.

"I suppose you've read my book? There was no need, it's all bullshit. The violence of the Ururu is a myth, because it never gets the chance to declare itself: the adult males sacrifice themselves at the first sign of loss of balance or inverted vision. I invented the legendary violence of this population and did my best to spread the word. The tribe had to terrify people as much as it fascinated them, do you understand? People had to be afraid to come here, to confront these huge, powerful hunters. All over the world, people took me for a lunatic, a murderer, a bloodthirsty degenerate, but that image only served my purpose. It was necessary for people to fear us. This population is mine, and I'll never abandon it."

"Nature and nurture . . . culture versus genes . . . such huge debates. Has DNA forced the Ururu to adopt that culture, or has the culture of the Ururu modified their DNA? Chimaux was a great believer in the second answer, obviously. He had his own, purely Darwinist, theories about how the tribe worked: the Ururu are left-handed the better to fight their enemies, and this trait had been imprinted in their genes because it offers a huge evolutionary advantage. The males are born at the expense of their mothers, because they're stronger and sooner or later will conquer other women, whom they'll inseminate in turn. Girls don't kill their mothers in childbirth—they don't do the fighting, and this way the mother can reproduce again and perhaps have a son. The Ururu males die young because they reproduce young, like Cro-Magnon, and nature no longer needs them. The women die later because they have to take care of the offspring . . . For Chimaux, Ururu *culture really modified their genes and had created this magnificent evolutionary model. But I was convinced it was all primarily genetic, that their genes had determined a culture based on human sacrifice. The Ururu never had a choice: they had to kill the women who gave birth to boys or else watch them bleed to death in horrible agony. And the incomprehensible violence that affected the males when they reached adulthood, which triggered their own deaths, was purely genetic, buried deep within their cell structure, and not influenced by environment or culture. All those rituals were just so much window dressing and superstition."*

"So you and Chimaux decided to test out your competing theories by inseminating women here in this country."

Noland's jaws tightened.

"Chimaux had an outsized ego. He always thought he was right, but he was pathetically indecisive. The whole thing was my idea. I was the one who made the hard choices. It's my name people should remember, not his."

"Oh, people will remember it, all right."

The scientist pressed his lips together.

"The only thing Chimaux had to do was gain control of the Ururu. That's where the measles came in—my idea. I was the one who filmed those wasted bodies, not him. I was the one who did the dirty work so that he could take over the tribe."

Small bubbles of spittle had formed on his lips. Sharko knew he was facing one of the most perverse expressions of human folly: men who wasted their superior intelligence solely to do evil. The fabled figure of the mad scientist was right there before him.

"Then . . . Well, yes, I inseminated women without their knowledge. Cryogenics has existed since the 1930s; the frozen Ururu sperm traveled thousands of miles to get here. Good French couples came to see me because they couldn't conceive. Some of the women wanted to be inseminated with their husbands' seed. It was so easy for me to substitute the sperm of an Ururu. It was undetectable—the Indians were white-skinned and their features were Caucasian; the babies would all be born as Europeans. Only the lactose intolerance could give it away. And of course, the fact that the child didn't look like the father. But even then, the families always found resemblances . . ."

Sharko's hand tightened on the grip of his gun. Never had he had such a desire to pull the trigger.

"You even inseminated your own wife."

"Don't be so quick to judge. For your information, I never loved my wife. You know nothing about me or my life. You have no idea what the words 'obsession' or 'ambition' can mean."

"How many innocent women did you inseminate?"

"I tried to inseminate several dozen, but the failure rate was huge. It didn't work all that well—the technique was still in its infancy. It's also possible the sperm samples didn't hold up well in transit. Ultimately it only worked on three women."

"Your wife . . . the grandmother of Grégory Carnot, and one other, is that right?"

"Yes. Those three women each had a child, but they were all girls."

"So one of those girls was Amanda Potier, Grégory Carnot's mother, and the other was your daughter Jeanne, who produced Coralie and Félix . . ."

He nodded.

"Three girls with Ururu genes, who carried the virus, and who in turn gave birth to seven children among them—three boys and four girls."

The generation of children whose genetic fingerprints were inscribed in Terney's book, thought Sharko.

"As far as I was concerned, that was the generation that told the tale. Félix Lambert, Grégory Carnot, and five others. Seven grandchildren with Ururu genes, born into good families, who were raised with love and who, nonetheless, reproduced the tribal pattern. Their mothers died if they gave birth to sons, or lived if they didn't. The male children turned violent when they reached maturity. It started just about a year ago. Grégory Carnot was the first to demonstrate what I'd been waiting to see for so long. Carnot, age twenty-four . . . Lambert, age twenty-two . . . It seems the virus takes effect a few years quicker in our society, closer to twenty than to thirty. No doubt the mix with Western genes slightly modified its behavior."

He sighed.

"I was right all along: culture had nothing to do with it. It was purely a matter of genetics. Even more than genetics, because I later learned it was actually a retrovirus with an incredibly effective strategy, that had managed to find the ideal host in that quasi-prehistoric tribe."

Despite the tension, his eyes shone continuously. He was the kind of *fanatic who would remain so all his life, who would believe to the bitter end, whom no prison could truly hold.*

"*What was Terney's part in all this?*" *asked Sharko.*

"*At the time, I didn't know the virus existed. I couldn't understand what was killing the mothers. I thought it had something to do with the immune system, maybe some sort of exchange between the mother and the fetus during pregnancy. Terney was a fanatic, and paranoid to boot, but he was a genius. He knew DNA and the mechanics of procreation backward and forward. He helped me understand it all. He's the one who discovered the retrovirus. Imagine how I felt the first time I saw it under the microscope . . .*"

Sharko thought of the vile Portuguese man-of-war floating in its liquid. A killer of humans.

"*We decided to call the virus by the same name as the insemination project: Phoenix. I knew Terney would take the bait, that he couldn't refuse the chance to treat a mother who was carrying in her body a pure product of evolution. I had kept track of Amanda Potier; I knew she was pregnant. She was the living embodiment of Terney's entire quest, all his research . . . Grégory Arthur TAnael CArnot was in a way his child . . . With his reputation and contacts, it was easy for him to obtain blood samples of the seven children after their births, so that he could give me a better understanding of Phoenix.*"

"*Tell me about Phoenix. How does that filth work?*"

The Ururu male blew a powder into his wife's face, making her eyes immediately bulge out and turn glassy. Then he made her bite into a stick. Chimaux watched the macabre spectacle in fascination.

"The newborn will immediately be handed over to another woman of the village, who will then raise him. And so life is perpetuated among the Ururu. It's cruel, but this tribe has come down through the millennia with these rites. If it still exists, it's because, somehow, a natural evolutionary balance has been established. The Ururu tribe has not experienced the same decadence as the rotting societies of the West. It has not felt this absurd need to reproduce later and later, to prolong its life span for no real purpose, to live in the familial model we know all too well. Just look at the damage this has caused in your world: illness upon illness past the age of forty. Do you think Alzheimer's is a new disease? What if I told you it has always existed, but that it never declared itself because people died too young? It sat quietly in our cells, awaiting its moment. Today, everyone can know his genome, his predisposition to diseases like cancer. Vile probabilities guide our future. We're becoming insane hypochondriacs. Evolution no longer has a say in any of it."

"Why Louts . . ." murmured Lucie in a flash of consciousness.

"Louts came here with a remarkable theory, which might have been my own about twenty years ago: the combative culture of a population 'imprints' the trait of left-handedness on their DNA, thus forcing the descendants to be left-handed as well, so that they too will be better fighters. A collective memory that modifies DNA. She shared my concept of evolution. She was just like me."

He lowered the waist of his fatigues to show a large wound on his groin.

"I nearly died five years ago. Noland wanted to take this way too far. When he and Terney identified the virus and figured out how it worked, he started talking about this large-scale project. If you'd known him, you'd know what words like that can mean in his mouth. I wouldn't go along with it, because this time it wasn't just about a few dead, but about injecting a living virus into the genetic heritage of the entire human race. A kind of AIDS to the tenth power, that would clean everything out. So he tried to kill me. Since then, I haven't left the jungle."

He readjusted his clothes and took another sip. Lucie struggled to memorize his words. A virus . . . Noland . . . She had to fight it, but the fog enveloped her, devoured her thoughts, erased her memories.

"When Louts came to see me, I had an idea. I wanted to know if the first symptoms of the virus had struck any young adult males. If some of them had become ultraviolent, and if Terney and Noland's theories had panned out. So I used her; I asked her to go visit the prisons, to find young, violent left-handed offenders who had complained of balance problems. All she had to do was bring me back a list of names and their photos; I knew I'd be able to recognize the Ururu grandchildren, and if so, that Noland had been right. When she didn't come back, I knew she'd succeeded too well. Her perseverance had cost her her life. Noland had killed her."

Lucie was floundering. Images continued to overlap in her head. Everything was mixed up, while the sound of female screaming rose from near the fire. Clear voices from the past blended with those of the present. Cops shouting, charging toward a house. Trembling, soaked, Lucie clearly saw herself rushing forward with the lawmen. They broke down the door and Lucie followed them in. Carnot flat on the ground . . . She ran up the stairs, met the odor of charred flesh. A door, a room. Another body, its eyes still open.

Juliette, dead, lying before her, with wide staring eyes.

Lucie rolled on her side, hands clutching at her face, and let out a long scream.

Her fingers clawed at the ground, her tears mixed with the ancestral earth, while in front of her blood-soaked hands lifted high the newborn ripped from its mother's womb. In a final flash of lucidity, she saw Chimaux leaning over her and heard him murmur in an icy voice:

"And now, I shall inhale your soul."

Noland spoke calmly, sponging the arch of his brow with small, precise dabs.

"Phoenix emerged from the womb of evolution and contaminated generations of Cro-Magnon, some thirty thousand years ago. I think that, in some way, it contributed to the extinction of the Neanderthals through a genocide wrought by infected Cro-Magnons, but that's another matter. Regardless, the competition between virus and humans, in the nascent Western societies, favored humans: the retrovirus became harmless over the centuries and was fossilized in our DNA. Nonetheless, it persisted in the Ururu tribe, with only slight mutations, as that isolated, quasi-prehistoric tribe slowly evolved. In Western societies, culture moves too fast; it guides genes, orients them, and gains the upper hand over nature. But not in the jungle. There, genes always stay ahead of culture."

"How does the virus work?"

"You just need a carrier, man or woman, for the child to be infected. Phoenix hides on chromosome two, near the genes that account for hand dominance. Its presence is what accounts for making the hosts left-handed. But to awaken and begin reproducing, Phoenix needs a key. And that key is something that any male on this planet has, his Y chromosome."

Sharko thought of Terney's title. There was no doubt it alluded to the Phoenix virus. More sleight-of-hand.

"When I inseminated the healthy mothers, more than forty years ago, they gave birth to an infected child—generation G1—since the virus was in the Ururu sperm, and thus in the child's genetic heritage. Let's suppose the G1 child turns out to be a girl, as was indeed the case every time, such as with Coralie's mother, Jeanne."

He was talking about the girl who was supposed to be his daughter, but who had none of his paternal genes. A stranger in his eyes, simply the product of an experiment.

"So Jeanne is a carrier of the virus. Some twenty years later, when her oocyte is fertilized by the spermatozoon of a Western male, it's up to chance to decide if the new fetus is female or male. Jeanne first has a girl, Coralie, and then a boy, Félix. Two infected children of the second generation, G2. In Coralie's case, the Western father has transmitted his X chromosome and the virus isn't triggered in Jeanne; the lock has remained shut—though this does not prevent Phoenix from being transmitted genetically to Coralie through chromosome two. In Félix's case, the father donates his Y chromosome. The Y enters into the composition of the placenta, which interacts with Jeanne's organism. At that point, the lock that is holding back the virus on Jeanne's chromosome two snaps open. Proteins are manufactured in the mother's body, and the virus proliferates with just one goal: ensure its own survival and its propagation in another body. The expression of the virus is characterized by a hypervascular placenta, alongside a sharp decrease in the mother's vital functions. The virus has won it all: it kills its host and propagates itself via the fetus, thus guaranteeing its own survival . . . you know the rest. Félix grows up, becomes an adult, probably has sexual relations. He transmits the virus in turn, if there are any children. Then the same thing happens that happened to the G1 mother: the virus reproduces inside Félix and kills him, this time attacking the brain. The same pattern obtains in every scenario, whether it's the mother or father who's infected, a boy or girl who's born. Phoenix has applied the same strategy as any other virus or parasite: survive, spread, kill. If it survived in the Ururu, it's because both humans and the virus found the advantages outweighed the drawbacks. A young, strong tribe, evolving slowly, its size self-regulated, experiencing no need other than to survive and ensure its continuity. The rest—especially old age—is merely . . . superfluous."

He sighed, eyes toward the ceiling. Sharko felt like disemboweling him.

"I've written all this down, apart from a few details. The analyzed sequences of Phoenix in both its mutated state and the nonmutated version from thirty thousand years ago. You can't possibly imagine the impact the discovery of the Cro-Magnon had, a year ago in that cave. An isolated individual who had massacred Neanderthals . . . the upside-down drawing . . . I had there an expression of the original form of a virus that only three people in the world even knew existed, and on which we'd been laboring for years. Stéphane Terney made arrangements to steal the mummy and its genome."

"Why not just steal the computer documents? What good was the mummy?"

"We didn't want to leave it in the scientists' hands. They would just have established its genome again and combed over it. Ultimately, they would have spotted the genetic differences between the ancestral genome and ours, and would have ended up discovering and understanding my retrovirus."

He clicked his tongue.

"Terney wanted so much to keep the Cro-Magnon in his museum, and I had to twist his arm a bit so that we could get rid of it. Then we exploited the genome. Our work was moving at a fast clip, thanks especially to an explosion of knowledge in the field of genetics. And then Terney called me in a panic at the beginning of the month to tell me about a student who was sticking her nose into left-handers and violence. Eva Louts. So I checked her out, and I discovered she'd been to the Amazon. Clearly Napoléon Chimaux was somehow involved. So I decided to do some housecleaning—things were becoming much too dangerous. Terney's paranoia was putting him in a serious panic. I killed them both, and I burned the tapes that recorded the Ururu rituals, the samples we'd taken, and the inseminations. I erased every trace. My biggest mistake was letting Terney photograph the Cro-Magnon and not removing those three pictures from his wall. But I never thought you'd make the connection."

He squeezed his fists.

"I wanted . . . to give life to the true Phoenix, see what it could do vis-à-vis its Ururu cousin, but I didn't have the chance. You have no idea how hard I've worked, the sacrifices I've made. You, you common street cop, you've ruined everything. You don't understand that evolution is the exception, and that extinction is the rule. We're all fated to die out. You first of all."

Sharko leaned close to him and shoved his gun under the man's nose.

"Your granddaughter would have died right before your eyes, and you knew it."

"She wouldn't have died. She would have played the part nature reserved for her. It's nature that should decide, not us."

"You're an irredeemable fanatic. For that alone, I should pull the trigger."

Noland found the strength to stretch his lips into a cold smile.

"Go ahead. Shoot. And you'll never know the names of the four remaining profiles. Or at the very least, you risk finding them too late, when the worst has already happened. And believe me, Inspector, you will know what that worst is."

Sharko gritted his teeth, struggling with his darkest demons, but finally removed his finger from the trigger. He lowered his weapon.

"The woman I love had better come back alive, you piece of filth. Because even in the depths of the prison where you'll be rotting for the rest of your days, mixing with the lowest refuse of your goddamned evolution, I swear I will know how to find you."

Lucie's eyes snapped open. The landscape was pitching and tossing, as if set on air cushions. The rumbling of an engine . . . silt in their wake . . . vibrations in the floor . . . She sat up, a hand on her head, and took a few seconds to realize she was back on the *Maria Nazare*. The boat was now moving with the current.

She was going home.

Pale, she dragged herself to the railing and vomited. She vomited because, like a sordid truth, she saw, as clearly as she could see the surrounding landscape, the toys still in their packaging in the twins' room . . . Then herself, alone at the school fence that first day, with no one to bring . . . The cell phone lying unused in a corner . . . Her walks through the Citadelle, alone with Klark. Her mother's searching looks, her allusions and her sighs . . . Alone, alone, always alone, talking to the dog, to a wall, to nothing.

Lucie's stomach heaved once more. The jungle, the drugs she'd been given, had made her see that both her little girls were dead. That for the past year she'd been living with a ghost, a hallucination, a little creature of smoke who had come to give her support, see her through the tragedy.

Staggering, Lucie raised her cloudy eyes toward Pedro, who was leaning on the prow, chewing some tobacco. In front of them rose the FUNAI outpost. No one tried even to stop them; the man with the scars signaled for them to keep moving. He stared at Lucie without moving, his eyes glacial, then quickly returned inside the hut.

The guide came up to Lucie with a smile.

"You're back among us."

Lucie breathed in painfully, then wiped away her tears with her fingers. She felt as if she were returning from beyond the grave.

"What happened? I remember walking . . . smoke . . . then it's like a black hole. Just images in my head. Such intimate, personal images . . . But . . . where's Chimaux? Why are we heading away? I want to go back there, I . . ."

Pedro laid a hand on her shoulder.

"You saw Chimaux and the savages. They brought you back to the boat after three days."

"Three days? But . . ."

"Chimaux made it very clear: he doesn't want anyone to go back there. Ever. Not you and not me. But he had a message for you. Something he asked me to convey."

Lucie ran both hands over her face. Three days. What had they done to her head? How had they managed to open her mind so wide?

"Tell me," she murmured sadly.

"He said, 'The dead can always be alive. You just have to believe in them, and they return.'"

With those words, he went into the wheelhouse, sounded a proud blast of the foghorn, and gunned the engines.

Several hours later, the boat reached the small port of São Gabriel. Amid the crowd of locals stood a European, beautiful gray shirt half open, sunglasses over his eyes.

Sunglasses with one stem glued back on.

Lucie felt her heart flip and her eyes fogged up once again. With a sigh, she stared silently at the black, tenebrous waves, beneath which thousands of species abounded. From the depths of her sorrow, she told herself that the greatest darkness could also bring hope and life.

Epilogue

The northern sky laid its silvery hues on the graves. Lucie made a sign of the cross before her children's burial vault, raised the collar of her jacket, and slid her arm under Franck Sharko's. A chill wind, down from the north, ripped the final leaves from the poplars, promising a harsh November. Word was, the coming winter would be rough. For Lucie and Sharko, it wouldn't be nearly as rough as summer had been.

Alone in the wide alleys, the couple finally left the cemetery and returned to the center of Lille on foot. That midafternoon, the huge shopping centers remained full, the homeless begged for change or warmed themselves over subway grates, buses and trolleys shuffled their daily allotment of workers, students, and strollers: each one following his or her own path, unwitting participants in the great laboratory of evolution.

Franck and Lucie had planned to go to Café de la Grand-Place to talk, but on an impulse the inspector took his companion by the hand and led her to Rue des Solitaires, on the outskirts of Old Lille. They walked into a small, unassuming bar called the Nemo; the sign was new, the place having recently been bought by a retired trucker. The minute he walked through the door, Sharko felt his heart contract. He breathed in the good smells of old brick and porous cement. They sat down under a small, dimly lit archway. Sharko looked around with shining eyes.

"This is where I first met Suzanne. I was in the army. I haven't been back here in so long."

He took Lucie's hands in his. His fingers had regained their thickness, his wrists their solidity.

"This place means so much to me—I wanted it to be here that I tell you I love you, Lucie."

They looked at each other without a word, as they often did, then ordered two hot chocolates that were quickly served. Sharko ran his finger around the edge of his burning cup.

"Yesterday I heard you went to see your old captain and asked about coming to work at Quai des Orfèvres. Paris Homicide. Kashmareck likes you a lot. He seems to be going all out for you, and it's a good bet your application will sail through. Why are you doing this?"

Lucie shrugged.

"I just want to be near you. I want us to be together, all the time. For us to be on the same team."

"Lucie . . ."

"Manien's squad has been cleaned out, thanks to your revelations. There are empty spots to fill. I've got no reason to stay here in Lille . . . too many memories."

She sighed sadly and added:

"So as long as you haven't resigned from the force, I'll go where you are."

"I can't resign. Not now. Someone killed Frédéric Hurault, and made sure it was near enough to number thirty-six for me to catch the case. They found my DNA on his clothes, and I'm pretty sure I wasn't the one who left it there. Hurault was the father of twin girls. I'm convinced this someone knew about Clara and Juliette. The murder was for my benefit. Now that I'm thinking more clearly, I'm convinced someone was using the body to send me a message."

Lucie shook her head.

"You're thinking *too* clearly. You know the power of coincidence as well as I do. And that's all it is, a coincidence, nothing more. Nobody's got it in for you. That murder is just one more lousy back-page item."

"Maybe. But now that they've reinstated me, I can't leave again without solving this one last crime."

Lucie poured sugar into her chocolate and stirred it.

"Then I'll do the same. And you're the one I want to work with. If they'll let us."

Sharko ended up smiling.

"Jesus, two months ago, we both swore to give all this up!"

They fell silent as they drank their chocolate, each staring into the void. The memories of their last case were still so close to the bone . . .

Georges Noland had finally given up the names corresponding to the remaining genetic profiles in Terney's book. One man and three women, all young, who at that very moment were undergoing tests, ultrasounds, MRIs, unable to understand what was happening to them. Of course, Noland had talked, but who could be sure he hadn't conducted other experiments, other inseminations, that weren't recorded anywhere? And what if he'd had accomplices? How far had he gone in his lunacy? Had he told the police the whole truth, or was he still concealing a portion of it in his diseased brain?

As for Napoléon Chimaux, he was still out there somewhere, hidden in the jungle. Dislodging him and making him admit his share of responsibility would not be easy.

Coralie Lambert could not be saved. By the time she was hospitalized, millions of tiny men-of-war had already invaded her body; the retrovirus had multiplied as of the first months of pregnancy, initiating a process of inescapable death. Her baby had been born in perfect health but harboring within him a sleeping monster. They could only hope that the geneticists, biologists, and virologists would find a way to annihilate the virus before this innocent infant would someday turn into another Grégory Carnot or Félix Lambert.

Assailed by memories, Sharko pursed his lips. Evolution built marvelous creations, but it could also be extremely cruel. The cop often repeated to himself what Noland had told him during their last face-to-face: *Evolution is the exception. Extinction is the rule.* He was right. Nature was constantly trying things out, testing out millions, billions of combinations, of which only a small handful would endure through the millennia. In that alchemy, there were necessarily some monstrosities: AIDS, cancer, GATACA, the great plagues, serial killers . . . Nature didn't distinguish between good and evil, it merely tried to solve an exceedingly complex equation. One thing was certain: it had taken an awful risk by creating mankind.

A couple entered, two kids holding hands who went to sit at a small round table. They looked at each other shyly, and Lucie could read the gentle glow of a nascent relationship. One day, perhaps, their chromosomes would embrace, their genes mix together. His blue eyes, her blond hair . . . the curve of a nose, the oval of a cheekbone, the little hollow of a dimple. Chance would decide who, between father and mother, would transmit which physical or mental particularity to the child. Their love would engender a thinking, intelligent being, capable of accomplishing beautiful things, who would prove that we were not merely survival machines.

Lost in her reverie, Lucie gazed absently at Franck Sharko and caught herself wondering, for the first time since they'd known each other, what the fruit of their union might be like. There would certainly be a bit of Clara and Juliette somewhere in that future being.

Yes, Clara and Juliette were inside of her, deep within her DNA, and *not* out there, six feet underground. It would take only a small spark to bring a part of her two treasures back to life.